NICOLE CONWAY

AUTHOR OF THE BESTSELLING
DRAGONRIDER CHRONICLES SERIES

Month9Books

MAD MAGIC by Nicole Conway
All rights reserved. Published in the United States of America by Month9Books, LLC.
No part of this book may be used or reproduced in any manner whatsoever without written permission of the publisher, except in the case of brief quotations embodied in critical articles and reviews.

Trade Paperback ISBN: 978-1-945107-86-3
EPub ISBN: 978-1-946700-14-8
Mobipocket ISBN: 978-1-946700-15-5
Hardback ISBN: 978-1-946700-13-1

Published by Month9Books, Raleigh, NC 27609
Title and cover design by Danielle Doolittle

Month9Books

To Dr. Jerome Ward and Beth Fuller,
who were two of my greatest mentors.

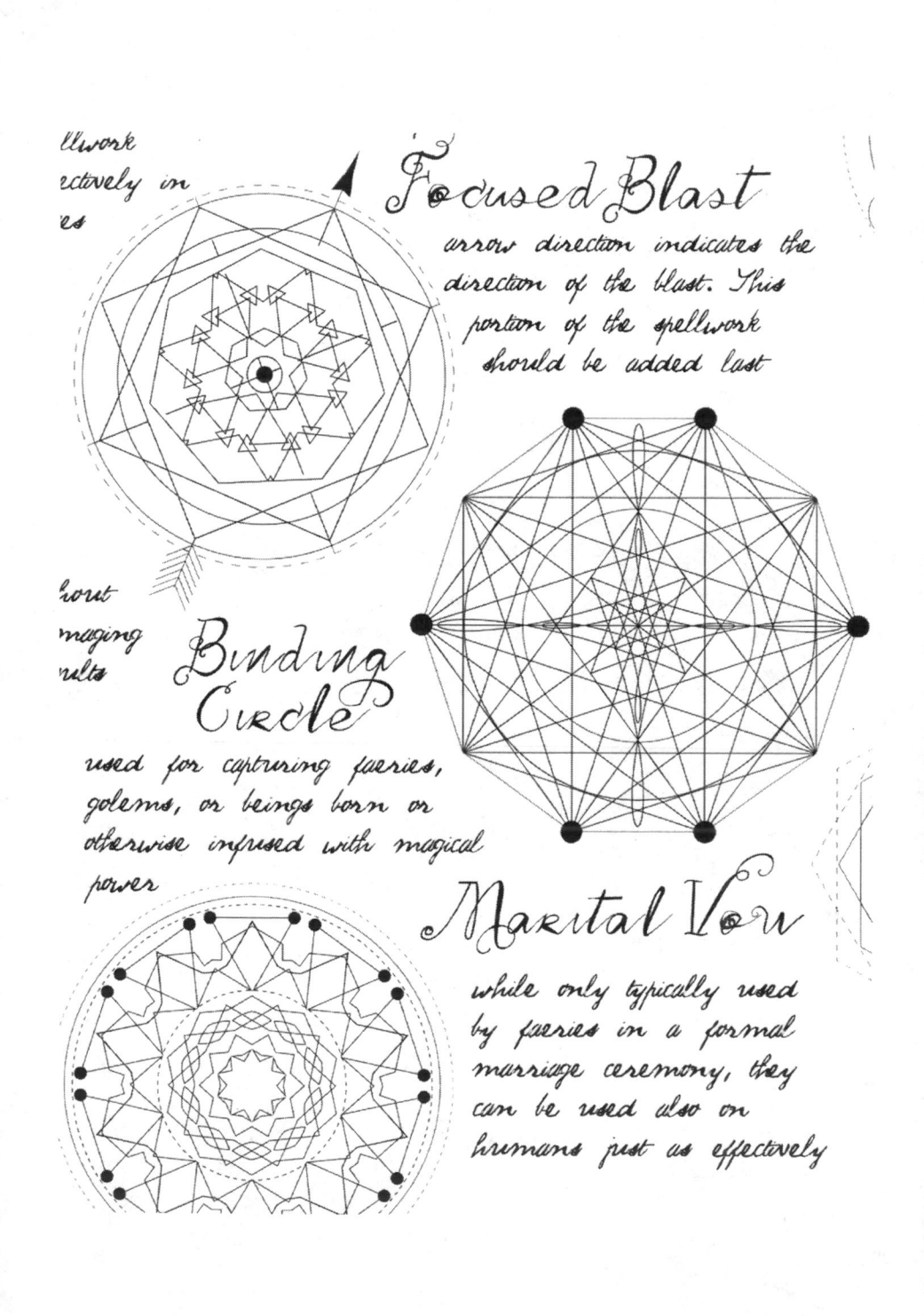

llwork
ectively in
es

Focused Blast

arrow direction indicates the
direction of the blast. This
portion of the spellwork
should be added last

hout
maging
ults

Binding
Circle

used for capturing faeries,
golems, or beings born or
otherwise infused with magical
power

Marital Vow

while only typically used
by faeries in a formal
marriage ceremony, they
can be used also on
humans just as effectively

Fibbing Gate

spellwork for this portal
must be extremely precise
or results will not be effective
Also see page 24 of red journal
for directions on exact placement of
the stones

this
comp

Glamour

this is used
primarily as
a bewitching
spell for
limited
enthrallment
and mind
control

for
cha
lus

Animate

highly effective in bringing objects to
life with limited capability for

I wanted today to be a normal, quiet day. I wanted to go to school, take my tests, turn in my homework, eat lunch, and walk home without any major catastrophes. But, as usual, that was too much to ask.

I, Josie Barton, could not do normal.

So, for the third time this week, I sat in Ms. Grear's office. She glared at me over the top of her thick-framed glasses, but I knew better than to meet her gaze. Instead, I focused on the glass nameplate on her desk. It had the words *School Counselor* engraved on it.

Ms. Grear didn't like me. None of the faculty did. I saw it in the way they watched me with smoldering, disapproving glares. I got the sense from all of them that they were trying to figure out what, exactly, was wrong with me.

That question was getting harder and harder for me to answer these days.

For starters, I was a "problem student," a troublemaker, prone to outbursts at the worst possible moments. I caused scenes in my classes— like I had today. It used to only happen every now and then. But lately, it seemed to be happening more and more often, and I couldn't do anything to stop it.

I didn't blame the teachers for getting fed up with me. I was pretty fed up, too. I certainly didn't want to be this way. I mean, who actually *wants* to be crazy? I practically had a reserved seat outside the principal's office. I was really on a roll this week.

"Well, Josie, I'm not sure what you expect me to do with you anymore." Ms. Grear spoke in a vicious, bitter tone.

I wasn't sure how to answer her, or even if I should try. Ms. Grear already thought I was totally out of my mind, after all, and had let me know that many times before. She'd even said I was a waste of the school system's valuable resources—but of course, not in those *exact* words. She'd phrased it very professionally. Something about how I was "wasting time that hard-working teachers could have spent on other students who actually appreciated it."

It was hard to hear stuff like that. But what hurt the most wasn't how they looked at me, or even the things they said. The absolute worst thing was the fact that I was so incredibly alone.

"It's been three years since the incident, and I feel that we have all been very considerate of your situation. We've given you plenty of time and space to deal with your personal issues. But, you've become a major distraction to the other students. You won't take your medications. You insist on disrupting every class you attend." Ms. Grear leaned back in her chair. The metal hinges on the seat creaked like they were screaming in pain under her weight. "Sooner or later, you are going to have to start taking responsibility for your outbursts."

"Yes, ma'am." I was hoping agreeing with her would save me from hearing this speech again.

Ms. Grear narrowed her eyes dangerously. Her mouth pinched up, and for a few terrifying seconds, she looked like an angry Buddha statue. Then she started raking through the papers in her desk drawers.

"I have been trying to offer this suggestion to your legal guardian, but since he is so *difficult* to get in touch with, I will give it to you instead." She shot me another accusing glare. "Be sure you pass it on to him."

I cringed instinctively and managed to nod.

She finally pulled a pamphlet out of a drawer and handed it to me. "Davner's is a school for mentally unstable children, like you. They take in students who can't function in normal society. It's a nice place. You'll like it. They'll keep you on the proper medications and give you the structure and constant attention you obviously require. You can make friends with other children who have the same issues you do. This school comes very highly recommended, and they will know exactly how to manage you."

I carefully took the pamphlet from her, handling it as though it might be explosive. There was a picture of an old-looking brick building on the front flap. Inside, there were lots of pictures of smiling nurses, pristinely clean classrooms, and happy-looking teenagers all hugging each other. I only skimmed the text, but the words *schizophrenia*, *bipolar disorder*, and *sociopathic tendencies* caught my eye right away.

My stomach began to get queasy.

I looked back up at her, mustering all my courage to try and argue my case. "But I don't want to transfer. I'm supposed to graduate soon. I can finish out the year. I just have to try harder. It's only a few months."

As Ms. Grear folded her chubby hands on the veneer desk, her thick fingers reminded me of pudgy, pink sausages. "Well, to be perfectly honest, you are on everyone's last nerve. Here at Saint Augustine's, we have standards. We have the highest test scores in the district. We are the most coveted private school in the city. Everyone else looks to us to set the bar, even when it comes to dealing with troubled students. I've already met with the rest of faculty, and we are all in agreement that this is the best option for you. All the paperwork is in order. All we need is the signature of your legal guardian. What was his name? Ben?"

I looked up again only because of the distinct flavor of sarcasm in her voice. She was grinning. It wasn't hard to imagine her with little horns and a pitchfork to match her evil smirk.

I wasn't sure what she thought was going on, but I knew she didn't think Ben was real. Even I doubted his existence sometimes, so I could understand why she might think I was making him up. He was barely in my life at all; just a spectator on the sidelines who stepped in every now and again when there was a problem I couldn't fix on my own. Beyond that, he was a shadow.

Maybe that was why I felt so isolated.

After my dad passed away in a house fire three years ago, I was completely alone in the world. I was fourteen then, so I couldn't legally be left on my own. I didn't have any extended relatives—no uncles, cousins, or grandparents who could take me in. My mom had died when I was really little, and my older brother not long after that. The only person still standing there after the funeral was over and the dust had settled was a mysterious figure that called himself my benefactor; I called him Ben for short. It sounded better than "Random Stranger Who Pays My Bills," since I didn't know his real name.

He wasn't a relative. In fact, I had never even seen his face. Right after my dad passed away, I was sent into foster care for several weeks while the police investigated the fire. During that time, a lawyer in a snazzy, black suit had come to visit me at the hospital. He had all the right paperwork with my dad's signature naming Ben as my new legal guardian, but all of it was sealed and beyond my understanding. It was like something from a mob movie.

Before I knew it, I was sitting in a fully furnished apartment with all that remained of my family's belongings that hadn't been burned to a crisp. I had a credit card in my wallet, and an acceptance letter to an expensive private school called Saint Augustine's. What else could a teenage girl ask for?

Answers, for starters. But those were hard to come by.

Apparently, my dad had made these arrangements for Ben to take care of me a long time ago, if anything bad were to happen. Ben was supposed to support me until I turned eighteen, and then I wasn't sure what would happen to me. I suspected I'd be left on my own to either sink or swim. For now, Ben took care of everything. He paid my rent and all my expenses. I had a credit card I could use for groceries and anything else I needed. Occasionally, we exchanged emails or text messages. But as far as communication went, that was where Ben drew the line. He never answered the phone when I called, and had never agreed to meet me—not even for holidays.

Ms. Grear talked me into circles about him all the time, like she was trying to catch me in a lie. She knew as much about him as I did. He didn't answer the phone when she called either. He had, however, sent her emails that she claimed sounded "youthfully voiced," which I guessed meant she was accusing me of writing them instead. In a few months, it wouldn't matter—I was about to graduate and turn eighteen. After that, I would be able to make all my own decisions, and wouldn't be anyone's burden to bear. I could move somewhere else, meet new people, and make a clean start.

I tried clinging to that idea as I looked back up at Ms. Grear. She scared me. She must have known she did because she always made a big show of it when she took me out of class for meetings like this. I think she liked watching me squirm as I sat across from her. Honestly, I was just trying to keep it all together. Meanwhile, her beady little eyes watched my every move, the corner of her mouth twitching with a sneer.

"I'll give him a call when I get home," I promised.

She scoffed and rolled her eyes, as if she couldn't believe I was still trying to keep up this charade. "Fine. You're dismissed." She jabbed an angry finger toward her door.

I gathered my backpack and hurried out of her office. The hallways were filled with students all dressed in school uniforms like mine—white button-down shirts, navy-blue knit sweaters, and blue plaid skirts or pants. We weren't allowed to wear makeup or excessive jewelry. I think it was to prevent anyone from feeling superior, like we were all equals or something. It didn't stop cliques from forming, though. There were the bookish kids, the popular and pretty ones, the athletes, and the gamers like at any other school.

Of course, I didn't have a niche. I didn't have any friends here at all. I was a pariah—thanks to my numerous outbursts—and it wasn't unusual for a room to clear whenever I entered.

It still hurt.

I intentionally avoided making eye contact with anyone as I dropped my books in my locker. The inside of my backpack still smelled like smoke from my last episode in chemistry class. I had been in the lab, paired up with one of the more popular girls to do an experiment. We were mixing chemicals, and things seemed to be going well. I had been trying my best to act as normal as possible, and she had been unusually nice to me, too. Like an idiot, I had begun to hope I might make a friend.

Then it happened again.

I was attempting to light the Bunsen burner to heat one of the chemicals when the flames flickered strangely. They flickered and danced, turning blue, pink, and purple. They'd moved almost like they were coming alive. I turned away and tried not to see; I'd always hoped it would go away if I ignored it. Then I saw the flames begin to take form—the shape of a fiery hand—and reach for my lab partner's ponytail. I screamed and dove at her, knocking her out of the way before her hair caught on fire.

Of course, no one else had seen the fire turn into a hand. All they had seen was me screaming and throwing myself at a perfectly innocent lab partner. The Chemistry teacher grabbed me by the collar and dragged me out of the lab while all my classmates watched. They stared at me with wide-eyed, shocked expressions—I got that look from them a lot. Some of the boys in the back snickered and I noticed a few of the other girls going over to console my former lab partner.

So much for making a friend.

I tried not to dwell on it too much as I left the school and walked home alone. I had other, much worse things I should have been worried about. But my thoughts got tangled up in Ms. Grear's words about transferring to a special school. Maybe she was right. Maybe things would be easier at a place like that. At least then I wouldn't have to live in that apartment anymore …

It was freezing outside. The sidewalks were slick with ice and soggy slush puddles. Fortunately, my apartment was only a few blocks away so I didn't have to walk far. Ben had put me as close as possible to the school so I could get back and forth easily, which was especially useful when the weather was bad.

My apartment was right smack in the middle of the historic part of the city, where doctors and lawyers usually moved to retire. The buildings were all neatly huddled together on either side of the street, tall and skinny like different colored puzzle pieces. Some had small, perfectly-manicured gardens out front and iron fences with elaborate gates. There was a line of square-cut shrubs down the middle of the divided street, and a few blocks away was a collection of quaint shops and a family owned grocery store. It was everything you might need conveniently within walking distance.

I should have been grateful. Ben had given me a beautiful, quiet, and seemingly safe place to live. Instead, I felt guilty because the sight of it filled me with dread. Once I crossed the threshold of my front door, things always got worse.

Not that Ben had any idea about that. For all he knew, I was perfectly happy there. The rent was probably outrageous, and he was the one paying for it. I'd already tried asking if I could move somewhere less expensive. I didn't mind walking longer or even taking the bus. Every time I brought it up, Ben insisted I should focus on my schoolwork and "enjoy my high school experience."

Yeah, right.

It was bad enough spending a stranger's money, but what made it even worse was despite everything he'd given me, I wanted something more from Ben. I wanted to *know* him. I was lonely, and he was the only person in the whole world who cared about me even a little, teensy, tiny bit. I had apologized to him plenty of times for being a burden, and he always replied right away to tell me it was his pleasure and privilege to take care of me. Those words never made me feel any better, though. Words on a computer screen weren't very comforting. Frankly, they were cold, distant, and impersonal. I was still desperately clinging to the hope that one day he would allow us to meet, and I'd see someone smile at me again as though they were happy to see me.

I tried not to dwell on that as I climbed the icy front steps of my building, gripping the iron railing so I didn't slip. It looked as if it had originally been built to be a colonial townhouse, but now, the top two floors had been converted into two apartments per level.

The landlord, Mr. Bregger, lived on the first floor. There were two other tenants living there besides me. One was a sweet elderly lady who lived alone on the second floor. She was deaf, and always smiled whenever I passed her in the stairwell. Sometimes, when it was a warm day, she sat out on the sofa in the mailroom with her big, fluffy orange cat in her lap.

Then there was the guy who lived directly across the hall from me.

He was standing in the common foyer, casually checking his mail, when I ducked inside. My entrance sent a blast of cold winter air through the foyer, but he never so much as shivered. I slipped off my mittens and scarf, hurrying to close the door before all the warm, inside air escaped. I made a lot of racket, most of it intentional, and he still didn't give me a single glance. He never did.

I shuffled right past him to check my own mail.

He didn't say a word.

Maybe that shouldn't have bothered me. After all, he looked exactly like the kind of person your parents might advise you to intentionally avoid while walking home alone. His shaggy, dark brown hair came down almost to his shoulders, and there were colorful-tattooed sleeves covering both of his beautifully sculpted arms. Even if tattoos weren't usually my thing, his were amazing. They were brightly colored and riddled with rich, intricate details of flowers, vines, feathers, fish, and splashes of water. I blatantly stole glances of them whenever I spotted him wearing something sleeveless.

Creepy? Probably, but I couldn't help myself. Something about him drove me absolutely nuts, and the fact that he seemed to be intentionally ignoring my existence made it even worse.

He'd moved in here a couple of months ago, and at first glance I wondered what someone like that was doing living in a place like this. But the more I saw of him, the more my brain bubbled with mystification. Who was this guy? Why was he living here, when he could have moved to one of the trendier neighborhoods downtown?

So far, I had no answers. And whether it was the long hair, the tattoos, or the fact that he apparently didn't own any jeans that didn't have ragged holes in them, there was an air of reckless danger about him that drew me in like a gnat to a bug-zapper. It didn't help that he was insanely good-looking. He had one of those hard, chiseled jawlines you seldom see outside of department store advertisements. He was a lot older, probably in his mid-twenties, and I was just a high-school girl in a dorky uniform that stared at him like a deer in headlights every time our paths crossed. It probably freaked him out. And yet, despite what seemed like a committed effort on his part to appear as unfriendly as possible, he had never said anything mean to me. He'd never said anything at all. Maybe it was a good thing he ignored me. If our eyes met, I might suddenly combust into an inferno of girlish embarrassment.

Despite his silence, I had learned a lot about him by watching him in passing. I'd gotten good at reading people that way. Call it the curse of the incredibly bored.

For instance, I knew he had to be a heavy smoker. I saw him standing outside the apartment finishing off one of his weird cigarettes early in the morning as I left for school every day. Mr. Bregger didn't allow smoking in the building, but my tattooed neighbor had built a regular bird's nest of burned-out cigarette butts in the flowerpots out front. Clearly, it wasn't a casual habit—not that I was any kind of smoking expert.

Normally, I would have found a smoking habit like that a total turn-off. But there was something different about the cigarettes he smoked.

They were wrapped in a cream-colored paper, almost like parchment, and I'd noticed the butts were stamped with a small, gold-foiled design in the shape of a crown. That wasn't a brand I recognized. Their smell was different, too. It was floral, almost like incense.

I also figured he had to be a bouncer or worker at a nightclub. I didn't know what else he could possibly be doing from 6:00 PM when he left, until 5:00 AM when I heard him climbing the stairs to our floor every night like clockwork.

He was also single, or at the very least not in a serious relationship, because I never heard anyone else come back with him. No girlfriends, no drunken one-night stands—nothing. I'd never seen him with any friends or visitors, and he never went out of town or away on vacation. In fact, he seemed to be almost as reclusive as me.

I was discreetly trying to sneak a peek at some of his mail while slipping my key into my own box. Okay, so maybe I was being a little creepy. I just wanted to find out what his name was. What's the harm in that?

And then the lock on my mailbox made an awful clanking noise.

I groaned. It only made that sound when the lock jammed. I tried not to curse aloud as I fought to get my key free. I tried wiggling it, twisting it, and beating on the mailbox door. Nothing. The lock refused to budge or let go of my key.

I was about to resort to something more violent when a big hand suddenly eclipsed my view.

"You're gonna break it if you keep jerkin' on it like that," a deep voice murmured right behind me. My tattooed neighbor muscled his way into my space, sliding me out of the way while he worked the lock.

I gaped at him in stunned silence, trying to wrap my mind around the fact that he'd spoken to me. He had an unlit cigarette between his lips, and his sharp eyes glanced my way for a brief second before he turned his attention back to my mailbox.

That was enough, though. That one, short glance sent a jolt through me like I'd stuck my finger in an electrical socket.

He had to have been wearing contacts. Either that, or I was seeing things again. His eyes looked *purple*. That couldn't possibly be real, right? I guess when you took the rest of his bizarre style into account, it didn't seem so strange that he might be wearing colored contacts, too.

He jiggled the lock a few times, twisting the key and finally popping it loose. Then he dropped the key back into my hand without a word and began walking away.

I stared at his broad back. It was almost too late when I finally remembered to call out, "Thank you!"

He didn't answer. He just raised one of his hands in a casual gesture without ever looking back and sauntered out the front door.

Wow.

It had all happened so fast. I was dazed as I climbed the stairs to my apartment. My frazzled brain churned, replaying every second. His tone had been so casual, like we knew one another already. And like an idiot, I had blown my perfect opportunity to ask his name. I was so busy mentally kicking myself about that, I had almost forgotten to be on guard when I arrived at my front door.

As soon as I realized where I was, I froze with my hand on the knob. I sucked in a sharp breath, and braced myself as I cracked open my door.

The things I saw at school were unpleasant. They were usually embarrassing and terrifying. In the past, doctors had diagnosed me with post-traumatic stress disorder. They said it was because my dad had died so suddenly and in a traumatic way, and that it would take time for me to recover. They prescribed all kinds of medications to help with the anxiety and hallucinations. Their diagnosis seemed to make perfect sense … until I got to my own front door.

That's where the real world seemed to stop.

Some things couldn't be explained away.

I opened the door slowly and as quietly as possible, leaning to peek inside before I dared to turn on the lights. The lamps lit around the room when I flipped the switch, revealing the chaos I'd been dreading. My couch was turned over with its cushions thrown everywhere. All the pictures had been ripped off the walls again. The drapes had been yanked off the windows, and the TV was face down on the floor.

I stepped carefully over broken glass on my way to the kitchen. There, I found the fridge door wide open and food strewn everywhere. It was as if someone had intentionally sprayed the walls in ketchup. A chill crept over my body, making my skin prickle as though I were walking into an icy dungeon. I stood there for a few moments, shivering and staring at the mess.

The doctor had assured me that it wasn't uncommon for people with PTSD to have episodes like this and not remember them later. He'd called them "blackouts." I didn't remember doing anything like this to my apartment. Everything had been neat and orderly, the way I liked it, when I left for school that morning. Anyone else probably would have immediately called the police and reported a break-in, but I knew better than that.

The police couldn't help me. No one could.

It took me all afternoon to clean things up. I scrubbed ketchup off the walls and cabinets, swept up broken glass, and hung all the pictures back on the walls. Thankfully, I'd already taken all the photos with any sentimental value out of the frames a long time ago. These were just generic snapshots—some of which had come with the frames. Before, I'd adorned my home with every snapshot I could find of my family. Having them there, smiling at me, made me feel less alone. But after a similar incident where all those images had been torn from their frames and my dad's face was scratched out of each one, it wasn't worth the risk. I didn't want to lose the few I had left.

When everything was clean and tidy again, I collapsed onto the couch and let out a sigh. It was getting late. I was exhausted, and yet I still had lots of homework to do before I could even try sleeping.

I took a quick shower and braided my coppery colored hair into a long, soggy rope down my back. I changed into pajamas, which were a pair of old sweatpants, socks, and one of my dad's old t-shirts. Then I curled up on the couch with my usual blanket and pillow, propped a textbook in my lap, and prepared to study.

Of course, sleeping in my bed or even stretching out across it to do my homework would have been nice, but I had given up on that a while ago. I couldn't sleep in my bedroom at all anymore, and I hated going in there. More things seemed to happen there than anywhere else in the apartment. The living room was the only place that even felt remotely safe. I knew it was only a matter of time, though. Slowly, but surely, I was being driven out of every room in this apartment. If things kept going at this rate, I'd be sleeping out in the hallway in the next few weeks.

I only made it halfway through my homework before nodding off. My face met my book a few times, and I finally gave up. Placing my textbook and notes in a stack on the coffee table, I bundled myself up in my blanket and drew my legs in toward my chest. All the lights in the apartment were still on, which made me feel a little better and the shadows less intense.

It wouldn't last, though. It never did. The darkness was my enemy, and I knew better than to think I would be safe just because there were a few lights burning.

My mind wandered back to that special school again. If I did decide to transfer, Ben would want to know why. He'd find out about my incidents at school, that I'd been seeing a few doctors secretly—basically everything I'd been hiding. I couldn't let that happen. I had to make it to graduation. It was only a few more months. I could do it.

Visions of colorful tattoos swirled in my head as my body slowly relaxed, pulled under by the stress of the day. I drifted off, after one last glance at the clock.

It was only midnight. I still had a few hours left to sleep before 3:02 AM.

13

The sound of something like glass smashing in the kitchen made me bolt upright. The room was pitch black. My heart began pounding at a frantic pace. I panicked and a cold sweat made my whole body shiver.

It was here.

Something else broke, crashing against the floor right next to the couch.

It was too dark to see what it was. My chest got tight. I struggled to breathe and dove under my blanket for cover. Reaching down, I pulled my cell phone out of the pocket of my sweatpants. I clung to it as the screen glowed. It was the only source of light in my apartment now.

I had to calm down.

I had to think.

I tried some of the coping techniques the doctors had taught me for dealing with panic attacks. Breathe, count, and claim the area around me as my personal safe space. I started counting, taking deep breaths with every number.

One … Two … Three …

Another loud crash made me scream. It sounded an awful lot like my television hitting the floor again. I curled up into the smallest ball I possibly could, hugging my knees to my chest, and squeezing my phone desperately.

The pictures on the walls were rattling. The legs of my wingback chair made scraping noises as it slid across the floor. Down the hall, I heard my bedroom door slam shut, over and over again.

Then it touched me.

Icy cold fingers wrapped around my ankle.

I screamed, and tried to kick away, but it was strong—much stronger than me. It yanked me off the couch and onto the floor like a ragdoll. The back of my head cracked against the floor. My vision spotted. I was only vaguely aware that I had dropped my cell phone.

Something dragged me across the floor. Still dazed, I managed another desperate, garbled scream. I grabbed the leg of the couch and yelled. I knew no one would hear me. It didn't matter how loud I was, or how long

I screamed. It was like being trapped in a bubble, an unbreakable cone of silence, where no one else could reach me.

I fought with all my might. It grabbed my braid, snatching my head back suddenly. I cried out as my fingers slid away from the couch leg.

It dragged me down the hall by my hair. I clawed at it, to get my hair free, but all I touched was empty air. There was nothing but deep, terrible darkness all around me.

It hauled me toward my bedroom. The door was still slamming repeatedly, like the chomping mouth of a hungry beast. I managed to grab the edge of the doorframe as it pulled me inside. I clung with all my strength, screaming at the top of my lungs for someone to help me.

The door slammed again, smashing my fingers and forcing me to let go.

The darkness swallowed me, gulping me down. The bedroom door slammed and locked. I screamed his name with all my might; I didn't know anyone else to cry out for.

But Ben never came.

I was shaking in the dark.

The cold was so intense. It felt as though someone were squeezing my lungs in clenched fists, preventing me from taking anything but short, frantic gasping breaths. My hands and feet were numb, although not enough that I couldn't feel the aching pain where the door had slammed on my hand.

I was only vaguely aware of strong, cold fingertips on my skin, gripping my throat. Not enough to choke me, though. It was just enough to let me know if it truly wanted to kill me—it could.

I should have been dead, but instead, everything seemed to be spinning. I felt weak and tired, like I could have slipped off into an eternal sleep.

And then suddenly, there was light.

The closet doors opened one by one. The grip on my throat vanished in an instant, and I gasped like I'd been holding my breath for an eternity. At that moment, I didn't know how I'd wound up in the closet—I couldn't remember anything except the darkness. It was all confused, terrifying chaos.

Looking up, I hoped to see my dad. I'd dreamt of a moment like this, when he would come home, smile at me like he used to, and rescue me from this nightmare.

But it wasn't him.

A pair of warm hands touched my face, patting my cheek like they were trying to revive me. Then he grabbed my shoulders and picked me up, pulling me out of that dark place. I heard his deep voice, but it was so muffled I couldn't make out what he'd said. He cradled me in his arms like a child and kept talking, as though he were trying to get me to answer. I couldn't. The world around me was still hazy, and yet his warmth was all too real. It made me instinctively cling to him.

My tattooed neighbor from across the hall carried me, holding me against his chest as though I were something precious. No one had ever carried me like that, especially not a guy.

As soon as we left my bedroom, everything seemed to get clearer. I could breathe easier, and the coldness ebbed away from my extremities. I could see him, his strange violet-colored eyes sharp and dangerous as they focused straight ahead.

His face was drawn into a look of quiet fury as he picked his way across the debris. Glass from the broken picture frames crunched under his shoes as we passed through the living room. My front door had obviously been kicked in. It was dangling off the hinges when he carried me across the hall. He didn't even bother trying to shut it.

When he opened the door to his apartment directly across from mine, the smell of him—that deep, musky, man-smell—hit me with startling force. I realized how long it had been since I was close enough to anyone to recognize his or her smell like that.

I looked up at him with my thoughts tangled like Christmas lights. Usually, I didn't like it when anyone touched me. It probably had a lot to do with adults dragging me places I didn't want to go. It made me feel small and powerless.

His touch wasn't like that. He was gentle, but firm. His arms felt sturdy and cautious as he carefully sat me down on his sofa.

I was feeling much calmer … right up until I heard him go back and lock his door.

What the *hell*?

I sat up immediately. Our eyes met from across the room. He walked toward me with purpose in every step.

Alarm bells screamed in my head. I didn't know him. I didn't know what he planned to do that required locking the door. And I did *not* want to find out.

As he got closer, I scrambled to the opposite end of his couch and snatched the remote control off the end table, holding it up like a weapon.

He stopped a few feet away, glancing at my poor excuse for a defense, and raised one of his eyebrows. "Calm down. I'm not gonna hurt you," he muttered.

"Why did you—" I started to ask.

He cut me off quickly, "You were screaming bloody murder over there. I'm sure everyone in a two-block radius heard you."

"A-actually I was going to ask why you locked the door." My voice came out like a terrified squeak.

He snorted and crossed his arms. "Because I live here, and I don't want whoever broke in and trashed your place trying the same thing here. What did you think?"

I didn't want to answer that. It seemed like a stupid accusation now, anyway. I glanced down at the remote control in my hand and slowly put it back on the table.

"You alright?" The concern in his deep, gruff voice surprised me.

I was still trying to figure that out. There were cuts and scratches all over my arms. Some of them even looked like bite marks. They stung whenever I moved. My ankle had finger-shaped bruises on it, and my neck still hurt from being dragged around by my hair. Then there were my fingers— three of them were turning an unsettling shade of blue where the door had smashed them. All told, I was a mess. My face grew hot with shame. How was I going to explain this?

"I'm fine," I managed to answer. Unfortunately, I had never been a very good liar. "Please don't call the police."

His forehead creased as he came closer, towering over me, and pointed at my arms. "Let me see."

He didn't give me a chance to refuse. He grabbed my wrists, turning my arms, and looking at the marks. Most of them were on my forearms, as though I'd been wrestling with an angry cat or something. Then he examined my fingers one by one. I winced as he probed at them, as though he were testing to see if any were broken.

Finally, he let me go and sighed. "It doesn't look that bad. I'll get you some antiseptic and gauze for those cuts."

I barely heard what he'd said. I'd seen him from a distance plenty of times, but this was my first chance to examine him up close. He had defined, squared features that struck me as classic—almost like one of those young Greek heroes in old renaissance paintings. There was a dusting of short, dark stubble on his sturdy jaw, and his strangely colored eyes were so serious and mesmerizing.

When he looked at me again, I couldn't speak. His gaze scrambled all my thoughts.

He didn't seem to notice though. "Sit tight."

I nodded, watching as he disappeared down the hall. After a few minutes, he came back with a spool of medical gauze and a tube of antibacterial cream. He sat down on the couch beside me and held out a hand expectantly.

"Arm," he demanded.

I put one of my arms in his hand. He smeared cream on all the cuts, scrapes, and bites. Then, he carefully wrapped both of my forearms in gauze. He seemed entirely focused on his work, and completely oblivious to how I kept staring at him.

I didn't understand why he was going to so much trouble. Why had he come in to get me in the first place? Why hadn't he just called the police? Anyone else would have dialed 911, complained about the noise, and left it at that.

Suddenly I realized—he had *heard* me. No one had ever heard me before. Why him? Why now? Wasn't he supposed to be at work?

I glanced over at the digital clock on his microwave. It read 3:37 AM, so he was home early. I knew his work hours kept him out all night. Most likely he'd never been home to hear me during one of those attacks.

It was painfully awkward to sit in silence and stare at him, but I didn't want him to ask about what was happening in my apartment. In my experience, once people got to know me, they tended to act like my brand of crazy might be contagious. With him, I had a clean slate—at least for a little while. I wanted to savor it while it lasted, so I didn't dare say a word.

He glanced up at me so suddenly I startled. His bizarre eyes caught in the dim light of the room and shimmered in hues of soft lavender and vivid violet.

"What?" he asked with a frown.

"Nothing! It's uh … I don't even know your name." I blurted out the first excuse I could think of.

He rolled his eyes, looking back down at my arms as he finished tying off the last strip of gauze. "Zeph," he answered. "Zeph Clemmont."

Zeph. I'd never heard that name before. It sounded kind of exotic. Then again, he wasn't exactly what most people would call average-looking.

"Your eyes are kinda strange," I blurted again before I could stop myself.

His eyes narrowed slightly, making one corner of his mouth scrunch as though he wasn't sure if he should be insulted.

"I-I mean I've never seen anyone with purple eyes like that." I frantically tried to explain myself. "I bet people ask you all the time if you wear contacts."

Zeph shrugged as he gathered up his medical supplies. "It's a genetic thing," he mumbled. "Is there anyone you can stay with tonight? A friend or something?"

"A friend?" I gaped at him for a moment like he was speaking a foreign language. Then I remembered normal people had those. I slowly shook my head. "N-no. It's fine, though. I can just go back to my apartment. I'll give my cousin a call tomorrow. He looks in on me sometimes."

The corner of Zeph's mouth twitched into a smirk, as though he wasn't buying one inch of that story. "Cousin, huh?"

"His name is Ben," I said as convincingly as possible. "He exists. Don't look at me like that. I'm not lying."

"Whatever you say, princess. You should probably let someone know what happened, though, even if you don't want to call the cops. Not a good idea for you to stay there tonight since I busted your door down. It isn't safe."

I wanted to tell him it didn't matter if I had a front door or not; I was never safe over there. I hung my head instead, watching out of the corner of my eye as Zeph stood up and went into the kitchen. He rooted around in his cabinets and finally came back with a jumbo-sized can of sliced peaches, a fork, and a big glass of milk. He sat down next to me again and gulped down half the glass of milk in one noisy slurp.

"I guess you can borrow my couch for tonight," he offered so casually that at first, I didn't realize what he'd said.

Then it clicked. "Wait, what? You mean I can stay here?"

"Well, it's that or you sleep in the hallway, right?" He had a mouthful of sliced peaches.

"But you don't even know my name," I protested. He was right, though. I had nowhere else to go.

He glanced sideways at me through some of his long, messy bangs. "So what is it?"

"Uh," I stammered. It was hard to answer when he was looking at me like that. "It's Josie."

"Josie who?"

I was really hoping he wouldn't ask me about my last name—or anything else specific about my life. If Child Protective Services ever got wind of my living situation, I knew they'd pull me out of school and send me to live with strangers. I'd gotten a small taste of foster care after Dad died, and I was not eager for seconds.

But I couldn't lie. Not when he was glaring at me like that. "Josie Barton."

"And you live alone?" I could feel his gaze moving over me, sizing me up from the other side of the couch.

My face began to get hot, and I looked down at my lap. I didn't want to answer that. "I-I need to go find my phone," I tried to change the subject. I was already wondering how I could explain all this to Ben.

Zeph leaned over to one side and pulled his cell phone out of his back pocket. He tossed it into my lap and went back to his dinner of peaches and milk. "Call whoever you need to. I'll stop by Mr. Bregger's tomorrow and let him know I'm paying for the door, since that one's my fault."

The door was the least of my worries. Hadn't he seen the rest of my apartment? It was an absolute wreck. It would take me all day to clean it again. I'd have to buy new picture frames and restock the refrigerator. I was worrying about all those things as I picked up Zeph's cell phone. It was still warm from being in his pocket, and there was a picture of a beautiful night skyline as his background image.

"Is it okay for me to send an email?" I asked. "It's probably too early to call him. I don't want to wake him up."

Zeph shrugged again and went on eating his peaches.

I logged into my email account and quickly typed a message to Ben. I tried to keep it as vague as possible, telling him there'd been an accident at my place. I told him it was my fault, but everything was okay now. I was going to stay with a friend for the night, so he didn't have to worry.

It was a lie, of course. Calling Zeph a friend was a huge stretch. I doubted Ben would catch on, though. At least, I hoped he wouldn't. I wasn't confident in my skills of deception, even though I had never told him anything about my personal life. He didn't know about the trips to the principal's office or my visits with a doctor. I'd been careful about that, using cash to pay for the appointments so he wouldn't see the charges on the credit card. He didn't know anything about my PTSD outbursts, or how I saw things that weren't there. I guess part of me was afraid that if he did find out, he might send me off to one of those mental hospitals himself.

"I'm going to bed," Zeph announced as he swallowed the last slice of peach. He left all his dishes and the empty can on the coffee table as he stood and stretched. Then he held a hand out to me, wiggling his fingers like he wanted me to take it.

I was stunned.

It looked like an invitation. Was he ... asking me to go to bed with him? I opened my mouth to speak, but all I did was make choking sounds.

"My phone," he growled, frowning like he wasn't sure why I was taking so long.

Now I was even more embarrassed. Way to go, Josie. Jumping to *that* conclusion right off the bat.

"Thank you for letting me stay here," I squeaked as I handed him back his cell phone.

"Don't worry about it." He went to a closet in the hall and took out a spare pillow and blanket. He tossed them at me before disappearing down the hall. Somewhere out of sight, I heard a door shut.

For a moment, I sat there and stared around his apartment. It wasn't much bigger than mine, although the layout was different. The kitchen and living room were combined, and the walls were painted a dark, soothing slate blue. His furniture was simple, just a dark brown leather sofa and two matching chairs. There were no decorative pieces anywhere—no pictures on the walls, only one rug that was too small for the room, and no artwork. There was nothing personal about the place at all, nothing to tell me about his life or who he was.

There was a stack of magazines on his coffee table, though. The first few were what I would expect a guy to have—about cars and fitness—but the third one down had a big picture of a busty woman straddling a motorcycle on the cover. The one after that had two busty girls in string bikinis posing on the hood of a sleek black car. I stopped there because I was blushing like crazy. Did all guys keep these kinds of magazines lying around in the open like this?

Curling up under the blanket, I tried not to think about what had happened in my apartment. Whenever I closed my eyes, my skin crawled. It was as though I could still feel those cold fingers squeezing me.

I wished I hadn't dropped my cell phone. I wished I could send Ben another message to make sure he believed me when I said everything was okay. I was terrified of him finding out how miserable I was. He'd told me once that there was no shame in asking him for help when I needed it. He was probably right, but that didn't make the situation any less terrifying. I was already a financial burden to him. I didn't want to be an emotional burden, too. I didn't want him to think I couldn't handle living by myself. If he found out about the things I saw, he might ship me off somewhere much worse than a special school.

The problem was ... I needed help so badly I couldn't stand it. My stupid pride and determination to be mature and rational about this was crumbling. I couldn't handle this on my own for much longer. Things were getting way out of control. I'd been screaming for help for years now, praying someone would come.

Zeph Clemmont was the first person that had ever heard me.

I couldn't remember the last time I had slept so long without being disturbed or woken up by something terrible ripping my apartment to shreds. Zeph's apartment felt safe. It was quiet, warm, and everything stayed peaceful for the rest of the night. I slept like a log.

The sound of traffic woke me late the next morning. I squinted at the digital clock on the microwave again. At first, it didn't matter to me what time it was. I didn't care. I was comfortable in that hazy state of bliss, clinging to the first good dream I'd had in months—which happened to be about eating sushi from one of those neat restaurants with the conveyer belt that went around with seemingly endless delicious options. I'd never actually been to one, but seeing them featured on the cooking channels always piqued my interest. Yes, I dreamt about food. Go ahead, judge away.

Then it hit me.

It was almost noon.

All my delightful visions of a brightly colored sushi parade evaporated. My head popped off the pillow immediately. I bolted upright, snatching the blanket off my legs. I was late for school—extremely late. I'd already missed morning detention, which was a sentence leftover from another one of my outbursts earlier in the week, and most of my morning classes. Ms. Grear was going to be angry enough to breathe fire by the time I got to her office. Getting written up two days in a row was a new low, even for me.

"So, you're alive." A deep, masculine voice made me jump. Zeph was leaning on the kitchen counter, sipping a cup of coffee with a scheming grin on his face. "I was beginning to wonder if I needed to check for a pulse."

"Oh no. No, no, no, no ..." I couldn't even put a sentence together as I scrambled to my feet and rushed to his door. "I'm late! I am *so* late!"

Zeph didn't try to stop me as I unlocked the door and then flung it open wide.

I didn't even get one foot outside. When I saw all the workers filing in and out of my apartment, I was too surprised to move. Men in matching uniforms were fixing my door, while others were carrying out bags of trash and mopping up the spilled food in the kitchen.

I stood in the doorway with my mouth open, staring, until I heard a loud sipping, slurping sound. Zeph was standing right behind me, drinking coffee like there was nothing at all strange about this.

"That cousin of yours works fast," he observed casually. "They've been here all morning. I went ahead and told them I'd pay for the work on the door."

"H-he didn't have to do all this," I whimpered. I was mortified at having all these people in my house, touching my things, and looking at the damage. It was like being violated somehow. "I could have cleaned it myself."

Zeph snorted. "So I take it you won't be filing a police report for a home invasion after all? Afraid CPS will come for you?"

I flinched at that accusation and shot him a glare. "It's none of your business."

"It wasn't," he corrected me as he went sauntering back into his apartment. "Until I had to come rescue you and let you sleep on my sofa. Now, I'm involved."

I slowly shut the door so none of the workers would overhear us. "Zeph, please don't tell anyone about this, or that I'm living by myself. I turn eighteen in a few months, and then it'll be legal for me to live alone. I can't go into a foster home. It'll ruin my school year and—"

"Can the waterworks, princess." Zeph plopped down onto his sofa and started flipping through one of his non-pornographic magazines. "I'm not telling anyone. It's your business, not mine."

I sank back in relief, leaning against his front door and letting out a deep sigh. "Thank you."

"You can thank me with some favors." He took another noisy drink from his mug. "My silence won't be free."

I frowned as my relief swiftly devolved to suspicion. "Wait, are you *blackmailing* me?"

He shrugged slightly. "That's an intense word for it. Let's just say a few favors on your end would ease my guilty conscience about letting a little high-school girl live all by herself in an apartment that's been vandalized."

"It wasn't vandalized, I … I did it myself!" I couldn't keep my voice steady. It was easier to agree with the doctors and Ms. Grear—to blame myself rather than trying to explain the things I saw.

"Right. Sure." He cocked an eyebrow.

I marched over to stand in front of him. "What kind of favors are you suggesting, exactly? It better not be anything like your gross magazines!"

He made a sarcastic snorting noise and shot me a cunning grin. "I was thinking more along the line of chores, actually. But if we're going that route—"

"No! No we are not," I interrupted. "Chores? You mean like doing your laundry?"

"I was thinking more like cooking." He flashed me another appraising glance with those mesmerizing eyes before going back to his magazine. "I'm a vegetarian, though. So keep that in mind."

I'd seen plenty of vegetarians before. Zeph did not look anything like a man who lived off broccoli, carrots, and kale salads. He had a robust, sturdy build even for a man of his height. His arms and chest were very toned beneath the thin, cotton undershirt he wore. I could see faint veins in his forearms and biceps as he sat there, nursing his coffee mug.

I narrowed my eyes suspiciously.

"Just leave whatever you make by the door."

"How did you know I like to cook, anyway?"

He didn't even look up from his magazine. "I can smell it when I leave for work. Smells good. And since you live alone, you must do your own cooking."

I blushed a little because that almost sounded like a compliment—a watered-down, vague compliment. "And that's it? You just want me to leave a bunch of food sitting outside your door?"

"Or bring it in. I don't care."

It was hard not to read too much into that. Was that an invitation come over and visit? I dared to dream. "Fine. I guess I'll have to read up on vegetarian recipes."

He grunted in agreement.

For a few minutes, everything was quiet except for the noise of the traffic outside and the workers fixing my apartment. I couldn't help but realize what a total wreck I was. My long red hair was frizzy and falling out of its braid. I was still wearing pajamas that weren't even remotely attractive. It made me even more self-conscious as I sat down on the opposite end of the couch from him.

"I guess I'm not going to school today," I muttered to myself in defeat. I couldn't even get inside my apartment to take a shower or retrieve my uniform. To be honest, my heart wasn't in it anyway. I didn't have the courage to endure another visit to Ms. Grear's office.

"Don't worry about it," he grumbled. "One day won't kill you."

"In my case, it might. My school counselor absolutely hates me, and so do most of the other teachers and people at my school."

Zeph finally glanced up from his magazine. He looked surprised. "Why? What'd you do?"

I looked down, fidgeting with my hands. "Well, you know. I'm crazy."

"Crazy how?"

I forced a laugh, trying to play it off like it wasn't a big deal. "Come on, you saw what I did to my apartment."

He'd been referring to it like it was a real home invasion, but surely he didn't believe that. Nothing was stolen. I hadn't been murdered or kidnapped. So what would have been the point of anyone breaking in? Besides, it was a lot more believable for me to have a mental breakdown than to try to convince anyone there was an angry, dark spirit haunting my home.

He was scowling. "And?"

"And it's like that all the time. I don't remember doing it, but it had to be me. It couldn't have been anyone else, right? It happens at school, too. I see things that aren't there. The counselor says I'm causing a disturbance, and she's right."

"Your counselor sounds like an idiot." He snorted. "You're not crazy."

"H-how can you say that?"

He went back to sipping his coffee as nonchalantly as ever. "Because, believe me, I *know* crazy. You're weird, maybe even a little ditzy, but you're not crazy."

Before I could stop it, a grin wriggled up my face.

Being called crazy was terrible. I'd heard it whispered at my back so many times I'd lost count. It was like having a disease that everyone else was afraid of catching. All of a sudden, nothing about you was credible. But weird? Ditzy? Those were words I could live with. Those were tolerable things.

I'd never been tolerable to anyone before.

"That's a creepy smile."

I wrinkled my nose at him. "I'm going home."

"Whatever you say, princess." He yawned, waving his hand off toward the door dismissively.

Even though it made me feel a little stupid, I kept smiling at him. I couldn't have handpicked a more inappropriate person in the entire world to become friends with, but for the first time since my dad passed away, I didn't feel alone anymore.

As I stepped out his front door, I glanced back to where Zeph was stretched out on the sofa with his feet propped up on the edge of the coffee table. He was gruff, a little rude, and rough-looking with the long hair and all those tattoos on his arms.

But it was too late.

I already liked him.

The workers left an invoice and receipt taped to the door with an envelope that had a new key inside it when they were finished. They had fixed everything and had even given me a new knob and deadbolt for my front door. I wondered how long this one would last.

Inside, everything was clean and smelled like fresh paint and bleach. All my decorations had been placed carefully around the rooms. Not all of them were in places I liked, but it was nice to come into a neat, orderly apartment. Even my cell phone was left sitting on the kitchen counter, waiting for me.

I took a shower and fixed my hair, taming my wild red curls with a few swipes of a straightening iron before changing into casual clothes. I sent Ben a text message to tell him that the workers had done a great job. After thanking him profusely, I promised it wouldn't happen again. Lies, lies, lies.

I was layering up my socks so I could brave the cold and buy fresh groceries when my phone began beeping and vibrating, announcing I had a new text message.

```
BEN: Glad everything is all right now. More than
anything, I'm thankful you're all right. I know you
don't want to tell me what happened, otherwise you
would have in your email, but I am here for you
regardless. Please remember that. Don't be afraid
to ask me for help when you need it.
```

Guilt immediately made my stomach bind up in knots. I stared at the screen, reading his message over and over. I felt bad for not telling him the truth, and yet at the same time, messages like this always sort of pissed me off. He was responsible for my well-being and survival, but we might as well have been total strangers. He kept himself anonymous and carefully set apart from my life, except to reach in like the proverbial hand of fate to move things in my favor now and again.

I had no right to be angry with him. I couldn't point fingers at the person giving me a roof over my head just because he didn't want to share it with me. It was his choice to keep his distance. My dad had asked him to be there for me in these few, specific ways, and Ben had been faithful to that agreement. I should have been content with the way things were.

After all, someone wanting privacy wasn't a new concept for me. My dad had been extremely private about his work. I knew absolutely nothing about what he did except that it involved a lot of bizarre research. He spent a lot of time buried in old books, most of which were written in foreign languages. A few of them had even survived the fire, and despite my best efforts to read them, I couldn't make heads or tails of the strange pictures, diagrams, and spidery handwriting etched in them. So I had packed up all of those books and stuffed them away in the guest room. They'd been so important to him, getting rid of them felt wrong.

I'd always suspected that Ben was somehow involved with my dad's work. It was the only reason that made any sense as to why Ben didn't want me to know anything more about him. Maybe they were in a secret line of work, like the CIA or FBI, and Ben couldn't get any closer to me than this because it would put my life in danger. That was part of the reason why I'd never just come out and asked to meet him, although I had hinted heavily at it plenty of times. That and … I knew what the answer would be.

I quickly typed back a message, assuring him that I was fine and everything was going swimmingly in my perfect teenage life. Sooner or later, I knew he was going to find out that wasn't true. Then I would have to confess to him about what was happening at school. If things with Ms. Grear kept going downhill this quickly, I wasn't going to come close to making it till graduation.

I couldn't tell him yet. I was too embarrassed by it all. Not to mention I was absolutely terrified he might agree with Ms. Grear and ship me off to some school for the mentally disturbed.

His reply came back so quickly, it made me nervous even before I read it.

> BEN: What happened last night? Is there something you aren't telling me?

My throat went dry. He'd never asked me anything like this before. He never pried.

My fingers hovered over the buttons while I desperately tried to come up with a convincing story. Maybe I could tell him I threw a wild party? Didn't other high school kids do that kind of thing sometimes?

I couldn't do it; I couldn't lie to him again. That wasn't the kind of person I wanted to be. Cramming my phone into my pocket without answering, I finished getting dressed. My thoughts were scrambled, torn over the difference between lying to him outright and covering everything up like always. Either way, it was deception, and either way, he was probably going to be seriously angry when he found out what was really going on.

I went back into the kitchen to grab a quick bite of breakfast and make a grocery list before I left. I was hoping that at least some of my food had been spared from last night's chaos.

Zeph was sitting at my kitchen table.

I screamed and fell back against the wall.

I wasn't expecting to see anyone sitting there. I didn't get many guests, especially not of the friendly, visible variety. When I recognized him, I tried to catch my breath.

Zeph crossed his arms over his chest like he'd caught me doing something terrible. He waved the Davner's pamphlet in front of my nose like a battle flag declaring war. "What's this?"

I was mortified.

Immediately, I dove to snatch the pamphlet back from him. "Don't go through my stuff! What are you even doing here? How did you get in?"

Faster than I could react, Zeph yanked the pamphlet out of reach. His violet eyes smoldered dangerously. "I came to leave you a check for the busted door. It's not my fault you left it unlocked. No wonder you had a break in."

"That does not mean you can come prancing in here anytime you like!" I fumed. "Give that back!"

"Not until you answer my question," he growled as he quickly stuck it under his rear end and sat on it. "What the hell is it?"

I wasn't about to go digging around under his butt for the pamphlet. "It's a special school. My counselor wants me to transfer there since I've been causing so much trouble." My eyes began to well up. "It's supposed to be for people ... like me."

Zeph pulled the pamphlet out from under him and immediately tore it into a hundred little pieces. He crumpled them all together in his palm, molding the shredded bits of paper into a marble-sized ball that he then dropped into my hand.

"You don't need to go to any special school."

I stared down in quiet mortification at what was left of the pamphlet. The tears that rolled down my face felt cool against my flushed cheeks. I clenched my teeth and stifled a sniffle. "Y-you're wrong. You don't know anything about me! I see things all the time that don't exist. I see monsters in the halls at school and shadows that move on the walls here at home. I hear things moving and growling in the dark. There is something wrong with me. I *am* crazy!"

Zeph stared at me with an eerily neutral expression. It was like the calm before the storm, and I wasn't sure what he might do.

I swallowed hard.

Suddenly, Zeph stood up and walked right past me. He left without saying a single word and slammed the door behind him hard enough to make the windows rattle.

Trembling and still holding the little wad of paper in my hand; I couldn't tear my eyes away from the door. Five minutes must have passed, and he still hadn't come back to finish our argument. I had made him angry—really, *really* angry. He might not ever come back, and that absolutely terrified me.

I was determined not to cry anymore. I wasn't going to do it. Somehow, it seemed like crying would be the same as letting him win. So, I threw what was left of the pamphlet away and snatched my coat off the rack by the door.

There were only a few things that brought me any comfort when I was this upset. Usually cleaning was enough to soothe me after a particularly rough day, but the workers had left everything in perfect order. So that left only one other option.

I cooked everything I could possibly think of that a nosy, vegetarian bachelor might want to eat. The smell of a few loaves of bread, vegetable stew, and more cookies than any sane person would need at one time filled my apartment. I wrapped everything up neatly in a brown paper bag, then scribbled a note on the side that said, "*Sorry I made you angry. Here's your first payment. I promise there are no laxatives in this.*"

I left the bag on Zeph's doorstep and rang the bell before running to the stairwell. Peeking around the corner, I waited for him to come out. I wanted to see how he would react to my peace offering.

He never came.

I left our apartment building disappointed, and sat down on the front steps to watch the evening traffic roll by. People walked home from work or rode by on their bicycles. A few happy couples wandered by, laughing and holding hands. I wondered what that must be like. I'd never had a boyfriend before. I'd barely even had a real friend until …

I flushed and fidgeted with my hair. Thinking about Zeph left me baffled. Why had he gotten so angry about me changing schools, anyway? Why did he care about that? It wasn't any of his business.

My phone buzzed in my pocket, sending a fresh pang of dread through my body. I'd forgotten all about Ben's text message from earlier. Seeing his name pop up on the screen with another message made my stomach twist.

> BEN: I'm sorry if my previous message seemed intrusive. I didn't mean to upset you. My primary concern is your safety. I want to respect your privacy while also providing you the security I promised your father I would. It's a difficult balance for me to strike sometimes. I trust you will tell me if there is something serious happening that I can help with.

How could I be so stupid? I should have answered him sooner. Now he was worried about me. I'd been so quick to tell him everything was fine that it must have sounded like I was overcompensating.

I quickly typed a message to thank him for his concern and support. I told him how much I appreciated everything he'd done for me, and promised to be more responsible with telling him when I needed help in the future.

Alone on the steps, I watched the sun set over our quaint neighborhood, as the streetlamps hummed to life. The air got colder and the wind blew through my hair. I'd watched the end of the day like this so many times, and it always made me think about my dad. I knew he wouldn't have enjoyed living somewhere like this. He didn't like cities. Dad had preferred the rolling countryside, like where our old house had been before it burned. I hadn't been back there in years. I missed it. The smell of the woods, clean air, and the sound of the wind in the trees were still etched in my memory, fragments of a childhood that had gone up in smoke.

Finally, I stood up and went back inside.

On my way back to my apartment, I walked past Zeph's door. The bag of food was gone. I smiled with relief. He didn't hate me, at least. If he'd hated me, then surely he wouldn't have taken the food, right?

I nibbled on my bottom lip, wishing I had been there to watch him discover it. Had he smiled? It was hard to imagine him smiling without also picturing devil horns on his head, though. Maybe some fangs, bat wings, and a pitchfork, too.

Everything in my apartment was still clean and orderly when I went inside. I ate a late-night snack, changed into my pajamas, and made my bed on the couch in silence. I should have been happy. My house was clean. I'd taken a day off from school. Instead, all I could think about was how unbearably quiet it was.

My gaze kept wandering back to the chair at the kitchen table where I'd discovered Zeph that morning. Why did my apartment feel so empty without him in it? Why was I hoping he'd come storming back through my front door to finish our argument?

Staring down at the screen of my phone, I scrolled through all of Ben's old emails and messages to reread each one. I still had them all saved, including the very first one he'd ever sent after my dad passed away. Sometimes, reading them helped ease my loneliness and anxiety about what was to come. After all, nothing had changed. I still wasn't safe here, even with Zeph across the hall.

I fluffed my pillow and tucked my blanket around me. Today was the first normal-ish day I'd had in a long time. I hoped that would extend through the night, too. Maybe it was over now. Maybe I could finally get a good night's sleep. After all, my apartment seemed quiet and calm.

I should have known it was too good to be true.

Something was breathing on me—a hot, moist breath, puffed right in my face, tickling my cheeks. I squinted and twitched my nose. Only it smelled awful—almost like … dog breath.

When I opened my eyes, there was nothing there.

A cold shiver ran through my body.

I sat up straight, snatching the blanket against my chest as I looked around. The room was completely dark again. The lamps had been extinguished. I couldn't even see the furniture.

Then I saw a glowing pair of silver eyes hovering in the corner of the room.

I froze. My breath caught in my throat. A sound like a dog snarling cut through the darkness. I gripped the blanket so hard my fingers went numb.

The monster in my apartment had never revealed itself before. Something was different—and very wrong.

As fast as I could blink, the creature moved closer. The eyes were a few yards away, then a few feet, and then suddenly, jagged teeth came into view.

It wasn't a dog. It was a wolf—a huge wolf with fur of pitch black that seemed to melt right into the rest of the shadows in the room. The edges of its body licked like dark flames, wavering and shifting as it prowled toward me.

I had to move. I had to get away. *Now!*

I crawled over the back of the couch as the creature pounced, bellowing in fury.

I screamed, kicking away from the animal as I scrambled to the other side of the room. The wolf stalked after me, its bottomless silver eyes glowing like two moons with an eerie, ethereal light. They shone so brightly I could see the saliva dripping off its fangs.

The beast backed me up against the living room wall, prowling closer and closer. There was nowhere to run, and nothing I could use as a weapon. I trembled, trying to find my voice so I could scream for help.

Suddenly, my front door burst open with a loud crack. Shards of wood went flying. The black wolf whipped its huge head around, and we both stared at the figure standing in the doorway.

The light flooding in from the hallway was too bright to make out anything more than a tall man's silhouette.

I knew it was Zeph. I could feel it.

I was afraid he wouldn't see the creature. No one else ever saw the things I did. Why would he be any different? But when Zeph raised his gaze to meet mine, his strange eyes glowed like fiery amethysts. In an instant, his attention flicked from me to the wolf. His mouth twitched and curled into a vicious snarl that displayed prominent, pointed incisors.

Panic squeezed the breath from my lungs. It wasn't possible—it couldn't be real. Was he some kind of demon? I opened my mouth to scream, but a strangled panicked squeak was all that would come out.

"You." Zeph pointed at me. "Don't freak out. Deep breaths. Got it?"

I squeaked again.

"And you," he snarled, his focus back on the wolf. There was power in his voice that made me tremble. "Eldrick, you worthless scumbag, I should have known it was you starting shit over here. You've got a lot of nerve."

As he came into the room, his shadowed form warped with every step. His head rolled to the side slightly as two tapered, spike-shaped horns emerged above long, pointed ears. His powerful shoulders flexed, hunching forward as two huge feathered wings seemed to unfold from somewhere within him. They glowed with a faint lavender light and shimmered as though each feather were made from beveled glass.

He walked right toward me. As he got closer, I could see strange markings on his powerful arms and chest coming to life like they were glowing under a black light. It was some sort of writing, but not in any language I recognized. It reminded me a little of the writing from my dad's books, though. It was intricate and elegant, like spirals and swirls that flowed beautifully over his darkly tanned skin.

I was paralyzed with awe—torn somewhere between terror and mystification. He couldn't be a demon. No, he was something else—something I didn't have a name for.

The wolf growled and then recoiled. It flicked a glance back at me, as if it was trying to decide whether to attack.

"Do it," Zeph sneered. "Give me an excuse to kill you."

The wolf bristled and licked its teeth tauntingly, then answered Zeph in a breathy masculine voice, "As if you could."

"Oh? Feeling cocky, are we?" Zeph laughed as he flexed again, making his broad wings stretch out farther and filling the room with that eerie purple light. He had a menacing smirk on his lips. It made a shiver run down my spine. "What's your problem, anyway? You've always been a dick, but at least before you had some kinda reason. This girl's not a threat to you."

"What would you know about it?" The wolf's body trembled with rage. "You think I am here by choice?"

Realization dawned on his face, making those violet eyes go round for a second. "Ah, I get it. How ironic. So you're stuck in a—"

"*Do not say it!*"

Zeph's mouth curled into a wicked smirk. "Not that I wouldn't enjoy giving you the public ass-whipping you deserve, but watching you bow to a mortal will be much more satisfying."

The wolf growled even louder. I saw his legs coil beneath him. His fangs flashed. I squeezed my eyes shut and prepared for the worst.

"Josie!" Zeph shouted. "You can control him! He has to obey you! Give him a command!"

I threw my hands up to shield my face and screamed, "Stop it! Don't touch me!"

I tensed up, waiting to feel his teeth clamp down on my skin, or worse. The wolf didn't attack.

He stayed crouched, still growling, his eyes boring into mine with scalding hatred.

Zeph grinned smugly. "Good, now tell him to sit, like a good little mutt."

Was he serious? I swallowed hard, steeling myself. "S-sit."

The wolf's ears pressed against his skull. His snout wrinkled as he showed me all his pointed teeth. But he obeyed. He sat back on his haunches, his shaggy pelt trembling with fury.

"Excellent. Nice to see you back in your place." Zeph was practically purring with satisfaction. Then he whirled around and started for me at a purpose-driven pace.

I screamed.

He looked like something out of a twisted thriller movie with fangs, spiked horns, and radiant wings. I didn't understand what he wanted from me, and the fact that he seemed to know that wolf so well wasn't reassuring at all.

"Josie," he said my name in a disturbingly calm voice. "I'm not gonna hurt you."

"S-stay away!" I couldn't control my shaking. I tried to get away, but there was nowhere else to run. All I could do was squeeze my eyes shut.

I could feel how close Zeph was even before I opened my eyes again. It was like his body gave off an invisible electric current that made every little hair on my arms stand on end.

When I did dare to look, he was crouched down right in front of me, his gleaming violet eyes staring right into mine and his voluminous wings closing around us like a cocoon.

It was too much to take in—the fear, the confusion, the giant shadow-wolf that apparently wanted to kill me, and the glowing, purple-eyed, vegetarian angel-monster living across the hall. I couldn't breathe. I leaned back against the wall as spots danced in my vision. My ears were ringing and my fingertips tingled.

"Looks like we need to talk." He arched one of his dark eyebrows. It was the same cocky expression he had given me the day before. Somewhere under all that purple, glowing, otherworldly strangeness, he was still the same Zeph.

"This is real." My own voice sounded far away. "I-I thought I was ..."

He smirked. "What? Crazy?"

I couldn't answer. My arms dropped back into my lap like two overcooked noodles. I couldn't keep myself conscious anymore.

I opened my eyes to the sound of my cell phone's alarm going off on my nightstand. I was lying on my bed amidst rumpled blankets, warm and comfortable. Soft sunlight filtered through the thin, lacey curtains over my bedroom window. Outside, I could faintly hear the sounds of morning traffic passing in front of the apartment building, and birds singing in the trees right outside.

This wasn't right. I didn't have mornings like this.

I sat up and scooted to the edge of my bed, leaning over to see down the hallway and into the living room.

There was no one else here.

My skin prickled with a cold chill.

I crept out of bed and down the hall, peeking around every corner before going from room to room. Nothing was broken. Nothing was cracked, flipped over, or spilled. Everything looked exactly the way it should have. My pictures were still on the walls. All the cabinets were closed. There was no grouchy tattooed man sitting at my breakfast table and no giant, evil wolf waiting to rip my throat out.

I stopped in the middle of the living room and scratched the back of my head. Had it all just been another nightmare? That was the only explanation that made sense ...

Until I saw the feather.

Out of the corner of my eye, I spotted something sparkling on the coffee table. It was a slender, delicate feather that looked like it had been cut from thin purple glass. I held it up, watching it shimmer and shine in the morning light.

It hadn't been a dream.

The wolf, Zeph, and everything else I had seen these past few years had all been real. That one little feather shattered the dam of doubt and fear that had been building in my mind. This wasn't PTSD or an anxiety disorder. I hadn't imagined any of it.

I wasn't crazy.

Still wearing my pajamas, I bolted out the front door and ran across the hall to ring Zeph's doorbell repeatedly.

My mind was a tangled net of questions. If I wasn't crazy and if all of this was real, then why was I seeing it when no one else could? What was Zeph? What was that wolf and why did he have to do what I asked? What was he even doing in my apartment in the first place?

There was only one person who had those answers, and he wasn't answering the stupid door.

"I know you're home!" I yelled, trying the knob; but it was locked. "Zeph! Open up!"

I knocked as loudly as I could and rang the bell a few more times. Minutes crawled by, and I planted myself stubbornly on his doorstep.

He never answered. In fact, I didn't hear a single sound coming from inside his place.

I glanced down at the beautiful feather still in my hand. It caught the light and sparkled like transparent purple glass, and yet it bent easily with a silky softness that tickled my palm. I wondered if the rest of his wings were as soft. Had they been? I couldn't remember now. All my thoughts were hazed as I looked back up at Zeph's door.

He had to come back sometime. I could be patient until then.

I twirled the feather between my fingers as I wandered back across the hall to my apartment. This shimmering, delicate gift was the only evidence I had that I wasn't out of my mind. It was my prize now, so I placed it in an empty bud vase on the windowsill behind the kitchen sink. I stood back to admire how it caught the sunlight and sent a riot of bright reflections glittering across the room.

Then my phone started buzzing again. It was my secondary "seriously, get up now" alarm. There was no way around it this time; I had to go to school today.

Yanking a clean uniform out of my closet, I quickly got dressed. The pleated skirt, button down blouse, and tie weren't very flattering on me. If anything, they made me look younger. I felt ridiculous until I pulled the thick, navy blue knit sweater over my head and straightened my collar out on top of it. Somehow wearing that helped a little. It at least disguised the fact that I basically had no boobs.

I scarfed down half a peanut butter and jelly sandwich before brushing my teeth and racing out the door. The sky was cloudless and crisp blue and the wind was cold, but bracing. I dared to smile as I strolled the sidewalk on my way to school. Maybe this would be a fresh start. If Zeph had chased off that wolf for good, then I didn't have to be nervous about going home anymore. Maybe the strange things that sometimes happened at school would stop, too.

One look and all my hopes came crashing down around my ears.

Through the line of other kids filing into the building, I spotted Ms. Grear's puffy, bulldog face glowering in my direction.

It was going to be one of *those* days, after all.

I was in for it this time. Anger wafted off her like a gust from a furnace as I walked up the front steps of the school. Her eyes locked onto mine, and every muscle in my body went tense.

Ms. Grear opened her mouth, and I cringed as I waited for the inevitable verbal smack down I was about to receive in front of all my peers.

Out of nowhere, something heavy fell onto my shoulders.

I glanced up in surprise—right into the face of an extremely good-looking boy I didn't recognize. He was gazing back down at me like there was nothing at all out of the ordinary about him holding onto me. Even though he was wearing our school uniform, I was sure I'd never seen him before. I would definitely have remembered a face like his. He had perfect, glossy, golden hair that fell over his eyes like he should be walking down a fashion runway. His smile immediately made my insides gelatinous. He winked at me like we were sharing an inside joke. My breath caught—he had beautiful, enchanting, *purple* eyes.

My heart hit the back of my throat so hard I literally choked out loud.

"You okay there, babe?" he asked casually, standing there with his arm draped around my shoulders. Then he turned to Ms. Grear, who looked like she might be choking, too. "This is your counselor, right?"

I made some unintelligible, panicked sound like a mouse that'd just been stepped on.

"Ms. Grear, it's so good to meet you. Thanks for lending Josie to me yesterday. Man, having her there at the hospital was such a lifesaver. I don't think I could have made it through all that without her." He gave another bewitching smile that made my whole body shudder with embarrassment.

"I'm sorry, I don't believe we've met," Ms. Grear finally spoke. Even she looked a little flushed. "Who are you?"

"Oh, I'm sorry! My name is Joe. Joe Noble. I'm new. I was supposed to start last week, but then my mom got diagnosed with an aggressive illness, and yesterday she had to have emergency surgery. It's pretty complicated. The doctors are still trying to figure out what's wrong," he explained, giving me a little squeeze that made me squeak out loud. "Lucky me, Josie was there at my side the whole time. I told her I would explain everything to her counselor, since she didn't get a chance to call. I know I made her miss detention and class yesterday. I hope we can work something out. Can't you let it slide? Just this once?"

He blinked innocently—those big lavender eyes that suckered even me right into believing that crazy story.

"Is this true, Josie?" Ms. Grear's voice cracked, and she had to look away and fan herself a little as her flabby cheeks turned bright red.

"I-I-I ..." Joe elbow me in the ribs, and I managed a panicked, "Yes."

"Very well, then." Ms. Grear sighed, pointing back into the school. "Both of you inside, now. Joe, please come with me to the central office so we can get you settled into your classes."

"Great! Thank you so much. I owe you one." Joe laughed and combed his fingers through his perfect, glossy, blonde bangs. He bent down, and before I could react, he planted a firm, warm kiss on my cheek. "See you later, babe."

Oh, god. Had he really just ...

It took a few minutes for my brain to start working again after that. I didn't remember walking into the school or the entire hour of detention. I finally remembered how to breathe again once the bell for my first period class rang, and realized that somehow I had ended up at my desk.

"*Pssst,*" someone whispered from behind me.

I glanced back, surprised to see one of the popular girls sitting directly behind me, leaning forward.

"Is it true? Is that cute new guy really your boyfriend?" She cupped a hand over her mouth so no one else would hear. "Is it true that his family is loaded? You're so lucky!"

I blushed. "N-no, I think he must have me confused with someone else!" More like he was some deranged relative of Zeph's that had been coerced or blackmailed into being my boyfriend. He'd said the eye thing was genetic, right? That's the only explanation my frazzled brain could come up with.

The classroom door opened, and every head in the classroom turned as Joe Noble swaggered in.

My stomach did a spastic backflip as our gazes met.

Joe waltzed right down the aisle of desks and stood in front of the popular girl sitting behind me. "Hey, sweetie. Can I have this seat? I want to sit by my girlfriend, if you don't mind."

He flashed her that charming grin and the poor girl tripped all over herself to give him the seat. Joe plopped down in the seat behind me, looking very pleased with himself.

All through class, I could feel his gaze on my back like a tingling heat. Was my hair straight? Had I ironed this shirt? Was there lint on my sweater? Had I remembered to put on perfume this morning?

When the teacher finished giving his lecture, we were allowed to talk quietly while we finished our worksheets. I finally got up the nerve to turn around in my seat and look at Joe again. He leaned back his chair, his hands folded behind his head and a bewitching grin on his perfect lips. It was like a snapshot from a magazine.

"Why are you doing this?" I asked him as quietly as I could. "I don't even know you. I've never seen you before in my life. Are you related to Zeph?"

"Seriously?" He asked, like I'd just asked the stupidest question ever. He arched one of his brows up in an eerily familiar way. Even his voice sounded a little familiar, like maybe …

My heart hit the back of my throat. But—when—how—what the *hell*? It couldn't be! It was impossible!

"Zeph!" I practically screamed.

Everyone in the room looked up with varying expressions of terror, bracing for the school psycho to have another meltdown. The teacher narrowed his eyes at me, and I instinctively shrank down farther in my seat.

"Nice," he mumbled with a sly grin. "No wonder everyone thinks you're nuts."

"Zeph, how are you … When did you …" I tried to settle on just one question to ask first, but I was having a hard enough time coming to terms with how Zeph had somehow made himself look like an incredibly cute teenage boy.

"Call me Joe," he reminded me. "And keep it down. You must love detention or something."

"Joe," I forced myself to whisper. "Why are you doing this?"

He just shrugged, like it was no big deal. "You said you didn't have any friends and the counselor was giving you a hard time. You were right about her, by the way. She's scary as shit."

"Is this some kind of mask? Like in a spy movie?" I poked his cheek with my pencil just to make sure.

"Pfft. Don't be ridiculous. I'm way cooler than that."

"You can't just barge in here and not explain any of this to me," I insisted, my voice growing louder as I lost control of my nerves. "You said we were going to talk. What about last night? What about that wolf? And your wings!"

Zeph put a hand over my mouth to shut me up. From across the classroom, the teacher was glaring at me again.

"Geez. Do you have any common sense at all? We can't talk about that here. Wait till after school. Now turn around and do your schoolwork'n crap. Go on. Shoo."

I scowled and slowly turned back around in my seat.

Even if he was being a jerk about it, it was … kind of nice knowing he was sitting back there. Somehow, it made me feel so much safer. It was the first day all year that I had gone from class to class without feeling terrified of what might be waiting for me around the corner.

Not that everything was normal. No, I wasn't *that* lucky. But when I noticed one of the big ivy plants on the windowsill in my English teacher's classroom beginning to move, stretching out like it was going to grab the girl sitting in front of me—Zeph appeared like he'd just materialized on the spot. He paused on his way down the aisle of desks and stared at the plant. His eyes narrowed. One corner of his mouth curled into a dangerous half-snarl. The leaves shivered as though a breeze had passed through the room. Slowly, the plant recoiled back into its pot and became perfectly still. Zeph gave an approving snort, and I never saw the ivy move again.

My mouth fell open.

He had seen it, too! Now I knew it wasn't just a fluke that he'd been able to see the wolf in my apartment. Whatever he was, he could see and sense the same things I could.

I wasn't imaging any of it.

That realization put tears in my eyes. Relief washed over every inch of my body. I hid my face with my hair, keeping my head down as I struggled to keep it together.

Someone poked me in the back with the eraser end of a pencil.

"Hey," Zeph whispered. "What's wrong?"

I shook my head slightly and rasped, "Nothing. I'm fine."

Apparently, "Joe" had done a real number on Ms. Grear, as well. He had charmed her into putting him in all the same classes I was in, and made a point to sit right behind me in each one—even if that meant he had to bat those dazzling purple eyes at the teacher to get the seating chart rearranged. Each time he did that, I got a strange chill. Sometimes I heard something, too, like a whispering melody in my ear. It came and went so quickly, though. Could I even be sure it had anything to do with Zeph?

By the end of the day, the school was buzzing with rumors about my new "boyfriend" and how cute we were together. I didn't understand that at *all*. It's like they'd forgotten all about me being a walking disaster. Did Zeph have something to do with that, too?

After the last bell, we left school holding hands. I kept my head down, trying not to make eye contact with any of my peers as we left. It probably confused anyone else who saw us. Why wouldn't I be thrilled to be holding hands with an attractive guy like that?

It wasn't until we rounded our street corner that he finally released me and let out a huge, growling groan. "I forgot how much high school sucks."

Yeah, school sucked. He had no freaking idea! He wasn't the one who had to pretend everything was perfectly fine while plants and fire were coming to life and attacking anyone who stood too close. I gritted my teeth, biting back a scream. I'd been patient enough. I was done waiting. He owed me some answers, and I wanted them *now*.

I waited until we were alone, standing in the hallway between our front doors, then I whacked him over the head with my purse. "What is going on? You said we would talk! I deserve some answers!"

He dodged my purse as I swung at him again. "Calm down. It's not that big of a deal."

"Not a big deal? Are you kidding me? I've been tortured every single night by that—that monster in my apartment! Then you show up! And at first you look like a grunge rocker, then a glowing violet angel-vampire, then like some model from a clothing advertisement!" I yanked my purse back, and went to shove him instead. "So you better start explaining this to me right now. I'm not even close to kidding!"

Zeph lunged at me suddenly, his jaw clenched and teeth bared. I caught a glint of those pointed canines again.

I panicked and tried to run back down the stairs, but he grabbed the back of my coat and picked me up like a crash test dummy. He threw me over his powerful shoulder and carried me into his apartment.

I yelped and struggled until he set me back on my feet. Then I got a good look at the rage skewing his handsome features. He slammed his front door and backed me up against it, looming over me with a smoldering glare.

I dropped my purse as he planted his hands against the door on either side of my shoulders, leaning in to put his face uncomfortably close to mine. His heavy breaths puffed against my cheeks, and his earthy scent sent a warm shiver down my spine. My fingers slowly curled into fists.

I couldn't look away.

His features shifted. His body shape changed, growing taller. His hair became a different style and color. In a matter of seconds, he was back to looking like the tattoo-covered, delinquent Zeph I'd known before.

"H-how did you do that?" I whispered.

"Magic." He pushed away from the door and turned his back to me.

"No, I'm serious. How?"

"I *am* serious." He stormed away into the kitchen and began rummaging through his cabinets for food. I got a little twinge of satisfaction when I saw him pull out one of the containers of cookies I'd made for him. "I'm not like you, in case you hadn't noticed. I'm not human."

That was the understatement of the century. "Oh, I noticed. The glowing wings and fangs were a dead giveaway."

He returned my dirty look even as he crammed a whole cookie into his cheek like a hamster, and chewed loudly.

"So what are you, then?" I walked around the kitchen island to stand in front of him, grabbing the container of cookies and plopping it on the counter so I had his full attention. "I need to understand. Please, Zeph."

He chewed, swallowed, and avoided my gaze like a rebellious child. His face turned a little pink over his nose. "You won't believe me. Or you'll laugh. Or both."

"I was almost mauled to death by a giant wolf in my living room last night and I just saw you transform into a completely different person right before my eyes. I'm pretty sure I'd believe anything you tell me at this point."

I grabbed one of his big, rough hands and squeezed it.

His cheeks and nose turned a dark shade of red, and he scrunched his mouth up uncomfortably.

He took in a slow, deep breath. "I'm a faerie."

I struggled to keep my lips sealed tight until I was sure I could talk without a giggle slipping out. "A faerie? You mean like Tinkerbell?"

"Is that supposed to be a joke?"

"I just, um, I'm trying to wrap my mind around it. What do you mean, exactly? What kind of faerie has wings, horns, and fangs, anyway?"

"It's complicated," he snapped defensively. "Humans understand next to nothing about us, which is generally better for everyone."

A thick silence settled between us as I stood watching him cram an inhuman amount of cookies into his mouth.

If this was some kind of psychological game of chicken, I wasn't going to lose. I wanted to know more about him, and more importantly, I wanted to know why I was involved in all this. Unfortunately, he didn't seem willing to tell me anything more.

"So it's some kind of secret?"

He made a flustered, growling sound. "I don't have time for this. Besides, we shouldn't be talking about that kinda thing here."

I frowned. "What? Why not?"

"You wanna know about the fair folk? You're going to have to come with me then. I've got work to do. We can talk there," he grumbled sheepishly through a mouthful of cookie. "Go change into something that makes me look less like a pervert."

Glancing down at my school uniform, I couldn't help but agree. It was bound to look strange for someone like him to be seen walking with a high school girl in a short, pleated skirt and knee-high socks. Someone might call the cops.

Zeph stood waiting for me in the hallway when I returned. I'd taken my time dressing in a much more sophisticated outfit with skinny jeans and a nice sweater. I'd even put on a little makeup and fixed my hair into a long French braid.

I was hoping for some praise, or at least some acknowledgement as I walked up to him. I should have known better. Zeph never looked up from where he was typing away on his cell phone. He had one of those strange cigarettes between his lips and the collar of his black wool coat turned up, hiding his neck.

I cleared my throat to get his attention, wrapping my favorite wool scarf loosely around my neck. "Where are we going?"

He crammed his cell phone into his back pocket with a sigh. "Angry Hank's Bar and Grill down on 31st. I bartend there some nights."

I nodded, suppressing a proud smile. I was right about his job, after all. No wonder he kept such strange hours.

He stopped right outside the door to fish through his coat pockets. He pulled out a silver metal zippo lighter, lit his bizarre parchment cigarette, and took a few deep puffs of it. The smoke was much more delicate, fragrant, and earthy—not like something that might be illegal, rather something that had been made without a hundred dangerous toxins added to it. Now that I'd been around him for a little while, I actually found myself liking that smell. Where did he get those things, anyway?

I caught him glancing down at me. "What?"

"They say smoking kills, you know," I baited.

Zeph snorted like that was funny. "Maybe smoking that shit you humans make does."

I shrugged. "Some people think it's gross."

"So is picking your nose, or biting your nails. I've seen you do both, by the way."

My face flushed and I tripped over my own feet. "T-that's—I would never—"

It made him chuckle. "I'm just teasing. Lighten up. You get ruffled way too easily."

He might have been right about that. But I wasn't used to this—having someone to talk to, joke with, or even walk next to. Already his presence beside me felt comfortable, as though he belonged there.

"There's that creepy smile again. What's wrong with you?"

"Nothing, according to you," I deflected. "So why are we going there? Is it safer to talk at a bar?"

"That's what Hank claims. Anyway, I already told you, I have work to do. I need to restock the bar before the start of tonight's shift." Zeph shrugged as he began walking down the sidewalk again.

It was still early in the afternoon, well before rush hour, so the streets weren't crowded. I kept close to him anyway, stealing glances up at his face whenever he wasn't looking. We walked in silence for several blocks. I tried to think of something to say, something not weird or related to him being a faerie, but my mind just kept going back to all the strange things I'd experienced in the past twenty-four hours. There was so much I wanted to ask him, and I wasn't sure where to start.

"So this cousin of yours, does he have a last name?"

A bolt of panic coursed through my body.

I couldn't meet his eyes as I scrambled together the best excuse I could think of. "O-of course. Same as mine. We're cousins, after all."

"Anyone ever mention that you're a terrible liar?"

"Oh, shut up. I don't know his real name, okay? He's always just called himself my benefactor. I call him "Ben" for short. He's never told me what his real name is. That was part of the deal he struck with my dad, apparently. He'd take care of me, but I wasn't allowed to know who he was."

"And you never asked?" Zeph sounded even more suspicious now.

"No," I admitted. It was embarrassing to even think about it, let alone say it out loud. "It's not like he'd tell me, anyway. It was made pretty clear to me at the beginning that I would never have a relationship with him. He doesn't share his personal information with me."

He made a thoughtful noise as he puffed more smoke into the cold evening air. "So why is he taking care of you? Where are your parents?"

I winced, and then steeled myself against the pain. I knew Zeph wasn't trying to be hurtful; maybe he just didn't know any better. Anyone would wonder that after seeing how I lived.

"Dead." I turned my face away so he wouldn't see my chin trembling. I bit down hard to try to make it stop. He was right; I wasn't a good liar. And I wasn't good at hiding my feelings, either.

I could see him leaning around to peer at me out of the corner of my eye. I expected to see pity or sympathy, since that's usually how people respond to that kind of news. Instead, he just looked confused.

"Both of them?" He flicked his ashes onto the sidewalk.

I nodded. "It's sort of a family curse, I guess. My mom died when I was little. I don't remember anything about her. My big brother, William, was killed in a car accident when I was in middle school. And then my dad …"

My voice died in my throat as the more recent memories of my dad's death clouded my mind. Time had numbed me to the pain of losing my other family members, but the loss of my dad was still fresh in my heart. Just the thought made my insides burn like they were on fire. It was a deep, aching pain that rose up and made my eyes well with tears. God, I missed him.

"That's … uh, strange."

"Not any stranger than being a glowing demon-faerie-thing."

He didn't retort.

We walked in silence again, passing block after block with a weird tension in the air between us. We passed apartment buildings, shops, restaurants, and bus stops. Other couples walked by on their way to the downtown business district, but they looked a lot happier than we did. They were holding hands or leaning on one another. It wasn't hard to imagine that they were going out for a nice evening together, maybe for dinner and a movie.

My hand was empty, and even though Zeph was walking close beside me, I could imagine how he might react if I reached out to him. Still, my fingers ached, wishing I could cross that tiny bit of distance between us. It was a purely selfish desire, though.

Zeph grabbed the hood of my coat, snagging me before I stumbled into the busy street like a dog on a leash. "Watch it," he murmured before letting my hood go. "Where's your head?"

I wasn't sure. I looked up at him through bangs frizzed by the chilly wind. I was remembering how he had kissed me on the cheek earlier that day. Sure, I knew it probably hadn't meant a thing to him. The whole Joe Noble ruse was probably just to jerk me around and snoop around in my personal life. And when he'd kissed me, it was most likely just to make his story more convincing.

But that was the first time in my life a boy had ever kissed me.

"Zeph."

He glanced down at me, taking the last few puffs from his cigarette before flicking the butt onto the sidewalk. "What?"

"Why are you doing this?" I dared to ask. "Helping me, I mean. Going to school with me. Rescuing me from monsters in my apartment. You do realize there's nothing I can do to repay you. I ... I don't have any money."

Zeph looked shocked for a moment. Standing there, just a few steps away, we stared into each other's eyes. There was something strange in his expression, almost like he was trying not to panic.

"I just feel sorry for you, I guess." His tone was stiff and uncomfortable as he turned away to cross the street.

That jerk—he was an even worse liar than I was!

There was a large neon sign over the door of Angry Hank's, depicting a stomping bull with a ring through its nose. Even from a distance, I could sense that there was something strange about the place. Just looking at it made my insides get all jittery.

Zeph starting picking up the pace as we crossed the street. He was practically jogging by the time we got to the door. He hurriedly unlocked the door then shoved me inside ahead of him before locking it behind us. Overhead, an old brass bell jangled to announce our arrival.

Once we were inside, he let out a relieved sigh and switched on the lights. He shrugged out of his heavy winter coat and draped it over the back of one of the tall, leather-backed stools.

"Fantastic. He's not here yet. Let's get this over with." He talked to himself as he made his way behind the bar.

I followed slowly, letting my eyes roam over the dimly-lit room. The old wooden floors creaked as I walked after Zeph, and the glass panes on the big windows facing the street looked wavy and ancient. A dozen matching barstools lined the bar where Zeph stood, flipping through a notepad for an empty page.

"Take a seat, small fry." He pointed at one of the stools with the end of a ballpoint pen. "I have to take inventory and restock. It won't take long."

"Okay." I struggled to get comfortable on one of the barstools. Unfortunately, my legs were so short and the barstool was so tall that my feet didn't even come close to touching the floor.

I caught Zeph grinning as he quickly filled a glass with ice and soda.

"No alcohol for the short girl," he teased with a roguish grin, winking as he topped the drink with a straw before sliding it toward me.

I was beginning to suspect that his habit of calling me annoying pet names was some bizarre way of showing affection. Two could play at that game.

"No tip for the butthead."

He laughed, which caught me off guard and completely stole my thunder. He had a wonderfully deep, rich laugh. I loved it instantly. "Good one. All right, sit tight. I'll be right back."

I sipped at the soda as he disappeared into the back room through a pair of saloon doors. When he came back, he had brought out boxes of imported, bottled beers and liquors, packages of straws, boxes of limes and oranges, and other materials.

"Can I ask questions now?" I leaned over the bar to watch him work.

"Sure," Zeph grunted as he squatted down to open a huge freezer door hidden under the bar.

My heart beat faster, and I chewed furiously on the straw in my drink. "What are you, exactly? I mean, I know you said a faerie before. But, what does that even mean?"

"Faerie is a broad term. It's like calling you a mammal." His tone was relaxed and casual as he distracted himself with refreshing the materials behind the bar. "There are lots of different kinds of fae, and history has slapped its own labels and explanations on us. Most of them are completely false. Every culture calls us something different: gods, angels, demons, ghosts, yōsei, mermaids, werewolves, spirits, vampires ... blah, blah, blah. You get the idea."

"What kind are you?" I interrupted.

He was quiet for a moment, like he was trying to decide whether or not to answer. "A changeling," he spoke at last in a quiet, reluctant voice.

"Changeling ..." I repeated that name. "And what does that mean, exactly? Is that why you can change your appearance? I thought changelings were swapped with children or stolen babies or something."

His lips thinned and his brow crinkled slightly as he leaned over the liquor bottles. "No. There are lots of stories about my kind. Most of them aren't true. Not that it matters. Humans tend to believe what they want to believe regardless of what the facts are."

"You said it was magic. So magic is real?"

Zeph turned and pointed a finger at me with a mischievous smile. "Nuh uh. You get one question, and then I get one. That way it's fair. I'm not gonna have you pilfering through my personal life unless I get some payback. Got it?"

I frowned and sank down in my seat a little. I could guess what he was going to ask about, and I didn't want to talk about that anymore.

"Come on, don't sulk like that. I'll be nice about it. Scout's honor."

I sighed. "Fine."

"Why'd your dad leave you in the care of someone you don't know? Do you even realize how bizarre that is? It sounds like you don't know anything about him at all. He could be a drug lord for all you know."

So much for being nice.

I slammed a hand down on the bar top angrily. "My dad would never leave me with someone like that!"

"Probably not, but you don't know that." He arched a brow at me, giving me that candid, skeptical expression that was so unique to him. "Why haven't you ever asked Ben about any of this?"

"I don't want to invade his privacy. Like I said, after Dad died, the lawyers made it very clear to me that I wasn't being adopted. I wasn't Ben's child." It sounded like a pitiful excuse, even to me. "And besides, Dad promised he was a good person. He said Ben would take care of me. That's all I need to know."

Zeph shook his head and looked away.

"Hey! You didn't know my dad, okay? So don't act all cocky. My dad was a wonderful man! I may not understand why he chose Ben to be my legal guardian, but I have faith in his decision." My hands curled into fists. "And it's my turn again. Tell me about magic. What is it? How does it work?"

"You might as well ask me to explain the meaning of life to you." I got another scathing, exasperated Zeph-glare from over one of his broad shoulders. "Magic isn't what you humans think it is. It isn't sparkly dust that makes you fly or happy thoughts, rainbows, or wishing on shooting stars."

As he began putting new liquor bottles up on the shelves behind the bar, the muscles of his back pressed against the fabric of his shirt. There were no traces of wings there anymore, and no horns hiding in his messy dark hair. I'd seen three different versions of him so far, and I had to wonder ... which one was the *real* Zeph?

"Magic is like water. It's required for all things on this earth to live and it cycles through the world to be reused over and over again. Some things, even some people, soak up more of it than others or require more of it to live. Children are usually more attuned to it than most. They soak it up like little sponges." Each word from his lips carried a weight I could feel hanging in the air. "Any being on earth is capable of using it, although humans lost interest and forgot how to do that a very long time ago. Most of them can't even see it or feel it anymore. Their minds have turned to things of metal. It can be that way for faeries, too. In fact, a lot of us have fallen from our former glory to be fed by the machines of the modern world."

A strange, wild hunger rose up in me so suddenly it made my body stiffen. If magic was real, then surely it had something to do with all the strange things that had been happening to me. I needed to know more—I needed to understand.

"Where does it come from?"

"The moon." He paused, holding a liquor bottle in each hand as he turned to look me in the eye. "Or at least, that's what the old songs say. No one knows for sure. But magic is raw energy that we can use as we choose. Even a small amount can accomplish miraculous or even terrible things."

I swallowed hard, already poised with my next question.

But Zeph interrupted with his own. "So, when did you start seeing things?"

I thought back for a moment. "A few months after my dad died. The doctor told me I had post-traumatic stress disorder. At first, it was just dreams. I had nightmares every night, and when I would wake up, my clothes would be soaked with sweat. Actually, last night when you rescued me from that wolf, it was the first time I had seen something so clearly. Before then, it was just shadows."

I stared down into my lap as I listened to the glassware clinking while Zeph put things away. "The wolf I saw—it wanted to kill me, didn't it? Was that a demon?"

"What, Eldrick?" Zeph sounded surprised. "Well, like I said before, it's not that simple. He's not a demon. He's a puca."

"A puca?"

He nodded. "An ancient spirit of darkness."

"And he's evil?"

He snorted, suppressing a chuckle. "Oh, he'd love for you to think that. But no, I said dark, not evil. The two things don't always go hand in hand. Misguided, stupid, arrogant—Eldrick is a lot of things. But he's not evil."

I had to let that sink in for a moment before I could speak again. "Then why was he trying to hurt me?"

Zeph smirked as he came back to the bar and began making lists of all the supplies he had restocked onto the notepad. "That was kinda your fault. Well, it was probably more your dad's. He should have warned you about him."

"W-what! My fault? I didn't do anything to him! And my dad never mentioned anything about a puca!"

"Exactly." Zeph pointed his pen at me accusingly again. "Look, spirits like Eldrick are a type of faerie, too. And all faeries, at one point or another, ran wild in nature—some of them for hundreds, maybe even thousands of years. Some still do to this day. And after all that time, they've absorbed massive amounts of magic from the earth. It's rare, but if Eldrick is living in your apartment, then it's because he's somehow bound to it—or to you. Believe me, if he could leave, he would. Faeries don't like being trapped like that. Eldrick is old, way older than me, and very powerful. To be living in a human dwelling like that, your dad must have caught him in a contract somehow. It's the only explanation that makes sense."

My head was spinning. "What are you talking about? What contract?"

Zeph shrugged again and went back to writing. "It's in a lot of the old stories. I'm sure you've heard that old wives' tale that if you catch a faerie, he has to grant you a wish, right? That's a contract. If you capture a fae, even an old powerful one like Eldrick, he is obligated to do something for you in exchange for his freedom."

"That wolf—er, Eldrick—had a contract with my dad?" Somehow, hearing that he had been basically held prisoner in my apartment, made me feel a little sorry for him. Not too much, though, since he'd been torturing me for the past several years.

"Most likely," he agreed. "You'd have to ask him about it, though. It must have had something to do with you; otherwise your father's death would have released him from the contract."

"That's why he has to do what I say?"

Zeph gave me a playful wink. "Now you're gettin' it."

"I can't believe it's that simple," I murmured. "It's just … if I'd known sooner. If he'd just talked to me about it once, maybe we could have avoided all this."

"Well, you gotta understand something about Eldrick. He hates humans, probably more than any other fae."

"Why?"

Zeph cleared his throat. His hand stopped scribbling on the paper and he flashed me a quick glance. "It's, uh, not really my story to tell. Let's just say that his past run-ins with the human race weren't exactly positive. Being caught in a contract is basically the most insulting thing that could've happened to him."

"Has anyone ever had a contract with you?"

He waggled a finger in my face. "Nice try, kid. You already slipped an extra one in there. It's my turn."

I frowned. Not again. Which painful or embarrassing topic would it be this time? Details of how my dad had died?

"Was that really your first kiss?"

My face instantly began to burn. My mouth hung open in total humiliation.

"Whoa, that's a yes." He laughed and poked my forehead tauntingly with the end of his pen. "What a shame. I should have made it more meaningful."

"H-how did you know that?"

"Aw, come on. Your face was even redder than it is now. You looked like someone had put a wig on a red party balloon." He kept on chuckling even as he finished his supply list.

I shut my mouth quickly. My heart pounded so loudly; I was afraid he might hear it.

"Okay, then. Why didn't you ever talk to me before? We've been neighbors for months, and you never said a word to me." I sat back in my chair proudly. If Zeph wasn't going to play fair by asking me embarrassing things like that, then why should I?

Immediately, his brows snapped together and his mouth set into a hard line. That question must have stung him—maybe even more than I'd intended. He leveled a no-nonsense gaze on me that made my skin prickle. "Because close to me is the worst place imaginable for someone like you. The things that scare you, beings like Eldrick, are attracted to me. Sure, my aura might frighten off the little ones, like the ones who have been picking on you at school, but there are other monsters out there. Creatures so horrible that there aren't even words for them in your human language.

My presence will drive them into the open."

Every hair on my body stood on end. "I might not be so scared of them if I understood them."

"No. It's not good for me to be around you. The closer we are, the more danger you'll be in. You being able to see us in our natural forms isn't going to make it any easier, either. In fact, it just makes it more fun for them to watch you be terrified." He looked away, his voice tight with frustration. "Most fae will ignore humans altogether. Some might try to protect them, if the occasion called for it, but there are others who don't like humans, and go out of their way to harm them."

I couldn't shake the feeling that he was trying to scare me off. He wanted me to be frightened enough to invite him out of my life forever, but that wasn't going to happen. For the first time in years, I didn't feel alone. Even if he teased me and acted like a jerk sometimes—I liked him. I wanted to get to know him, even if it was dangerous.

"You've protected me more than once, even though I never asked you to." I said quietly. It wasn't that I was looking for trouble, and I certainly wasn't trying to use him like a shield against Eldrick. I just didn't want to lose him. "Why? Why are you going to all this trouble for me?"

Zeph's expression hardened further. He stopped writing. "That's complicated, too."

"Well, even if this Ben guy is a felon or a CIA operative, you need to tell him what's been going on at school and at your apartment." Zeph had finished the restocking work and had shoved his list of supplies folded up underneath the cash register. "He's supposed to be taking care of you, right? How can he do that if you don't tell him anything that happens? He might even know why your dad was mixed up with Eldrick in the first place."

He was right, but I wasn't about to give him the satisfaction of letting him know that. "I'm already a financial burden to him, Zeph. I can't ask for more. Besides, what's there to fix at this point? You said Eldrick has to do what I tell him, right? So, I can stop him from torturing me. And if you keep coming to school as Joe, the faeries there won't bother me either, right?"

"What makes you think I'm going to keep going to school with you every day? I do have a job and a life, you know."

I grabbed his arm. "But, Zeph! I—"

He jerked away from me suddenly, like I'd shocked him or hurt him somehow. He looked almost … afraid. Was it something I'd said?

Zeph's shot his gaze toward the front windows. His broad shoulders tensed, and he moved away from me before ducking back behind the bar.

What was going on? Was he hiding from someone?

The brass bell over the door jangled, and a burly, mountain of a man stepped inside. Instantly, the atmosphere became much heavier. He was scratching at his scraggly, white goatee, staring right at me with ominous silence. The closer he came, the more detail I could see under the dim lights. He was impressively tall and dressed out from head to toe in black leather motorcycle cuts. The jacket he wore seemed old, and many of the patches sewn onto it were beginning to fray around the edges. He was nearly bald on top, but what remained of his hair was long and pulled into a ponytail at the back of his neck.

I slid off the barstool and shrank back against the wall. If anyone looked like they had the potential to turn into some big, scary faerie-monster, it was this guy. Zeph seemed too busy pretending to be busy rearranging glassware to notice my panic.

The massive man stopped right in front of me. He stared down at me with his dark eyes glittering. His crinkled, aged face was set deeply with wrinkles that made it impossible to tell if he really was scowling at me, or if that was just how he looked.

I yelped as he stuck a hand out toward me. "And who's this?" His voice was throaty, gruff, but surprisingly kind. When I dared to look at his face again, he was smiling down at me curiously.

"My neighbor," Zeph piped up from across the room. "I'm babysitting today. Don't scare her, Hank. She'll start crying again."

All the fear drained out of my body, chased away by a sudden burst of rage as I glared at Zeph's back. Babysitting? Crying? Was he serious?

Hank must have noticed my response because he let out a dry chuckle before turning around to make his way back behind the bar. "A little young for you, isn't she?"

Zeph's face went white. "Shit, Hank! Don't say that kinda stuff. I gave her some soda, that's it! I'm not into puny redheaded girls. Do I look like an idiot?"

Puny? Okay, so maybe I was small for my age. I was short and petite, so I got mistaken for being a freshman all the time. But I was almost eighteen—*not* a kid. It took everything I had to keep my mouth shut as I stood there, fuming.

"Yep," Hank answered with a snort. "And I can see you fooling around back there like one, too. If you're done, then get outta here. I'm not paying you to stand around and flap your gums."

"You barely pay me at all." Zeph snatched his coat from the chair and swung it back over his shoulders on his way toward the door. He grabbed the hood of my coat on his way out the door and dragged me along with him. "Come on."

"Hey," Hank shouted. His voice seemed to make the room shudder and my stomach flip.

Zeph came to an abrupt halt with his hand on the doorknob. He didn't turn around or even look back. I looked back to see Hank frowning ominously.

"I got wind of another case." The hushed somberness in Hank's voice made me anxious. "Just a few blocks from here. I have it on good authority that a few priests are already over there, trying to run them out. You could go lend a hand."

I couldn't see Zeph's face because of how he was holding onto my hood, but I could feel his grip on me tighten. "I can't get involved in that right now," he said through his teeth.

"I know you don't have much time left," Hank murmured. "I can go with you. Your presence alone might be enough to scare them out."

The two men exchanged a long, unblinking stare. A minute passed, and neither of them said a word. Gradually, Zeph's chest and shoulders grew tense. His jaw clenched.

"There's a kid involved," Hank added quietly. "I wouldn't be asking otherwise."

Zeph flashed him a dangerous look, his mouth twitching like he wanted to snarl. I held my breath, waiting for an explanation.

Zeph was eerily silent as he turned back to us, apparently thinking it over. "Fine." He sighed at last and let go of my hood. "Bring the car around."

Hank nodded and quickly left out the back entrance.

For a few seconds, Zeph didn't move. Then he stormed across the room and switched off the neon sign with a curse. He started haphazardly jerking the blinds down on the bar's windows, banging drawers and cabinets shut, and growling under his breath. He slammed the door hard, making the whole frame rattle, and locked it.

My hands trembled as I studied him, unsure what to say. We were both standing out on the curb, braced against the cold evening wind. My head was swirling with questions. What was a case? What did that mean—that a kid was involved? What had set him off like this?

Finally, I couldn't take it anymore. "Where are we going?"

Zeph was lighting up a fresh cigarette, puffing on it like a furious freight train. "*We* aren't going anywhere. You're going home."

I squared my shoulders, burying my hands deep in my coat pockets as I met his eyes with rebellion. I didn't want him to see them shaking. "What? I am not! I want to go with you. Quit treating me like a child. I can take care of myself."

"Not a chance. This isn't anything you need to get involved in."

I narrowed my gaze. "Maybe I should tell Hank about spending the night at your place, then? Seems like a *responsible* adult might want to know we live right across the hall and that you have a nasty habit of coming into my apartment whenever you want—day or night."

Zeph sputtered furiously, making sounds that could have been the beginnings of words, but I couldn't understand any of them. At last, he turned his back to me and fumed. "Fine. Just keep your head down and don't talk to anyone."

I grinned in triumph. Right on cue, an old, black Cadillac pulled up to the curb. Hank waved us inside.

Zeph put a hand against my back as he ushered me to the car and opened the rear passenger door. I expected him to ride shotgun, but instead he climbed in after me and practically shoved his way into the middle seat so that I was squished between him and the door. I would've been excited to be in the backseat with a handsome guy ... but there was nothing romantic about the way Zeph had me smashed against him. His elbow was practically in my chest, and not in a fun way.

Hank put the car in gear and pulled away from the curb at a startling speed. We weaved through traffic, and I found myself gripping the seat until my knuckles were white. We swerved just a little too close to every car we passed and zipped through intersections while the lights were yellow. Was he trying to kill us before we even got there?

"Is Freddy there?" Zeph asked casually as he cracked the back window so he could flick his ashes outside.

"I'm not sure." Hank made a grunting noise. "No one from the Seelie Court was on scene when I passed by earlier. Typical. This is a small matter. They won't bother with it."

Zeph held his cigarette between his teeth as he opened the center console of the car and began pulling out a series of strange objects—a long, golden feather, something that resembled a dream catcher with little bones tied to it, and bundles of a strange-smelling herb. "So, what are we dealing with? Bogles again?"

Hank nodded. "I think so. Two, maybe three. It was hard to get a good feel for it from such a distance. I'll have more to tell you when we get there."

I swallowed hard as Zeph handed me those strange objects one by one. He took his time inspecting each one. He smelled the herbs and tested the point of the golden feather before handing each to me.

"What is this?" I asked as I smelled the herbs, too.

"Sage." Hank smiled at me in the rearview mirror. "Fae find the scent very pungent. You can use it to drive them out of places you don't want them to go."

"I thought that was for keeping out demons?" I asked.

Hank's smile widened. "Sometimes there's not much difference between the two."

The sage didn't smell bad to me, but just a few sniffs of it seemed to make Zeph uncomfortable. His eyes watered and he sneezed. "Smells like butt to me," he murmured. "Keep that in your pocket, will you? At least until we get inside."

I nodded and stuck the little bundles of dried sage into my coat pocket. "We're going to fight dark spirits with sage? Can I use this to drive the puca out of my apartment?"

Hank let out another dry, hoarse laugh. "Sharp kid, isn't she? Nah, sweetie. Sage only works on weaker fae. Pucas are about as strong as they come besides sidhe. Besides, we don't want to have to fight anyone, if we can help it."

"We're just serving an eviction notice." Zeph had a menacing, scheming smirk on his face as we pulled onto a suburban street.

"So, if it bothers you ... does that mean you're a weak fae?" I stole a quick glance at Zeph.

He didn't answer. Instead, his jawline went tense and he turned his face away to look out the window. His hands slowly curled into fists, making veins stand out along his forearms. Confusion whirled through my brain, and I fought the urge to touch his hand. Anything to let him know I hadn't meant that as an insult.

We passed house after house, and nothing looked out of the ordinary. People were out walking their dogs, sitting on their front porches, or checking their mail. We were several blocks away from the hustle and bustle of the downtown area, in a neighborhood that clearly housed middle-income families. This didn't seem like the right place to find bogles or monsters.

Then I looked up at the front of the house. There was a car parked in the driveway, and two men dressed in robes like catholic priests standing outside it. They were talking to an older woman who stood with two younger girls on either side of her. One of them looked to be in her mid-twenties, while the other was probably in middle school.

Everyone in their group turned to stare as we parked on the street, right in front of their house. I got the feeling these people hadn't been expecting us. The mother and her daughters all looked concerned, maybe even a little afraid—not that I blamed them. Hank was officially the scariest looking person I knew, besides maybe Zeph. The priests, however, seemed irritated when they saw us getting out of the car. Their noses wrinkled with disapproval and they leaned together, muttering to one another secretively.

"Got anything for me?" Zeph murmured as he dropped his cigarette butt on the pavement and ground it with the toe of his shoe.

Hank grunted thoughtfully. "Three bogles. Smells like swamp spirits. They've made themselves a nice little nest in there. This is gonna be interesting. I'll deal with the family, you get it done."

"That's not what I meant, old man."

Hank scrunched his lips. I watched him go digging through his pockets and take out a small paper box about the size of a deck of cards. He passed it to Zeph, who immediately opened it to smell the contents. It was more of those strange cigarettes.

I arched an eyebrow. So that's where they came from. Interesting.

"Alright, then." Zeph nodded firmly. "Josie, you're with me."

The instant my feet hit the pavement, a fresh wave of pure anxiety washed over me. It made me nauseous just to look at the front door of the house, and the closer we got to it, the heavier the air became. A strange mixture of fear and excitement made my chest tighten, like I was about to go over the first big drop on a roller coaster. I wanted to grab onto Zeph, but he'd seemed so upset when I had done that before—I couldn't bring myself to try it again. Not to mention the only reason I was even here in the first place was because I'd insisted on it. Now was not the time to chicken out.

Hank went directly to where the family and two priests stood and struck up a conversation. The priests sneered as though they were already well acquainted and wanted nothing to do with him. The mother and younger daughter seemed curious, but the older daughter stared at Zeph with wide, love-struck eyes.

My eye started to twitch. Seriously? Didn't she see me walking *right* next to him?

If Zeph had noticed her though, it didn't show. He looked straight ahead, his gaze calm and focused. "Don't be afraid," he whispered to me.

"I'm not," I attempted to lie.

He slowly opened the front door, and we were met with a rush of cold air like we'd just opened a freezer door.

Inside, there was nothing but darkness.

"You can sense them, right?" Zeph whispered. He reached for my hand, lacing his warm fingers through mine, and drawing me closer to his side. It made my stupid heart pound sloppily again. "Tell me what you feel."

What did I feel? That idiot … I couldn't feel anything right then except how his hand was big, strong, and warm as it held firmly onto mine. I felt like I never wanted to let go. I felt like I wanted him to kiss me again. I swallowed hard and tried to focus. Now was not the time and I was not some love-struck little child.

I let out a slow, controlled breath and forced my mind to go quiet.

"It's different from Eldrick." A tingling warmth crept up my spine. "I think they know we're here."

A strange smirk curled up his lips. "Of course. I told you, my aura draws a lot of attention. They know I'm coming to kick them out, so they're gonna be pissed. Stay with me, okay? Don't leave my side."

My palms were getting sweaty. The sneer on Zeph's face kept me mute as he walked into the house.

"Don't talk to them," he warned. "Don't acknowledge them in any way. If I end up having to pull one of them off you, I'm going to be seriously pissed. You'll be making dinner for months as payment."

Wait ... what? Pull one *off* me? I dug in my heels, but he jerked me closer and shut the door. The darkness swallowed us whole. My pulse raced. Something wasn't right. I didn't belong here—in this situation. I was getting in way over my head.

The house was an absolute wreck from one end to the other, which wasn't an unfamiliar sight for me. Things were scattered all over the floors, furniture was upturned, and there were marks all over the walls as though someone had gone crazy with a permanent marker.

"Notice anything different?" Zeph asked.

I let my eyes wander around the room.

In my own apartment, the chaos had always been random, like the result of someone throwing a violent tantrum. But here, all the items on the floor were arranged in lines or strange, specific patterns. Spray bottles of household cleaner were arranged in a circle, stuffed animals had been placed in lines going around the room. Even the marks on the walls appeared to be writing of some kind.

"W-why is it like this?"

"Because they're trying to run those humans out of here. Someone had to have invited one of them in first, though. They can't just move in whenever they want. It's an ancient law; a fae can't take up residence in the dwelling of a human without a direct invitation. They'll sometimes play tricks to try to get an invitation. They'll take the form of someone familiar, pretend to be the ghost of a dead child, appear like a divine creature bringing some heavenly message—you name it, it's been done." He kept his voice low as we walked from room to room, surveying the damage. "By the contract, Eldrick is bound as your servant, so there'd be no point in him trying to run you out. He's just been throwing a fit—like the spoiled brat he is."

As we moved into the kitchen, the familiar sight of food spilled on the floor gave me an eerie feeling. There was a big, three-toed footprint clearly pressed into a mixture of ketchup and mashed potatoes right in the middle of the floor. My blood ran cold at the sight of it.

"What a lovely little nest they've built in here." Zeph held out his hand. "All right, let's get to work. Hand me the sage."

6

With his lighter, Zeph set two of the bundles of sage on fire, and quickly blew them out. The smoldering ends of the herbs released a fragrant gray smoke, and he handed them to me before quickly covering his nose. His eyes were watering again, and he took a few big steps away.

"Well if that doesn't stir them up, I don't know what will."

Suddenly, a wave of nausea made my skin clammy and my throat go dry. Something was watching us. I didn't know how I knew it—I just did. I couldn't see anything strange in the room yet, but I could feel it as though someone were breathing down the back of my neck.

I gagged as a terrible smell wafted past my nose. It was like a mixture of burning hair and old vomit. Disgusting.

"What is that?" I coughed and sputtered, waving the sage around so the scent of the smoke would help clear away the stink.

"Hank was right." Zeph shed his long wool coat and flexed his thick arms like he was about to get into a fistfight. "Swamp spirits. Stand back."

"Oooh, look who it is," a whispery voice echoed through the room, seeming to come from every direction at once. "Zephiel has come to play.

And he brought us housewarming a gift!"

Zeph's body rippled like a mirage. Then he made a deep, snarling noise—a sound that should have come from a beast, not a man. His faerie form unfolded before me just like it had when he saved me from Eldrick. His shirt seemed to melt away like liquid as glowing violet runes ignited on his body, shining brightly in the dark house. His muscular back twisted, and beautiful angelic wings took form—filling the kitchen and brushing against the floor and ceiling. Black spike-like horns grew from his head and his ears became long and pointed. His fingernails grew into claws. His features sharpened, his purple eyes glowed, and he bared his fangs at the darkness.

Even though I had already seen him like this once, it still terrified me. I stumbled back, tripping over a pile of pots and pans, and landed squarely on my rear end. It made a ruckus, and Zeph snapped an annoyed glare back at me as if I was ruining his cool entrance.

"She's just a waif, look at her," the cold whisper sneered. "But her power ... can you smell it, my brothers? Such power!"

"Yes," another voice agreed, seeming to come from right beside me. "Not in five hundred years have I smelled it!"

I winced as a rancid breath puffed right in my face.

"Zeph!" I screamed, dropped the sage, and thrust my hands into the empty air in front of me. I was stunned when I touched a solid mass—something I couldn't see. It felt scaly, slimy, and alive.

And it was right in front of me.

The creature belted out a booming laugh of pleasure.

I scrambled across the floor to get away, not daring to look back.

"That power!" It roared with delight. "Give it all to me!"

A huge, scaly hand grabbed my foot and dragged me back. I kicked and flailed, screaming for Zeph again. Where was he? Was he just going to let them take me?

The monster kept laughing, reeling me in inch-by-inch. "That's right! Scream for him! He can't protect you, just like he couldn't protect your father!"

"Hey! Don't talk about me like I'm not here!" Zeph's voice suddenly boomed over me. He appeared like an angel of vengeance, and there was an awful crunching sound. The monster released my foot.

I scrambled away, my whole body shaking in terror. I shambled to the closest wall and tried to stand as my legs threatened to buckle. Before me, the creature wavered and solidified.

It looked like a humanoid lizard—a mixture of monster and man—with a long scaly body and jagged teeth in its oversized mouth. Zeph had it by the neck, holding it above the ground with one hand as the creature squirmed and shrieked. It clawed at Zeph's arm frantically, snapping its massive jaws and lashing its long tail.

"You dare touch what belongs to me?" Zeph roared like a lion and squeezed the monster's neck. There was another gory, cracking sound, and instantly the monster's body went limp.

A chorus of yowls screeched. I clamped my hands over my ears. The kitchen windows began to crack and burst. Two more of the scaly creatures were crouched in the stairwell that led to the second story of the house. They wailed and spat in dismay, but didn't dare to come any closer.

"Get out." I didn't realize Zeph was talking to me at first.

Then he cast an icy glare in my direction.

My legs were numb with terror.

"I said go! *Now*!" His voice was so loud it rattled the whole house.

Before I realized what I was doing, I found myself running for the front door. I bolted outside and went straight to the car. Hank was still there, talking to the family and the priests in the driveway. They all watched me go sprinting past, running with my head down so I didn't have to make eye contact with anyone. I shut myself in the backseat of Hank's old Cadillac and curled up, drawing my knees to my chest.

I counted my breaths, shutting my eyes tightly and letting my forehead rest on my kneecaps. My pulse was still racing, and my foot still throbbed from where that awful creature had grabbed me.

That's when I remembered.

The monster had said something about Zeph protecting my dad.

That *liar*!

It wasn't true. It couldn't be. Tears filled my eyes as I tried to rationalize it. Zeph hadn't known my dad … had he? How could he? My dad had died almost four years ago, before I even lived in that apartment building.

I got angry just thinking about it. If Zeph had known my dad, then that meant he'd been lying to me about it all this time. He'd been asking those questions, probing me for information like he had no idea what was going on or who I was. He'd been deceiving me from the start—and I'd fallen for it!

By the time Zeph emerged from the house, looking like a normal, human delinquent again, I had already worked myself up into a fit of rage. I tested out a string of insults I fully intended on hurling at him as soon as he got in the car as I peered over the edge of the window he had left cracked open.

Hank got into the car first, and cranked the engine. He didn't say a word to me as he drummed his fingers on the steering wheel. We both watched as Zeph made his way down the driveway toward us, putting on his coat and adjusting its collar. He took his time, pulling a fresh cigarette out of his coat pocket, and holding it between his lips. Relishing the victory, probably. Although, I noticed the expression on his face was closer to one of total exhaustion than smug satisfaction.

Then that girl, the oldest of the two daughters, stopped him.

They were only a few feet away from the car, close enough that I could hear every word. She still had that flirty, doe-eyed expression on her face. I hated her instantly. I could practically feel my blood boiling in my veins as she stroked his arm to get his attention. It was way more than just a friendly gesture.

What was there to like about him, anyway? Couldn't she tell he was a jerk? Sure, he was handsome, but obviously hadn't brushed his hair or bothered to shave in a few days.

"I can't thank you enough for helping us," she said. She kept touching her hair, tossing it from one shoulder to the other. "It means so much to me."

Zeph gave her that once-over glance I'd seen other men give an attractive female, like some kind of full body scan to see if she had any glaring flaws. His annoyed expression never changed, though. "Yeah, well, whatever. It's fine."

She wasn't fazed in the slightest. She just kept batting her eyes at him. "Maybe we could get a drink sometime? You know, so I can thank you properly?"

My cheeks were so hot they would have sizzled to the touch. I looked around, wishing I had something to throw at them. I was practically snorting steam as I peeked through the car window, watching his every move.

Zeph stared at her as though she were out of her mind. Then he shook his head. "Sorry. I'm only interested in puny redheads." Those words rolled out of his mouth like it should have been obvious, and he walked back to the car without looking back.

My mouth hung wide open.

What? But ... at the bar, he'd said ...

In a matter of seconds, all the anger drained from my body. I felt like a deflated balloon, leaning against the car window. Too late, I realized Hank was watching me in the rearview mirror. I could tell by how the corners of his eyes were crinkled that he was smiling at me.

I wanted to melt into the seat, and scrambled back to my side of the car, pulling my hood up over my head to hide my red face. When Zeph got inside, I couldn't even look at him. I didn't want him to know I'd heard him.

We pulled away from the house, leaving that girl standing in her driveway, blinking owlishly with shock. She was pretty, so maybe she wasn't used to being rejected like that.

No one said a word as we drove back downtown. It was just after dark when Hank dropped us off in front of our building. He and Zeph shook hands, exchanging a few muttered words I couldn't make out, and then he was gone. Zeph and I were alone. We stood on the curb watching his taillights disappear into traffic as he drove away.

Anger roared in my veins. I didn't even want to look at Zeph, despite the fact that I was fully entitled to an explanation about how he knew my dad.

I finally got up the nerve to glance over at him. He stood, staring at me as though there was something he wanted to say.

Nope. I was 1,000% done with him today.

I did an immediate about-face and began speed-walking toward the front door of our building.

I was still alone as I rounded the last set of stairs leading up to our floor. A tangled mess of emotions coiled and twisted in my brain. Why wasn't he chasing after me? Why wasn't he yelling, cursing, or trying to justify himself? Wasn't he even going to try to deny that he'd been lying to me all this time about knowing my dad?

When I got to our hall, Zeph was already standing at the top of the stairs, leaning against my front door like a living barricade. His arms were crossed, and his mouth scrunched into a stubborn frown.

I staggered to a halt. "How did you get up here?"

He arched an eyebrow. "She asked the faerie gifted with magical power."

His tone was so sarcastic, so pompous … I gnashed my teeth to keep my chin from trembling. No angry crying. Not now.

"Move, idiot. I'm going home. I've had all I can stand of you today."

"We need to talk." He didn't move an inch.

"I have nothing to say to you, so move."

"Well that's fine, cause I've got lots to say to you."

No. Not right now. My eyes were welling up. I couldn't hold it together much longer, and I was *not* about to let him see me cry. Whatever he wanted to say, it could wait. I had to get away.

When I tried shoving him out of my path, he grabbed me by the back of my coat and plucked me off the floor like a naughty puppy. "Quit that."

"I don't want to hear it, Zeph!" I yelled, wrestling myself free of his grip. "You lied to me. You lied right to my face!"

He took a step and reached out as though he was going to embrace me. No. Freaking. Way.

I reared a hand back, ready to slap him if he came any closer.

"What the hell did you expect?" He shouted suddenly, flailing his arms. "Fine, you're pissed at me. I get that. But at least let me explain!"

I swallowed the lump in my throat and forced myself to sound calmer. I wasn't about to give him the satisfaction of seeing me cry. "Go away, Zeph. Just leave me alone. I never want to see you again!"

As soon as the door clicked shut and I was alone again in my apartment, I hated myself for saying that to him. I didn't want him to leave. I didn't want to fight with him at all. He was the only person in the world who seemed to care what happened to me other than Ben—and I'd never even looked Ben in the eye.

I hoped to see him sitting at my kitchen table as I stumbled through on the way to my bedroom, but my apartment was empty and uncomfortably quiet. I stormed to my bedroom and slammed the door as hard as I could, hoping he would hear it.

After all, I knew better now than to think any door I shut would actually keep him out.

I collapsed onto my bed with my face in my pillow. My stomach growled and ached, but I had no desire to cook anything. Chocolate probably would have worked toward solving all my problems, emotional and physical, but I didn't have any on hand.

My skin still felt clammy. My body was still trembling. Just the thought of Zeph made my fingers and toes curl, my throat ache, and my breath catch with a sob.

I needed to clear my head.

I forced myself to get up and go to the bathroom. A long shower would be good. It might even wash off any residual stink from those lizard monsters.

I let the shower run until the whole bathroom was fogged with steam. Leaning against the shower wall, I let my head loll back so the hot water ran through my hair and down my back. At last, the pressure inside me seemed to ease.

But I still couldn't close my eyes without seeing his stupid, lying face.

I stood at the bathroom counter for a long time with my hair dripping wet, staring at the circles under my eyes through a small hole I'd wiped in the fog on the mirror. I wasn't as pretty as that girl who'd flirted with Zeph today. Her hair had been so silky, while mine looked like a frizzy mane of red curls. It reminded me of how my dad had jokingly called me his Raggedy Ann when I was little. That girl also had a more shapely, grown-up body. Me? Well, I was still wearing an A-cup that I didn't even fill up all the way. Her skin had been smooth and clean like something from a makeup ad. I had freckles—lots and lots of them.

But Zeph had said he liked "puny redheads."

Remembering those words made my heart do that weird fluttering, shivering thing deep in my chest. I didn't know why he'd said that. Maybe he knew I was eavesdropping and said it just to tease me? That definitely sounded like something he would do.

Then again, maybe not.

I stood at the mirror, chasing down my racing thoughts until the steam finally cleared from the room. None of what Zeph did or said made any sense. He was constantly contradicting himself. Why? What was the point? To drive me nuts? If so, he was doing a fantastic job. With a sigh, I wrapped myself up in my favorite pink, fluffy bathrobe and went back to the bedroom.

I opened my bedroom door and screamed.

There was a man in my room. It took me a few seconds of absolute terror and gripping the doorframe to realize I knew him.

Zeph sat on the floor, leaning back against the side of my bed. He rested his elbows on his knees, and his head bowed low to his chest. He didn't even look up as I struggled to regain my composure. It took me a minute or two to work up the energy to be furious with him.

"I told you not to do this! Don't come in here without asking! You scared me to death, you moron!"

His expression was so bleak and dejected as he sat there, staring at the floor. It made me very uneasy. Slowly, he raised his head to gaze up at me, and I could tell just by the look on his face that he'd come here to talk—whether I liked it or not.

"I'm sorry," he said quietly.

"Sorry?" I didn't quite believe that. He'd never been sorry for breaking into my home before. "Did you break my door again?"

"No. I'm not talking about that." He went back to staring at the floor. "I mean about your dad. I'm sorry … I should have told you. I just didn't think he would have wanted you to get mixed up with me. I know it looks bad now, like I was just lying to be a prick, but I'll tell you whatever you want to know."

I took a few cautious steps into the room. I was beginning to wish I had dressed in the bathroom. Him showing up in my home all the time was going to be an adjustment. I'd have to make sure never to walk around in my underwear. "Mixed up with you? Why not? What's wrong with you?"

Zeph smirked, like I'd made a joke. He scratched at the back of his head nervously. "A lot, probably."

I took a deep, steadying breath and went to my dresser. I tried to keep things as casual as possible, hoping he wouldn't notice as I went digging through my underwear drawer for the most adult-looking undergarments I owned.

At last, I turned around. "I need to change, so close your eyes. No peeking."

"Hah. As if there's anything there to see."

I narrowed my eyes. "Of course. Puny redheaded girls do nothing for you, right?"

His face flushed a little, and I reveled in my victory. Strange as it was, hearing him be sarcastic and rude again was comforting. Plus, knowing I could beat him at his own game made it much more fun.

Zeph was quiet then, sitting obediently on the floor with his eyes closed and his head leaned back against the side of my bed. "Your dad was a good man. He didn't deserve what happened to him. He always made the people around him want to be better and work harder so that we could restore peace." He pursed his lips. "I guess I'm not a shining example of that, though."

I quickly finished dressing, pulling one of my dad's old t-shirts over my head and slipping on a pair of gym shorts. I plopped onto my knees on the floor in front of him, making enough noise to let him know I was done changing.

"Yeah, you are pretty disgusting."

Zeph snorted and his mouth quirked into a half-cocked smirk. "Keep it up, princess. Next time, I'll let the bogle chew on you a little longer."

"So why wouldn't my dad want me to get involved with you? What was that bogle talking about? Why were you protecting my dad?"

"It's a long story," he admitted. "It goes back to the old Seelie and Unseelie dispute. Thousands of years ago, all faeries used to live together in harmony with humanity. We were ruled over by one fae who had been given dominion over all other faeries by the vessel."

I inched a little closer. "Vessel?"

"The vessel is a human gifted with the blessing of the moon. They're like a walking fountain of raw, untapped magical energy. They have the power to share that energy with others if they choose," he explained. "Legend has it that the vessel signifies the bond between fae and humanity—how we are supposed to share and help one another. That's why only the vessel can choose the next faerie ruler."

"You mean like a king or a queen?"

He nodded. "We lived in peace that way for a long time. But, as the world of humankind began to grow and change, turning away from magic and forgetting the old ways, the faerie court was split." His jaw tensed for a moment. "Some of them believed that we should remove ourselves from human sight altogether. They thought we should never use our magic except when a human life was in mortal danger—and sometimes not even then. They called themselves the Seelie Court, and decided to remain strictly devoted to the old laws."

Zeph hesitated, and then stretched out his legs and let his hands fall back into his lap. "But others began to hate humans for destroying the forests and poisoning the wild places of the world where faeries had lived in peace for so long." He dragged a finger through his bangs, brushing them away from his eyes. His gaze was distant. "They didn't want to obey rules for regulating magic that the Seelie Court was determined to uphold— rules that they believed conflicted with their ability to defend themselves and their homes. They call themselves Unseelies and are regarded as rogues, vigilantes, or even evil spirits. Not all of them are, but it only takes a few to give the whole lot a bad name."

I sank back on my heels some. "Like the bogles from today?"

"Yep. Exactly. The two courts have been at war for a very long time. The Seelies like to pretend they're the magic police. They try to apprehend and punish Unseelie fae who have broken their laws. Meanwhile, the Unseelies are some of the most pretentious, self-serving idiots you'll ever meet. Most of them have found ways to hide in plain sight while simultaneously exploiting the greed and vices of humanity. Some have progressed to committing even more heinous acts, even against their own kind." He smirked again, as he gave a shrug. "Your dad wanted to find a way to mend our differences so we could deal with the only real villain this world has ever known."

"My dad never talked much about his work," I admitted. "I had no idea he was involved in anything like this."

Zeph sighed. "He was one of the few humans who had dared to try it in a long time. But he understood the threat Fir Darrig poses, not just to the faerie world, but to the human world as well."

"Fir Darrig?"

His smirked disappeared. The mischievous light in his eyes died, and I saw his whole body tense. "Big trouble," he answered softly.

Things were slowly beginning to make more sense. If my dad had been poking around in the faerie realm, which I now knew could be extremely dangerous, then it wasn't surprising that he had gotten in over his head. I knew he had passed away in a house fire when I was fourteen—a fire I had only narrowly escaped from, although I didn't remember it. The smoke had been so intense that I lost consciousness in the hallway trying to escape, and woke up in the back of an ambulance hours later.

Had Fir Darrig caused that fire?

The memory replayed before I could stop it. It consumed me—the smell of the smoke, not being able to breathe without choking, and the roar of the flames. A heat so intense I couldn't even open my eyes without blinding, searing pain.

"Hey, you okay?" He was looking at me with his brow drawn up with worry.

I forced a teasing smile. "Fine. So which are you? Seelie or Unseelie?"

He arched his eyebrow at me with that candid expression I was beginning to enjoy so much. "You think I'd follow anyone else's rules?"

"Unseelie it is, then." I managed to laugh.

He laughed, too, reclining back against the side of my bed and closing his eyes again. He looked strangely innocent sitting there with his expression calm. It made him even more irresistible.

I scooted in a few more inches. My pulse frenzied, and I held my breath as I reached out to touch one of his cheeks. "Falling asleep?"

Zeph caught my hand right before I could grab him, holding it in a warm, firm grip. His purple eyes opened, looking directly at me with an expression that made my heart skip a beat. "You're a mean kid. No wonder you don't have any friends."

I was trying to come up with a snappy reply, but he took my hand and pressed it up against the side of his face. I stifled a gasp, watching the way his eyes rolled back. He seemed to enjoy the way my palm felt against his rough, stubbly cheek. My fingers followed the contour of his face until he turned his head into my palm, and I felt his warm, soft lips graze the side of my thumb.

For a moment, I couldn't breathe.

Somewhere in my twisted mind was the foolish hope that he might try something more, like kissing me again. I wanted that—I wanted it *badly*.

Finally, he released my hand and stood. "It's late. You have school tomorrow."

I deflated. That was the last thing I wanted to think about right then. "You'll come with me tomorrow, won't you? As Joe?" I asked as I crawled into my bed.

He hesitated. "I guess I don't have much of a choice now. At least, not until we come up with a better solution. Word'll spread that you're involved with me. You'll become more of a target from now on. Like it or not, that knucklehead of a puca is going to have to start carrying his weight around here."

That wasn't comforting at all. I didn't want Eldrick at my side—I wanted *him*.

He sighed, shoving his hands in the pockets of his worn-out jeans. "Go to sleep. I won't let anything get you." He showed me another roguish grin before starting toward the door.

One glance across the room to my closet gave me chills. Eldrick might be in there. He could be anywhere in this apartment, just waiting for the chance to ...

"Zeph?" I gulped, studying the pattern on my comforter. "Will you please stay here tonight?"

"That's not ... I mean, you're still too ... uh, technically. I can't ..."

"For crying out loud! I turn eighteen in a few months." I sulked.

"Besides, I didn't mean it like *that*. You have a dirty mind."

"What the heck am I supposed to think?" He face went red.

"You're not even human, so what does it matter? You're probably a thousand years old, right?"

Zeph didn't argue that, which surprised me more than it should have. I didn't know how old he was, but maybe I had been closer to the right number than I thought.

"I just don't want to be alone," I confessed, quickly changing the subject. "I keep thinking about what else might be in my apartment that I can't even see."

His tense expression began to fade, steadily becoming something much gentler and yet profoundly uncertain. Had I struck a chord?

"Fine." He sighed in defeat. "But you better not tell anybody about this, got me? Not Hank. Not the landlord. Nobody."

Zeph walked around to the empty side of my bed and sat down. He started untying his shoes and muttering under his breath. I couldn't make out most of what he said, but I did hear him say something about not getting under the blankets.

"Good. Your feet probably stink anyway," I quipped.

He made the whole bed jostle as he flopped back with his hands behind his head, stretching out with a satisfied groan. He was so tall that his feet hung off the end of the mattress.

"I'm only sitting here until you fall asleep. Then I'm going to the couch," he mumbled. "It's not up for debate, so don't give me lip about it. Got it?"

"Sure." I fought a smile as he sat up long enough to rearrange the pillows.

I could just barely lie next to him without touching. He was close enough that I could feel the warmth of his body. Occasionally, I caught a waft of his earthy smell. It was strange and soothing to have another person near me—a person who seemed to want to be around me. I'd only been able to sleep whenever he was around, keeping the invisible monsters at bay.

"You better not snore," I mumbled as I closed my eyes.

"Just go to sleep," he replied, and I could hear the smile in his voice.

Zeph snored loud enough to wake the dead. So much for going to the couch. Sitting up, I frowned at where he was stretched out on top of the blankets, sound asleep.

Zeph had mentioned fae were often mistaken for angels. Knowing that, I wondered where the expression "sleeping like an angel" had come from … because there wasn't anything beautiful about the way he was snoring like a freight train. He was sprawled on his belly, arms straight down at his sides, with his bare feet still hanging off the end of my bed. His dark hair was mashed flat on one side, and sticking up on the other. His clothes were rumpled, and his face was buried in the pillow. He looked dead except for the fact that I could hear the muffled sounds of his deep, wheezing breaths. How could he even breathe at all like that?

Leaning over the edge of the bed, I dragged my laptop off the nightstand and pulled it onto my lap. While it booted up, I tried to think of what I could say to Ben about what'd happened yesterday.

I twirled a lock of Zeph's lengthy hair around my finger as he went on snoring and wheezing. He didn't even twitch. Too bad I couldn't sleep that deeply.

It took a few seconds for my email inbox to load. A hard knot formed in the back of my throat when I saw I already had a new email from Ben.

Josie,

I received an email from a so-called friend of yours. He told me he got my address when you used his phone. He explained the situation at school, that you've been having a hard time with a certain guidance counselor and that you are afraid to tell me about these problems because of the complexity of our relationship. If I have ever made you feel uncomfortable about coming to me with these kinds of issues, please let me apologize. I am very sorry. That was never my intent. Your father asked me to be his replacement to the best of my ability, and I have obviously failed in that because you don't feel like you can be honest with me. I hope you'll give me the opportunity to do better. I will have a discussion with your guidance counselor and, if need be, I will relocate you to a different school of your choosing.

As for the "friend" who sent me the email, while I appreciate his interest in your well-being, I want to advise you to be careful. He wouldn't give me his name or explain how he knows you. I won't tell you not to trust him, that's a choice you are fully capable of making on your own, but I want you to be safe. In any case, I'm happy you've found someone who is apparently concerned about you. Just remember to protect yourself. There are terrible people in this world.

Yours,
Ben

I stopped twirling the lock of Zeph's hair. I debated on ripping it right out of his head. He sent Ben an email about me? Of all the nosy, crooked, sneaky things to do!

But as fast as my temper caught fire, it began to fizzle out just as quickly. I untwisted his lock of hair from around my finger, and stared at the back of his sleeping, dumb head. Just what was his problem, anyway?

Based on what I had seen of him, Zeph didn't get involved with other people if he could avoid it—or unless his boss forced him. Otherwise, he might have taken that pretty girl up on her request for a date. He never had people over, which I knew because I had been basically stalking him before all this. Even Hank seemed to regard him with a sort of gruff, almost cautious friendliness.

So why was he meddling around in my business?

Unless … he was genuinely worried about me. The more I thought about it, the more it made me smile. I guess he did like me, after all.

Shutting the computer down again, I slipped it back under the side of my bed and leaned over to plant a kiss on the back of Zeph's head. He didn't stop wheezing, even when I slid out of the bed and ducked out into the hall.

I hurried through my morning routine, trying not to make too much noise. I fixed my hair with a little extra effort, and dabbed on some makeup. It was against school rules, but the risk was worth it for the boost of confidence. Funny how a single swipe of eyeliner can make you feel bolder.

I crept down the hallway to the kitchen, acutely aware that I had my work cut out for me in there. Trying to fix breakfast without making too much of a racket was a challenge. After whipping together some vegetarian-friendly biscuits, I cut up a few slices of watermelon and pineapple and tossed them into a bowl. I poured two big glasses of milk and spread everything out neatly on the table, setting two places with plates and utensils.

Just as I took the biscuits out of the oven, my bedroom door opened. Heavy footsteps echoed down the hall, and Zeph came staggering into the room with his hair rumpled up like he'd just walked through a hurricane. He looked at me, then at the table, and then at the big pan of golden-brown biscuits I was holding. His eyes squinted at them suspiciously.

"It's five in the morning," he complained in a hoarse voice. "What's all this for?"

"You," I said proudly. I brought a little dish of cinnamon butter I had prepared and the quart-sized jar of organic, raw honey I'd bought at a local farmer's market. It still had a big slice of the comb inside. "To thank you for yesterday."

"For lying?"

"No, for telling the truth. And for agreeing to stay with me." I removed my cooking apron and sat down across from him.

He wasn't listening anymore. The instant the jar of honey hit the table in front of him, his gaze was fixed on it like he'd just seen the Holy Grail. His eyes grew wide. He wasted no time on ceremony.

I watched in quiet horror as he plucked four biscuits from the pan, slathered them with honey until they were sopping, and ate them with his fingers. He did the same thing with the entire bowl of fruit, making sure each slice was covered completely in golden honey before he wolfed it down.

"Stop that!" I caught him right before he was about to stick his whole hand in the jar. "What's wrong with you?"

He looked at me like he might bite me for getting between him and the honey jar. "It's my favorite."

"That doesn't mean you go sticking your dirty hands in it." I took the jar and put it on the opposite end of the table. "You probably scratched your dangly man parts or something. If you want more, use a spoon."

He scowled at me before he snatched up a spoon again and went back to funneling the rest of the honey into his mouth. Without meaning to, I had stumbled across something that guaranteed his unfaltering cooperation. I pondered that as I plucked a biscuit out of the pan before he could go back for more.

Zeph gulped down his glass of milk and two more biscuits somewhere between bites of honey. He cleaned out the entire jar, then pried the comb out of it and began chewing on it like a dog with a rawhide bone. I didn't fight with him over that. I had a feeling I might lose a finger if I tried to take it away.

Sipping on a glass of milk in between bites of my own breakfast, I thought about the email he'd sent to Ben, and wondered exactly what it had said. I doubted Zeph would want to tell me. Maybe that was for the best.

"Is Hank a faerie, too?" I asked as I poured us both a second glass of milk.

Zeph was busy licking his fingers. "No. He's human, like you. Remember, I said some humans still remember the old ways. Usually, it's people with a cultural heritage tied directly to us. Hank is a shaman. His family came here from Mongolia generations back, but they continued to honor their ancestral traditions. His culture is steeped in our laws and practices, and has been for as long as any of us can remember. So he's able to see and sense us."

"And you two just go around saving people from bogles in your free time?" Hank had called it a case—as though this was something they treated like a job.

"Only if it's serious. And it's not always bogles. There are some Unseelies who cross the line from mischief to ... well, worse things. We've dealt with that a few times before," he explained between sips of milk. "Sidhe are the ones you don't want to mess with. Most of them stayed true to the old ways, with the Seelie Court, but there are some who don't. They're like first-class citizens in the faerie world. Their power is rich and ancient, and they're usually the ones you see depicted in artwork. You know, looking all pretty'n crap. They're easier on the eyes than most of us, I guess."

I thought about that for a moment. "What about changelings?"

Zeph hesitated as he glanced at me from across the table. He may have been trying to give me a silent warning, but it was completely ruined by the milk mustache he had on his upper lip.

Suddenly, a chilled breeze swept through the room. My skin prickled and my breathing hitched. I *knew* that feeling.

"Changelings are regarded as common miscreants, instigators, deceivers, and thieves. Distinctly unintelligent, some might say," a deep, eerily familiar voice growled.

I sat up straight in my chair, unable to hide the panic as I dropped my glass of milk. It shattered on the kitchen floor. I recognized that voice, even if I hadn't heard it in a few days. It was unmistakable.

Eldrick stood in the kitchen doorway, watching us with eyes that shimmered like two silver moons. I'd never seen him in daylight before and never looking like a person. But he was no less menacing than when he looked like a big angry wolf.

He appeared much younger than I'd expected. The way Zeph had talked about Eldrick before, as though he were someone incredibly ancient, made me think he would be bent, wrinkled, and elderly. But the tall, leanly-built man before me couldn't have been any older than Zeph.

Nothing about Eldrick looked friendly or inviting. Sure, he was beautiful, just like Zeph—albeit in a much different way. He had broad shoulders and a cold intensity to his sharp features. Deep set eyes the color of liquid platinum leered at me through his styled, pitch-black hair that fell around his ears and swept across his brow. His olive toned skin was a flawless, and there was an almost obsessive perfection about how his clothes were arranged. The charcoal colored knit sweater he wore was rolled neatly up to his elbows, and his dress slacks were tailored to fit his lean build with a sense of modern style. A silver band shimmered on his right thumb; it was a ring cut in the shape of a crown.

"Nice of you to join us, loser. Tired of hiding under the bed?" Zeph sneered without giving the puca a second glance.

I took a trembling step toward Zeph, broken glass crunching under my shoes.

Eldrick watched my every move with his creepy, pale eyes. "She's afraid of me. How pathetic."

"Probably because you've been acting like an asshole. What was all that? A desperate effort to get her to kick you out? Pretty damn pathetic, even by your standards."

Eldrick's lips drew back in a snarl. "I suppose you would know all about desperate efforts, wouldn't you?"

"You wanna say that again?" Zeph slammed a fist down on the table, making all the dishes rattle. "Or should I just go ahead and beat your ass right now?"

"Guys, please, stop fighting. Ben just had this place fixed up after last time." I steeled my nerves and met Eldrick's gaze. It seemed like this kind of strangeness was going to become commonplace in my life now, so I would have to grow a thick skin and learn to deal with it. "Do you want anything for breakfast?"

The dark spirit stared at me with oppressive, eerie eyes. For the briefest instant, he looked genuinely surprised. "Why would *you* do anything for me?"

"Yeah," Zeph agreed. "Are you thick in the head? He's been torturing you for years. Make him grovel a little. Make him rub your feet or something."

"Shut up," I snapped at both of them. "You said it was my fault, right? Because my dad was the one who caught him and forced a contract on him? I … I guess I can understand why he would hate me. Anyway, someone in this situation has to be the adult, and since neither of you two are stepping up to the plate, I guess that leaves me."

Eldrick pressed his lips together uncomfortably, but his eyes never left me.

I quickly cleaned up the mess from my broken glass and got to work tidying up the rest of the kitchen. I was bent over the sink, rinsing the last few dishes, when I felt a cold puff of air on the back of my neck.

When I turned around, Eldrick was standing right over me, backing me up against the counter while he invaded my personal space.

I sucked in a sharp breath.

Even Zeph looked surprised as he stumbled to his feet, his fists balled up like he was ready to be the hammer of justice at the first sign of trouble. He might have looked intimidating if not for the giant ball of honeycomb that was still in his cheek.

"Your father was a fool to think I would serve such a pathetic human girl," Eldrick hissed, venom and fury burning in every word.

"He was smarter than you, apparently. He must have been if he tricked you into a contract, right?" I countered. It was just a guess. All I had to go on was what Zeph had told me.

His expression tightened, like he was debating whether or not it would be worth whatever physical punishment Zeph might give him if he ripped my throat out.

"And now you have to do what I tell you, right? So shut up, sit down, and eat. Zeph, let him have that last biscuit," I commanded. Eldrick didn't have to like me, but for now, he had to obey me.

He sat down in my seat, eyeing the single biscuit that was left in the pan. He curled his lip in disgust. "Human food is vile."

Great. Somehow, I'd become the only mature individual in the kitchen—which was pretty sad considering I was the youngest by probably a few centuries.

"Look, take one bite. If you still don't like it, then you don't have to finish it," I bargained with him. "How do you know if you like something or not if you won't even try it?"

If looks could kill, Eldrick's glare would have burned me to cinders right where I stood. He muttered something that was probably profanity in an ancient language and took a *tiny* bite of the biscuit.

I turned my back, deciding not to watch in case he chose not to finish it purely to spite me. No point in putting more wind in his sails. I finished the dishes, setting them out to dry, and went back to finish clearing the table.

The biscuit was gone.

Across the table, Zeph sat with his arms crossed and a big, smug grin on his lips. The only evidence of what had happened were a few crumbs left on the plate and the sour look of rebellion still on Eldrick's face.

"You should try it with the honey next time." Zeph's voice had a definite tone of sarcasm as he got up and rubbed his belly. "I'm going back to bed."

"But what about school?" I grabbed the back of his shirt to stop him. "You said you would go with me."

"Hey, I have grown-up stuff to do, you know. I do have a job." He swatted my hands away and strolled back down the hallway to my bedroom as if he lived there.

"You said worse things would start targeting me now. And everyone at school will ask me about Joe!" I pleaded as I followed him.

"Take sourpuss in there. He has to do what you say, right? So tell him to go." Zeph groaned as he flopped back down on my bed.

"He doesn't look anything like Joe. Remember what happened with that ivy plant? What if he can't stop those kinds of things from happening?"

"Of course he can. Relax. He might be a pain in the butt, but he's old and powerful. It'll be fine." He twirled a finger in the air. A musical sound floated past my ears, like the faint chime of bells. It made me shiver a little, and I glanced back over my shoulder as a loud thud came from the kitchen.

This was *not* what I had in mind. Eldrick hated me. I didn't want to have to spend all day being followed around by someone who was looking for any excuse to rip my head off. I chewed on my bottom lip, thinking it over while Zeph wrapped himself up in my blankets like a man-burrito.

"What have you done to me?" A roaring voice boomed from the doorway.

I squeaked in panic, whirling around to see Joe—a new Joe—standing there with a look of wrath smoldering in his eyes.

"See? Problem solved," Zeph murmured from inside my bed. "Go forth and have school."

"You insolent worm! Change me back immediately!" Eldrick bellowed.

"No! Please don't fight!" I jumped in between them, planting my hands on his chest to stop him from going any further.

Eldrick jerked away from me violently and staggered back a few feet, his face blanched with fear and silver eyes were wide.

Was he … afraid of *me*? Why? What could I possibly do to someone like him?

Zeph just yawned. "Oh, relax. It's not permanent. It'll wear off after 3:00 PM."

"It had better," Eldrick threatened.

Awkward didn't even begin to describe it.

Eldrick strode beside me, looking like the golden-haired Joe who was supposed to be my boyfriend. At first, he wouldn't walk any closer than a few feet away. But as we ventured out of the apartment and approached the front of the school, his movements became rigid. Something wasn't right. His face had that wild, pasty look of terror again as he slunk closer to my side. His silver eyes tracked the other students passing us on their way inside, cringing away if anyone strayed too close.

I leaned over to whisper. "Are you okay?"

He stopped. His jaw clenched and his brow locked into a frown. "Do not pretend to be concerned about my welfare. I don't need the help of a human."

"I'm not pretending anything." Moving slowly, I held out a hand. "Stay near me, you'll be fine."

He twitched his mouth as he studied my open palm. At last, his large hand grasped mine, but his expression was one of absolute misery. He looked like he might actually be sick. He stared at the ground and followed me into the school, gripping my hand like a corpse with *rigor mortis*.

"I'm really sorry about this, Eld—I mean Joe," I said quietly. "I'll tell him not to change you again unless you say it's okay."

As much as I wanted to be angry with Eldrick, which he certainly deserved after everything he'd done to me, I understood his frustration. Why would anyone want to be bound to me? He'd probably been well respected amongst his kind. Now, he was basically my servant. Talk about being knocked off a pedestal. It wasn't my fault, but someone had to take the blame. My dad was dead, so that meant I was the only one he could be angry with. Lucky me.

"Eldrick, I'm sorry my dad trapped you. I don't know why he did it, or what kind of contract he made with you. For the record, I'm not exactly happy with you either, but can't we just put all that aside for today?"

He flicked me a glance, remaining silent.

"Maybe you could tell me about the contract? I-I'm sort of new to this stuff. I don't know how it works."

His brows knitted and a vein stood out against the side of his neck. "It stipulates that I must reside in your dwelling and do your bidding until such time as you release me."

"That's it?"

He nodded once.

I frowned. What was the point of that? Why would my dad want this guy stuck around me all the time? So far, it had only made both of us miserable.

Eldrick didn't say much of anything for the rest of the day. My classmates noticed "Joe's" sudden change in demeanor right away. The guy they had all met the day before had been cheerful and charming. This Joe was anything but. He sat in the seat behind me, doing his work quietly. When we changed classes, he walked a few feet behind me, staring down at the floor with a somber expression.

That is—until a group of other students rushed up, clamoring to greet him and ask about his mother and how his family was doing.

By the look on Eldrick's face, you'd think they were rushing him with pitchforks. He shied away, ducking behind me while the color drained from his face. Wild terror flashed in his eyes as he stared at them, his mouth set in a twitching frown. His chest heaved with frantic breaths, hands balled into fists.

His reaction made everyone pause—including me. The other students were glancing at one another, beginning to whisper.

"Sorry, guys." I forced a smile. "It's a bad day, you know, with his mom. He needs a little space."

That did the trick. The crowd began to disperse, offering a few sympathetic smiles as they went. I let out a sigh of relief.

Crisis averted.

All of a sudden, I felt a warm, strong hand clasp mine.

Eldrick was standing next to me again, his face angled away so I couldn't see his expression. He was holding onto my hand like someone gripping a life preserver. I wondered what scared him so badly about being around other people. He was supposed to be ancient and powerful, right? Why would a being like that be afraid of humans? What could they possibly to do someone like him?

"What's up with Joe's mom?" A group of popular girls cornered me outside the lunchroom. "He seems so sad today. Is his mom okay?"

I had almost forgotten about the story Zeph made up to explain my absence from school. "O-oh. Yeah. You know, it's just hard on him right now. They're still trying to figure out what's wrong with her. It isn't looking good."

"That's awful." One of the girls gave me an awkward side-hug. "We should get her flowers or something. Would you take them to her?"

When I agreed, I just assumed they weren't being serious. People said that kind of thing all the time without meaning it, right? A week ago, none of these girls would have even agreed to sit at the same lunch table with me.

By the end of the day, a bunch of the students and faculty had collected donation money, and I wound up walking home with a giant bouquet of roses and daisies in my arms. It was so big I could barely see what was in front of me. The porcelain vase was heavy, but I was determined not to ask Eldrick for help.

We were almost back to the apartment building, crossing the last intersection, when I tripped.

I stepped off the curb without expecting it, and fell face-forward onto the pavement. The vase smashed into a million pieces. Out of the corner of my eye, I saw the wheels of a car screeching right toward me.

My body went stiff with terror.

It all happened so fast; I didn't have time to respond.

I shut my eyes, cringing for impact, and then I felt two strong hands grab me by the waist. Someone snatched me off the asphalt just in time. The car zipped past, barely missing me, and smashing all the flowers that were lying in the street.

I expected it to be Zeph. I wanted it to be him.

But when I opened my eyes to see who had saved me from becoming a road pancake, I was stunned. Eldrick had his arms around me, holding me protectively while he glared in the direction the car had gone. He didn't look like Joe anymore. He was himself again, complete with silky black hair blowing perfectly over his angular cheekbones.

"I almost died," I gasped.

Eldrick seemed to realize the awkward position we were in, and immediately stepped away from me. He smoothed out the front of his black sweater, plucking off pieces of dirt with a grim frown.

"You are an astounding amount of trouble," he scolded.

"So much for the flowers." It was a little sad to see them all smashed into the pavement. "I can't believe the jerk in that car didn't even stop to see if I was okay."

Eldrick put his hands in the pockets of his black, dress pants. "Humans rarely care for the well-being of anyone besides themselves. You care nothing for the suffering of others." He spoke like he had personal experience in that department.

"We're not all like that," I muttered.

"Hah!" He scoffed. "I've yet to meet a single one that isn't. You are all the same—driven by ulterior motives. Every last one of you is fueled by greed and so numbed by your own narcissism you feel nothing but warped desire."

I sighed. I wasn't in the mood to argue with him. He didn't seem to take anything I said seriously, anyway.

When we returned to my apartment building, Zeph wasn't there. His front door was locked, and my bed was empty. He'd mentioned needing to go to work, though, so I wasn't too worried about it.

But without him my apartment seemed so empty. The silence was deafening. Even with Eldrick skulking around in a less terrifying form, I felt alone.

I sank down on the sofa and turned on the TV for background noise, and began reading through the last email from Ben on my phone again. First, Zeph had gone out of his way to fix things at school by sending Ben that email, and now he had set me up with a new stand-in boyfriend-guardian to keep watch over me while I went about my everyday life. At least, that's how it looked from where I was standing.

A cold pang of realization hit me square in the gut—was he trying to get rid of me? With all my problems apparently solved, he had no reason to ever bother with me again. Was our previous routine of occasional awkward glances in the mailroom about to resume again? It's not like I had any right to ask him to come back over here. I wasn't his problem.

"I guess that's it, then," I whispered to myself.

The sofa shifted as someone else sat down. I looked over, stunned to see Eldrick sitting beside me with a coffee mug in his hand. Granted, he was as far away from me as possible, perched on the complete opposite end of the sofa. But still …

"Zeph has been trying to get rid of me all this time, hasn't he?" I dared to ask. It was a personal question, but at least I knew Eldrick wouldn't lie for the sake of my feelings.

The dark spirit took a quiet sip from his coffee cup. "I've never understood the motives of his species. They're far too emotional. Far too changeable. Hence their name."

Great. That was *not* helpful.

He stared at the television like I might as well be invisible. Then he spoke up again, "Perhaps you should ask yourself this question, human. If he is a changeling and his nature is to constantly change, then is it even possible to ever truly know him?"

Ouch—heavy question.

I sank a little lower in my seat. Part of me knew immediately that Eldrick was right. I didn't know Zeph—not really. I'd admired him from afar. I'd only spent a little time with him. I'd begun to learn about him and this strange world of faeries he was part of. But when it came down to the cold hard facts, I didn't know anything about him. I just knew what I felt—even if it wasn't rational at all.

I opened my phone, quickly typing up a text message to Ben.

JOSIE: Do you know Zeph Clemmont?

It was just a wild guess—a hunch that since they had both known my dad, they might also know each other.

I put the phone on the coffee table, crossing my legs under me while I stared at the TV screen. On the other end of the sofa, Eldrick looked as composed and elegant as ever, as if he should have been teaching advanced English at some snobby private college. Remembering how he'd cringed away in fear of a bunch of high school students … it just boggled my mind. He didn't look like the kind of person who'd be intimidated by anyone.

I decided to press my luck. "Can I ask you something?"

He gave a tight, annoyed exhale. "If you must."

"Why are you so afraid of humans?"

Eldrick's grip on the coffee mug stiffened, turning his knuckles white. No answer.

"I'm sure you have a good reason. And I guess it's stupid, considering what we've been through up to this point, but I'd like for us to be friends."

Still no answer.

I stared at him, hoping he'd somehow be able to tell I was telling the truth. "For the record, I'm not going to hurt you or order you to do something bad. I'm not like that."

His sterling gaze slowly panned over to meet mine. "Why?" His tone was sharp with disdain.

"Why what?"

"Why would you *ever* want to befriend me?"

I blinked. "Because if we're going to be stuck with one another for a while, we might as well make the best of it, right? I'd like to start over and get to know each other properly this time. What do you think?"

Eldrick swallowed. His hold on the coffee mug relaxed some. Looking away, he gave one quick nod.

I smiled. It wasn't much, but it was progress. "So was Zeph right? Have you been living under my bed this whole time?"

"No." He puffed up slightly as though that were insulting. "The closet."

Right. Cause that's ... way better than under the bed.

"I can get the guest room ready for you, if you want," I suggested.

Eldrick focused his platinum-colored eyes back on the TV. "That would be satisfactory."

I giggled.

His stern brow furrowed in irritation. "What are you laughing at?"

"You sound like a robot when you talk that way."

He snorted, pursing his lips a little as though he were sulking.

"I wish I had known more about you before now. It would have been nice, you know, to not be alone all the time. Maybe you'll never be my friend. But at least we can be sort of like ... roommates?"

"That's hardly an appropriate term when I have to do your bidding night and day," he said with a twinge of disdain in his voice again.

"I'm not going to treat you like a butler, if that's what you're thinking. I don't need a servant. I don't even need a fake boyfriend. For now, I just need someone to make sure I make it to graduation without being locked up in an asylum or strangled to death by an ivy plant. Then I'll figure out how to break the contract Dad put on you, and you can leave. I won't be anyone's problem anymore."

I blinked tears out of my eyes, trying my best to smile so my words would be convincing. When I couldn't keep up the façade anymore, I stared back at the TV screen, and hoped he wouldn't notice.

Eldrick didn't answer. I felt his gaze on me like the glare of a spotlight. The room became quiet except for the murmur of the TV.

Then my phone buzzed on the coffee table.

BEN: Yes. Do not get involved with him. That man is very dangerous.

With my heart beating out of control, I quickly sent a reply.

JOSIE: Why? I don't think I can do that.

His reply came so quickly I nearly dropped the phone in surprise. He wasn't usually so prompt. Mentioning Zeph must have gotten his attention.

BEN: Why not?

I hesitated. Telling the truth might not be a good idea in this case, but I was in too deep, now. Ben had said he wanted to know what was going on with me. He had told me in that email that he wanted me to trust him.

JOSIE: I think I'm falling for him.
BEN: You don't know him like I do. He's not good

for you. You need to stay away from him. Please say
you will.
    JOSIE: I can't. I'm sorry.

Ben didn't reply.

Zeph was a jerk. It didn't take a psychology degree to figure that out. He was quite possibly the rudest, most arrogant, immature person I knew. But I couldn't change how I felt. I couldn't deny how touching him made my heart race, or how hearing him say he liked "puny redheads" made my spirit soar. It had only been a few days, and already I didn't want to imagine what my life would be like without Zeph in it. It didn't make sense, even to me. No one had ever gotten under my skin the way Zeph Clemmont did.

Minutes passed, then an hour.

I sat on the sofa with Eldrick, watching the commercials with baited breath while I waited for Ben to send a reply. He never answered. Finally, I tossed my phone back on the coffee table. It didn't matter what he said, anyway. My mind was set.

The sofa lurched again as Eldrick stood. He disappeared into the kitchen, and I craned my neck to see what he was doing in there. Dishes clinked. After a few minutes, he returned holding two mugs. His was refilled to the brim with coffee. The one he handed to me, however, contained hot water and one of my favorite herbal tea bags suspended in steaming water.

I gaped up at him, stunned.

"Are you going to take it or not?" His brow furrowed slightly.

"I-I ... thank you." I cautiously accepted the warm mug. The fragrant smell of chamomile and vanilla was relaxing.

He made a grunting sound and sat down again. "I've often found tea, while less enjoyable than coffee, to be far more soothing when dealing with frustration."

"You think I'm frustrated?"

Eldrick cast me a knowing glance. "Generally speaking, anyone exposed to Zephiel's company for an extended period of time is prone to become … intensely frustrated."

Tell me about it.

I smirked down into my mug of tea and took a long sip before placing it on the coffee table. "Fair enough. But *I* have a better way to deal with stress."

His expression scrunched suspiciously, eyes narrowing as I bounded over to the TV cabinet. I took out my favorite video gaming system—which was outdated enough to be called vintage now. Still, the old games were my favorite. Playing them with Dad was one of my favorite childhood memories.

And it had been forever since I had anyone to play with.

"Okay, you better prepare yourself." I tossed Eldrick a controller and grinned.

He caught it in one hand, arching an eyebrow. "And this is?"

"The sign of your doom, puca." I booted up the game system and darted back to sit on the couch beside him. "I'm about to get some sweet revenge."

A long, miserable week passed, and I didn't hear anything from my scruffy, across-the-hall neighbor. I didn't even see him coming or going out of his apartment anymore. More than once, I stood outside his front door and rang the bell so we could talk about this like two mature adults.

Then I remembered, this was Zeph I was dealing with.

Ben must have been furious with me as well because his messages were very tactful and cold. He kept the conversation strictly on how I was doing and didn't go off topic. He'd never acted this way toward me before. I could sense his disapproval, even though he never mentioned Zeph in any of his messages. It made me sad to think that I'd upset him, and it made me wonder what it was about Zeph that he distrusted so much.

Strange as it was, the only person who brought me any comfort was Eldrick. He couldn't keep going to school with me as Joe, not without Zeph there to cast some changeling magic on him, but he did walk me there every morning. Sometimes he even told me to stay out of trouble, which could have been mistaken for caring about my welfare. I tried not to read too much into it, though. He waited at a coffee shop across the street all day for me to return, and then he walked me back home.

Whether it was his presence in the vicinity or the lingering memory of Zeph still fresh in the minds of those mischievous spirits, I didn't see anything strange while I sat in my classes. It was my first taste of real normality. I'd even come up with a good excuse for Joe's absence. With the whole sick mom story still playing on everyone's sympathies, it was easy for me to say that he was spending every day with his family as they rallied around his poor, suffering mother. Whatever magic Zeph had cast on the people at school was still in full effect because they believed anything I said without question. The only downside to that story was that it meant everyone began overcompensating for how cruel they had been to me before. The popular kids left flowers on my desk or brought me cookies during lunch. Some of them sat with me, but our conversations were always about Joe. The teachers all asked me to pass on my sympathies to sad, wonderful, sweet Joe. Even Ms. Grear stopped me once to ask how he was doing.

It was a painful reminder that Zeph was gone. I had nothing to suggest I'd ever see him again.

And then late on a Friday afternoon, everything changed.

I stood in the kitchen stirring a pot of vegetarian spaghetti—since my new houseguest also didn't eat any kind of meat, either. I hadn't gotten around to asking him if that was just a personal preference, or a faerie thing.

Eldrick sat at the kitchen table reading one of my dad's old books, which—according to him—were all about faerie lore and how to make magical spells.

Eldrick had discovered my stockpile of Dad's research in one of the boxes stacked in the guest room closet. It was full of journals, stacks of papers, and even a few scrolls made of leather—all things that had survived the fire. Most of them still smelled of smoke, were a little singed, and nearly all of them were written in a weird language. The letters looked like little thorny vines, snaking across the pages in complex patterns. I couldn't read it, but Eldrick seemed quite interested in them. He'd already finished several of them and reluctantly admitted that my dad had been very talented with creating new spells—"for a human," anyway.

I wanted to ask him what all those books were about. I wanted to know why my dad was so interested in faerie lore and making spells, and what it had to do with me. I'd already begun to suspect that the house fire that had taken his life was no accident, but to be honest, I was terrified of what the truth might be. Dad had obviously gone to a lot of trouble to make sure I didn't get involved and yet he'd basically chained Eldrick to my heels. It made no sense whatsoever.

Anyway, this was usually how we spent our evenings now. I cooked a nice vegetarian meal while he sat nearby and read. It was beginning to almost feel normal—well, as normal as it can be to have a puca as a roommate.

Eldrick and I both looked up when the doorbell rang.

"Should I get it?" he asked, studying me.

"No, no. It's fine. Here, come stir the sauce for me, please. I'll get it." I wiped my hands on a dishcloth, and handed him the spoon and my cooking apron. "It's probably just someone selling something. No tasting! It's not finished, yet."

It wasn't a salesman.

My heart hit the back of my throat.

Zeph was leaning against the doorway, his mouth sagging in a defeated frown.

A painful knot of anxiety formed in my stomach. I'd missed this idiot more than I wanted him to know. I'd thought about him every single day. But now the sight of him made all my emotions scramble. I couldn't decide if I wanted to hug him or slap him and slam the door in his face.

"I've been thinking," he announced in a strangely apprehensive tone. There were heavy circles under his eyes, and his stubble was a bit longer than usual.

"Shocking. I hope you didn't hurt yourself."

"Fine. Maybe I deserved that."

"You tattled to my legal guardian and passed me off to Eldrick like an old piece of luggage, you've been avoiding me, *and* you left me to explain to all your adoring fans what happened to Joe Noble." I let go of the door so I could cross my arms.

Zeph let out a long, annoyed groan and raked his fingers through his messy brown hair. "I screwed up again. I get it. I was stupid and dumb, and I probably hurt your feelings. And I'm sorry. Okay?"

Pathetic—even by his standards. "Why did you even come here?"

"I need your help," he confessed. "I've got another case. It's a bad one. I need a hand with it."

"Why not ask Eldrick? Or I'm sure you've got other friends who would be happy to let you use and lie to them for a little while."

Zeph frowned harder. "I need your ... particular brand of help."

I raised my eyebrows. "Is that so?"

"Yes. Shake a leg, princess. Clock is ticking."

"You mean we're going right now?"

"Yeah. Hurry up. Hank called a few minutes ago. All he would say is that it's critical. He's gonna meet me downstairs in five minutes."

"I never said I was going." I dug my heels in and glared at him.

Zeph pursed his lips.

We stared one another down like gunslingers.

"Fine," he grumbled. "What do you want, then?"

I hesitated. After all, this might be my last shot at getting anything out of him. I had to shoot to kill.

"A date," I replied at last.

His eyes widened. "With me?"

"Well certainly not with Hank."

Zeph was silent, gaping at me. His face slowly began to flush. Suddenly, he snapped his mouth shut and glared down at the floor between us. "Okay, then. A date it is."

I smirked in triumph. "Good. I need a second to change."

He followed me inside, waiting while I hurried to my bedroom and put on a pair of jeans and several long-sleeved shirts. It was freezing outside, so I added a few extra layers to keep me from winding up a redheaded popsicle.

When I came back to the kitchen, Zeph was biting his lip like he was trying hard not to laugh. I couldn't figure out why.

Then I looked at Eldrick.

He was standing at the stove, apparently oblivious or unconcerned with whatever we were doing, stirring the spaghetti sauce—wearing my frilly pink cooking apron. I realized now he must have gotten the wrong idea. I'd handed him the spoon and the apron at the same time, but I hadn't meant for him to wear it.

"Let's go." Zeph elbowed me.

I nodded. "Be right out."

While he went to the door, I quickly dug my phone out of my pocket and snapped a picture of Eldrick. Thankfully, he didn't seem to notice. I had a feeling that sort of thing might make him hate me more than ever. Worth it, though.

"Eldrick, would you mind watching the house for me for a bit? I'll be back in a little while." I still felt bad for ordering him around. It was better to ask, I thought, even if he never said no.

"What should I do with this?" He held up the pot of steaming red sauce.

"Keep stirring for a few more minutes, until it gets thick. Then pour it over the pasta over there. Don't forget to turn off the stove." I came up behind him, leaning around to watch how he was stirring. "Think you can handle it?"

Eldrick stiffened, his expression flustered as he flicked me a glance. He still freaked out like that whenever I came too close, but he didn't try to shove me away anymore, so I counted that as progress, too.

"I'll manage." He was focused on the sauce again.

"Thank you. Eat as much as you want, okay? I'll be back in a little while." I waved as I left, grabbing my thickest winter coat and scarf from the closet by the front door on my way out.

Zeph was still smirking when I found him idling in the front foyer of our building. He took one look at me, his face red like he couldn't stand to hold it in anymore. Then he erupted, laughing so hard I thought he might choke. There were tears in his eyes by the time we got to the sidewalk.

"Only you." He snickered, wiping his eyes with his coat sleeves. "Only you could get the crowned Prince of Nightmares himself to wear a pink apron and stand there, stirring away like little Suzie homemaker."

"Don't tease him, Zeph." I swatted his arm.

"What's this? A change of heart? Don't tell me you like that idiot?" Zeph gave me that taunting, signature smirk of his. "Oh man, if only his dad could see him. I think he would literally vomit if he saw his only son and heir doing housework like a freakin' maid."

"Stop it. He's not my maid. You have no idea how much work it's been to get him to talk to me at all. Who is his dad, anyway?"

"The one and only Bogeyman," Zeph laughed darkly. "Or boogeyman, as you probably know him. Human names for us tend to change over the years."

"The boogeyman … is a faerie?"

"Of course. And besides Fir Darrig, he's the most notorious Unseelie fae in the world. As the King of Nightmares, he has quite the reputation."

I gulped.

It wasn't difficult to imagine that Eldrick came from a long line of horrible things that went bump in the night. He had terrorized me, too. And even now that we were on semi-good terms, I still wondered if he might turn on me in a second if he ever got free of my dad's contract.

I was lost in thought when a familiar black Cadillac pulled up to the curb. Hank honked the horn, and Zeph grabbed my elbow and pulled me into the back seat.

Once we were squished in the car again, Zeph's good mood fizzled. He wasn't smiling or laughing anymore.

Hank peeled away into traffic with alarming speed. I could see his face in the rearview mirror, and there were deep creases of worry around his eyes. He was gripping the steering wheel so hard the veins in his hands stood out.

"She's not ready for a case this bad," Hank grumbled.

"Like we have a choice? If I have to do a purge, I'm going to need a boost of power. I don't have the stamina for that anymore and you know it." Zeph was all business now, lighting up a cigarette as he slid across the seat to the other side of the car and began rifling through the central console of the car again.

Hank met my gaze in the rearview mirror. "Josie, you need to follow our instructions *exactly* this time. Do you understand? This is very dangerous. I can't prove it yet, and this is purely a hunch, but I have a feeling Fir Darrig is somehow involved. We have to be extra careful."

I nodded. "I understand."

Zeph took a long drag from his cigarette, blowing the smoke out the crack in the window as he spread out his tools on the seat between us. This time he had a different set of weird-looking odds and ends. "So, brief me already. What are we dealing with?" he asked as he picked up a box of multicolored sidewalk chalk.

"I got a call from a worried neighbor about an hour ago. A family of five, formerly of six, living in a small farmhouse just outside the city limits. They've heard voices, footsteps, and witnessed moving objects. All signs point to fae mischief," Hank replied. "My source thinks there may have been winged shadowmen, but the family never mentioned anything about their shape. One of the children, a thirteen-year-old boy, has already been killed. He shot himself in the head less than two weeks ago after showing signs of extreme depression and personality shift. They also suspect he may have been dabbling in the occult. Now, the boy's twin brother is beginning to show the same symptoms."

"Dammit." Zeph shook his head angrily. "So what you're saying is, it's probably a sylph. Well, this is going to suck big time."

I decided to pipe up before I got lost in all their business jabber. "Excuse me, what's a sylph, exactly, and why is that so bad?"

"A wind spirit," Hank began to explain. "Normally, they ally with the Seelie Court. They're powerful, and notoriously hard to catch. Unfortunately, one of their best-known tricks is their ability to possess the body of other beings in their sleep. Sylph possession is usually mistaken for sleepwalking. Sometimes they just do it as a prank. You know, to mess with humans for a laugh. That kind of thing is harmless. But every now and then, we come across an Unseelie sylph with a taste for violence."

"They're bad news," Zeph interrupted. "They do some pretty sick, twisted stuff. Whatever you do, don't listen to the chimes."

The more they explained, the more I began to realize this might be a terrible idea. I didn't have any experience with these kinds of things. I didn't know much at all about faeries and what they were capable of. Yet, here I was, sitting beside Zeph while he crammed his pockets full of sidewalk chalk.

"This isn't a good case for rookies to be cutting their teeth on," Hank muttered like he could read my mind.

"She can handle it." Zeph patted my knee. "Besides, I'm going to need a good tether."

Hank snorted disapprovingly. "A tether? Using her for that is a little excessive, don't you think? That's like shooting mice with a Gatling gun."

I didn't know what a tether was, but I didn't get a chance to ask. Hank's phone rang as he pulled the car off a dark highway that led out of town, and we went bouncing down a gravel driveway. He was talking loudly with someone, asking for directions and trying to give our location. We passed several houses that stood far off the road, nestled into the rolling countryside. The trees on the side of the road stood close together, their branches naked of all their leaves.

When Hank turned onto one of the dirt driveways, he hung up the phone and switched on his bright lights. They illumed the farmhouse sitting atop the crest of a sloping hill. It looked somber against the dreary gray sky. There were no lights in the windows, and as we got closer, I saw that the whole family was sitting out on the front porch. Well, most of them anyway. Two children were missing from their group—the pair of twin boys Hank had mentioned.

Hank popped the trunk of the car, and the three of us stood, bathed in the moonlight, staring down into the large duffel bag he had stocked full of gear. Most if it were things I recognized—bundles of sage and other herbs, feathers, more boxes of chalk, candles, and bottles of olive oil. Then I noticed the one long black case lying at the bottom of the trunk. Hank went after that one first, and Zeph gave him a wide berth when he opened it and took out a double-barreled shotgun.

"Iron shot," Hank explained when he saw me eyeing the gun cautiously. He handed me one of the strange looking shells he'd begun loading into the rear of the barrel.

I'd never seen a gun in real life before unless it was clipped to a policeman's belt. "Why iron?"

"Fae can't stand it. Burns the hell out of them. Has that effect on anything magical. Magic can't cross it or pass through it, and if you pierce a fae's body with it, the wound will most likely be fatal unless they get to a healer in time. If you want shoot to kill when it comes to fae, always use iron." Hank plucked the shell out of my hand and crammed it and a handful of others in his pocket.

"But we always try to capture, first," Zeph interrupted. "Hank's gotten handy at rehabilitating and pacifying fae so they can be released. One of the many useful talents that his ancestors have passed down through the generations. If we can avoid having to kill anything, that's always the best option."

Hank's features darkened. "Sometimes there's no other choice, though. Some fae get a taste of blood and things get ugly real fast. It's like they go mad for it."

The family looked at us with pale faces and big, haunted eyes as we made our way up the front steps. They had already lost one child to this sylph creature, and now another one's life was in danger.

The oldest child was a boy who looked like he might be close to my age. Next to him, his sister couldn't have been more than fifteen. She had braided pigtails and a big coat on over her nightgown. Both of them were stiff with fear as they stared at me. I tried to give them a reassuring smile.

Hank pulled the parents aside, talking to them in a hushed voice. I wondered what he was saying. More importantly, I wondered if we could actually help these people.

"What do you feel?" Zeph whispered suddenly, his hot breath touching my ear.

"Like I'm going to hit you if you keep sneaking up on me like that," I whispered back. "What are we doing here? These people … What if we can't help them? What are they going to do? Can't we call the police and explain what's going on?"

"Human police can't do anything about this, princess. You know that better than anyone, right? Besides, I'm here to kick some sylph-butt." He gave a menacing, toothy smirk. It was like a reminder; the creature inside the house wasn't the only monster on the premises. "And you're here to help me do it. And if we both fail, Hank'll use that gun to blow that sylph away. One way or another, this ends tonight."

"You said the Seelie Court is supposed to be policing people who abuse magic, right? Why aren't they doing anything about this?" I kept my voice down as we walked past the family, making our way up the porch toward the front door of the house.

"Because they are disillusioned into thinking they've got it all under control. It's a political game, Josie, just like with humans. They have their own favorite villains—usually the Unseelies they want to see behind bars because it makes them look good. They've been ignoring threats like Fir Darrig and his cronies for a long time because of his social standing, leaving the victims of his brutality to fend for themselves. He's one of the five original pilgrims, and back in the day—before we came to your world—he was highly respected amongst our people. There are still a lot of fae who don't want to cross him, regardless of whose side he's on. So, we have to do what we can, while we can."

I shivered. It was so unfair. How could anyone be so cruel and callous? People were suffering—dying—and the Seelie Court wouldn't even look twice?

"Zeph," Hank called out as he walked toward us, shotgun resting against his shoulder. His expression was bleak. "They have the boy restrained upstairs. They had to tie him down because he tried to chew off his own fingers. I need to stay with the family. I'm going to move them away from the house. There's too much fear in them. Even if you manage to drive out the sylph, they're all so weak that any one of them would make an easy target. If that thing comes for us, I'll have no choice but to shoot."

My stomach rolled, my hands got clammy, and a cold sweat made me shiver.

Zeph nodded. "Right. I can handle this alone. Do what you have to."

Hank looked at me apprehensively. "You're sure? You could call Freddy. He would help."

"No!" Zeph snarled suddenly, his violet eyes flashing like flames for a few seconds.

Hank just frowned. "Don't let pride cloud your vision, changeling. He's your brother—and he has great talent. He could ensure our success."

"Stay the hell out of it. It's none of your damn business, old man." Zeph shoved past us and stormed to the front door. He snapped his fingers at me like he was calling a dog. "Come on. Let's get this over with."

Hank didn't reply, although his mouth sagged with uncertainty.

A smog of grief and bitterness filled the house, threatening to suffocate me if I took another step. My body shivered, cold sweat sliding down the sides of my face as I reached instinctively to grip Zeph's hand. He squeezed it back.

The silver wash of moonlight through the windows was all we had to see by. The old wooden floorboards creaked with every step. My skin prickled, as the temperature plummeted. My breath hung in the air like white wisps of fog. Every shred of common sense screamed in my brain. This was a terrible idea. Why had I let Zeph drag me into this?

"W-why isn't there any electricity?" My teeth chattered and I inched closer to Zeph's side.

His arm was tense, every muscle rigid as he stared straight ahead. "Common fae trick. Most humans are spooked by the dark, and strong emotions like fear make you easier prey."

"Prey? For what?"

"Remember how I said children soak up magic easy? For a faerie looking for an easy jackpot of magical energy, stealing it off a kid is the best way to score. Shitty thing to do, though."

"How do they do it?" The back of my neck tingled. All the tiny hairs on my arms stood on end. I couldn't shake the sense that something was watching me.

Zeph's voice deepened. "You'll see."

We made our way down a long hallway, passing portraits of family memories—of smiling faces and sunny vacations. They hardly resembled the family huddled outside on the porch. There was no more happiness here now.

"Upstairs," Zeph reminded me, nodding toward a staircase.

The moment we arrived at the bedroom door, the thick, coppery flavor of blood hit me so hard I gagged. My body went cold and I stopped.

Zeph looked back when my hand tugged against his as I backed away. His face crossed a beam of moonlight spilling through the window at the end of the hall. "It's okay, princess. I won't let it hurt you."

More than anything, I wanted to believe that. I took in a deep breath of the frigid air and steeled myself.

Zeph pulled a small flashlight out of his pocket and pointed the beam at the door. He was breathing heavy as he twisted the knob. It creaked, and the old hinges groaned as he pushed the door open.

I covered my mouth to keep from screaming.

The boy screeched as soon as the light touched him. He hissed, his body warped and disfigured like a tangled mess of twisted limbs in the middle of the mattress. He'd broken one of the bonds his parents had used to tie him down. His clothes and mattress were soaked with blood.

I couldn't move. I couldn't breathe. I stood in terror, watching the boy writhe. Two of his fingers were nothing but bloody, gnarled stumps, and there was meaty gore between his teeth when he snarled at us.

My stomach rolled. I gagged again. I covered my mouth and shut my eyes.

"Zeph," I whimpered. "We need to call an ambulance! He could bleed to death!"

"Calm down. You don't die from losing a finger. Remember what I said," Zeph's voice was strangely calm. He touched my wrist, his fingers leaving trails of warmth on my skin. I dared to meet his gaze.

I noticed that he had deliberately put himself between the boy and me, like he hoped to shield me in case something went wrong. "Don't listen to the chimes. Don't talk to it. It will try to tell you things, to make you feel anger or fear. Negative emotions give it strength and make you vulnerable to possession. Do *not* let it touch you. Got me?"

What? What chimes? *It?* Was he talking about the boy? My mind tangled with confusion as Zeph turned away. His hand slid out of mine.

He took off his coat, but not before fishing the box of sidewalk chalk out of the pocket. He began drawing curling, spidery letters paired with weird little shapes on the floor with chalk—things similar to what I had seen in my dad's old books. He made a series of them between the doorway, in front of the bedroom window, and finally in the shape of a two large circles, close together like a figure eight, on the floor. The last design he drew was a triangle within a circle. Once he finished, he pulled a little baggie of salt, and sprinkled it all around the outside perimeter of the design.

It took everything I had not to glance back down at the boy for more than a second or two. Every time I tried, my stomach churned and my heart wrenched with the desire to help him. The noises he made didn't sound human. His head was twisted around at an angle that looked like it should have only been possible for someone with a broken neck, and his glazed, milky eyes bored into mine. I shuddered. I had to force myself to remember—this was a child, not a monster. A faerie had done this to him. The family downstairs loved him, and they were counting on us to save him.

When I looked back at Zeph, he'd shed his human shape—and his shirt. His bare shoulders flexed, and two shining wings filled the room with a gentle glow, and his brawny upper body rippled with strength. He stooped to take off his shoes and socks, tossing them into the growing pile near the door. Then Zeph turned, and his eyes were intense as he stared at me with purpose. "Ready?"

Um, no. Of course not.

"Look who came to pay me a visit …" The voice coming from the boy's body clearly wasn't his. It didn't even sound like a child. It sounded more like an old man's throaty, raspy sneer. "I've been expecting you. My master will be so pleased."

"I bet." Zeph smirked at the boy's twisted form. "When he gets here, I'll beat his ass, too."

"You talk so big, but we all know your secret. You're a dead-man walking, changeling. How sad." The voice gave a hissing, scratchy chuckle. "You've only got a few months left, don't you? Who will protect her then, hmm? Not that puca runt, I'm sure. He'll go whimpering back to his father with his tail between his legs, just like last time."

Zeph prowled closer, his wings brushing the floor as he walked. He grabbed one of my arms, pushed up the sleeve of my coat, and began drawing on my skin with the piece of chalk. He drew more of those strange little runes, making them spiral up both my arms and across my forehead. I tried my best to hold still, but I couldn't make my body stop trembling.

"Don't be afraid," he whispered.

"I-I'm not. I'm just cold," I lied through chattering teeth.

"This'll be over soon. Just hang in there. You asked me what a tether is, remember?" He took my hand gently and led me over to stand in the middle of one of the circles on the floor.

I nodded. "Y-yes."

"Oh, she likes it when you touch her doesn't she? Look at that. I bet her little body just aches for you," the monster hiding behind that boy's skin laughed again.

I flushed. How could that creature possibly know that?

Zeph ignored him. He kept his attention focused on me as he stepped into the circle next to mine, still holding my hand tightly. "I have to do what we call a purge. It's like a cleansing, or an exorcism, but much more focused. It'll only take a minute or two, but I need enough power to flush the boy's body entirely, which will drive out the sylph. He won't be able to disobey me then. It's the only way we can save him. I'm going to need to borrow power from you to do it, though. You'll be the tether that binds us as one so we can share that power."

"Borrow from me?" I didn't understand how I could possibly help with something like that. "But I can't do magic. I'm not a child. If I had power like that, I'd know it, wouldn't I?"

His smile was tender and strangely sad. "You can do a lot more than you realize, Josie. Every living thing on this planet has magic in them, whether they realize it or not. Some have a lot more than others. Just trust me, okay? I won't let anything bad happen to you."

I did trust him. Looking up into his strange, otherworldly face, I knew there would never be anyone I trusted more. He was a terrifying, beautiful creature. The dazzling light from his wings chased away the thick shadows and washed over me, extinguishing my fears.

He reached for my other hand. "It's going to hurt a little. But not for long. It'll be a lot worse on my end."

I took a deep breath. "I'm ready. Let's do this."

Zeph stared down at me, his mouth scrunched like there was something else he wanted to say. His brow crinkled and he stole a glance over at the boy. "You know how I said strong emotions make for easy prey? It's because those powerful feelings sort of bring all that stored magic to the surface so you can tap into it—or so a fae can steal it."

I frowned. "Why are you telling me this now?"

"Because to get the burst of power I'm gonna need for this, I have to do something more effective than scaring you."

"What is that supposed to—"

Suddenly, Zeph pulled me close. He grasped my face and pressed his lips against mine.

I froze. My stomach dropped, my knees went weak, and my heartbeat thrilled. All I could think about was the warmth of his mouth moving against mine—delicious and addicting. I wanted to get closer. I wanted to touch him, maybe run my fingers through his hair. I started to take a step.

Zeph held me in place. His grip on my face tightened.

A strange tingling sensation sizzled through my fingers and toes. That was normal for a first real kiss, right?

It spread, becoming more and more uncomfortable like the dull ache whenever one of my legs fell asleep. My head swam, and the tingling began to hurt as though I'd been buried in burning hot sand.

Zeph jerked away, his face blanched and screwed up with pain. His body convulsed, and the chalk marks on the floor lit up like white paint under a black light. He let out a booming roar, flexing to spread his wings wide. All around us, the shape of the room seemed to flex with him as though the universe were made of rubber.

His body warped into something stranger than ever. More of those dazzling runes began gleaming down his back, abdomen, and across his chest—covering him like ultraviolet stripes. His wings unfurled to fill the room, growing greater in size and more vivid in color. All his glassy feathers sparkled in radiant hues of violet, crimson, and gold. The horns on his head were longer and curled, like ram's horns. His ears became long and pointed again, and his legs morphed and twisted, evolving into a furry and feline shape. His feet were paws, each tipped with a curled claw, and I could have sworn I saw him sprout a lion's tail.

Whatever Zeph was—I'd never seen anything like it. But the sight of him in that form didn't startle me. Instead, my eyes roamed his physique, admiring every detail and wishing I had the nerve to reach out and touch him.

I didn't get to enjoy that distraction for long.

"He doesn't want you to know, little girl," the sylph screeched over the sound of Zeph's rage. "He's keeping secrets from you again. Lies! So many lies! Can't you feel it?"

I clamped my hands over my ears.

Zeph walked to the bedside, his lips drawn back in a snarl as he glared down at the child who kicked and flailed, trying to get away from him. He put his palms on either side of the boy's head, forcing him to be still. The child's body went rigid. His eyes glowed like a car's headlights as a strange sound whispered through the air. Something musical, maybe. Chimes?

"Look how hard he's worked to cover up his lies! So many years of desperate work. So many tears. So much blood," the sylph wailed. "All these broken years spent toiling just because he doesn't want you to know the truth!"

"Stop it!" I screamed back, shutting my eyes tightly. I wouldn't listen, no matter what. I had to be strong this time.

"He doesn't want you to know ... he's your benefactor. Your sweet, sweet Ben."

The air seemed to suck right out of the room—becoming a vacuum of eerie calm.

The boy lay silent, his chest rising and falling with peaceful breaths. His body was bloodied and bruised, but no longer bent in horrific ways. He even had color in his cheeks again.

On the other side of the room, Zeph was weaving on his feet. The marks on his body were beginning to go dark. His face was dripping with sweat, and he looked like he was in pain. He managed to keep his composure though, walking to the foot of the bed where the circle lined with salt was drawn on the floor.

In the center of it, hovering like a column of black smoke, was the sylph.

Two white eyes burned amidst a formless, flickering dark mass like smoldering embers. The creature let out a shriek like the cry of an eagle and threw itself against the edge of the circle. It made a loud buzzing, zapping sound. The salt circle glowed with power, sending up a sizzling cylindrical column of golden energy. Trapped inside, the sylph leered at me. Its shape was much more solid now and reminded me of a harpy, like the ones I had read about in my English class when we studied Ovid's *Metamorphoses*—only this one looked like a male rather than a female like in the stories.

The short, ugly creature shifted on its scaly, bird-like legs as it eyed its glowing prison as though searching for some way out. It had the wings of a bird where its arms should have been and long, pointed ears, and a hooked nose.

The sylph leered up at us with beady dark eyes glittering with malice, baring pointed teeth. It flailed against the barrier again, clawing and hissing furiously. The salt circle held firm, though.

Zeph seemed satisfied. The sylph apparently couldn't escape that circle, and as soon as he finished making sure of that ... he crumpled into a heap on the floor. His wings and horns melted away, vanishing into a fine mist that dissipated almost as quickly as they appeared.

Immediately, I pulled out my phone to dial 911. If we acted fast, maybe they would be able to save some of the boy's fingers. I was trying to explain to the 911 dispatcher where we were, which was becoming more and more frustrating, when Hank and the rest of the boy's family came running into the room.

"Eli!" The mother let out a frantic sob and rushed to the bed, throwing her arms around her son.

The father and the rest of the siblings stood back, though. None of them said a word. Their expressions were still pasty with horror, eyes wide and wary.

As soon as he walked over, I shoved the phone into Hank's hands and rushed to Zeph.

He was lying on the floor, sprawled out and gasping for frantic, shallow breaths. His fingers twitched, almost as though he'd been electrocuted, and his face was ashen.

Oh god. Had something gone wrong? Was he dying?

Zeph's eyes flew open as I reached to touch his shoulder. He barely made it to his hands and knees before throwing up violently. I reeled back to avoid the spray.

125

Vomit went everywhere—all over the floor, rug, and my shoes. I backed farther away and got to my feet. The sound of his retching was unbearable, but I couldn't look away.

Zeph was Ben.

He'd been lying to me *again*. The emails ... the text messages ... and now this charade of friendship, acting like he was some kind of guardian. All this time, he was just screwing around with my head, toying with me and tugging on my heartstrings just to watch me dance. How could he do this to me? Losing my whole family wasn't enough?

And the worst part was I'd fallen for it. Ugh, I'd even told him that I had feelings for him!

I stormed toward the door.

"Josie!" Zeph's weak, hoarse voice called after me. "Wait! Please!"

I glared back at his desperate, puke-covered face. "I'm going to get you a bucket, you moron," I snapped bitterly.

Any betrayal I had ever experienced paled in comparison to this. He deserved to suffer. He deserved to puke until he died—but I wasn't going to let him do it all over someone else's house. This poor family hadn't done anything to deserve having to clean up his mess.

When I came back with a small plastic trashcan, I slammed it down in front of him. My face screwed up as I bit back angry sobs.

"He'll be fine. It should pass in a few hours." Hank came to join me as I watched Zeph leaning into the trashcan. "He just used too much magic at once. It's a shock to his system, after not being at his full strength for so long. It's like giving an emaciated person too much to eat after they've been starving."

I narrowed my eyes on my benefactor. I'd give him a shock, all right.

Hank nudged my arm. "Come on, let's help him to the car."

I didn't want to help Zeph do anything, but it wasn't fair to leave Hank with all the work.

The boy's father joined in the effort to clean up our mess while Hank dealt with the sylph. He used what looked like a quilt made of a patchwork of animal skins, leaves, and brightly colored silks. He cast it over the salt circle, and the shape of the sylph vanished. Hank gathered the quilt up until it was folded up into a small star-shape. He handled it carefully, and I knew the sylph must be trapped inside that cloth somehow. He locked the cloth inside a lunchbox-sized case that looked like it was made of solid iron. Interesting. It must have had something to do with what he'd told me before, about how iron couldn't conduct magic.

I'd never seen anything like it ... I *had* to learn how to do that. Whatever it took, whoever's arm I had to twist, I needed to learn more about this. I wanted to fight these faeries and help people the way Hank did.

The ambulance arrived as we loaded Zeph into the back of our car. I sat beside him in the back, holding his coat while he stayed hunched over with the trashcan between his knees. The family had let him keep it—not that I blamed them. As we pulled away from the house, Hank rolled all the car windows down so the smell of fresh vomit wouldn't be so bad on the drive back home.

Zeph was obviously miserable. He was still heaving so hard and often that he couldn't speak, but I couldn't bear to look at him. Every time I did, betrayal cut through my chest and brought fresh tears to my eyes. I bit down hard on my bottom lip to stifle any sound. Breathe—I had to breathe.

We slipped through the empty downtown streets. At this hour, the only traffic was a few taxis roaming around for late night fares. The city was calm—a tranquil contrast to what was going on in the seat next to me as we pulled up to the front of our building.

Hank helped Zeph climb the stairs to his apartment. I walked ahead, leading the way and unlocking his front door with the set of keys I found in his coat pocket. After depositing him on his bed, Hank stood back with a grimace. We both watched silently while Zeph hugged his trashcan again. The sounds he made were almost as bad as the smell.

"The symptoms are like the stomach flu, but they should clear up soon," Hank said, like he was trying to reassure me. "Next time, it won't be like this ... hopefully."

I wasn't so sure there would be a next time.

"I'll be fine. Go on, I'm sure you've got more important things to do."

He cast me an apologetic look. "You sure about that?"

I nodded.

"Here, this'll help." He reached into one of the pockets of his black leather vest and handed me another pack of Zeph's favorite cigarettes.

I narrowed my eyes. "Seriously? Now is not the time for—"

"They're for the pain," he interrupted.

"Pain?"

Hank nodded. "I make them myself. It's nothing illegal, so don't worry about that. They're my own combination of medicinal herbs and a bit of spellwork. Gives him a boost on the days when the pain's dragging him down. Using too much magic usually sets it off in a bad way."

I swallowed hard and looked down at the small box. So … all the times he was smoking … it was because he was suffering? "I-I didn't realize."

Hank shrugged. "Once you get him settled, take a few and put them in a bowl. It's the smoke you're after. Think of it like incense. You're gonna need to let them burn a little and then blow them out."

"Okay."

"And you're sure you don't want me to hang around?"

I closed my eyes. I wasn't sure of anything anymore. "I'm okay. I'll manage."

Hank wrote his cell phone number down, just in case I needed any more help, but didn't stick around for me to change my mind. I walked him to the door and leaned my forehead against it after he left, listening to his footsteps retreating down the stairs with my hand still resting on the knob. Slowly, I took a deep, slow breath.

As much as I wanted to hate Zeph, there was something I wanted more. I wanted answers, to know why he had lied about this for so long. What did he possibly stand to gain from jerking me around like that? How could he have been living right across the hall all this time? Why hadn't he intervened with Eldrick sooner? The questions streamed in my head, suffocating me. I needed answers, and I needed them now. Unfortunately, I knew I wasn't going to get anything out of him other than undigested food at the moment.

Right now, he needed my help.

But that didn't mean I had to be nice about it.

"Come on. We're going to the bathroom," I announced when I came back into the bedroom. I carried his nearly-full trashcan as I walked him to the en suite bathroom. He was so heavy I could barely manage on my own. I was silently grateful the bathroom was close by because if it had been a few more feet away, we both might have ended up lying in a pile of something extra gross on his bedroom floor.

I emptied the trashcan into the toilet, and flushed it before I bent him over it so he could throw up again. Each time he heaved, it was so violent it made his body shudder. I couldn't watch.

Soaking a washcloth in cold water, I draped it over the back of his neck. He felt feverish to the touch and was shaking. My quiet rage was the only thing that prevented me from feeling sorry for him. I wanted to leave him here to suffer by himself—it's what he deserved. But I couldn't, and trying to rationalize why only made me more angry.

The hours dragged by so slowly it was almost unbearable.

Zeph couldn't talk, and he was growing weaker by the minute. I kept the rag on the back of his neck, rinsing it over and over to keep it cool. I made him some ginger tea with honey, forcing him to drink it whenever the vomiting let up for any length of time. It was a slow, grueling process.

Finally, at about four in the morning, he started to get better. I took that opportunity to force him into a warm shower.

Zeph could barely stand up on his own, so I had to go across the hall and change into a swimsuit so I could help him bathe. Eldrick watched me come and go, eyeing me curiously as I stomped angrily through my apartment, but he didn't ask questions. Frankly, I was in no mood to explain.

I put on my least attractive swimsuit—a polka-dot one piece with a dorky fringed skirt from middle school which, sadly, still fit. I didn't want any part of Zeph's brain that might still be functioning to get any pleasure out of this.

It was hard not to blush as I stripped him down to his underwear, letting him hold onto me as he climbed into the shower. Zeph stood under the water, looking dejected and miserable, while I scrubbed as much of him as I dared. I washed his hair and helped him rinse, then assisted him out of the shower. He sat on the toilet, the trash can between his knees just in case, while I toweled him off. I roughed up his hair to get as much of the water out of it as I could. It was strangely intimate, touching him like that. I'd never been this close to anyone before, let alone a man.

The only thing I made him change by himself were his now-soaked, boxer shorts. He almost killed himself doing just that. I turned my back long enough for him to struggle into dry ones, which thankfully he did before his legs gave out and he fell against the wall.

Once I had him up again, I pulled a clean, dry shirt over his head. He wobbled dangerously again, and I was too afraid he'd fall on me and crush me into the floor. So I gave up on trying to put sweatpants on him.

It took all my strength to help him stagger back into the bedroom. There, Zeph sat on the edge of his king-sized bed with the plastic trashcan still within arm's reach just in case. He watched in silence as I opened the pack of Hank's homemade faerie cigarettes, stacked four of them into a cereal bowl, and lit them. After they were burning nicely, I blew out the flames and let them smolder on the nightstand. Bluish smoke curled up from the little parchment-wrapped sticks, filling the room with a fragrant, herbal smell I knew well.

Instantly, Zeph's body relaxed. His eyes rolled closed. Maybe it was just a coincidence, but their scent made me feel calmer, too. I wondered how Zeph had managed before whenever he got sick like this. Somehow, I couldn't see Hank going to so much trouble.

Zeph's sheets were thin, rumpled, and looked like they hadn't been washed in months. Was that typical for a bachelor? After I tucked him in, I went to my apartment again to change out of my swimsuit, and bring back a few old quilts. I layered up as many blankets as I could find on top of him, but he was still shaking. My stomach twisted into knots. I didn't know if this was normal or serious. Hank hadn't seemed too worried, and he had mentioned the symptoms would be like the stomach flu.

All I could do now was wait.

Sitting down on the bed beside him, I pressed a hand against his forehead. I couldn't tell that he felt any warmer than usual, though. So why was he shaking like that? Was it the pain? I could try burning more of those cigarettes, but if something more was wrong, I didn't know what to do. Maybe sending Hank away had been a bad idea, after all.

Worry made my thoughts race. I'd almost convinced myself to call Hank I heard him rasp out a few words.

"I'm so sorry, Josie."

I flinched. My pulse went into overdrive. "Stop it. Shut up. You don't get to say that to me."

"I didn't do it to hurt you," he tried to continue, his voice weak. "I swear. I would never do anything to—"

I slapped a hand over his mouth, forcing him to be quiet. "No. You have *no* idea what I went through." My throat seized up. I bit back a sob and looked away. "It's not true. Tell me it isn't. Right now, Zeph. Tell me you're not Ben."

He blinked twice. As I pulled my hand away, his eyes saddened and his mouth screwed up.

Angry tears blurred my vision. I didn't expect to see so much pain in his eyes as he stared back at me. It wasn't fair. He didn't get to be the one hurt by all this—it was *his* fault!

"All this time … you've been sitting here, right across the hall from me, while I went through hell by myself?" The angry words began pouring out of me. "Why? Why would you do that to me?"

His chin trembled.

"And after Dad died—you wouldn't even let me know who you were? What the *hell*? Did you think you could just send me a check and a few text messages every month, and I'd be fine?" I clenched my hands. "Birthdays and Christmases came every year and I was completely alone. You wouldn't even let me hear your voice!"

"Josie, please," he begged and reached to touch my arm. "I had to—"

I jerked away.

His features crinkled in distress. "It wasn't my choice to make. Whatever I felt for you, whatever I wanted—none of that mattered. I had to keep you safe."

"*Safe?*" I screamed. "Eldrick tortured me! He nearly drove me out of my own home! And you let him do it! How the hell is that keeping me safe?"

His expression closed up. "I didn't know about that, Josie. I swear. Your dad never said a word to me about it. All you had to do was tell me, just once, that something was happening. I would have fixed it—there isn't a force on earth that would have stopped me from getting to you. But you always said everything was fine."

"So, you moving across the hall from me? What was that?" I didn't want to believe any of it. "Pity? Coincidence? You better not say love. I swear to god, I'll punch you."

"I …" He looked away and his brows drew together. "I can't tell you that. Not yet."

I leaned over, burying my face in my hands as I sat on the edge of the bed. He was still hiding things, still keeping secrets. What other lies was he hiding from me now? "You're an ass. I really can't stand you right now."

"I know." His voice sounded completely broken. "Just tell me what you want me to do. I'll never speak to you again, if that's what you want."

I whirled around to grab his face in my hands so that he was forced to meet my gaze. "No. Absolutely not. You're not getting off that easy, you big idiot. No, you're going to pay me back in *full* for all those years I had to live by myself. You're stuck with me *forever*. Birthdays, Christmases, Valentine's Days—every single holiday, no matter how stupid you think it is. I better get a present for each one of them, too. And it better be something good and expensive. You owe me big, and believe me; you're going to pay."

There was a confused furrow in his brow. His eyes searched mine, as though he were trying to decide whether or not I was being serious.

I had only just begun to get serious.

"You aren't allowed to call me a 'kid' anymore—not in any way, shape, or form. I'm the only mature person living on this floor. And you are going to school with me again; I don't care how you feel about it. It's not fair for Eldrick to be picking up your slack." I sat back, wiping the tears from my face and trying to compose myself again.

He swallowed hard and gave me a small nod.

"And as for my date—don't think I'm going to forget about that."

Zeph's eyes widened. One corner of his mouth twitched like he was trying not to smile. "You mean ... you still want me to?"

I shot him a glare. "It better be the most romantic thing that's ever happened to anyone."

The twitching stopped. He started chewing on the inside of his cheek as his gaze drifted away, as though he were thinking.

Minutes passed, and I tried to sulk. But at last, my anger gave way to exhaustion. The soothing, fragrant smell of those smoldering cigarettes was calming. My shoulders sagged, and I rubbed the back of my aching neck.

Zeph had picked the perfect time to get sick. If I hadn't felt so sorry for him, I would have demanded even more, or tacked on a few days of silent treatment just for spite, but he looked pretty pathetic, lying there with his eyes closed and his face flushed.

Seeing him that vulnerable made me want an excuse to touch him. I tested his forehead again for fever, pulled the blankets up to his chin, and combed some of his soft hair out of his eyes. He let out a heavy sigh, his body finally relaxing into the bed.

A strange sense of peace and security settled over me like a warm ray of sunlight.

That was when I realized ... I was so glad he was Ben.

He'd done a rotten job of it, but he had taken care of me. He'd given me a safe place to live, gotten me into a good school, and tried to be supportive. As much as I wanted to blame him for the situation with Eldrick—I couldn't. Not completely, anyway. I'd intentionally kept that stuff from Ben. He was a liar. But I'd been lying to him, too.

And when it mattered the most, when I needed someone to find me in the dark, Zeph had been there.

Thinking about all the messages he'd sent as Ben, demanding that I stay away from him, made me smile. What a moron. Did he really think that would be enough? Sure, he was right—there were things in his world of mad magic that absolutely terrified me. Things I wasn't prepared for. Things that could hurt me. But none of that scared me more than the idea that I might never see him again.

Without a word, I slipped into the bed beside him and burrowed under the blankets to muscle my way under his arm.

He groaned and rolled his head over to squint at me. "What're you doin'?" I could have sworn he was blushing.

"Go to sleep," I said, mimicking his voice. I was so embarrassed I couldn't bring myself to look up at him for very long.

He didn't give me a choice, though. He snaked his arm around me tighter and pulled me close against his side. "You're warm," he murmured, his deep voice echoing against my ear as I laid my head on his chest.

"Zeph?"

"Mmm?" He was barely awake.

I wondered if he even knew what I was saying. Then I decided it didn't matter. I just needed to say it—as though the words were gnawing and clawing their way past all my better judgment.

"I love you."

When I woke up late the next afternoon, Zeph was still snoring like a chainsaw. He hadn't let me go all night. The color in his cheeks was back to normal, and there weren't any dusky circles under his eyes.

I breathed a sigh of relief.

Besides betraying Zeph's big bad secret about being my legal guardian, there was something else that sylph had said last night that was still bothering me. It nagged at my brain whenever I let my thoughts wander.

It hadn't seemed so important at the time. After all, that awful creature had said a lot of cruel, taunting things, and I had tried my best not to listen to any of it. But the sylph mentioned how Zeph only had a few months left. I didn't know what that meant, and somehow, I doubted Zeph was going to tell me.

After being so ill most of the night, I didn't want to wake him up to interrogate him. I slipped out of the bed as quietly as I could, tiptoeing into the living room and out the front door. I was looking forward to taking a shower and changing clothes, and maybe even getting something to eat before starting my Saturday errands.

As soon as I opened my front door, Eldrick was standing right in front of me. He wore a dangerous, disapproving scowl, his arms crossed. He loomed over me, raising both eyebrows as though he were waiting for me to explain myself.

"What's wrong?" I glanced around the living room.

"We are out of coffee," Eldrick announced so seriously, you'd think he was telling me the president had just been shot.

I stared at him, trying to figure out if there was more to the story than that. But no, that seemed to be the only reason for his distress. "We can buy more. I need to go to the grocery store anyway."

"Excellent." He appeared satisfied. "Also, the spaghetti is gone."

"You ate all of it?" I brushed past him on my way to the bedroom, kicking off my shoes and socks as I went.

"You said I could eat as much as I wanted," he said as he followed me.

Well, he was right about that. I should have known there wouldn't be any leftovers. I was going to have to start buying a lot more groceries if I kept feeding two bachelor faeries all the time. They were eating me out of house and home. "Looks like we're going out for dinner too, then."

"Will the lowlife changeling next door be joining us?" Eldrick hesitated in the doorway of my bedroom.

"I don't know. He's still asleep." Digging through my drawers, I took out a fresh pair of jeans and a few layers of shirts to wear underneath a cozy wool sweater. I was busy spreading everything out on the bed, and for a moment, I forgot all about Eldrick.

He cleared his throat. "Did you … have intimate relations with him?"

I dropped the shirt I was holding up. "A-absolutely not! Why would you care about that, anyway?"

He picked at imaginary lint on his perfectly ironed V-neck sweater. "It's just highly inappropriate, and he is a poor choice in a mate."

"Why?"

Eldrick looked surprised. "Because of his curse—"

"My ears are burning." Zeph appeared in the doorway, wearing only his t-shirt and boxers. "Can't you two knuckleheads come up with something more interesting to talk about?"

My insides cringed and twisted into anxious knots as I fidgeted with my outfit. I couldn't keep my expression from screwing up in panic, and I didn't want either of them to see it. What did Eldrick mean by that?

I needed to know, and I knew Zeph would never tell me. Straightforward honesty clearly wasn't his thing. I'd have to try asking Eldrick the next time we were alone.

Zeph jabbed an accusing finger at Eldrick. "And you, why are you so interested in who she's sleeping with? You jealous?"

"Don't be absurd!" Eldrick snapped.

"I think you are. Geez. I leave you two alone for a few weeks and you're already falling in love. How precious."

Eldrick's face turned an alarming shade of red.

This was about to devolve into a fight, which I was not prepared to deal with until I'd been adequately caffeinated. "Okay, boys, calm down. Hurry up and get dressed, Zeph. I need to do some shopping, and then we're going out for dinner."

He suddenly appeared right in front of me, inches from my nose. "Nope."

I frowned. "What?"

"Tell that guy to do the shopping," he pointed a thumb back at Eldrick. "We're going on a date, remember?"

"Today?"

"Yep."

I blushed. "B-but, I mean, I'm not—"

"Relax, I've got to get ready, too." He had a roguish grin on his lips when he turned away. "You said it had to be romantic, right? So do that female thing and get yourself all fixed up, then meet me in the hall."

I waited until I heard my front door close to let out a sigh. Great. Of course I wanted to go on a date with him—just not right this minute. I was still exhausted from last night's ordeal. Zeph probably was, as well. After everything he'd thrown up, I didn't see how he could bear to be up, walking around, and even heckling Eldrick, as though nothing had happened.

Nibbling on my bottom lip, I stared back down at the outfit spread on the bed. Maybe this wasn't a good idea. Too bad those herbal cigarettes didn't seem to have the same effect on me, I might have tried one to get rid of the headache that was pounding right between my eyes.

"You don't seem pleased." Eldrick was still leaning in the doorway with his arms folded. "If you don't wish to go, then I suggest you tell him."

"It's not that," I mumbled as I picked up my clothes and started for the bathroom.

"Then what is it?"

I paused as I passed him in the doorway. Our gazes locked, and it was as though his sterling eyes could see right down into my soul.

I turned away. "We'll talk about it later."

He was right. There was something bugging me—something I needed to know. But asking about the curse would just have to wait.

First, I had to survive a first date with Zeph.

I took a quick shower, washed and styled my hair, and put on a little more make up than usual. It took me four times to get my eyeliner right because my stupid hands wouldn't stop shaking. Did my clothes look okay? Were skinny jeans and an off-the-shoulder sweater too plain? I didn't have a lot of fancy clothes to choose from. I'd never needed any before this.

As I stood back and scrutinized my reflection in the bathroom mirror, a familiar pain rose up in my chest. I wished my mom were here. I missed her, but moments like this were when I needed her so much it made my whole body ache. I wanted her there, standing right next to me, telling me that everything would be fine.

Tears blurred my vision until I couldn't see my reflection anymore.

Someone knocked softly against the bathroom door. "Are you ready?"

I recognized Zeph's voice.

"I-I'm fine. Uh, I mean, yes. Almost ready." My throat seized up.

The knob rattled. "You don't sound fine. Is everything okay?"

"Yes! I'll be out in a minute." I took a few deep breaths and steadied myself.

When I emerged, Zeph was waiting in the kitchen, dressed in his usual pair of holey blue jeans and a t-shirt, and sneakers. He'd brushed his hair a little, but apart from that, I couldn't tell he'd made much of an effort at all.

"Is that the same shirt you wore yesterday?" I frowned. "What exactly have you been doing this whole time?"

Zeph glanced me up and down. It was that same once-over scan he'd given the pretty girl on our first case with the bogles. This time, however, his lips parted slightly. He swallowed, and when our eyes met, he was blushing a little. "Cut me some slack, would you? I've been working hard. Doing this stuff isn't as easy as it used to be. Not to mention I had to give that bonehead Eldrick directions to the grocery store. He couldn't find his ass with both hands even if someone drew him a map."

"Doing what stuff?"

"You'll see." He smirked as he stood up and led the way out into the hall, stopping just long enough for me to put on my shoes.

"Leave it, you'll be fine," he said when I started to grab my coat.

"But it's freezing out."

"Not where we're going."

Oh no. What was he up to this time?

I followed Zeph across the hall into his apartment, looking around for anything suspicious. Nothing jumped out at me, though.

That is, not until he closed the door.

On the back of his front door, Zeph had drawn the most complicated display of spellwork I had ever seen. The intricate spell was filled with hundreds of symbols of all shapes and sizes, positioned within rings that spanned outward from the doorknob. Some of it had even been scrawled onto the brass knob itself.

"What is this?" I traced my fingertips over some of the designs.

He shrugged. "Something I was toying around with back when I worked with your dad. We called it an 'anydoor,' but it still needs some tweaking. I think this'll work just for today, though."

I smiled. "It's beautiful."

"Pfft. You haven't even seen what it does, yet." Zeph held a hand out for me to take. "Come here, princess. Let's give it a whirl."

Zeph gripped my hand tightly as we stood in front of the door. He reached out for the knob with the other, and hesitated. He combed some of his bangs away from his eyes, rubbed the back of his neck, and took a deep breath.

I cleared my throat. "Is everything okay?"

"Uh, yeah," he mumbled. "Look, I haven't tried this one in a while. Fair warning."

"You're not going to start throwing up again, are you?"

He laughed hoarsely. "No. I mean, probably not. But, uh, there's a slim chance we could end up on Mars or something."

"W-what?"

"Hey, I said it was a *slim* chance. It's probably fine. I'm pretty sure I got it right."

"Zeph Clemmont, if we die in the vacuum of space, I swear—"

He grabbed the knob and twisted. The runes ignited one by one, shining brilliantly across the door with a crescendo of chimes. My skin tingled as a warm shiver climbed my spine. Zeph's hold on my hand tightened. His jaw went rigid and he squeezed his eyes shut as he pulled the door open.

I shut my eyes, too.

There was a rush of bitterly cold air, and for an instant, I felt weightless. My stomach swam, and I squeezed Zeph's hand with all my strength. The harmony of the chimes was still echoing in my ears with a cadence like an ocean tide. Little by little, their sound began to fade. Something else sounded in the distance—a different kind of tune. It almost sounded like ... country music?

Suddenly my feet struck solid ground again.

"Are we on Mars?" I whispered, my eyes still pinched shut as I clung to Zeph's arm.

"Not unless Mars has started serving funnel cake," he rasped.

I cracked an eye open. Zeph was doubled over, looking pale again. He was fighting for breath, coughing and wheezing. Oh god. He'd overdone it! I should have known better than to let him try something like this after what we'd been through.

"Zeph," I tugged on his arm. "Does it hurt? Do you have any of Hank's cigarettes? Here, sit down, keeping taking deep breaths. I'll try to find you something to—"

He shook his head. "I-I'm fine, princess. Just gimme a second."

I fidgeted with the sleeves of my sweater, watching as he steadied himself against the door. A sudden roar and squeals of laughter made me turn. Was that ... a roller coaster?

Warm sunlight caressed my face and the savory flavors of popcorn, fried treats, and cotton candy wafted past my nose. Hundreds of people were walking around in shorts and t-shirts, munching on tasty treats, and standing in lines for game booths and carnival rides.

We were standing right next to a small building, and behind us was a door marked "Employees Only." Was that the door we'd just come through? But—*how*? We'd been in Zeph's apartment only seconds before.

I blinked up at him, breathless and dizzy.

"Cool, huh?" He chuckled, the color back in his cheeks. "Let's go. I don't wanna miss the pig races. I've got money on number four. He's a sure thing."

I stumbled along as Zeph took my hand again and we jumped in line to get our tickets. "Is this a carnival?"

He cocked an eyebrow. "Not just 'a' carnival. This is *the* best carnival, ever. It's the Florida Strawberry Festival."

"We're in Florida?"

Zeph's expression dimmed a bit. "Yeah. Is this okay? I just thought—"

"No! I mean, yes! It's amazing. It's perfect." I was still coming to terms with the fact that we'd walked through his front door and somehow wound up on the other end of the coastline. This whole magic thing was going to take some getting used to.

He smirked and looped an arm around my shoulders, drawing me in against his side. "Good. I didn't exactly have time to come up with a Plan B."

He didn't need one. Bathed in the warm Florida sun, we walked the fairgrounds hand in hand, sampling all the delicious treats and trying out the game booths. I won a cute stuffed lion on my first try at a shooting gallery game. Turns out, my aim was dead on.

Zeph was smiling nervously as we wandered back into the crowd, my toy lion sticking out of his pocket. "Remind me never to piss you off again."

"I'll try but you'll probably do it anyway." I laughed.

We rode the roller coaster and took a tour through the big livestock arena where all the pigs, cows, sheep, and other animals were waiting to be judged. I breathed in deeply the musky scent of the hay and animals. That paired with the way Zeph's sturdy fingers wove through mine made every part of my heart warm. I couldn't remember the last time I'd been this ... happy.

I didn't want to lose this—not ever.

"Hey? You okay?" Zeph was studying me, looking totally ridiculous in a foam hat shaped like a giant strawberry.

I sat down on the bleachers next to him, waiting with the rest of the crowd for the pig races to begin. "Just wondering what you're going to do with that hat after today."

He grinned. "If my pig wins, Hank has to wear it all night at work and he owes me twenty bucks."

"Lucky number four?"

"Yep." He offered me the basket of fresh strawberries he'd just bought. He'd been cramming his face full of them nonstop. This place was a vegetarian faerie's paradise.

Swiping a few, I sat back to watch as six little pigs were lined up in a miniature starting gate like racehorses. Each one was wearing a felt coat stitched with a number on it. Number four was a small, fuzzy piglet with orange spots. When they loaded him into the chute, Zeph stood up to shout.

I whipped out my phone and snapped a sneaky picture. Zeph in that dorky strawberry hat was going to make the perfect background wallpaper.

The rest of the crowd stood up as an announcer over a loudspeaker gave a countdown to a gunshot. The chutes opened, and six little pigs came racing out onto the track while everyone cheered. Zeph and I screamed, jumped, and waved our arms as the pigs charged past. The group was clustered at the first turn, tripping all over one another. But as they came around the last corner, lucky number four had taken the lead a snout-length ahead of the rest of the pigs. He darted over the finish line, locking in first place.

Zeph whooped and yelled, waving his hat in the air.

I giggled—right up until he suddenly whirled around, snagged an arm around my waist, and planted a triumphant kiss on my cheek.

My body tingled. I blushed, glancing up at him as he beamed. It was nothing, just a silly kiss on the cheek. But it made my heart race and my thoughts scatter.

He was still strutting and chanting about his victory when we left the bleachers, headed for the Ferris wheel. The sun was beginning to set. We couldn't stay much longer. But I wanted to do this—no, I *had* to. I would get Zeph on that Ferris wheel if it killed me. Maybe I didn't know much about romance or dating, but I knew the rule of Ferris wheels. If anything romantic was ever going to happen on a date to a carnival, that was where you had to be.

As soon as we got close to it, my heart sank. There must have been two hundred people waiting in line.

Zeph glanced down at his phone and sighed. "Doesn't look like we've got time for this. I'm supposed to be at work in an hour."

My shoulders sagged. "Okay. Should we go home, then?"

"Nah, let's do one more thing." He rubbed his chin and looked around. Then his eyes widened. He pointed to the dunk tank. "That one."

I arched a brow. What was the big deal about a dunk tank, anyway? As we got closer, though, I saw what had him so worked up.

The grand prize was a freshly baked strawberry pie.

The game was easy enough; all you had to do was hit the target with a beanbag hard enough to trigger the collapsing platform. Nothing new there. But as we went to pay for a round, the lady selling tickets waved us off. "Sorry. We're closed."

"Seriously?" Zeph frowned.

"The tank guy is on break."

"Pfft. Closed my ass," Zeph snatched off his strawberry hat and took my stuffed lion out of his pocket, shoving them both into my arms along with his nearly empty basket of strawberries. "I'll be the damn tank guy."

I blinked. "Wait, it's not a big deal. Let's just find a different game. I'm sure there's other places to get pie."

It was too late. Zeph stripped off his shirt, balling it up and adding it to the stack of stuff in my arms.

My throat went dry. I noticed a few other women standing nearby staring at him, too. Bronze skin, corded arms, and a perfectly sculpted torso—it was hard to ignore a physique like his.

"It's a matter of pride," he said as he kicked off his shoes and went to climb into the tank.

The ticket-lady didn't even protest. She was too busy gawking. Her eyes never left him as I put our stuff down, paid for three beanbags, and took my place in front of the target.

"Okay, princess. Let's see some more of that wicked aim," Zeph taunted.

I narrowed my eyes, reared back, and hurled the first beanbag. It sailed wide, missing the target entirely.

He smirked. "Ooh, that's too bad. Maybe try a little less checking me out and a little more hitting the bullseye."

"Oh, shut up." I drew back again, slinging the second beanbag.

It smacked the target dead on. The platform dropped, dumping Zeph into the water. He came up laughing and sputtering, wiping his hair out of his eyes. I cheered, running over to do a victory dance in front of him as he climbed out of the tank.

He took his shirt back and used it to dry his face. "Yeah, yeah. No one likes a showoff, you know."

"You're soaked! Look at your jeans."

"Hmm. Yep, looks like I'll need some help drying off." I caught a flash of his mischievous grin half a second too late. Zeph grabbed my arm and dragged me in, hugging me against his wet body and lifting me off my feet.

"Ah! No, stop! This is my favorite sweater!" I giggled as I tried to wriggle free.

Zeph spun me around once and then he put me back down. But he didn't let me go. His muscular arms stayed wrapped around me, and his gaze flickered to my mouth. My stomach fluttered. I could feel my pulse in my throat.

Yes … *yes*! Our lips were so close. Just kiss me, you idiot.

"We should go," he murmured.

The wind rushed out of me all at once. "We still have time."

He wouldn't meet my gaze again. "No, Josie. We don't."

As he let me go and began putting his shirt back on, I struggled to figure out what had gone wrong. It wasn't just me, right? That moment—the way he'd held and looked at me. He had wanted it, too. Why was he throwing up walls now?

The answer pierced my mind like a cold spike.

It had to be because of the curse.

Z eph sat down on a bench to put his socks and shoes back on. His jeans were still soaked, and his shaggy dark hair was dripping onto his face and shoulders. I watched him for a moment, biding my time. I was going to ask him. Surely he wouldn't lie to me again, not about this.

I took in a deep breath.

"Zeph, will you—"

The wind gusted right in my face all of a sudden. It snatched the foam strawberry hat right out of my arms and sent it skipping across the ground.

"Crap! Hang on, I'll be right back."

"Hey, wait!"

I ignored him and darted after the hat. It blew across the ground right out of my reach, disappearing into a crowd of people standing around a performance stage. The music was loud, and the people smashed in around me as I ducked through, searching for the hat.

Someone stepped right into my path.

I leaned around, trying to see which way the hat had blown. "Excuse me, I'm just trying to …"

A cold chill shuddered over my body.

I looked up into the flat gaze of a young woman with long hair white as frost. Her pale skin caught the sunlight like porcelain as she tilted her head slowly to the side.

My adrenaline spiked. Something wasn't right about her.

The woman's glacier blue eyes never blinked, but one corner of her mouth curled into a sneer. Suddenly, she snapped a hand out and touched my forehead with a finger.

My body went rigid and my chest spasmed as though my breath had frozen in my lungs. I couldn't move. My knees buckled.

I toppled forward, but in one fluid motion, the tall woman crouched and picked up my limp body. I heard something—a cutting sound near my ear—right before she hefted me over her slender shoulder effortlessly and began striding away into the crowd. There were hundreds of people standing around us, staring at the stage, clapping and singing along with a country music tune. Not a single one of them looked our way. Couldn't they see me?

Oh god, no. What was happening? Who was this woman? Where was Zeph?

My pulse thrashed in my ears. Tears welled in my eyes. I was hanging there, helpless, unable to make a sound as the woman walked calmly through the exit gates and into the parking lot. The two security guards watching the gates never even looked at us.

My throat burned, but I couldn't scream.

We were halfway across the parking lot when a crashing sound made the woman stop short.

"Lumi!" Zeph's voice boomed over the noise of the fairgrounds. "You've got something that belongs to me."

"Are you still alive?" The woman's voice was calm. "Pity. You must be running short on time by now, though. How many more months is it? Two? Three?"

Zeph growled low. "Put her down and walk away. Last warning."

147

"Or what?" She snickered.

"Or your mistress is gonna have to come scrape what's left of you off this asphalt. Then again, maybe you're Fir Darrig's bitch, these days?"

The woman's shoulder tensed under me. She growled—a canine sound that reminded me strangely of Eldrick. The temperature started to plummet. Chills swelled over me and the eerie echo of music whispered in my ears.

The air exploded around me like a blast from a deep freeze.

I was flying through the air, arms and legs flailing out of my control, until I smacked against something hard. A car? My numb body slumped to the ground and I landed on my back, staring up at the endless blue sky. My vision went fuzzy, I still couldn't move anything, but all around me the sounds of combat raged—metal crunching, glass shattering, and two beasts snarling and bellowing. Chimes blared through the air as though someone were slamming their fists onto a piano, and each chord came with an explosion of energy sizzling in the air.

I couldn't even turn my head to watch. What was happening? What had that woman done to me? Was I ... dying?

Darkness closed in, swallowing me whole.

A second passed. Maybe two. Or was it longer? Time seemed so irrelevant in that blackness.

A sudden primal scream shattered the darkness. Light poured over me, blinding me for a moment.

Through the haze, I saw him.

Zeph was crouched over me, his mouth forcing breath into my lungs and his hands working my chest. CPR? He drew back, his expression twisted and his eyes wild. Blood oozed from a deep cut across his forehead.

I sputtered and sucked in a frantic breath. Instantly, my head cleared. My vision snapped into focus. "Z-Zeph."

The next thing I knew, his arms were around me. Zeph was shaking all over, gripping me tightly against him. Soft feathers from his wings brushed my cheek.

"I-I can't move my legs." My throat was raw. Every word was agony. "What happened?"

Somehow, we were back in the hallway outside Zeph's front door. Oh god, how long had I been out? What had I missed?

My front door burst open and Eldrick stormed out, his chest thrumming with a beastly growl. His shoulders were hunched, his sterling eyes flashed, and his teeth were bared in a snarl as he glanced down the hall both ways. "I smell her—where is she? Where is Lumi?"

"Forget her and get your ass over here." Zeph's voice was choked with emotion. "She tried to petrify Josie. I can't undo it all the way."

Eldrick bent down, grasping my chin in his fingers as he peered into my eyes. "Can you see me, Josie?"

"Y-yes," I rasped.

He gave a quick nod before flashing a look at Zeph. "She'll be fine. I can undo the rest of the spell. Bring her inside."

Zeph carried me silently through the apartment into my bedroom. He was still shaking and his chin was twitching like he could barely keep it together. As soon as he laid me down on the bed, he backed away to lean against the wall. His jaw clenched and he put his face in his hands.

I tried to reach for him. "I-I'm okay, Zeph. It wasn't your fault."

He snapped a cold glare up at me, his hands curling into fists. His eyes blazed and a throbbing vein stood out against his neck. I waited for the yelling to start. Cursing. Flailing. Pitching his usual fit. I would have taken any of it right then just to know he was still himself.

But he didn't make a sound. Zeph bolted from the bedroom with a flurry of violet feathers, slamming the door behind him.

My heart sank.

"That imbecile," Eldrick muttered under his breath.

My tears felt cool against my flushed skin. "It wasn't his fault. I wandered away from him at the fair—I wasn't paying any attention."

Eldrick snorted. "He should have known better than to take you out into public like that."

149

I didn't want to argue. It wasn't Zeph's fault, though. I had insisted on a date. He'd only taken me there because I demanded something romantic. He was trying to make me happy.

I tried to swallow back the stiffness in my throat. "Whatever that woman did to me, you can fix it, right?"

"Indeed," Eldrick sighed and approached the bed, leaning over to inspect me again. His silver eyes darted all over, as though he were scrutinizing every detail. "Petrification requires a skilled touch. Ideally, this sort of spell would render the victim perfectly incapacitated and alive, making them easy to take advantage of. Lumi must have botched the spell. Amateur."

"O-oh."

He stretched a hand over me, his fingers spread wide as his palm hovered right over face. "You'll most likely feel weak for a few days, and there may be some lingering numbness in your extremities. But the effects won't be permanent."

"Thank you," I whispered.

He frowned, his expression sharpening for an instant. "You ... do not need to thank me for this."

What? Why? What had changed? I wanted to ask, but my body felt so weak. My thoughts became hazy again as a gentle, soothing melody hummed in the air. It washed over me, relaxing every part of my body as though I were drifting in a pool of cool water.

I didn't care about anything, then. Where Zeph was, why that woman had tried to kidnap me—none of it mattered. My eyelids got heavier and heavier as I took in deep, comfortable breaths. I let the faint smell of eucalyptus and the whispering of chimes carry me away.

By Sunday, everything was back to normal.

Well, it was for me, anyway.

Eldrick's efforts at removing the petrification had worked. I didn't have any more numbness or tingling in my fingers and toes. I felt fine. Zeph, on the other hand, was still haunting my steps with his gaze darting at every sudden sound. He wouldn't tell me why Lumi had attacked me like that, no matter how many times I asked. Was it really because I had been with him? Somehow … that answer didn't satisfy me anymore. This wasn't just some silly ivy plant or Bunsen burner acting up.

That woman had nearly killed me. I needed to know why. But if I was going to get any useful information out of Eldrick, it would have to happen after Zeph went to work.

I glanced at the clock on my phone again. Not long now.

Eldrick was scowling into the refrigerator. "Are we out of milk *again*?"

"I was thirsty," Zeph mumbled.

"That doesn't entitle you to drink the entire gallon in one sitting." Eldrick slammed the fridge door and stalked over to the coffee maker.

I stuffed my phone back into my pocket. "Why are you guys vegetarians, anyway?"

"All faeries are," Eldrick scoffed. "We cannot eat anything that contains or is tainted by the blood of a living being. It makes us violently ill."

I was now well acquainted with what "violently ill" meant by faerie standards, and I was *not* interested in repeating that experience. Just thinking about it made me cringe.

"*Most* of us, not all," Zeph corrected.

Eldrick snorted in agreement. "True. There are an infamous few whose souls have been so befouled and utterly warped by hatred, they actually crave it. It's repulsive."

I wondered if that was where legends about vampires had come from. Zeph had mentioned something about them being associated with faeries before. "What about eggs?"

"Eggs are good," Zeph replied from where he was sitting at the table, nibbling on a fresh peach. "Basically no meat. And pure foods like milk, fruit, honey, and some vegetables are the best."

"Pure foods," Eldrick explained, like he knew I was about to ask what that meant. "Those are products of nature that don't require any living creature to suffer by taking them—including plant life. We can stomach plants, however, because of their lack of blood."

"Oh." Well, that explained why Zeph had devoured the entire jar of my expensive organic raw honey. "Where is the best place to go out to eat, then?"

The two faerie men glanced at one another, as though they were sharing some private, telepathic conversation.

For an instant, I wished I wasn't the only human in the room.

Zeph shrugged and whipped out his phone. "It doesn't matter to me. I can't go anyway."

I gave him what I hoped would be a convincing frown. "Work?"

"Yep. Hank texted me earlier. He's swamped at the bar tonight." He didn't sound very excited about it.

I picked at my fingernails. "So … if Eldrick and I go out for some dinner, should I bring something back for you?"

Zeph cut me glare. His brow creased and his eyes narrowed.

"It'll be fine. Eldrick will be there. We won't go far."

He pursed his lips, gaze flickering over to Eldrick—who was still preoccupied with pouring himself a fresh cup of coffee.

"And we'll come straight back after. I promise."

"Ugh, fine." Zeph sighed and rubbed his forehead "Straight back here, though. I mean it. It'll be late when I get back. Eldrick, make sure she stays out of trouble."

The dark spirit leaning against my kitchen counter casually sipping coffee, shot him a dirty look. "You have no authority to give me orders, changeling scum."

They bickered right up until Zeph shut the front door behind him. I didn't say a single word until he was gone because I refused to pick a side.

If this was a matter of one of them establishing himself as the alpha dog, then they were just going to have to sort it out on their own. I just hoped they figured it out soon because their childish arguing was going to drive me nuts.

"Are we going?" Eldrick was watching me with a puzzled expression.

Standing at the kitchen sink, I realized I'd been staring at the sparkling purple feather—Zeph's feather—that was still inside the vase on the windowsill. Something about the way the moonlight caught it made my head feel fuzzy.

"Sure." I forced a smile and grabbed my coat and scarf off the back of the sofa on my way to the door.

"Wait," Eldrick snapped suddenly. He caught the back of my coat, yanking me to an abrupt halt. Then he grasped my shoulders and spun me around to face him.

I was a little alarmed. He wasn't usually so eager to touch me, or anyone else for that matter.

He had a pensive frown against his sharp features as he took my scarf and began tying it into a complex knot around my neck. "You always wear it wrong," he insisted as he finished tucking the loose ends under the collar of my coat. "If you're going to wear a scarf, tie it like this."

I blushed. "Thank you."

He made an impatient, huffing noise and nodded toward the door. Eldrick almost never wore a coat, even though it was freezing outside. I didn't understand it. After all, Zeph wore one. Did faeries get cold? Or was it just a fashion statement? Somehow, I doubted Zeph dressed with any regard for style.

Eldrick, on the other hand, seemed to care a lot about how he looked. Once again, he was wearing all black—black pants, black dress shoes, and a black sweater over a black button-down dress shirt. His clothes were so formal—or at least, they seemed that way to me. I wasn't used to being around someone who cared anything about looking fashionable.

Eldrick walked beside me out into the chilly night, his stride brimming

153

with a sense of proud elegance. Zeph had called him a prince before. When he walked like that, he certainly looked like nobility. He had his broad shoulders back, his head held high, and his hands tucked into his pockets. It made him seem sophisticated.

"Don't you get cold?" I finally decided to ask as we began our casual stroll downtown.

He glanced down at me through his feathery black bangs. "No."

"Because you're a puca?"

"Yes, I suppose that is the simplest explanation."

"I'm sorry. I know I ask a lot of questions," I mumbled. "I don't understand the world you come from. And now it seems like Zeph was right; the closer I get to him, the more dangerous things are."

Out of the blue, Eldrick grabbed my arm and pulled me closer against his side. His eyes met mine. My stomach fluttered. His face was so close. He had never tried to touch me like that before.

It wasn't that I didn't like him or find him attractive. He was frighteningly handsome, if not a little intimidating. And while we had gotten off to the worst start imaginable, things were different now. He was becoming the closest thing I had to family.

But I couldn't think of him *that* way.

I was trying to think of a nice way to pull my arm away without offending him when someone on a bicycle went zipping past us, narrowly missing me.

Once again, he'd saved me from being run over.

"You have the resources to learn about our world, if you desire. Your father left many valuable texts behind," he said casually, as though nothing had happened—but he hadn't let go of my arm.

"I can't read any of it. It's all written in the faerie language."

"Humans can learn to read our language. It is the voice of the earth. All beings have an innate understanding of it. It is what you would call instinctual." He kept talking while he looked straight ahead.

I grinned at him hopefully. "Will you help me learn?"

"If you desire."

"It's just … I don't want to be afraid anymore. If something bad happens again, I want to be able to handle things myself instead of relying on you and Zeph to come to my rescue."

Eldrick flicked a strange look down at me. I almost mistook it for concern. "Does our presence displease you?"

I blinked in surprise. "N-no! That's not it at all. I just, well, I suppose I still keep asking myself if I'm going to wake up one day and you'll both be gone. Then I'll be alone again. And I'll have to figure out some way to survive on my own."

I was uncomfortable admitting that. I didn't want to cheapen their efforts—especially Zeph's—in keeping me safe.

I cleared my throat. "What does the faerie language sound like?"

Eldrick's tense, furrowed brow went slack. His expression became as serene and blissful as the cool surface of the moon. "Music," he breathed the word as though it were ecstasy.

"You mean like the chimes?" I knew that sound well.

He nodded slowly. "Ages ago, some called it the music of the spheres. Your father possessed an exquisitely intimate knowledge of spellsongs. He could hear the tones and translate the harmonics into the human language." We paused at a corner, letting a few bicyclers pass on the sidewalk. "To be perfectly frank, I'm impressed he was able to do such a thing. The details of our language, particularly the ancient spellsongs that comprise spellwork, are difficult for even an elder fae to discern. I've never seen so many texts about us in the human language before."

My head spun with questions as I tried to keep up with Eldrick's long strides. "What's a spellsong? And what does it have to do with spellwork?"

"A spellsong is, as you described it, the chimes. The use of magic of any kind has a unique sound. A song, if you will."

My lips parted—that was why I heard that sound whenever Zeph or Eldrick worked magic!

"Some are more distinct and obvious than others, usually depending on their desired effect. But each note, each melody, can be paired with a unique shape, line, or design—something your father quite skillfully deciphered." He stopped at the edge of a crosswalk and turned to face me. "It isn't unlike how humans write sheet music. You need to see the notes in order to understand how a song is made."

"Do faeries have to write down all their spellwork, too?"

He smiled and opened his other hand. One twist of his wrist, and a beautifully intricate ring of bright runes appeared. It hovered in the air above his open hand, glowing softly while the details, designs, and smaller rings within it moved like the inner mechanisms in a pocket watch.

My breath caught as the familiar tingle whispered over on my skin. I heard the soft, whispering of bells in my ear.

Other people were walking and cycling by, passing us on the sidewalk. But no one else even seemed to notice. It was as though they couldn't see it at all. It was just the same as when Lumi had kidnapped me—they were blind to it.

"Most faeries do not require a knowledge of how a spell is made. For us, it is innate—comparable to someone who can play by ear rather than requiring sheet music. But there are instances where we must know how to read spellwork, such as in the case of learning a new spell, or performing a ritual that would be otherwise unnatural to us," he explained, snapping his hand closed and extinguishing the spell. "Apparently, your father had begun developing some of his own spells; a dangerous endeavor for a human. His journals are full of them."

The light turned green and we crossed the street together. I clung closer to Eldrick's side, taking refuge from the bitter wind against his tall frame. "If it was so dangerous, then why would he go to so much trouble?"

Eldrick's expression became stony and impossible to read. His lips pressed together as though he'd tasted something bitter. "We once had our own written records of our history, and catalogues of every spell known in our world. But such things aren't valued anymore. Most faeries now care more about their own survival than trying to preserve our history."

I nodded. "Zeph said something like that, too."

Eldrick's brow creased. "The minds of my kind are changing rapidly, turning from the old ways and caring little about the harmony of the earth. It can't be helped, since so much of our existence now depends on the activity of humans. We are following you on your path to self-destruction like lambs to the slaughter."

So much for progress.

We'd come to a small, familiar bistro on the street corner near my school. It was the same one where he waited for me while I was in class. They had a nice menu on display by the curb, and while the food definitely sounded delicious, I knew the real reason he had chosen to come here had nothing to do with the food. This place served lots of expensive, house-roasted coffees.

No one liked coffee more than Eldrick. I didn't know exactly how many cups he drank on a daily basis, but considering how much more I had to buy now just to meet his demand—I was willing to bet it was in the twenties. He snubbed all the cheap bargain brands and always went straight for the exotic gourmet dark roasts.

Eldrick held the door for me, then took my coat and scarf to carry it to a table near the back of the restaurant. He held a chair out for me as we settled in. It was so formal. I wasn't used to being treated this way. A waitress brought us menus and glasses of water. Eldrick ordered an appetizer of hummus and sliced vegetables to share.

But as hungry as I was, I couldn't think about food yet. This was my chance. We were alone, out of Zeph's earshot. It was time to get answers.

"Can I ask you something in confidence?" I used spreading my napkin across my lap as an excuse not to meet his gaze.

"By that, I assume you mean you would prefer that I didn't relay any of this to your lover?"

It took a second for me to collect my sanity, which he'd just smashed like a glass Christmas ornament. "No—well, yes. But we aren't lovers. In fact, I'm not even sure he thinks of me that way."

"He does." Eldrick sounded extremely sure about that.

"H-how do you …"

He rolled his silver eyes. "Don't be childish. A man doesn't do the things he has for someone he doesn't have feelings for. That he is willing to jeopardize his own life should be evidence enough that his feelings are amorous." Eldrick picked up a slice of cucumber from the appetizer tray and popped it into his mouth. "I doubt he would go to such lengths for anyone else."

"What lengths has he gone to?" I wasn't sure I was ready to know, but the way he said it made it sound important. "Does it have something to do with the curse you mentioned before?"

Eldrick didn't answer right away. The waitress came back to our table, and he ordered a large black coffee. I ordered one of their signature sandwiches, even if the current subject had completely ruined my appetite.

"I take it this is the question you'd like to keep between us," he said after the waitress had gone.

I was hoping he would be able to read the answer in my eyes. Zeph didn't want me to know what was going on. He'd already gone to a lot of trouble to lie and hide his identity from me. Now, I could sense that he was keeping secrets again. The past two times I had figured things out the hard way. I didn't want to go through that again.

This time, I wanted to be prepared.

Eldrick sat forward in his chair, folding his arms and resting his elbows on the tabletop. His eerie, platinum-colored eyes stared into mine. "Zeph is a great deal younger than I am. He wasn't born in our world; he was born in yours—the human world—so his perspective is not something I can claim to comprehend. But I do know that he spent a large part of his life alone. Apart from a now estranged younger brother who has apparently sided with the Seelie Court, Zeph has no other family that will claim him. I can only assume that meeting your parents and becoming involved with them made him believe he had found a place where he was wanted."

I sank back in my seat, taking it all in. "You mean, he doesn't have anyone else? What about his parents?"

"His father is a notorious troublemaker, a shapeshifter known as Hedley Kow. His mother ... to be perfectly honest, I'm not sure he knows who she is." Eldrick's jaw tensed and his brow creased as he stared down at his coffee mug. "My understanding is that his brother has nowhere near the ability that Zeph has when it comes to wielding magic. No doubt, this is by design. The Seelie Court likes to keep its prodigies under the tightest control. I assume this is because their initial complacency is what caused them to lose Zeph in the first place."

"You mean ... Zeph was a Seelie?" Under the table, I kept wringing my hands until my fingers were slimy and sweaty.

"It came as a surprise to us all. He doesn't seem the type to enjoy submitting to anyone's authority. Perhaps he recognized the need for some accountability when it came to using magic. He's witnessed the very worst of what can happen without some semblance of control over it." He shrugged and took another sip of coffee. "Whatever the reason, he tried to persuade the Seelie Court into taking action against Fir Darrig, who had only recently begun causing more serious trouble than usual. The Seelie Court didn't agree. Many of them have close ties to Fir Darrig and are willing to overlook his behavior. This must have incited some rage in Zeph, because he attempted to apprehend Fir Darrig himself."

I swallowed. "All alone?"

Eldrick nodded. "A brave gesture. Perhaps even a noble one. But stupid, nonetheless. In the process of his pursuit, he turned his back on the Seelie Court and became a vigilante, acting on his own accord. It caused quite an upset. Until that moment, Zeph had been something of an authority figure and there were many who admired his skill. When it comes to changeling magic, Zeph's talent is indisputable."

That wasn't hard to believe. Zeph's temper was almost as bad as mine—*almost*. I could imagine him trying something like that, but hearing that he had been respected, admired even, was a shock. It was a cold reminder of how little I actually knew about him.

"Fir Darrig is not to be trifled with. He's become so notorious his name is all but synonymous as a term for those who like to play gruesome pranks—which has always been one

of his favorite pastimes. His many years of life have made him quite powerful." Eldrick shifted uncomfortably. "He was, after all, one of the original pilgrims who came here to sing the first songs. Add to that his uncanny ability to rally weaker minds to his cause and his intricate knowledge of the complexities of spellwork, he becomes quite the monster. The horrible grudge he bears against humankind makes him all the more dangerous."

I wondered if that was something he and Fir Darrig had in common. After all, when we first met, Eldrick wouldn't even come near me. It had taken weeks to earn his trust. Even now, I wasn't sure if he liked me or just tolerated my existence. He still preached about the evils of humankind with every other breath, but it was difficult to tell if it was just the voice of some past pain or how he truly felt.

Across the table, Eldrick had almost emptied his first cup of coffee. He was casually swirling a carrot around in the hummus, the dim light of the café catching in his glossy black hair. I couldn't help it. Deep down, it hurt to think that he might still resent me as much as he did the rest of humanity.

"Fir Darrig has no love left in his heart, not even for his own kind, and Zeph was ill prepared to challenge him alone. Many who stood a far greater chance than Zeph have already tried and failed. It's as though Fir Darrig has found some way to make himself immortal." His voice carried a chilling sense of finality.

I tipped my head to the side slightly. "You mean, faeries aren't already immortal?"

A bewitching smirk curled up his lips. "Hardly. Our lifespan simply exceeds that of humans. I assumed you knew this."

My cheeks grew hot and I dipped my head slightly. I briefly debated asking how old he was. But then Eldrick began to continue his story.

"Fir Darrig could have destroyed Zeph easily. Perhaps he found it amusing that Zeph was so juvenile in his hope that he could actually overpower him in a duel of magic. Fir Darrig placed a curse on Zeph to publicly humiliate him: another example of his morbid sense of humor." He curled his lip at the thought. "It was a disgusting, shameful thing to do. The most sacred of our old laws stated that no fae should ever use that sort of magic against another. By doing that, Fir Darrig was essentially mocking all our sacred traditions."

My body tensed as a sudden coldness sent shivers over my skin. This was it—the curse—the one everyone kept mentioning!

"It was an appalling event, and times have grown darker, even since then." Eldrick's scowl softened as he studied me. "Now, Unseelie faeries use that sort of binding magic against one another practically every day. It's become commonplace, thanks to Fir Darrig. Now, I see that even Zeph is guilty of that crime when he goes on these so-called cases. I suppose he is more or less justified in those instances, however. If the Seelie Court is not going to appropriately police this kind of activity, someone else should."

Under the table, I squeezed my sweaty hands into fists. I couldn't lose my nerve. Not now—even if the answer terrified me.

"What was the curse?"

Eldrick hesitated. He shifted in his seat again, chewing on the inside of his cheek. "I wasn't there in person. I've only ever heard rumors about it."

He was stalling.

I planted my hands on the table firmly. "Tell me."

Eldrick cleared his throat, glancing away before he spoke in a stiff tone, "The curse stipulated that if Zeph did not deliver the vessel to Fir Darrig by the next Singing Moon, then he would perish."

Memories pricked at my mind. Zeph had told me about the vessel before. It was supposed to be a human brimming with magical energy, and they were the ones who chose the next faerie king or queen. But … what did this vessel person have to do with Zeph? How much time did we have left to find them before the Singing Moon? Why wasn't Zeph out there looking for them right now?

"The Singing Moon only occurs once every five centuries. All full moons are cause for some celebration amongst our kind, but the night of the Singing Moon is a holiday held dear by all faeries," Eldrick continued. "It used to signal the coronation of a new king or queen. With every passing day, the Singing Moon draws nearer, and more of Zeph's power diminishes. Soon he will be too weak to defend even himself."

My chest began to feel tight. Worry spread through every inch of my body with a cold shudder. "When is the next Singing Moon?"

Eldrick stared at me so deeply I could see tiny reflections of myself in his eyes. "In approximately three months."

11

"There are some unique aspects of the vessel that are consistent throughout time, making them fairly easy to identify. First, they have an innate ability to sense and see magic that far exceeds a normal human. Second, and much more distinctly, is that their birthdate always coincides with the night of the Singing Moon. So, Josie, you need to ask yourself a very important question." Eldrick's voice had become hushed and deep. "Who is the vessel?"

"Who is the vessel?" I repeated the question in a whisper.

A strange heat prickled in my chest. It made my breathing hitch and my lips part. My heart dropped into the soles of my shoes.

I knew who the vessel was.

"It's not possible." I squeezed a hand against my chest where that tingling warmth still buzzed. "It can't be. I-if I were something like that, I would already know!"

Eldrick frowned. "Don't be foolish. You *do* know. I can see it in your eyes."

I shrank back into my chair, unable to stop my heart from racing out of control. All this time, Zeph had been my benefactor, but he'd also been keeping me at a distance. Whatever feelings he had for me, he was still refusing to let them show. And this—*this* was why! Because of his curse, because of what I was, it was dangerous for me to be near him.

"He knows I'm the vessel." I gasped. "He's known it all along."

"Based upon what I've read of his journals, your father knew it, too." Eldrick stared down into his coffee mug again. "He was fixated on finding a way to destroy Fir Darrig. Clearly he has designs upon claiming you."

"Why? He's already so powerful, and you said he's immortal, too. What would he need me for?"

"With your power as the vessel fused to his own, Fir Darrig would essentially become a god. He would be unstoppable in every sense of the word. Presently, the only hope for thwarting Fir Darrig has rested in the hands of the Seelie Court. Their united front might be enough to undo him if they could ever be convinced to try." His face twitched, as though he were resisting a snarl. "However, as it stands, there is only person on this planet with enough magical power to rival Fir Darrig. That is you, Josie. If he were to use your power, there would be no contesting him. I shudder to think of what he would do not only to our kind, but to yours as well."

Horror strangled all the breath from my lungs. I had stared into the eyes of fae who wanted to hurt me. I knew what they were capable of. But bogles and sylphs—they were nothing compared to Fir Darrig. What could I possibly do? I didn't know how to cast any spells.

Yet.

"You said my dad's old books have information about fighting Fir Darrig?"

Eldrick shrugged. "Not exclusively, but your father was experimenting with offensive spellwork, enchanting items for use in battle, and different ways of binding fae."

"You mean like the salt circle we used to capture a sylph?" I recalled.

"Indeed. Your father must have had some excellent tutoring ... I suspect from a certain changeling vigilante with a grudge against Fir Darrig."

Eldrick flicked me a suggestive grin.

That was it—that was why they had been working together! The shattered pieces of my strange life were beginning to finally fall back into place. "So Zeph and my dad were looking for a way to stop Fir Darrig."

"That is certainly a plausible deduction," Eldrick agreed. "Your father had a vested interest in destroying him, since Fir Darrig's desire for supreme power over the faerie world would inevitably involve acquiring you as his pawn. However, simply destroying Fir Darrig wouldn't affect Zeph's curse. Curses are peculiar and difficult devices. Still ..." He stopped mid-sentence, tapping a finger on his chin.

"What?" I pressed.

Eldrick shrugged again. "I wonder at the amount of trust your father put in Zeph. Allowing him to be your legal guardian seems like a gamble. It's astounding to think he would be willing to trust a changeling with something so precious to him, especially since Zeph's species is known to be inherently selfish and deceptive. If Zeph were to simply surrender to the terms of his curse and deliver you to Fir Darrig, he would be a free man."

That truth knocked the breath right out of me again. If Zeph wanted out of his curse, then all he had to do was drop me at Fir Darrig's feet. It was simple, and yet ...

"Perhaps this is the evidence you've desired that he does have great affection for you. Apparently, Zeph would rather die the slowest and most agonizing death a faerie can suffer than surrender you over to Fir Darrig."

I wanted to believe that. God, I wanted desperately to know Zeph felt that way about me. I loved that idiot and all of his antics. But how could I be sure he felt that way, too? Sure, it sounded good. But this was all speculation. Zeph had never told me that he loved me. I didn't want my first leap into romance to be a jump to the wrong conclusion.

"You're making that face again," Eldrick grumbled.

"What face?"

He went back to sipping his coffee. "You frequently get this strange expression of uneasiness, as though you're about to become ill. Are you really that concerned that your feelings are unrequited?"

I swallowed hard. "Sorry. I'm just nervous. I've never been in love before, so I don't really know the rules."

He arched a brow curiously. "Rules?"

"Yeah, you know. Like what I'm allowed to ask, or when I should expect him to give me an answer about how he feels."

Eldrick eyes gleamed with a wry grin. "Hasn't anyone ever told you that all is fair in love and war? There are no rules. I think you have vastly underestimated the influence you have over that moron."

I'd heard that quote before, although I had never understood what it meant. "So, I should just ask him outright?"

Eldrick's smug grin made my stomach squirm. "It isn't like you to be so timid. Those who are timid in love are the ones who will inevitably end up brokenhearted and alone."

Those words were still sinking in long after we had finished dinner and started walking back home. It was so easy to be quiet with Eldrick, though. He didn't push awkward conversation just to seem sociable. Words weren't necessary with him. He was strolling calmly at my side like nothing was wrong, seeming perfectly content.

"Can I ask you something else?" I asked as we stood at a crosswalk, waiting for the light to change.

"Of course."

I wasn't sure if bringing this up would be a good idea. It might upset him, but I was too curious to let it go. "What happened to you? What made you hate humans so much?"

The light at the crosswalk turned green, and the crowd waiting on the sidewalk with us began to move forward ... but Eldrick held still. I looked up at him, slightly afraid of what kind of expression I might find on his sharply-featured face.

Maybe it had been a bad idea to ask about this.

His brow was furrowed a little, as though he were searching for the right words. When he began to answer, he avoided my eyes. "I was not born in your world, Josie. My mother and father brought me here when I was a child. We were refugees, desperate for safe harbor and ignorant of human nature. Even then, long before the faerie court was ever split, there were mixed opinions among my kind about whether or not humans could be trusted. Some of us, my parents included, preferred not to mingle with them. But I ... chose not to listen to their warnings."

The light changed again, and more people gathered around us on the curb. Eldrick was silent, his eyes slowly shifting to stare down at me with an intensity I didn't understand. When the crowds moved to begin crossing the street again, he still didn't take a step.

"There was a small human village near my father's first estate. He had already made a name for himself as a notorious evil in that part of the world. Most of it was merely a ruse, a reputation he propagated in order to keep humans away." His head bowed and his eyes fixed upon the pavement with a vacant stare. "But in my childish naivety, I thought that reputation wouldn't extend to me. I wanted to see humans up close. I wanted to walk among, learn from, and be close to them. I hoped they would be accepting of me. That was not the case, however."

I could see his face under the dim glow of the streetlamps. His jaw had gone tense, and I could see his pulse throbbing in the side of his neck. "When they saw me, they initially treated me with kindness. They invited me into their village. They offered me gifts—food, toys, and trinkets—and I trusted them without question. I left that village certain that my parents were wrong; humans and faeries could be allies. We could be friends. We could love one another."

A cold wind blew between us, biting at my nose and making his dark hair blow over his brow. It numbed me to the bone, but I didn't dare take my eyes off him.

"The humans in that village laid a trap for me. When I returned, they captured me. I was too young to know better, and too inexperienced with my own magic to fight back. I'd never had to defend myself from that kind of threat before. It went against every ounce of my nature to want to hurt them, and yet they bound me in an iron cage in their village square. They tried for three weeks to burn me alive. Being what I was, I could regenerate quickly enough that I survived. It takes more than mere flame to kill a fae. But that is not to say that we don't experience pain."

"They … they tortured you." A lump lodged at the back of my throat.

"I begged for mercy. I pleaded with them. And when that failed, I cried for my parents to come set me free," he murmured. "They did, at last. My father broke me from that prison and took me home. I never went back into a human city again. That is—until your father captured me."

Tears slid down my face, freezing against my cheeks. I wanted to touch him, to comfort him, and at the same time I was terrified. No wonder he hated me. No wonder this contract between us had made him so feral.

He had been afraid of me.

"Your father said the terms of our contract would be simple. I am to be your faithful servant, obedient to your every whim, until the day you choose to set me free. You are the only one who can break our contract."

With a sigh, Eldrick faced me again. He frowned and brushed a hand over my cheek, wiping some of the tears from my face. Neither of us looked away as we stood at the crosswalk, the light changing over and over.

"That's why you scratched his face off all the pictures in my house," I whispered.

He looked away.

"Eldrick, you have to know, I would *never* do something to hurt you," I continued.

"Not even after what I have already done to you?"

Once again, we both got quiet.

I didn't know what to say. I could understand his side of things now, but he was right—it didn't excuse what he'd done to me. He had robbed me of any security I should have had in my already messed-up life. My home was supposed to be my refuge, and he had turned it into my own personal hell.

Suddenly, Eldrick put his big hands on my shoulders. He pulled me in, holding me firmly against his body. Before I could respond, I felt him press his lips against the top of my head.

"Forgive me," he murmured against my hair.

I was too stunned to move, much less make a sound.

"Can you? Would you?"

"I-I …" It was as though someone had packed all my brains into a blender and hit frappe.

He held me even tighter, squeezing me so hard I could barely breathe. "I understand now why your father did what he did. You are precious, indeed. I find you vastly less repulsive than the rest of your species."

"Thank you, I think." My voice was muffled because my head was being mashed into his shoulder. "It's okay, Eldrick. I'm not angry with you."

"Are you certain?" His eyes were wide and bewildered as he released me.

"Yes." I stepped back and gave him a smile. "You're my friend. Whatever happened with those people before—as long as I'm alive, I won't let it happen again."

His expression faltered, twitching for a moment as he glanced all around. Had I broken him? Or maybe he was having some kind of internal meltdown? Was he about to explode?

Eldrick laughed.

I froze, gaping as he doubled over and wrapped his arms around his stomach. He had the most beautiful, deep, rich laugh I'd ever heard.

When he finally came up for air, his face was flushed and there were tears in his eyes. "Josie Barton," he said my name like he couldn't believe it.

"Yes?"

Eldrick leaned down closer, still chuckling under his breath. "You are the strangest person I have ever met."

Eldrick wasn't enjoying watching any of the movies I had chosen so far. Big surprise there. Unfortunately for him, this was *my* apartment and I was going to watch whatever it took to get my mind off where Zeph might be.

Sitting side-by-side on the couch, I was still glad to have his company—even though he was glowering at the TV screen with his lip curled. His noisy disgust was annoying, but it was helping to distract me from the way the hours were dragging by. My gaze wandered to the clock hanging in the kitchen again. Geez, where was he? It was well past midnight already, and Zeph still wasn't home.

Okay, no need to start panicking. This wasn't abnormal. He'd always worked late shifts before we met, so I was probably being paranoid.

"This is utterly ridiculous," Eldrick complained.

I threw a few kernels of popcorn at him. "Hush! This is a classic. Cinderella is one of the best love stories of all time."

"By whose authority? Why on earth would any faerie simply flutter in and grant this silly woman all her wishes for nothing? It makes no sense. And to make the spells only last until midnight? What good does that do anyone?" he protested. I couldn't take him seriously when he had popcorn stuck in his hair, though. "If she's supposed to be the godmother of this woman, why hasn't she been helping her before this? And why does everyone keep singing? God, the infernal *singing*—it never ends."

"This was supposed to be fun, you know." I sighed. "You're ruining the story."

"This story was forfeit long before I was forced to endure it."

I shot him a glare. "Keep it up and we'll watch it again."

Eldrick snapped his mouth shut. With his arms folded over his chest, he sank down into the couch and sulked. Just when I thought he'd given up, I heard him mutter under his breath, "Preposterous. A pumpkin is a terrible item to render into a carriage. The smell would be repugnant. This so-called 'faerie godmother' is obviously a hack."

I was debating on pouring the whole bowl of popcorn over his head when the front door burst open. Zeph staggered in, his shoulders drooping with exhaustion—or at least, it kind of looked like him. Something was off …

His hair was short!

It was still the same dark brown color, but it was trimmed and styled much shorter now.

Zeph dragged his feet all the way to the couch and plopped down next to me with a loud sigh. "Why are you guys still awake? You have any idea how late it is?"

My breath caught when he leaned over and suddenly laid his head onto my shoulder. I caught a waft of his smell as the stubble on his jaw prickled my shoulder.

"I-I guess we just lost track of time," I rasped.

"Is that so?" He raised his head and squinted at me, his mouth puckered like he didn't buy it. "Well, it's way past your bedtime now, jailbait. Mine, too."

As soon as Zeph mentioned going to bed, my dark wolfish friend cleared his throat. He muttered something under his breath as he stood and disappeared into the guest bedroom. The door banged shut.

"What's up with him?" Zeph gave me a suspicious look. "You two been makin' out? Did I interrupt?"

I glared at him.

"Oh I get it. He's been trying to work up the nerve to hold your hand this whole time. For a prince, he doesn't have much in the self-esteem department."

"Eldrick does *not* like me *that* way!" My voice cracked and my chest was tight and breathless as I shoved him off me. The fact that he would even suggest something like that made my blood boil. Zeph knew how I felt. He was taunting me on purpose—he had to be!

"Don't get your panties in a twist."

"Why would you even say that?" I looked away.

"I was just kidding."

"Well, it's not funny." I got up and switched off the TV. My feelings were already raw, and learning about his curse certainly hadn't helped soothe me any. What the hell was his problem? Why did he have to treat it like one big joke? Eldrick had seemed so sure that Zeph was in love with me. He'd acted like it should be obvious.

I wasn't convinced.

I needed to hear those words leave Zeph's lips before I would ever believe it. But as I stood there, looking into his indifferent stare, I realized ... that might never happen. He'd just keep stringing me on, dodging the issue, and sending me all these mixed signals.

Stomping back to my bedroom, I barely got inside the door when I felt a strong grip on my arm. Zeph pulled me to a halt, towering over me with a severe expression.

"What's the matter with you?" he demanded. "Did that prick say something bad to you? Did he threaten you? I'm serious, Josie. It's one thing for him to mouth off, but I'm not gonna stand by and let him make you feel unsafe."

I tried to squirm away, but he wouldn't let up. A hard knot burned in the back of my throat when I saw him shut the door behind us. As soon as he faced me again, his violet eyes meeting mine in the dim light of my bedroom, I couldn't hold it in anymore.

"Do you love me, Zeph?" The question tore past all my better judgment and left my lips before I could stop it.

Pain flashed in his eyes. His mouth twitched, and he let go of my arm. "Don't ask me that," his voice was unsteady.

"I deserve to know. So far, you've lied about every connection you have with me. Don't lie to me again—not about this."

He began avoiding my eyes and backing away toward the door like he might try to bolt. When I grabbed at the front of his shirt to stop him, he winced and hissed out a string of curses like I'd stung him.

When I drew my hand away, my fingers were dripping red.

"W-what is this?" I pulled back the front of his coat to see fresh blood running down his chest. The whole front of his shirt was soaked.

"It's not that bad." He tried to turn away so I couldn't see. "Honestly. It hurts like hell, but it's not a big deal."

I pulled his coat off his shoulders to get a better look. I wasn't sure what passed as a "big deal" in his world, but it certainly looked serious to me. There was a deep wound in his shoulder, right beneath his collarbone.

My throat went dry. "You're hurt!"

"It's not as bad as it—"

"You have to sit down!" I shrieked. "Right now, sit down and don't move!"

I bolted to the bathroom and ripped all the contents of the cabinet under my sink out onto the floor. I snatched up a first aid kit, several towels, and wet a few washcloths before I ran back to the bedroom. My hands were shaking. I couldn't stop it. There was so much blood. Was this even going to help? Should I just call 911?

When I came back in, Zeph shot me that signature annoyed glance with his eyebrow arched. He sat obediently on the floor beside the bed with his shirt off, pressing it over the wound as a makeshift bandage.

"Seriously, it's fine," he mumbled like I was wasting my time over nothing. "It'll be healed up by morning. Calm down. You look like you're about to have a heart attack."

I knelt down in front of him, frantically opening the kit of medical supplies. My vision blurred and I kept dropping things.

He grabbed my chin and turned my face toward him. "Hey. Look at me. I'm fine, okay? You're hyperventilating."

There was so much blood on his shirt … Nothing about that was fine. "B-but, Zeph—"

"I'll talk you through it. Get one of those washcloths and clean it out. You're gonna need some of that rubbing alcohol, too. It's a puncture, and it's pretty deep, so be sure you pour a lot on there." He explained each step in a calm, even voice. It was soothing, and I found myself able to concentrate as I cleaned his wound.

"Who did this to you? I thought you said you were at work?"

Zeph flinched, and his thick arms tensed up when I poured the alcohol into his wound. "I wasn't lying about that, believe it or not. A couple of biker gangs always pass through the bar this time of year as one of their regular watering holes. They know Hank pretty well, and they get rowdy once the booze starts flowing. We have a hard time keeping them under control. And tonight, they picked a fight with some of the local idiots. I just got caught in the crossfire while I was tryin' to break things up."

I pressed a warm washcloth against the cut. "Remind me to slap Hank for this. He shouldn't be using you like his personal muscle. You're a bartender, not a bouncer. There are people out there who are trained for this kind of thing. What did they stab you with?"

"A broken bottle. And hey, it's not like I care. I regenerate quickly. Better they stab me than someone important."

"You *are* important!" I began layering thick cotton bandages over the puncture. "Hank is going to get it, I swear. You just wait till I get a hold of him. What would I do if something happened to you? How am I supposed to—"

"Seriously, you need to take a few deep breaths," he interrupted. "I've been cut up way worse than this. It'll be fine."

I seethed quietly as I finished wrapping his shoulder in layers of gauze. It wasn't a professional job, but it was the best I could do. I was already reciting what I would say to Hank the next time I saw him, muttering it through my teeth like a madwoman.

Zeph laughed.

"It's not funny!"

"It kinda is," he snickered. "I know plenty of fae who would like to put a bullet between my eyes just for spite because they know it wouldn't kill me—it'd just really hurt. Simple human weapons usually won't do much damage, and most fae heal up fast anyway."

I sat back on my heels, staring down at my hands. I could see pink traces of his blood under my fingernails. He was always teasing me, always playing stuff off like it was one big joke. Now was not the time for that—

not when I'd just been wrist deep in *his* blood. My heart wrenched. Was that really how he felt about me? Was I just one big joke to him?

"Josie." Zeph's voice was serious again. "What happened while I was gone? What did Eldrick do? You were fine before I left."

"He didn't do anything," I whispered.

As we both fell silent, I forced myself to look up at him again. His expression caught me off guard. It was like a terrified little boy about to face his worst nightmare. I'd never seen him so vulnerable.

"Eldrick told me about your curse," I confessed. "About how you challenged Fir Darrig, and how only delivering the vessel to him by the next Singing Moon will save your life."

The child-like vulnerability vanished. His eyes flashed. "That nosy little jackass. Can't mind his own damn business! Has to pilfer around in mine every time I—"

"It's true, then?" I said quietly. "You're dying?"

Zeph's anger dissipated. He wiped one of my cheeks with his thumb. Until then, I hadn't realized tears were running down my face.

"Stop that, princess," he scolded me gently as he wrapped his rough, warm hand around the back of my neck. He pulled me closer until our foreheads bumped against one another. "Don't cry for me. It's not fair. Do you have any idea how hard I've worked to try to make you happy? Even if I did a shitty job at it."

"I won't let you die, Zeph," I promised. "I'll kill Fir Darrig myself, if that's what it takes."

"Keep saying stupid stuff like that, and you're gonna get me in big trouble." I could hear a smile in his voice.

I pushed my forehead harder against his. "You've been nothing but trouble since you first broke down my door."

"Yeah. I guess that's true."

Closing my eyes, I drank in the silence as we sat together. He was so close. So why did it still feel like he was worlds away? I had to cross that distance, somehow. I had to find some reason to touch him.

"What happened to your hair?" I ran my fingers through it. Wearing it shorter changed his whole appearance. It suited his squared features and sturdy jaw line much better.

"Hank happened," he muttered sulkily. "He said it was this or a hairnet. I'm *not* wearing a hairnet."

I giggled, teasing his bangs so they stood straight up. "I like it. If not for all those tattoos, you might pass for a respectable member of society now."

Zeph glanced at his bare arms in surprise, as though he hadn't realized the tattoos made such a difference. I couldn't keep my gaze from following the swirling, colorful designs that covered the skin from his wrists all the way to his pectorals—the shapes of flowers, koi fish, thorny rose vines, and feathers.

Suddenly, I realized—once again—he wasn't wearing a shirt. His chiseled physique was beyond intimidating.

"You don't like them?" he asked as he ran a finger over one of the marks on his bicep. It was shaped like a big green vine covered in red-tipped thorns.

My face flushed until I could feel my ears burning. I opened my mouth, but nothing would come out. Like them? Um, yes. I did. All teasing aside, they were unique and beautiful—just like the rest of him.

He began carefully sliding his hand down his arm. That eerie musical sound, like the faint chiming of bells, softly echoed through the air. My skin prickled. A shiver ran up my spine, spreading tingling warmth all the way to the tips of my fingers. I was completely captivated as he wiped away the tattoos on his skin like they were nothing but marker on a dry erase board.

With a flourish of his fingers, Zeph began running his hand back over his arm again. The chimes echoed through my bedroom, whispering over my skin and making me shudder. The motion of his hand left a trail of new designs on his skin—more intricate and colorful than ever before. They seemed to move, all squirming against one another for space until at last, they froze in place.

My lips parted as a skipping breath left my lips. I knew this was magic. It was the most intensely beautiful thing I'd ever seen.

"What's that look for?" He smirked and flicked the end of my nose playfully. "You're blushing again. Even your big ole ears are red."

"I don't have big ears!"

He chucked while he tugged on one of my earlobes. "You totally do. Like a baby cow or something."

"Stop that!" I tried to swat his hands away.

It didn't work. Zeph seized both my arms in his strong hands. He pulled me closer and closer, a dark, mischievous glint in his violet eyes.

My pulse raced, and I couldn't look away.

"Like I said," he growled deeply as he yanked me down onto his lap. "You're gonna get me in big trouble."

As he slid his hands from my arms to my waist, I got the feeling *I* was the one who might be in trouble. I was straddling his lap, trying not to freak out. I couldn't stop trembling. Every inch of me was flushed and extra sensitive at the places where our skin touched. Blasts of his hot breath puffed over my neck and his hair tickled my cheek.

"I must scare you." I could feel his lips brushing the skin right under my ear. "Is that why you're shaking? Or are you just trying to tempt me? That's a bad idea, you know."

I bit down on my bottom lip and closed my eyes.

His voice grew softer. "My willpower isn't that great."

Zeph hesitated. I felt his body tense for a second. Then he kissed the side of my neck. His warm lips pressed against my skin, sending waves of tingling adrenaline blooming through my body. My hips instinctively moved against his. His warm, musky scent saturated my nose.

I gasped as he began twisting his fingers into my hair, holding the back of my head and bringing me so close that I could feel his chest moving with every word he spoke. "You have no idea how …" I could hear the conviction in his voice, but before he seemed able to finish that thought, he suddenly pulled away. "We can't do this."

I was still in a daze. "Do what?"

He twirled a finger, gesturing to how I was sitting on him. "This. All of this, right here. You're too young, I'm too old, and I'm damn sure your dad wouldn't like it. Get up. You're supposed to be in bed."

My mouth fell open.

What the hell? He'd just gone from doing *that* to ordering me around like an overbearing babysitter in under a minute. I was too stunned to even protest as he slid out from underneath me and stood.

Zeph made a big, awkward show of tucking me in. He tried to laugh and be casual as he kissed my forehead and switched off the lamp, but I could see the nervous tension written all over his face. His smile was thin, fizzling before it ever reached his eyes. He closed the bedroom door, leaving me alone in the dark.

He was throwing up walls again—holding me out at a distance. I could feel it, like a growing rift tearing us apart. Before, knowing he was keeping his distance and holding back all those secrets had filled me with so much anger. Why would he lie to me? Why would he push me away? Why would he refuse to tell me how he felt?

Now, I knew exactly why.

He was still trying to protect me. He didn't believe he could break his curse, and he wasn't going to hand me over to Fir Darrig. Zeph thought he was going to die. He must have also thought that if he told me how he felt, if he let it show, or if I got too attached ... I'd somehow be dragged down with him.

But it was too late for that.

If he was going out like a dying star, then I was already doomed to burn in his wake.

Everyone at school was overjoyed to have Joe Noble back with all his charm, smiles, and dazzling charisma. The teachers showered him with praise. They couldn't stop telling him how proud they were that he was handling this difficult time in his life with such optimism and positivity. Our classmates tripped all over themselves to talk to him, and even the popular girls followed him down the halls between classes, asking about how our relationship was going.

Whether it was genuine or just the effects of some spell he'd cast over them, it was driving me nuts. I couldn't get a moment's peace no matter where I went. Zeph, on the other hand, basked in all the attention behind his Joe-disguise. He was eating it up, and simultaneously dragged me into the spotlight with him as the ever-supportive "girlfriend."

After a few weeks of that crap, I was kinda starting to miss being a social outcast.

"We were thinking, you know, since it's almost the end of the year, what if we dedicated the yearbook to your mom? You know, like, with her picture and everything." One of the girls in our calculus class had invited herself to sit on top of my desk so she could talk to Joe. She had become a familiar fixture there, although she seldom acknowledged my existence.

I could see her scheme from a mile away. It didn't take a genius to figure out she was up to no good. She batted her eyes a little too much, and was always twirling her hair or nibbling coyly on the end of her pencil when she eyed Zeph—er, Joe. Ugh. It's like she had no sense of shame at all.

"Wouldn't that be awesome?" She smiled hopefully.

"Sure, I'll ask her." Joe tossed his perfect golden locks out of his eyes and gave her a dazzling, Hollywood smile.

Seriously The *yearbook*? Had he completely lost it? I knew there was probably steam coming out of my ears, but I was determined not to get involved in a conversation with her. I kept my eyes on my homework.

"Great! We'll need a picture of her, too." The girl tapped her lips with her pencil suggestively, "I'm Anna, by the way. I hope you don't mind me asking, but are you two going to prom together? I mean, I heard you were a couple, but you don't really act like it. You never, like, hold hands or anything anymore."

I almost cracked my pen in half.

Behind me, Joe sounded genuinely confused. "Prom? I didn't even know you guys had one."

"Yeah, totally! The theatre kids always pick the theme. It's a masquerade ball this year," she added with a flirty giggle. "Do you have a date?"

"Of course. If there's a dance, I'm going with my girlfriend, Josie. She's the love of my life. We're getting engaged after graduation," he answered so fast it made my head spin.

"O-oh," Anna stammered. Her tone was as stunned as it was critical. "That's, um, so sweet. Congratulations."

This whole charade had just reached a new level of ridiculous. I waited until Anna gathered up the shattered pieces of her pride and moved back to her own desk, before I leaned back and whispered to him, "Are you insane? You can't let them dedicate our yearbook to someone who doesn't exist!"

"Oh, come on. What does it matter? It's a lousy high school yearbook.

Who cares?" he muttered back.

"I care! Don't you realize they'll probably want to meet this imaginary mother of yours?" I was having a difficult time keeping my voice down.

"Oh, gee, that should be a real problem. Especially for a guy who can change shape like, um, a changeling?" He mocked me in my own frantic tone.

"You can't just go meddling around like that, injecting yourself into people's lives and then going on your merry way!"

He snorted. "Of course I can. I've done it before plenty of times. This doesn't even come close to my best work."

"Best work? What are you talking about?" I snuck a glance back at him.

He leaned back in his desk, looking incredibly proud of himself. His violet eyes twinkled with mischief. "Let's say, I've made one small step for mankind."

I gaped. "W-what?"

"Well, faeriekind, to be exact." He winked at me. "I can't take all the credit, though. I didn't plan on doing it. I just happened to be in the right place at the right time. That Armstrong guy has the shittiest luck."

"You … You're unbelievable!" I covered my mouth to hide my horror. I didn't want anyone else around us getting suspicious. "You killed him!"

Zeph rolled his eyes like I was making a big deal out of nothing. "No! Geez, I'm not *that* bad. I just put him to sleep for a bit. You know, gave him a little magical faerie nap. It didn't hurt him, and he still thought he went to the moon, so no harm done. He just, well, didn't actually go. I did."

I put my head down on my desk. "Who hijacks a trip to the moon? You're a lunatic."

"Which makes you an even bigger one for wanting to be around me," he countered.

"What else have you done? Shot Kennedy? Crossed the Delaware?"

Joe laughed and tugged at my braid like he was playing with it. "No. But maybe you shouldn't look too closely at the statue of David."

"I think I'm gonna be sick," I buried my face in the crease of my textbook. I'd seen Zeph flaunt his powers before; he could change his whole appearance as easily as other people changed clothes. I hadn't thought about all the shenanigans he might get into if he used his magic to make himself look like someone famous.

"Get used to it, princess." He still sounded smug. "Mischief and magic is what I do best."

Those words were still buzzing around in my head at the end of the school day. The mental image I now had of the statue of David wasn't helping, either. Against his advice, I'd looked it up on my phone to see what he was talking about. The statue's face definitely bore an uncanny resemblance to a certain trouble-causing changeling. Now I couldn't think about it without imagining the David holding a cigarette between his lips.

Okay, fine. It was a *little* funny.

After school let out, we walked home together holding hands like a normal couple. Regardless of how much mischief he was stirring up at my school, I couldn't deny that holding his hand made me happy. It might not have meant much to him; grown men—er, faeries—didn't usually care about that kind of little thing, did they? Even though I knew he was keeping up the ruse of us being a couple, it always made my heartbeat fast with excitement to feel his fingers laced through mine. I couldn't hold back my nervous smile.

When we rounded the last corner, Zeph wheezed strangely all of a sudden. He stumbled and pulled his hand away from mine, gasping for breath and clutching his chest.

"Zeph? What's wrong?" I called after him.

No answer.

I chased after him as he ducked into a nearby alleyway, barely making it out of sight before his magical illusion began to fall apart. He melted back into his usual, human-looking shape with a sudden shudder. His face was ashen, and sweat beaded on his forehead as he clenched his teeth.

"Are you all right?" I reached for his arm to help him stand, but he brushed me off.

"I-I'm fine," he gasped as he doubled over, his shoulders trembling. "I-it's just hard to keep up the illusion all day."

"You're getting weaker." My heart twisted painfully in my chest. I knew it had to be because the night of the Singing Moon was getting closer. "Let's go home. You need to rest."

He was still huffing and puffing. "Just gimme a second."

"You can't keep doing this and working for Hank, too. It's a waste of your power. I can go to school without Joe. I've done it before." I tried to reason with him. "I'm not scared anymore. I can handle it by myself."

He stood up straight again, but his face still looked pale. "It's not about being scared, Josie. It isn't safe."

"So I'll bring Eldrick, instead."

He clenched his teeth and looked away. "I … I'm not sure I can cast the glamour on him anymore. It might not stick."

A weight settled over my body. Doing this for me was hurting him—I was hurting him.

Zeph touched my cheek, brushing a thumb over my chin. He gave me another hollow smile. "I'll be fine."

"Is it because of what happened with that woman at the fair?" I steeled myself as I met his gaze. "You said that woman, Lumi, might be working for Fir Darrig. Is that why all these things have been happening to me? Why you moved in across the hall? Fir Darrig knows who I am, doesn't he?"

Despite the way he was still panting and sweating, Zeph's face became steely. "We're not talking about that. Not another word. I mean it."

"I can't stand by and do nothing. I won't watch you suffer."

This was too much. When it came to losing people I loved, I knew exactly what kind of hell I was in for. I'd already gone down that road more times than anyone ever should—first my mother and brother, and then with my father. Now Zeph was withering away right in front of my eyes.

I couldn't go through this again.

"Don't overreact. I'm just a little tired." His hands were shaking as he took out his lighter and one of Hank's cigarettes. He could barely hold it steady long enough to light it. Once he'd taken in a few deep breaths of the smoke, he let out a deep sigh and his shoulders relaxed. "Let's go home."

"You're lying again! If it's magic you need, then let me give you some of my power. I know I'm the vessel. You said I could share my power with anyone I choose. Let me help you."

Zeph froze. He stared at me, eyes wide, and his mouth open slightly. "How did you …"

I bit the inside of my cheek. I knew because of Eldrick, but I wasn't about to throw him under the bus.

"No," he snapped and threw down his cigarette butt. It'd taken him less than a minute to burn through it.

"But I am the vessel, aren't I? You've known that all along. You even borrowed power from me before. That's how you were able to purge the sylph out of that little boy, isn't it? How is this any different?"

"Because I *refuse* to be like Fir Darrig!" He roared suddenly, his violet eyes flashing and his fang-like teeth emerging for an instant—giving me a glimpse of the monster beneath his human disguise.

Zeph took a step toward me, still snarling. "I know I've already fallen far. I've broken ancient laws and made myself a heretic in the eyes of my kind. But I won't use you like that. If it's to save someone else, then fine— I'll do what has to be done. But not for this, not to compensate for my own mistakes!"

I stumbled back, almost tripping over my own feet.

As soon as he noticed my reaction, he relaxed. His shoulders sagged and his expression drooped, looking to the ground as though he were ashamed. "Josie, I'm so sorry. Eldrick told you a lot, I guess."

I got a twinge of guilt. I didn't like having to go behind his back to get answers, but he'd left me no choice.

"Please, try to understand. I had to do everything I could to hide you from Fir Darrig and whoever else he might send to track you down. I … I knew coming here, living near you, would get complicated. But the closer it gets to the Singing Moon, the harder he's gonna try. I had to make sure you were safe."

"That's why you tried to ditch me, at first?" I crossed my arms.

"No, geez, I wasn't trying to ..." He rubbed the back of his neck and growled. "You gotta understand, at my side is always gonna be first place Fir Darrig will look for you. Maybe I should've told you about all this sooner, but I just thought it would be better if you could hang on to a few more weeks of your innocence. I hoped maybe you wouldn't get attached to me."

"Too late."

He sighed. "I know."

"Borrowing some of my power when you need it doesn't change anything, Zeph. Not for me. I don't see you as a mooch or a user, if that's what you're so afraid of. But if it's your pride getting in the way, well, you're just going to have to swallow it for a while—at least until we can figure this out."

His mouth flattened as he raised an unblinking stare to me. "It's not just that. Knowing what you are means things will start to change—the more of that power you use, the harder it'll be for you to hide. That's why you *cannot* learn magic. It's bad enough for me to use your power, but if do it yourself, you'll put off a powerful aura and start to draw more and more fae to you." He was searching my face, his violet eyes catching the sunlight as they moved. "The fact that you haven't used it yet is the only thing that still keeps you hidden. But on your eighteenth birthday, when the Singing Moon rises, not even that will matter. You'll be exposed, and Fir Darrig will come. With or without me, you'll have to face him."

"I'm not afraid," I repeated. "But if it's all the same to you, I'd rather face him together."

He swallowed. His cheeks began to flush.

I stretched a hand out toward him. "So don't give up. We can fight this together. Please, let's just try."

As he stared at my outstretched palm, Zeph's expression slowly darkened. The walls were coming back up, and there was nothing I could do to stop it. "No, Josie. You're not gonna fight. That's not what your dad wanted. It's not what I want for you, either."

"What about what I want?" I frowned.

He looked away and never answered.

Now I was the one keeping secrets.

Zeph crashed as soon as we came back from school every day. Sometimes he slept in my bed, sometimes on my couch, but he never went back to his apartment. I didn't know if that was because he'd run out of his food at his own place, or just didn't want to let me out of his sight, but I was betting on the latter. Paranoid? Yeah. A little. He still insisted on going to school with me disguised as Joe, but I knew he was stretching himself thin. The length of time he could hold the disguise together grew shorter and shorter. Going to school during the day and then working at night was just too much for him, even if he was too proud to admit it.

While Zeph slept, I cooked and finished my homework, playing the role of the meek little orphan girl, just like he wanted. Around 5 PM Zeph finally stirred. He was always grouchy and incoherent, but after I fed him a big dinner, he was able to drag himself to work at the bar. Hank let him change his hours, so he came home earlier, but it still put him working until midnight.

The second the front door closed and I was positive Zeph was out of the building, I snapped into action. Eldrick and I carried all our materials into the living room and got to work. I'd sacrificed one of my school notebooks entirely to practicing some of the spells I thought might come in handy. Sooner or later, I was going to have to start memorizing them. Baby steps.

First, I had to figure out how all this worked.

Eldrick was true to his word, and he had been helping me learn to read the faerie language. He was also teaching me the basics of spellwork, though he admitted it wasn't his specialty. I was his first student.

"As a faerie, my ability to cast magic is innate. My species doesn't often need to draw out spellwork, unless it's to mark our territory, use a spell that is unnatural to us, or to curse someone," he said as he carried in yet another big box of my dad's research. He placed it carefully in the middle of the floor and sat down. He took out books and old scrolls, spreading them out all around us. "But as a human, you will always have to use written spellwork. The details must be precise and perfect. Even one minor flaw could have catastrophic results."

I sat down next to him, armed with my notebook and a pen, as usual. Seeing all of my dad's work, years upon years of it, laid out before me always left me feeling very small. I'd never known he was working on something like this. He had been so careful to hide it from me when I was younger.

Now I needed to know—I needed to learn everything I could, and not just because of what might happen to Zeph. That was a huge part of it, yes, but I also wanted to learn to defend myself. If Fir Darrig came for me—now, tomorrow, or ten years from now—I was going to be ready. I was going to give him one hell of a fight.

"You were doing quite well yesterday," Eldrick commented as he handed me a thick, ragged journal. I had already begun reading it, although interpreting the faerie language was a real challenge for me at first. It was like trying to peek through all those spiraling, thorny, vine-like marks to see the real message hidden behind them. Eldrick was right; it did come to me as if by pure instinct, and the more I read, the easier it became.

For hours, while Zeph was away at work, I studied magic and spellwork. I read my dad's journals, and thumbed my way through all the old documents he had collected. So many of them contained intricate illustrations not only of spells, but also artifacts and maps. Reading them was like stepping off the edge of reality into a dream. I was immersed in that world. My soul was drenched with wonder at everything I learned. And with every page I studied, I found myself ravenous for more.

Time always seemed to blitz by, never leaving me in a good place to pause my work when it came time to hide everything again. I was learning so much about the faerie world, and more importantly, about my dad. Reading his journal was like crossing time and space to have a heart-to-heart chat with him. It was as surreal as it was precious to me.

I ran my fingers across the pages covered in my dad's handwriting. This journal was all about the history of Fir Darrig and a group of other faeries. He called them the pilgrims—a word I had heard numerous times now. According to his journal, the five pilgrims had been the first faeries to ever come to our world. They'd fled here after the destruction of their own world, somewhere far across time and space, and had come searching for a new place to call home. It reminded me of what Eldrick had said before—about how he had not been born in the human world. Now … I finally understood it.

I was surprised that of five pilgrims, I recognized most of the names. There were two I'd never heard of before, Aneira and Belisma, but I knew the name Gabriel right away. Dad's rushed notes said that he was a sylph lord of incredible beauty with wings of gold. All the sylphs running around now, be they good or bad, were his descendants. Then there was Erebos, which was a name I recognized from Greek mythology. Although Dad's journal explained he was apparently a type of faerie called a barghest. He was known by many other names and titles, including the "Bogeyman." Later that had somehow been changed to boogeyman, just as Zeph had said. Sometimes he appeared as a great black dog, often with three heads, and other times he was more wolf-like.

Erebos, I suspected, must be Eldrick's father.

Lastly, I recognized Fir Darrig's name. Written beneath it were lengthy descriptions and details, many jumped together as though they'd been added over time. Fir Darrig was a sidhe. He had been a beautiful, powerful faerie who served as an advisor in the courts of human kings and queens for ages. He was revered by his own kind, and loved by all as a wise and gentle spirit, represent the beauty and purity of nature.

But like in all faerie tales, something had gone wrong. My dad still hadn't been sure what it was exactly. He wrote that he suspected it had something to do with a human, a princess, that had done something terrible to Fir Darrig. My dad wasn't positive about all that, but he did seem very sure that this incident is what most likely led to the original split between the two faerie courts.

I stopped reading for a moment. "Eldrick?"

"Yes?" he answered from over the rim of a coffee mug, as usual.

"Did you know Fir Darrig before all this?" I held up the journal so he could see which part I was reading.

Eldrick scanned the page. "I knew of him, but I didn't know him personally," he said. "He's far older than I am. My father found him obnoxious, although apparently not enough to avoid marrying into his bloodline."

"Y-you mean ..."

"Yes." He leaned back in his seat again and went on sipping on his fifth cup of coffee. "My mother is one of Fir Darrig's daughters."

I had to let that sink in for a moment. "What about Zeph? I mean, I know you said his father was some kind of shapeshifter. But no one knows who is mother is?"

Eldrick flicked me a glance over the rim of his mug. "No. You see, Hedley Kow is a well-known philanderer, especially when it comes to lovely faerie women. He's been known to use his abilities to trick them into, well, I'm sure you can figure that part out for yourself. Among our people, there are few who could count themselves more lovely than the sidhe."

I blushed. Wow. I wondered if Zeph had ever ...

"You must understand that as a race, the sidhe are very proud. They possess a great deal of magical power that surpasses most other fae. They are the ones most often depicted in famous artwork, and they are frequently mistaken for angels or even gods and goddesses. But for all their beauty, they have one weakness."

I held my breath. "What is it?"

He smiled strangely, almost sadly. "The same weakness that all fae share, regardless of our particular species. We have an inborn, often uncontrollable, interest in humanity. We cannot help it. None of us are exempt from that innate desire to be close to humankind."

"Oh." I wasn't expecting that. "But Zeph told me before that there are lots of faeries who hate humans now. Even you did, right?"

"True. Our attachment to your kind consistently causes problems. It's an inconvenient instinct." He placed his mug down on the table. "To understand us fully, Josie, you must stop trying to compare us to humans. We don't think the way you do. We don't react the same way. You have to put aside that expectation."

I frowned. As much as I wanted to, I didn't understand.

"Take for example the beasts of your own world. In remote places where humans have yet set foot, wild creatures do not fear you. They often seek you out rather than running away, curious to learn what you are. That is their instinct—something entirely beyond their control," he explained, his brow crinkling with thought. "In that same way, our initial instinct is to want to be close to humans. However after generations upon generations of negative experiences, we have learned that not all of you mean well. Our curiosity has become caution and fear, which can evolve into hatred given the right … encouragement. This is what became of Fir Darrig, or so the rumor goes."

"This princess did something to him, didn't she?" I dared to ask. "To make Fir Darrig turn on everyone?"

Eldrick seemed to grow distant. He looked away, staring at the pile of scrolls and papers all around us. "I'm afraid I don't know exactly what transpired, but I can imagine that loving someone would make a person—or even a fae—blind to any ulterior motives. No one sees a dagger in the hand of someone they love until it is already planted in their back."

The journal in my hands suddenly felt heavier. I ran my fingers over the crinkled, weathered pages again. Eldrick's words were sad, but I couldn't deny their truth.

I went on reading. My dad had been searching for ways to bind or catch faeries, and he wrote down all of his experiments in great detail. In most of them, he'd used Zeph as his guinea pig. Lining spell circles in salt worked best for dealing with most spirits—just like with the sylph. Although, he had also been experimenting with the use of a variety of other things, as well—oils, wax, herbs, and even different varieties of gemstones.

Dad had found that certain stones contained crystallized magical energy that could be used to strengthen spellwork. Rubies, for instance, contained vast amounts of concentrated magical power, the most of any stone he'd studied. There was even a rare kind, a star ruby, that was basically the equivalent of a magical bomb. Opals, sapphires, and quartz were quite potent, too. Ironically, diamonds didn't contain much magic, so they weren't very valuable for spellwork. The problem with the stones was that they sort of behaved like a bullet for a gun. You could use them once, draw out their full power in a burst or even to contain something inside them, but after that … they were essentially useless.

Well, for magical purposes, anyway.

It also only worked if the stones were natural. They had to be formed in nature, cultivated over time to absorb magic. Gems and stones produced in a lab wouldn't contain any magic at all, and were also useless for spellwork.

I kept reading, burying my nose in my dad's words while the last few minutes ticked away. Zeph would be back soon. I'd have to make sure to have everything hidden before then. I didn't want to imagine how he'd react if he caught me studying faerie magic like this.

Despite all the research Dad had done, the pages upon pages of handwritten notes and illustrations, and all the time he had poured into trying out different combinations of spells and materials, at the end of the last journal, he admitted he still didn't think he had found something strong enough to contain a being like Fir Darrig. For that problem, Dad believed there was one solution—only one spell in the entire history of the fae that could possibly seal Fir Darrig away forever.

He called it the Fibbing Gate.

Even the word, written in the faerie language, curled upon itself as though it were trying to hide. It was a spell, some ancient tool for passing from one realm to the next. A portal. Dad wrote that he didn't quite understand it, but he knew it involved the use of a strange mineral called staurolite. In the middle of the page, Dad had sketched out what looked like a three-dimensional cross shape.

"A weeping stone." Eldrick was reading over my shoulder.

His closeness made me jump in surprise. "A what?"

"It goes back to our pilgrimage into your world," he explained. "A very, *very* long time ago, even before the first songs. Our kind came into this world through an ancient gateway, fleeing from an unspeakable terror that was ravaging our own realm. Our home had become a place of darkness and fear—a place without moonlight."

My skin prickled. "What … kind of terror?"

Memories flickered in the depths of his silver eyes. "There is no word for them in the human language. We called them skiia—the devourers. They cannot be bargained or reasoned with. Their only motive is to drain every drop of magic they possibly can, and as they do, they spread like a plague."

I swallowed and sank back in my seat.

"We came here as refugees after our own world was overrun," Eldrick murmured. "Humankind looked upon us with awe and adoration. We made our home here, eager to share this beautiful world with you, but not before sealing away the ancient gateway so that the evil destroying our own homeland would never find its way here."

"The Fibbing Gate," I whispered.

Eldrick's body shuddered at the name. "I was very young when it happened. My memories of it have all but faded to nothing. In that same way, such stories of the gateway have become myths. My father told them to me as a child." He ran one of his fingers over the drawing on the page.

"Weeping stones were said to guard it. They stones are made of iron, which as you know has incredible power against faerie magic, so that no one would ever be able to open it again."

"Why would my dad be interested in it?"

His expression steeled as he studied the page. "I don't know," he finally admitted. "But there's someone else who might."

"Who?" I waited anxiously.

"Zeph's brother, Frederic, gave up practicing changeling magic to become a scholar for the Seelie Court," he muttered quietly. "He's a guardian of the ancient songs, a keeper of the scrolls."

Suddenly, the front door burst open.

Zeph stood in the doorway, a tower of wrath. His violet eyes glowed with fury as he stormed into the room. "You," he roared and slammed the door with a violent crack. "What the *hell* do you think you're doing?"

Eldrick growled back, a beastly sound that brought back memories of when I had first seen him as that black wolf. Somewhere under his sleek, handsome exterior, that beast was still lurking. "She is the vessel, so she stands in both worlds. That means she has a right to know."

The outline of Zeph's body rippled. I could see traces of glowing runes beginning to peek through his clothing. "But you had no right to tell her!"

"Her father's words have told her, not mine. You are the one with no right—no right to keep his findings from her!" Eldrick's form began to waver, as well. In the blink of an eye, his human shape dissolved into a churning black mist. When it became solid again, he took the shape of that huge, silver-eyed wolf. His snout wrinkled as he showed his teeth.

"What's the plan, genius? You let her start slinging spells around and Fir Darrig will come here full force. You ready to fight him head-on?" Zeph snarled back, showing his own pointed canines. "Or maybe you *want* her to die so your contract will finally be broken?"

Eldrick's wolf ears slicked back, his body coiling to lunge.

"Stop it!" I stood up and put myself between them. "Zeph, it's my fault. Eldrick was just following my orders. You know he doesn't have a choice. He has to do as I say. Quit lashing out at him when I'm the one you're really pissed at."

Eldrick's growling ceased. He stared at me, his wolfish head cocked to the side.

"I'm not using you as a scapegoat. Besides, he was bound to find out what we were up to sooner or later." I smiled. "It'll be okay. I can handle this."

I turned to face Zeph again, ready to make my case. He never gave me a chance. Snatching me by the arm, he dragged me out of the apartment and tossed me into the hall.

"You can *handle* it?" he shouted.

I tried backing away, but there was only so far I could go. He pinned me against the wall, standing so close I could see tiny flecks of gold hidden in the violet color of his eyes. His nostrils flared, and a vein throbbed in the side of his neck.

"You have *no* idea what you're messing with. You stupid, *stupid* ..." His voice trailed off as though the rage were too much. He clenched his fists, making his strong arms go solid.

"Zeph—"

"How could you do this? I specifically told you not to! Don't get involved! Stay out of it! No magic—*none!*" He slammed a hand against the wall right next to me. "Are you just trying to screw with me? You think it's a joke? You want to die, is that it? You want to make me watch Fir Darrig take you?" His eyes flashed with blind fury. "What's the matter with you? Why are you doing this? Tell me!"

"FOR YOU!"

That shut him up.

For a few seconds, the only sound between us was our own furious, panting breaths as we glared at one another. Waves of anger roared through my body, making my fingers twitch and my vision spot.

"You know why I have to do this," I spoke again, trying a softer voice. "What I don't get is why you think you have to do this by yourself. You are not alone. I am here—right here—ready to fight for you. But I can't fight what I don't understand."

"I don't want you to fight at all! That's the whole damn point!" His voice broke and his shoulders seized. There was fresh agony in his gaze. "Everything I've done, everything I've sacrificed—all of it was so you could be safe! So you wouldn't have to fight! So you could have a normal life."

"Zeph, abnormal people can't have normal lives. And there's absolutely nothing normal about being a living battery for faerie magic."

"You could still be happy," he argued. "That's what you wanted. That's what you made me promise!"

"What? What are you talking about?"

"I know you don't remember. You were a kid," he rasped through deep, frustrated breaths and turned his face away. "You just ..."

"I what?" Reaching up, I gently grasped his chin so he would look at me again.

He squeezed his eyes shut, tears running down the sides of his face as he clenched his teeth. I'd never seen him this upset before. It made my insides bind up in anxious knots and any lingering flames from my temper instantly fizzled.

Slowly, Zeph took my hand and began moving my fingers around so that our pinkies were interlocked. "I used to babysit you and your brother sometimes. I probably wouldn't be anyone's first choice for a babysitter, but for some reason you would always beg me to play with you. You'd do this sad face thing where you rolled your lip out and ... well, I couldn't say no. The damn lip thing always got me."

He finally met my gaze again, tears still pooling in his eyes.

"One day in the summer the three of us were out playing in the yard. It was just around sunset. There were fireflies everywhere, so you and William wanted to run around and catch them. And you held my hand like this— with your little finger wrapped around mine. You asked me to promise that I would make you happy forever. That was the contract we made ... after you captured my heart."

My breath caught in my throat. I couldn't move. Even if I didn't remember any of that, there was no denying the brokenness on his face as he squeezed his pinky finger around mine. This wasn't a lie. This was the first real truth he'd told me. No more secrets. No more lies.

"I love you, Josie. I know it probably doesn't make any sense to you, but I have been yours alone ever since that day."

My whole body flushed as my heart seemed to freeze in my chest.

"There's nothing Fir Darrig or anyone else can do to me that will make me betray that promise. If it means I have to die to keep you away from him, then so be it. I'm not afraid of dying if it means you'll be safe. He can do whatever he wants to me. He can tear me apart—but he can't have you."

I grabbed his face, dragging him closer so I could press my mouth against his. It was clumsy and desperate, but I didn't care.

I wanted him so badly nothing else mattered.

Zeph sucked in a sharp breath and went stiff.

Oh no. Had I … just messed everything up? Had he meant a different kind of love? My brain swirled with anxiety as I began to pull away.

Zeph suddenly snagged his big arms around me. He backed me up against the wall and he kissed me back with a ferocity I wasn't expecting. The way his lips moved against mine was rough and passionate and dangerously deep. All the anger, frustration, and doubt that had built up between us shattered instantly.

I wrapped my arms around his neck, grabbing fistfuls of the back of his shirt. I could feel the thick rolling muscles of his shoulders underneath the fabric. His hold on me shifted as he lifted me off my feet, gripping my thighs and bringing my legs around his waist. The sudden contact of his hips against mine made me gasp and blush.

He broke away from our kiss and stared down at me, his expression wild and hungry as his chest heaved with ragged breaths. I could tell he was trying to make up his mind about what to do next. The question— the possibilities scrolled through his eyes like text on a news ticker: your bedroom or mine? Or maybe right here?

Every neuron in my brain was firing, screaming reminders of all my insecurities. Not pretty enough. Too short. Too skinny. No experience. Only the touch of his lips silenced those demons.

Zeph loved me—nothing else mattered.

I hooked a finger through one of his belt loops on the front of his jeans and tugged.

"That's dangerous," he warned. "I told you, my willpower isn't that great."

I smirked. "Good. I won't have to work very hard, then."

"Yeah?" He leaned in again. The stubble on his chin scratched lightly over my shoulder as he kissed the side of my neck.

I squeezed the back of his shirt tighter. It felt *so* good when he did that.

"Almost sounds like a challenge. I'm not sure you're ready for that. I'll work you harder than you can even imagine, princess." He opened his mouth and let my delicate skin scrape lightly through his teeth. It sent warm shivers of pleasure down my spine. My toes curled. An involuntary, elated sound slipped past my lips.

He chuckled darkly.

I let my eyes roll closed, my head tilting back as his lips roamed lower. "Zeph, I want—"

A loud, obnoxious buzzing noise came from Zeph's back pocket.

No ... *no!*

I deflated, slumping and opening my eyes again. He was gritting his teeth, flushed and disheveled. Zeph cursed as he put me back on the ground. He snatched his phone out like he might just hurl it into the stairwell and forget about it. Part of me hoped he would.

One glance at the screen changed his whole demeanor. He let out a loud, frustrated groan as he rolled his eyes.

"What? I'm sorta busy."

Hank's voice crackled on the other end, but I couldn't make out what he was saying.

"You can't handle that by yourself? Geez. What good are you?" Zeph was fuming as he backed away a few steps. "It's a dryad, genius. It's a freaking tree. You don't need me for that. Just use some Roundup. Or better yet, a blowtorch."

Hank's voice became louder. He sounded irritated.

"Fine, fine. I'll be there in a minute. Don't get your panties all in a twist." He muttered a few more angry curses and crammed the cell phone back into his pocket.

"A case?" I guessed.

"Yeah. I'm sorry." Zeph rubbed his forehead with the heel of his hand like he was trying to calm himself.

I stood on my toes to plant a kiss on his cheek. "Don't be. Go on, it's okay. I'll still be here when you get back."

I started for my front door when a hand smacked me on the rear end. I spun around, ready to shoot the culprit a teasing scowl, but he was already disappearing down the stairs with a cigarette between his teeth and a proud spring in his step.

Zeph didn't come back home until early the next morning. I was getting ready for school when he staggered in like a zombie. His clothes were caked with mud, and there were twigs and leaves matted in his hair. He looked as if a swamp creature had just gotten finished using him as a toothpick.

"I don't want to talk about it. So don't even start with me," he grumbled before I could even get a question out. "I'm going to bathe, then I'm going to bed. That's it."

"What? In my bed?" I called after him. "You do have your own place, you know!"

He fanned a hand at me. "Yours smells better."

Probably because I actually *washed* my sheets. "Well, don't use my pink towels. I don't want swamp stink all over them."

He tracked dirt all the way into the bathroom, leaving a slime trail like a slug. When was I going to have time to clean all that up? I stooped down to pick up a leaf that was dripping with brown, muddy goo.

"I'll take care of it." Eldrick's calm, deep voice came from behind me.

I startled and dropped the leaf. "Are you sure?"

He nodded. "You'll be late if you don't leave soon."

I smiled and pulled him into a side-hug that he only barely reciprocated. "You're the best!"

"I know," he replied in all seriousness. Then he handed me a small slip of paper. "Here."

"What's this?" I asked as I went to unfold it, but Eldrick stopped me.

"Wait until you get to school. Send one message with your location and a time, nothing more." He kept his voice hushed as he motioned to the bathroom where Zeph had just turned on the shower. "Do not mention where you live or anything specific about yourself. You must tread carefully. As far as I know, he is loyal to the Seelie Court now. However, someone in your position can never be too careful."

I didn't understand why he was acting so strangely until I sat down in my desk and took the paper out again. I unfolded it carefully, and then it all made sense. Written on the paper was a name—Frederic Everett—and a phone number. Eldrick knew we had to keep this a secret between us, but he also knew better than to trust a member of the Seelie Court with our location. Both he and Zeph were wanted men, technically.

I typed out a text exactly the way Eldrick had instructed. I gave the location of the bistro near my school where we had gone for dinner, and a time when I knew I could be there—right after school. My hands shook as I sent the message.

A few minutes later, my phone vibrated.

[UNKNOWN]: I'll be there.

I took a shaky breath, my whole body shivering as I tried to assure myself this was fine. I could handle it. I had to—Zeph's life depended on it.

I was a wreck all day, jumping at any sudden sound. My classmates asked about Joe, and I couldn't even come up with a decent excuse for his absence. When the last bell rang to release us from class, I tried to think of what I might do if things went sour. I knew a few spells now. I might be able to defend myself in a pinch … maybe.

Hopefully.

It began to snow as I walked to the bistro alone. Even though I was bundled up in my coat and scarf, my teeth wouldn't stop chattering. My legs were freezing thanks to my school uniform's skirt only coming to my knees, and my tall socks didn't do much to help. I desperately needed to invest in some stockings. Thankfully, it was a short walk.

I arrived a few minutes early. Knocking the slush off my shoes at the door, I asked the hostess for a table near the back. I sat down to wait. The longer I sat there, the more I wished Eldrick had come with me. I would have felt much more confident if he were sitting there, scowling, and sipping coffee like last time. Until that moment, I hadn't realized just how comforting his presence had become.

I sat up straight when the bistro door opened, craning my neck to see who was coming in. A man and woman standing arm-in-arm looked straight at me. Panic swirled in my stomach. Oh god. I wasn't expecting *two* of them. Moreover, I didn't understand why they both were staring at me—like they recognized me or something.

The man approached first, leaving his pretty, female partner by the door to wait. I studied him carefully. As he got closer, I knew it was Frederic; it had to be. He and Zeph didn't look a lot alike, but there were enough similarities to tell they were related. Their hair was the same dark brown color, although Frederic's was much curlier. He was tall, like Zeph, but not nearly as muscular or athletic-looking. They had a similar shape to their faces, but where Zeph had a rebellious cut to his features, Frederic's whole demeanor was much softer. Even his warm, amber brown eyes seemed gentle, although I wondered about them. Why weren't they purple like Zeph's?

He regarded me with a cautious smile. "Hello. I'm Freddy Everett. You're the one who sent the message, aren't you?"

I nodded. "Yes. I've heard a lot about you."

"You must be Josie Barton," he guessed.

"How did you know that?" I tried to keep a confident front up. Internally, I was freaking out. He knew me? How? Had Eldrick tipped him off?

"Ah, well. It's sort of a long story. Would it be all right if my wife joined us?" He gestured to the petite woman waiting by the door.

She smiled brightly and waved.

"Your wife? Oh, um, sure. That's fine."

Okay, so I wasn't exactly comfortable with it. I didn't like being outnumbered, but at least they seemed nice. They were both dressed in neat, conservative clothes, and they were wearing matching scarves—which was kind of cute. When the woman walked over to join us, they held hands again.

They seemed like a normal young couple, but I knew better. Freddy was supposed to be a changeling, just like Zeph. And this woman? Well, I didn't know what she was yet, but I was willing to bet it wasn't anything human.

"I'm Camilla," she said cheerfully. Light, polished, and effortlessly beautiful, she was everything I'd imagined a faerie would look like. Her long, sleek black hair had been flat-ironed to silky perfection, and her skin was pale and utterly flawless. Her dark eyes glittered like obsidian, and the air around her seemed to resonate with magical energy.

While they settled into the chairs across the table from me, I tried to think of where to begin. Having two of them there, looking at me expectantly, was intimidating.

"You look so much like your mother." Camilla gave a dreamy sigh. "She was an enchanting woman. She had the same red hair."

I blushed. "I-I don't remember much about her. I was a baby when she died. Wait—how did you know my mom?"

She giggled. "We knew both of your parents. The Bartons were very near and dear to us. Your father never told you?"

I gaped and slowly shook my head.

Freddy nodded in agreement. "I'm sure it's been a difficult journey for you to make it this far. But please believe me when I say how glad we are to see that you're alive and well."

"Oh. Well, thank you." I shifted uncomfortably. This was already not going as planned. "Well, that's only because of Zeph. He's been taking care of me since my dad died."

Freddy's expression suddenly became desperate. "You mean you've seen him? How is he?"

"Not great," I answered honestly. "That's actually why I'm here. I need your help."

"It's the curse, isn't it?" Freddy's voice broke and he leaned forward, putting his head in his hands. I wasn't expecting him to look so … upset. "He refuses to see me. He won't even take my calls anymore. It's been years since I even heard his voice."

Zeph was stubborn. I understood that better than most, but seeing Freddy look so worried broke my heart. I knew what it was like to lose a sibling, and I wouldn't have wished that pain on anyone. It was easier just to try not to think about William at all, or at least it had been. But after losing Dad, too, it was as though that tidal wave of grief had swallowed me completely. I was crushed to nothing—too numb to even know what to feel about William anymore.

"He won't let anyone talk about you when I'm around," I said quietly. "Why is he doing this? You're brothers, aren't you?"

"Because I didn't follow him when he turned his back on the Seelie Court to confront Fir Darrig." Freddy sat up slowly, shaking his head. "But I couldn't just leave. I had a responsibility to my wife. He was asking me to put her life in danger, too. How could I do that?"

I felt the weight of his guilt when he looked at me. Having to choose between loyalty to his brother and his wife's safety must have been difficult, and I knew how Zeph could be. When he got angry, he lashed out, and anyone standing nearby got burned.

"I'm sorry if I seem emotional. I'm not trying to put on a show for you,

I swear." Freddy gave me a hollow smile that was all too familiar to me. I'd seen Zeph look at me like that before when he was hiding his true feelings. "I just know things must be getting hard for him. I haven't seen him in a long time. I didn't even realize he was living here again. The Singing Moon is almost here, and his time is running out."

"So you must know that I'm the vessel, then?" I put all my cards on the table.

"Of course, dear. We knew your parents well. I even babysat you a few times, though I'm sure you don't remember it. You were such a precious baby. I used to braid flowers into your hair," Camilla said with a nostalgic smile. "From the moment you were born, we dedicated ourselves to finding some way to keep you safe from anyone who might want to abuse you for your power."

She and Freddy exchanged a look. His brow creased and she gazed at me again, her smile fading. "We knew you were going to need the best protection the faerie world could manage without breaking any of the old laws. But none of our efforts satisfied Zeph. He didn't think we were doing enough. It was odd. We had never seen him so … dedicated to a human before."

"He became a man obsessed, and no one could reason with him," Freddy agreed. "He was so furious he stormed off on his own, determined to confront Fir Darrig himself, no matter the risk. I tried to stop him. Tried to talk him down. But it was as though something happened that suddenly made him snap."

All my confidence began to seep away. In its place, a cold sense of realization settled on my chest like a lead weight. "I-I think I know what happened."

Freddy and Camilla both leaned forward with hopeful expressions. "You do?" they said in unison.

"Last night, he told me about something that happened when I was little. He said I captured his heart, and that I made him promise to make me happy." I flushed, looking away as I repeated the story. "I don't remember it. I must have been too young."

Freddy sat back in his chair like he was trying to process the new information. His mouth was open and his eyes as round as saucers.

"That's it," Camilla whispered. "It has to be. I don't know how I didn't see it before. That's why he became so reckless—he felt a heart-chord. What other explanation could there be?"

I glanced between them. "What's that?"

"It's quite rare," Freddy replied. "I'm not sure how much you understand about magic, but every living thing in this world has a soul from the tiniest ant to the oldest tree. And with that soul comes a song—not in the literal sense, though. It's more akin to what you humans would call an aura. The core essence of who you are. It resonates, and those who are more sensitive to the magic can pick up on it."

"Have you ever met someone and you just knew, at first glance, that something wasn't right with them?" Camilla asked.

I thought about Ms. Grear. "Um, yes. I think so."

"Their aura, their soul, conflicts with yours. Humans refer to it as intuition, sometimes," she said. "But when you meet someone whose soul creates perfect harmony with yours, the result is …"

"Magical," I breathed the word as chills swept over me.

Freddy chuckled. "For lack of a better word. We call it a heart-chord. A love song."

Camilla's dark eyes were misty. "He truly was made a fool by love."

"It doesn't make sense, though," I interrupted. "If I was just a little kid, how could he love me like *that*?"

"When it comes to a heart-chord, age, race, circumstance—none of that matters," Freddy explained. "It's a sense of rightness, of one being perfectly understanding another, not a sexual desire."

"So I guess it can … evolve into that kind of thing later?"

Freddy shrugged. "Sure. But that doesn't mean it always does. They could be a mentor, a friend, a sibling, even an animal like a pet."

"Besides, a person's soul doesn't change with age." Camilla gave me another affectionate smile. "That goes for every being of any species, not just faeries. We can live for thousands of years or just a hundred, but the essence of who we are won't be changed by time. It's always the soul of a person that matters most."

Freddy's soft laughter distracted us both. He was smiling to himself, rubbing his chin thoughtfully. "I can't believe I never put two and two together."

"I didn't realize it either." Camilla patted his arm. "But it's not like that sort of thing happens every day. And he always complained whenever we asked him to look after the children."

"Not to mention he's the last sort of person you'd think would ever strike a heart-chord with anyone." Freddy sighed. "He always insisted on taking on the role of the unruly rogue—never going to settle, never caring about anyone else."

I rolled my eyes. "He's not as suave as he wants everyone to think he is, for the record. He snores like a freight train. And sometimes he drools all over my pillows."

Suddenly, they both turned and stared at me, their eyes wide. Freddy was blushing and fidgeting his tie. Camilla covered her mouth with her hand.

"Y-you and Zeph have—" Freddy sputtered and choked on his own surprise. "I mean, I didn't realize you two were already ... intimate."

"That pig! Heart-chord or not, she's much too young for *that*!" Camilla gasped. She slammed a hand down on the table, rattling all the silverware. "If I find out he used a glamour to—"

"Now, now, dear," Freddy patted her shoulder soothingly. "She's almost eighteen, right? That's plenty old enough to make her own decisions about relationships. Besides, I seriously doubt Zeph would use a glamour spell to will her into bed with him."

"U-uh, no, he didn't," I stammered. "And we haven't, you know, done *that* yet. He just stays in my bed sometimes. Or on my couch. Basically, wherever he collapses."

They both seemed relieved.

"Well, thank heaven for that." Camilla fanned herself with the bistro menu, her lips still drawn into a frown. "It might seem silly, since we don't age the same as humans do, but we like to maintain a respectful stance on human laws. Especially when it pertains to marriage and love and legal consent to—"

"Josie, forgive me for sounding blunt, but why exactly did you contact me?" Freddy interrupted suddenly, and shifted awkwardly in his seat. His face was still beet red.

I was more than happy to get this meeting back on track. I hadn't come here to talk about my sex life—or lack thereof.

Not that I didn't like chatting with them. They both seemed so nice, so warm, and friendly. It was like a weird reunion with a long-lost family I'd never met before. I didn't understand why Zeph was avoiding them, or why Eldrick had seemed so concerned about me meeting them.

"I need to know about the Fibbing Gate," I said.

Freddy choked again. He glanced around, looking over his shoulder as though he were afraid someone might be eavesdropping. "How do you know about that? Did Zeph tell you?"

"No. In fact, he doesn't even know I'm here. But like you said, the Singing Moon is getting closer. He doesn't have much time left. I know my dad was researching ways to destroy Fir Darrig. I've been reading all of his findings," I explained. "I'm not going to let Zeph die because of me. I'm going to destroy Fir Darrig unless he agrees to break the curse. But I'm not willing to chance it on an empty threat, so I need to know about the Fibbing Gate."

"My, that's a tall order." Camilla looked worried. "Maybe it would be better if Zeph were here, too. It does concern him, after all. You know how angry he'll be if he finds out we've been meeting with her in secret."

I saw Freddy's expression fall again. His emotions were so transparent; it was easy to figure out what he was thinking. Unfortunately, I had to agree with him. I seriously doubted Zeph would ever agree to meeting with them. He wouldn't even talk about Freddy.

"Zeph isn't interested in saving himself." I sat up a little straighter. "He's being a stubborn idiot, as usual. So it's up to me. I know my dad was experimenting with ways of sealing away powerful faeries. The last thing written in his journal was about the Fibbing Gate."

Once again, Freddy looked uneasy. He winced and leaned in closer, whispering. "Josie, it's dangerous to speak of such things."

"Why?"

"Because Nagroot has forbidden it," he replied.

"Who's Nagroot?"

"He's is the Steward of the Seelie Court. He's the one who … well, he forbade us from making a strike against Fir Darrig. He won't allow anyone in the Seelie Court to act out like that. He holds to the old laws, which prohibit faeries from using magic against one another. If we try, then we are immediately treated as traitors and excused from the Court. That's why I didn't follow Zeph before. Once you're excused from the Seelie Court, you're doomed to live out the rest of your years as a rogue on the run—as an Unseelie."

I took a second to process that.

"Nagroot is very influential in the faerie world, sweetie," Camilla said quietly. "He's quite old, and a sidhe like Fir Darrig—one of his descendants, in fact. There are even rumors he might even be sympathetic to Fir Darrig."

"Shh, darling, don't say such things." Freddy was looking a little pale.

Camilla didn't share his apprehension. "By now I'm sure he's heard them, too. I, for one, suspect there's some truth to it. We petitioned him to help us protect you when you were a baby, and he refused. He said there was too much bad blood between the two courts now. He doesn't believe our differences can be mended by one human, even if that human is the vessel."

"No, that's not it," Freddy interjected. Those words must have stoked his temper a little because I saw a flash of rebellious anger in his eyes that reminded me of someone. "It's completely ludicrous. If anyone can bring peace to our world, it *would* be the vessel! He must know that. But now he's got his greedy crooked behind in a seat of authority. He doesn't want to let that go."

"You may be right. But we all must acknowledge that the tension between Seelies and Unseelies has never been greater." Camilla regarded her husband with a sad smile. "If we try to force everyone under one banner to fight Fir Darrig, other Unseelie might rally to him. We don't want to make a monster into a martyr and start a faerie war in his name."

Freddy rubbed his brow and gave a stiff nod. Unlike his brother, apparently he could listen to reason.

Camilla put a hand on his arm. Immediately, Freddy relaxed. "It's bad enough we've already got so many fae willing to cast foul magic against one another. A war would make the rift even worse. So Nagroot will do whatever he believes he must to prevent it, even if it means behaving foolishly."

I could see both sides of the argument, but without knowing Nagroot personally, it was impossible to decide who was right. Fortunately, it didn't matter. "I don't need his help or his approval. I'm not a faerie, so the laws don't apply to me."

Freddy and Camilla blinked at me in surprise. Then they both slowly began to smile.

"She really is like her mother," Camilla said.

"It's the red hair," Freddy agreed. "You know what they say about redheads. Too much fire in the soul is bound to leak out somewhere."

I blushed again. "So will you help me or not?"

They nodded in unison.

"Of course, dear." Camilla patted my arm gently. "We'll just have to be extra careful."

I exchanged numbers and email addresses with Freddy and Camilla as we finished our meeting. Freddy admitted he didn't know much about the Fibbing Gate, but he promised to send me any information he could find. He verified Eldrick's claim that it was a very old legend—one that was generally taken to be more fiction than fact.

"It'll take some time. But I'll see what I can come up with," he promised as they escorted me out of the bistro. "With any luck, I can at least figure out if the story is true or not. There has to be someone left who remembers. Or maybe there's something in one of the older texts …"

"Just be careful, dear," Camilla warned. "We don't want Nagroot to catch on."

"Or Zeph," I added. "I'm pretty sure he would blow a gasket if he knew I was here."

Freddy chuckled and patted my shoulder. "Don't worry. If he finds out, you can blame it all on us. He already hates us, so it won't make much difference."

Despite his smile, those words reflected such a deep sadness my heart sank. It wasn't right for Zeph to be so angry with them. He was being childish—again.

"Oh my," Camilla gasped suddenly. Her wide-eyed stare was fixed upon the door and her porcelain-perfect cheeks flushed.

Eldrick strode down the sidewalk wearing a long, black coat, his broad shoulders flecked with white falling snow. His bangs blew over his sharp eyes, and his steely gaze fixed squarely on me. As he crossed the street, standing tall and proud, every woman in a two-block radius seemed to turn around and gawk at him. Not even Camilla was able to resist ogling him, which earned her an elbow and sulky frown from her husband.

"It's time to go home," Eldrick announced in a firm, deep voice as he stopped right before me.

"You came to pick me up?" I smiled at him.

He curled a finger in my direction, calling me over to his side like a disobedient puppy. "You were taking too long."

It didn't bother me as much as it should have. I was so glad to see him, I skipped over to his side and looped my arm through his. "Better watch it. People are going to think you were worried about me."

"Don't be ridiculous," he scolded me. His silver eyes glanced at Freddy and Camilla dismissively, as though he didn't think they were worth his time.

"Eldrick Dorchaidhe," Freddy said his name like it was an accusation. "I can honestly say you are the last fae in the world I expected to see standing beside a human girl. Stepped down off your pedestal, have you?"

"Spare me the juvenile mockery," Eldrick replied dryly. "Lest you make your inferiority more obvious to your wife."

"Now, now. We can be civil, can't we? Behave yourselves in front of Josie. This isn't an elementary school playground." Camilla tried not to laugh, but she wasn't doing a very good job. "Eldrick, it's good to see you again."

He nodded, but didn't reciprocate her greeting. Instead, he pulled me out the door and down the street. I barely managed a wave goodbye.

"What was that all about?" I asked as soon as Eldrick let go of my arm. "Why did you come to get me? I was fine with them."

"It's getting late," he insisted with a scowl.

"Not *that* late." I glanced up at him, and I couldn't keep from smiling. Maybe he'd never admit it, but I knew I was right. Eldrick had been worried about me. "Is Zeph awake yet?"

He shook his head.

I leaned against his arm, hiding from the biting cold of the wind as we walked home together. So, I'd known Freddy, Camilla, and Zeph when I was little. They'd been close family friends ... and yet I didn't have a single memory of any of them? That didn't make sense. Surely I should have been able to recall something—any tiny detail. Especially if they'd spent so much time babysitting William and me.

Granted, a lot of my memories from back then were hazy, and most of them had been drowned out by the pain and sorrow of losing my family members one by one. I didn't even remember my mother's voice. I only recognized her face because I had seen it in photographs. I remembered more about my big brother, William, but he had passed away when I was in fifth grade. He was already in high school by then, so we hadn't spent much time together.

I let out a sigh. There had to be some other explanation—maybe something Freddy and Camilla, or even Zeph, hadn't told me.

"What's wrong with you?" Eldrick asked.

"Nothing," I lied. "I'm just restless. All we can do now is wait and see what Freddy can find out. I hate waiting." Okay, so that wasn't *all* a lie. I did hate feeling like I was just sitting on my hands.

He slipped his arm out of my grasp and planted a hand on my shoulder. I wasn't sure what to make of it at first, especially when he gradually pulled me closer to walk with his arm around me. "Humans are always impatient. Perhaps that is due to your short lifespan."

I rolled my eyes. "You're so charming. It's hard to believe you're still single." I was being sarcastic, but apparently, he didn't pick up on that.

"Yes, well, my social standing amongst my kin makes it necessary for me to be highly selective when settling on a mate. My father has many children, but so far I am the only one he has recognized as a legitimate heir."

"Riiight," I laughed. It was hard to imagine someone as chronically serious as Eldrick falling in love—his smile alone was as rare as a total lunar eclipse—but kissing someone? That was impossible to visualize.

"We should continue your studies," he continued. "You seem to have several spells memorized accurately enough, it's time for you to attempt to use them."

"You mean like a test run?" I swallowed hard. I wondered how angry Zeph would be if I accidentally set the apartment on fire. Maybe we should stock up on fire extinguishers first.

We were nearly back to my street, within sight of the last intersection where we had to take a turn, when Eldrick suddenly went tense. He moved like a blur, grabbing me by the arm and dragging me against his side.

"Hey, what's the—"

"Hush." His eyes narrowed into dangerous silver slits. Standing so close to him, I could feel every hard muscle in his body. His nostrils flared, as though he were scenting the air.

Eldrick's harrowing stare fixed upon an alleyway directly across the street from us. The two tall buildings on either side cast heavy shadows, making the alley pitch black, so I couldn't see anything in it. What was happening? Were they invisible? Or hiding in the dark?

I glanced both ways, but there was no one in sight in either direction.

"Behind me," Eldrick commanded. A low, rumbling growl came from somewhere deep in his throat.

I scrambled to duck behind him and clung to his coat. My whole body was trembling as I peeked around his arm.

Across the street, a pair of gleaming ice blue eyes winked to life in the darkness. I watched, breathless and terrified, as a huge white wolf came striding out of the alleyway. Its head raised and ears pricked forward as it watched us, black nose twitching. What was a creature like that doing in the city?

A blast of frigid wind cut right through me and I sucked in a sharp breath. Those eyes—where had I seen them before?

Eldrick's growling grew louder.

The white wolf let out a snort, snapping its jaws. It turned its head away as the air around me seemed to grow colder.

Eldrick spread his arms out, his shoulders hunched aggressively and his teeth bared. He tilted his chin up slightly in a challenging gesture, his jawline hard.

A wide, toothy grin spread across the wolf's mouth. "Hello, big brother. I see the rumors are true. Enslaved to that human whelp? How pathetic." It spoke in a soft feminine voice.

Eldrick didn't move.

"You should let me have her. One bite and I'll solve everyone's problems—even yours."

I cringed and squeezed the back of Eldrick's coat tighter. I'd heard that voice before somewhere. But where?

"Touch her and I will do far worse than one bite," Eldrick rumbled. "Walk away, Lumi. This is your only warning."

My heart stopped. Lumi? The woman from the fair?

A soft chime whispered in the air, sending chills over my skin. As quickly as it had appeared, the creature shimmered and changed, changing from a wolf into a beautiful young woman—the same one that had tried to abduct me at the fair.

My pulse raced and my throat seized up. I couldn't stop myself from shaking.

Lumi stood up slowly, the wind catching in her long white hair. Lithe and lean with skin like freshly fallen snow, she looked nothing at all like Eldrick. The only thing about them that was even remotely similar was the cold, ruthless way they were glaring at one another.

Lumi smirked as she adjusted the collar of her white leather jacket, her piercing gaze still fixed on me. "She reeks of fear."

Suddenly, Eldrick took a step toward her with his lips drawn back in a snarl. Cool chills tingled across my body as his form wavered, threatening to change.

Lumi jumped back with a yelp, landing in a defensive stance with her eyes wide. She flashed me another quick glare, clicking her teeth before disappearing into the darkness of the alleyway again.

The chimes in the air went silent.

"I-is she gone?" I whispered.

Eldrick let his arms drop. His body relaxed, but the fury in his sterling eyes didn't lose any of its potency. "For now."

"That woman … is your sister?"

He nodded slowly.

"Is she working for Fir Darrig?"

His lips scrunched. "I'm not sure. Lumi has been very loyal to her mother in the past. But, if Fir Darrig is recruiting other Unseelie to his cause … then I suppose it is possible."

"W-what if you hadn't been here? Oh god, what if she'd attacked us?" My knees went weak.

Eldrick seized my arms to steady me. "I *am* here." His expression was stern as he moved to take my hand. "Let's go."

Zeph still wasn't awake when we got home—which was a relief. It gave me some time to calm down. If Zeph found out where I'd been and that Lumi had tried to kidnap me again … I shuddered.

I was still trembling as we walked through the door. Eldrick hovered around me, silent and grim-faced as I hung up my coat and scarf. It was warm in my apartment, but the memory of Lumi's chilling stare still made me shiver.

Cooking always soothed my nerves. It kept my shaking hands busy and my mind focused on something else. I took my time making vegetarian lasagna, broccoli salad with cranberries and raisins, and crescent rolls glazed with cinnamon and honey. It made my whole apartment smell heavenly. Eldrick hovered over me, trying to taste everything to "ensure its quality." I had to chase him off with a wooden spoon.

I figured the smells would wake Zeph up and bring him staggering into the kitchen, bleary-eyed and ready to eat anything he could get his hands on. But after setting the table and letting everything cool off for a few minutes, he still hadn't appeared. My still-panicked brain immediately jumped to terrible conclusions.

Leaving Eldrick sitting at his place at the table, I crept down the hall and opened my bedroom door. Zeph was sound asleep in my bed, buried under all my blankets. When I pulled back the comforter, I found him curled up on his side, hugging one of my pillows to his chest while wheezing loudly.

I smiled. My beautiful, scruffy, mess of a man.

I eased down onto the side of the bed and began running my fingers through his hair. He twitched, but didn't wake up. His eyelids flickered like he was dreaming.

There were so many things I wanted to ask him, and so much more I wanted to tell him. He needed to forgive Freddy. Whatever had happened in the past, he needed to let that go. His little brother was obviously in pain, struggling to deal with their estrangement. Couldn't he just swallow his pride for once? Just for the sake of family?

I knew better than to bring it up, though. He'd probably growl and curse, call me a few names, and say it wasn't any of my business. He would be right about that. I had no right to get involved. Despite the fact that he rarely acted like it, Zeph was a grown man. He could take care of his own business.

"Hey." I rubbed one of his tattooed arms. "I'm about to ask a stupid question, are you listening?"

He made a deep, groaning sound and tried to hide his face against the pillow.

I bent down and whispered, letting my lips brush his ear, "Are you hungry?"

A violet-colored eye popped open to stare up at me. He groaned again, and looped an arm around my neck to drag me down into the bed with him. "What did you make? It smells really good," he murmured sleepily. "Just like you."

"Several things." I smiled and snuggled up against him. Wrapped up in his embrace, my whole body relaxed. My trembling stopped. I finally felt safe again—warm and secure in his arms. "And I was thinking of making some more of those cookies for dessert, if you want."

"Yeah. I like those." He closed his eyes again, giving groggy, sluggish responses in between yawns. "How was school?"

"Oh, you know. Uneventful. Everyone was asking where Joe was, as usual." I was determined to keep my meeting with Freddy and Camilla a secret. Maybe I'd never be as good a liar as Zeph, but I could try.

I must have been getting a little better at it, though. It was getting closer and closer to prom week, and Zeph had no idea. I'd been intentionally trashing all traces of prom fliers and catalogues before he could see them.

Sure, it was my senior year and I'd never been to a prom before—any other time I would have wanted to go. But right now, there were bigger, much more important things to worry about.

Like the welfare of the man who was curled up in my bed.

With my head resting on the pillow next to his, staring at him nose-to-nose, I found myself wondering about that childhood promise he'd made me. Did we really have a heart-chord? Could humans even hear or sense one? Even if I never remembered anything else from those days, I wished I could recall even a glimpse of that moment. I wanted to feel it, hear it, the way faeries did—the way Zeph had.

"You're creepin' me out, staring at me like that," Zeph teased.

"I'm waiting on you to get up! Eldrick and I are ready to eat. Dinner is getting cold."

"Fine, fine. I'm up." He grabbed my head suddenly, dragging me close into what I hoped would be a kiss.

It wasn't.

It was a noogie. A violent, horrible noogie that completely ruined my hair.

"You idiot! Stop!" I picked up a pillow and whacked him over the head with it. As soon as his grip loosened, I crawled frantically for the edge of the bed.

Zeph seized my ankle. "Oh no you don't," he chuckled as he dragged me back. "I'm not done with you."

He was on me in an instant, his big, firm body pinning me to the mattress. His nose grazed along my cheek. "Why does it seem like you're hiding something from me? You're so nervous. Did you think I wouldn't notice?"

I flushed and turned my face away. "I-I'm not."

"Liar."

"No worse than you." Tingly, excited heat buzzed through my body. I closed my eyes, my heart pounding as his breath tickled my neck. "Zeph, the door's open. Eldrick is—"

His lips touched mine with a gentle, soft kiss. "We'll have to be quiet, then."

My stomach swirled and fluttered as he pushed his mouth against mine again. I grabbed onto him, snaking my arms around his body.

The smell of his bare skin and hair—like warm cinnamon and evergreen—filled my nose. It made me hazy as he parted his lips, deepening the kiss and sliding his arms underneath me.

Why hadn't I shut the stupid door?

He moved away from my lips, nipping playfully at the side of my neck as he unbuttoned the front of my school uniform blouse.

I stiffened—I couldn't help it. As much as I wanted this, my teeth wouldn't quit chattering.

Zeph stopped.

Slowly, I opened my eyes. He was still fidgeting with one of my buttons, his brow furrowed and his ... was his hand shaking?

"I, uh ..." He cleared his throat.

"What's wrong?"

He wouldn't look me in the eye. "Sorry. I guess I'm nervous."

Seriously? *He* was nervous? I bit at my bottom lip.

"I just don't want to screw this up." He let out a deep, weighted sigh. "I've waited a long time. I wasn't even sure if you'd feel that way about me when you got older. I mean, I would've understood if you didn't. I'm not usually anyone's first pick—"

I slapped a hand over his mouth. "You are my *only* pick, Zeph."

Now he was blushing, too.

"If you intend on continuing, please at least have the decency to close the door. I'd rather not be forced to listen to this while I'm trying to eat." Eldrick's voice came from the doorway. He was scowling at us, twirling a fork between his fingers.

I snatched a hand over my chest to hold my blouse closed. "We're not!"

"We totally were." Zeph grinned.

"Well, not anymore. Come on, you need to eat something before you go to work." I quickly squirmed out from under him, giving one of his ears a little tug.

He was laughing proudly all the way to the kitchen. He seemed to have forgotten that he was only wearing his boxer shorts—not that I didn't enjoy the view—but it was a little distracting while I tried to eat dinner.

Halfway through the meal, Eldrick couldn't contain his disgust anymore. He scolded Zeph for not bothering to put on a shirt and that immediately stirred things up.

"Oh come on, it's nothing she hasn't seen before," Zeph said with a cheek-full of food. "I think the more important question is, are you a boxers or briefs man? You're so uptight, though. You seem like you might even enjoy a little pain and discomfort. So, maybe a man-thong?"

Eldrick gripped his fork like a weapon. "I am *not* having this discussion with you."

"Oh! Ladies and gentlemen, we have a winner!" Zeph crowed loudly.

Looking around my kitchen table made me strangely happy, though. I'd gone from years of sitting by myself every night, eating in total silence, to this in a matter of a few months. Now Zeph and Eldrick were arguing over who got the last crescent roll, and I had to move quick if I wanted more than a few bites of broccoli salad. It was loud and chaotic, but it was wonderful. I wanted to savor this moment. So, I took my phone out of my pocket and snapped a picture of them.

Both faeries shot me a dangerous glare.

"Hey, don't take naked pictures of me!" Zeph yelled. "That better not end up on the damn internet!"

Eldrick snorted. "As if anyone would want to see it."

"Says the guy who's been staring at me since I walked in. It's okay to be jealous."

"Me? Jealous of *you?*" Eldrick balked.

While they rolled right back into another argument, I saved the picture and put my phone away. I was amassing quite an album now.

One good thing about feeding two man-sized faeries was that there were never any leftovers. I didn't have to wrap up any of the food no matter how big a portion I made. Zeph could have doubled as a living garbage disposal. I wondered if his little brother had such a fierce appetite.

Eldrick came to the sink to help me wash the dishes. He was always helping me now by doing little things around the house, even though I never asked him to. He'd basically taken over doing the laundry, since he informed me that I did a bad job getting the wrinkles out of my school uniforms. I had to admit, the man could starch and iron like a professional. No wonder his clothes were always so neat and spotless.

I was stunned when Zeph appeared on my other side and started drying the plates. Normally, he ate anything he could find and then crawled right back into bed.

He caught me staring at him and frowned. "What?"

"N-nothing." I quickly went back to washing.

A familiar buzzing sound came from the kitchen table, and we all glanced back. I knew what it was even before I saw Zeph's cell phone slowly creeping across the tabletop every time it vibrated.

I was beginning to hate that sound more and more. Good things rarely happened after he got a call.

He left the room to answer, and I tried to focus on the dishes. My heart wasn't in it, though. Was it Hank calling with another case? Where would they go this time? Would Zeph be hurt when he got back? Was I going to have to stitch him up again? What if he didn't come back at all? Would Hank even tell me what happened?

I stood there and scrubbed the same plate for about five minutes before realizing what I was doing.

Eldrick took the plate from me carefully. "Your expression suggests you're unhappy."

"Hank shouldn't be asking him to go on any more cases," I whispered, hoping Zeph wouldn't hear. "He can barely hold an illusion for more than a few hours now. What if he gets hurt? He might not be able to regenerate. He could be killed."

"Then go with him," Eldrick suggested. "You are the vessel. You can restore his power long enough for him to survive whatever injuries he sustains."

That seemed like the obvious solution—which naturally meant Zeph would fight me tooth and nail over it. He was worried about Fir Darrig coming for me or that I might get hurt. How he had taken a silly childhood promise to make me happy to the extreme of thinking he was supposed to be my "human" shield was beyond me. Watching him suffer did *not* make me happy at all.

"What if I'm not ready?" I whispered. "I haven't practiced using any of the spells yet. I might mess up. I might hurt Zeph or Hank on accident."

"I could go with you." Eldrick's words were so quiet I barely heard them.

I swallowed hard. "I won't ask you to do that."

He flicked me a quick glance. "You don't have to."

14

I'd almost forgotten how absolutely furious I was with Hank until the moment our eyes met from across the car. I didn't say anything when he smiled at me. I gave him my iciest glare instead. Shaman or not, he should have known better. Zeph couldn't keep this up for much longer. He could barely make it through a school day in his Joe disguise, let alone fight other fae.

"Ouch." Hank looked surprised. "Someone's cranky tonight."

"Yeah, well, selfish old geezers who put the life of the man I love in danger tend to get on my nerves. I'm funny that way."

"Josie …" Zeph said my name like it was a warning.

Hank chuckled. "It's all right."

"No, it isn't." I turned in the passenger's seat so I could face him. I wasn't going to let him brush me off like some tourist who'd only come along to watch the show. "You know Zeph is getting weaker by the day, but you're still calling him for cases almost every night. Enough is enough. If you get him killed, I promise, I will become your very worst nightmare."

"Is that so?" Hank sounded a little annoyed.

"Absolutely." I narrowed my eyes. "I happen to know someone in the nightmare business."

I caught a brief glimpse of Eldrick smirking in the rearview mirror.

"Save your threats. You've made your point." Hank hacked a loud, smoker's cough. "In case you didn't know, it's your fault we've had so many cases lately. The more your power grows, the more faeries are being drawn to it. Hiding behind the auras of these two pinheads might be enough to keep most faeries and sprites confused about your location, or too afraid to approach you, but it won't for much longer. And when you are out in the open, there won't be a force on the planet strong enough to keep Fir Darrig from coming right for you. He's already putting out his feelers, sending his lackeys, and laying traps all around to try to catch you. The only reason you are sitting in my car right now is because leaving you alone with that silver-eyed troublemaker back there makes me nervous as hell. Contract or not, I know what his type is capable of."

"Don't pretend that you know me," Eldrick snapped from the backseat.

"Maybe I don't, but I know what stock you come from," Hank countered. "Nothing good has ever come from your father. Your mother, either, for that matter. Don't think I'm buying into anything you say just because this girl claims we can trust you."

Eldrick's expression went cold, but he didn't reply.

I sank back into my seat, my pulse still pounding in my eardrums. I bit down hard and stared out the window, clenching my hands into fists and hoping Hank wouldn't notice. He was right—this was all my fault. Maybe not directly, but it was happening because of me. I couldn't do anything about it, no matter how much I hated it.

Dad's journal verified everything Zeph had already warned me about. Every time I gave power to a faerie or used it myself for spellwork, my aura would grow and strengthen. It was like cutting off the heads of a hydra; the more I used, the greater the power would become. Soon, it would be impossible to hide it.

And on the night of my eighteenth birthday, I would glow like moonlight for all the faerie world to see.

"Circumstances being what they are, I don't see how you can be successful at all without my help," Eldrick retorted. "Josie is here only to ensure that Zeph lives to fight the next battle. But if he is unable to resolve this one, I am your last line of defense."

"I've got my own bag of tricks, puca." Hank flashed him a glare. "And I'm keeping an eye on you."

"That's enough, Hank." Zeph growled a warning from the backseat. "Let's just get this over with so we can all get back to our lives. Tell me, what are we dealing with?"

The old man shifted uneasily. "Well, I'm not quite sure. It's at a wedding venue just outside of town, an old vineyard backed up to the woods. They called in to the local police a few hours ago. A couple of kids went missing during the reception."

"Wait, who called?" Zeph's voice had a suspicious edge to it.

Hank sighed. "I've got a source in the police department. They've been on the scene looking for the kids, but so far can't find any trace of them. They called me to try to track them—said there's something fishy about the scene. They wouldn't tell me anymore than that over the phone."

Zeph flopped back onto the seat with a groan. "Cops? Are you out of your mind? You know how the cops feel about me."

"So wear a disguise, or change to your natural state," Hank huffed. "In fact, it'd probably better if you both did. Make yourselves scarce, fan out, and see if you can track down any fae in the area that might be causing all this. Miss Attitude over here can help me search for the kids. You boneheads can handle that, right?"

Zeph grumbled something that was probably profanity.

"And if the culprit is Fir Darrig?" Eldrick asked.

"Then we fall back to the car and make a stand long enough for you to get her out of here." Zeph jabbed a finger in my direction.

I twisted in my seat to look back at him. "Wait, what? Why can't I go with you?"

Zeph's head was bowed to his chest as he sat, fidgeting with his hands. "I'm … not sure I could outrun him now."

The hum of the tires on the highway filled the awkward silence.

My heart wrenched painfully and I squeezed the seat as I stared at him. He was risking so much to do this. His dignity. His life. My throat burned every time I swallowed. Even Eldrick was studying him out of the corner of his eye, his expression almost sympathetic.

I blinked the tears from my eyes as I turned back to sit in my seat. Reaching into the pocket of my coat, I squeezed my hand around the Sharpie marker I had stashed there just in case. My mind raced over the spells I knew—a binding circle, a focused blast—things that might be useful. If things did get bad, I could help. I could fight. I wasn't going to run.

We turned off a rural highway onto a narrow road marked with a sign that read "Josie & Mark's Wedding." I got a bad feeling. Was it a coincidence I had the same name as the bride?

The road wound through a snowbound forest, twisting and turning for almost a mile. Pretty glass lanterns dangled from icy tree branches on either side of the road, lighting the way toward the wedding ceremony.

As we got closer to the vineyard, I saw the flash of blue police lights blinking through the dark shapes of trees. There were squad cars parked everywhere, but I didn't see any police officers. Strange. Where were they?

Hank pulled the Cadillac off the road to park with the other wedding guests' cars. Ahead, there was an elegant, old colonial house, decorated with twinkle lights and candles that sparkled against the snowy night. Wreaths of evergreen and holly hung on every window and door. Right beside the house stood an old, whitewashed barn that was decorated for the ceremony, too.

The house and barn were surrounded by a dense hardwood forest. Beams of light moved through the trees—probably flashlights from the officers searching for the children. As we got out of the car, I heard men calling out and dogs barking. A blast of the frigid wind made my cheeks sting. I pulled the hood of my coat down over my head.

"This is bad," Zeph whispered. "It's cold out, too cold for humans to stand. I hope those kids were at least wearing coats."

Hank grunted with agreement. "Let's get to work."

"Indeed. I'd rather not waste my entire night here," Eldrick sighed as he opened his door and stepped out into the snow.

The instant his feet hit the ground, his shape began to change. Once, the sight of him in his natural form—a huge black wolf—had terrified me. Now I could only smile as he shook himself and leered around with those shining silver eyes.

I'd not seen him this way in a while. Now that the sight of him didn't make me want to faint with terror, I noticed more of the finer details. His pelt was black, yes, but when he moved I could see the shimmering of a faint, swirling silver pattern hidden in it. It was only when the moonlight struck them that those markings glimmered like mercury. There were sweeping black horns on his head, right above his wolfish ears. They reminded me of an elk's and had those same faint markings on them, as well.

"Won't someone notice him? What if one of the cops sees him or Zeph?" I asked worriedly. He was massive—almost as big as a horse. A wolf that size was bound to cause a panic.

Hank chuckled. "We're the only ones who can see him clearly. Cause I'm a shaman and you're the vessel, we both have the ability to see them in their natural forms. Most people can't. They just see shadows, ghosts, or whatever their minds will allow them to believe. Some don't see anything at all."

Zeph had told me something similar before; people all around the world called faeries different things because they were mistaken for something divine or otherworldly. Watching Zeph step out of the car, his natural form unfolding to light up the night with that eerie purple light, I could definitely understand why. I watched him take off into the night like a violet comet. Eldrick was right behind him, his beastly form flickering as though it were made of smoke.

"They'll be fine." Hank tried to reassure me.

I frowned and opened the car door. "It's not them I'm worried about. We should hurry. Those kids couldn't have gone far."

A young, nervous-looking police officer in a long wool coat met us outside the barn. He seemed confused when he noticed me standing there, dwarfed by Hank's massive stature. "Who's this?"

"My assistant." Hank gestured to me. "She's learning the trade."

I managed a weak smile.

The officer nodded. "We've been searching the woods for three hours already, even brought out the K-9 unit to see if we could use the dogs to track them. So far, nothing," the officer explained as he handed Hank a huge flashlight. "We've got the rest of the wedding guests secure in the house, for now."

"So what has you thinking this is a case for me?" Hank arched a brow.

The officer panned his flashlight away, his expression tightening with a worried frown. "Well, at first, it just looked like the kids wandered off during the party, but now ..."

"Now what?" Hank demanded.

"We found some tracks in the vineyard out back." The officer swallowed hard. "T-they're huge. I called you right away when we found them. Nothing indigenous to this area makes prints like that."

Hank switched the flashlight on, nodding for the officer to take the lead. "Show me."

We marched through the snow, following the young policeman around the property and behind the barn to an open field lined with wooden trellises for grape vines. The soil was packed under a layer of snow and ice that crunched under our shoes. Moonlight poured from the clear night sky, making the winter landscape shine like platinum.

I crashed into Hank's back. He and the officer had stopped to examine some of the tracks while I was looking around. Only, they didn't look like footprints to me. They were huge, round-ish compressions in the snow. There was no consistency to their shape at all. They were staggered sort of like footsteps, but they didn't look like the feet of anything I could imagine.

One glance at Hank's expression told me I was wrong about that, though. He squatted down in front of one of the prints, touching two fingers to it like he was feeling for a pulse. A prickle on the back of my neck sent chills over me. The whispering sound of chimes echoed past my ears, almost completely hidden by the wind.

"You need to call the rest of your men back from the woods," he said in a low voice.

The officer was looking more and more uneasy. "Hank, I-I don't have the authority to—"

"Do it," Hank growled through his teeth. "You're going to piss it off even more."

"I-it?" the officer stammered. "What is it?"

Hank slowly stood up, shining his flashlight across the field to the forest beyond. The tracks led away into the thickets, vanishing under a veil of shadows.

We left the young police officer yammering into his radio, frantically requesting that everyone fall back to the house as Hank and I headed into the forest at a brisk pace.

"What is it?" I asked again.

"Bad news," Hank muttered. "And it probably already knows we're here."

I didn't get any more information out of him as we walked to the edge of the forest. The instant the beam of his flashlight panned across the trees, I got nauseated. We both stood motionless, staring at the forest.

My breath caught.

The trees were *green*. How could anything be green this early in spring?

There were fresh leaves on them, and thick moss growing up their trunks. Flowers and grass bloomed all along the ground, and big vines clung to the branches like jungle snakes. Even the air that seemed to waft out of the forest felt warm and strangely humid. It was like getting breathed on by a big, hairy dog.

"How is this possible?" I whispered.

Hank's expression had gone dark and ominous. "A lot of old magic. Older than you. Older than me. Older than both of your faerie pets."

"It's Fir Darrig, isn't it?"

The forest seemed to shudder at the sound of that name. A fierce, cold wind rustled through the leaves, making sounds as though the trees where whispering.

My skin prickled. Where was Zeph? Eldrick? Had they seen this yet? Were they okay?

Hank cleared his throat. "Could be. Hard to tell. Unseelie's don't usually leave signatures on their handiwork, but anything that bends nature is nearly always the work of a sidhe."

Together, we entered the forest with slow, cautious steps. Sounds seemed to come from all around us. A chorus of crickets and frogs sang sweet summertime melodies. Owls hooted from the treetops. Somewhere in the dark, I could hear the faint echoes of bells tinkling in a beautiful harmony. It made my head fuzzy. I was getting dizzy, and my steps became sluggish. First, my feet wouldn't obey me, and then my eyelids grew heavy. I was so … sleepy.

"Don't listen to the chimes," Hank said suddenly. He grabbed me under the arm and shook me roughly.

My head cleared, although my fingers and toes still tingled. "It's a spellsong? Can you tell which one it is?"

"My ears aren't that keen, but I've heard this one before. We call it an enthrallment." He let me go and kept walking slowly and carefully through the trees. "It'll pull you into a trance. Makes you real easy to catch if you're just standing there drooling on yourself."

I fell in step beside him, and tried not to listen. The chimes were so beautiful, so alluring. It was difficult to ignore. No—I had to be stronger than this. I had to focus. "Can I ask you something?"

He made a grunting sound that I took as a "yes."

"Why do you go on these cases? Is someone paying you?"

"Who'd be paying me?" He gave a raspy chuckle. "I just do what's been passed down in my family for generations. Granted, I don't do it the way my ancestors did. In fact, I'm sure there are some who would condemn my methods as dishonorable, but that's a price I'm willing to pay. Things are different here. The spirits are more hostile now—smarter and more desperate. If I'm going to be of help to anyone, be it the spirits or the people here, then I have to adapt," he said quietly. "A shaman can use the energy from the earth—what the faeries call 'magic'—to bring healing and harmony, amongst other things. We can sense the spirit world and channel it. We do battle where no one else dares to, with things the rest of the 'civilized' world refuses to acknowledge."

I studied his face. Somehow, in this light, he looked ancient—like he might be something ethereal himself. "And you help some faeries? Like Zeph?"

He nodded. "Not all of them have bad intentions. In fact, I'd say most of them are regular folk, like you or me, just trying to live out their lives in peace. But for those who aren't, I have a duty to stop them, drive them out, and set things right."

He crouched down to look at another deep track pressed into the soft, loamy soil.

I could understand that. What I was doing—learning about my dad's spells and reading his journals—wasn't so different. I was only beginning to understand magic, and yet I felt a sense of responsibility to be here. This fight was mine, too.

"How did you get mixed up with Zeph?" I asked.

"Our paths were bound to cross. He was an Unseelie faerie looking for work and a place to hide from Fir Darrig. My bar is probably the most heavily-warded structure in the city. If I activated the warding spells, no faerie would be able put a toenail over that threshold without my say-so, no matter how powerful or old they were."

I hesitated. So the bar where Zeph worked was some kind of faerie bunker? "Why? I mean, why do you need something like that?"

Hank chuckled. "I always like to have an ace in the hole. There are spell lines eight layers deep keeping all energy contained under that roof. Took me a long time to build it. If the Seelie's found out about it, no doubt they'd assume I was up to no good since what can keep a faerie out can also keep one locked in."

"They wouldn't want you to have it?"

"No, they wouldn't like it one bit. Not that I blame them. They've had a lot of trouble in the past with people keeping fae as slaves, using them for foul reasons," he explained. "It's my backup plan—something I keep in reserve for emergencies only."

"So you just gave Zeph a bar keeping job and what, decided to have him be your personal faerie bouncer on the side?"

He stood and scratched his white beard thoughtfully. "More or less. I needed some help managing all the cases that were suddenly popping up— someone who could go bare knuckles against the worst of 'em. Zeph has never had a problem holding his own in a fight. Eh, until recently, anyway."

I had a new appreciation for Hank. He obviously knew a lot about the faerie world and ancient methods of dealing with it. I knew there was probably a lot I could have learned from him. Even with Eldrick's help, I had only learned a few spells. It was incredibly difficult, even if Eldrick and Zeph made it look so easy. The shape of each mark, the position of every line, every tiny detail demanded utter perfection for a spell to work.

"Here." Hank picked up a few thumb-sized acorns off the ground from around his feet and dropped them into my hand. "Hang on to those."

"What for?" I tucked them in my coat pocket.

He grunted as he stood up again. "They make pretty good messengers."

I wasn't sure what to make of that.

Hank carefully picked his way through the forest, leading the way. The hot, stagnant air was making me sweat under my thick winter coat.

Suddenly, something made me stop dead in my tracks.

Voices. Giggling, like two children's voices, echoed through the trees.

Something fluttered by like fabric darting through the shadows.

"Hank! Look!" I yanked on his sleeve. "The children!"

But they were gone. I stood, totally confused. I knew I hadn't imagined that.

Hank frowned in the direction I was pointing. "What did you see?"

"I-I thought I saw them. I know I heard laughter. They were right there just a second ago."

For several uncomfortable moments, we stood perfectly still, listening to every sound. Hank stood firm, like a grim, biker version of Santa, scowling into the dark. His eyes narrowed with concentration, and I strained to hear anything above the sound of the chimes.

Then I heard it again. More laughter. It was definitely children's voices. Out of the corner of my eye, I saw movement again. This time it looked like two little figures, running together between the trees.

"There!" I shouted, spinning around. As soon as I turned to face them, they disappeared again.

Hank made a deep, disapproving sound in his throat. I thought he didn't believe me.

"I know I saw it. I'm not making things up," I insisted.

"I believe you," he growled deeply. "This isn't good. Hand me one of those acorns."

"Should we go after them?" I fished out one of the small, oval-shaped nuts and handed it to him.

"Absolutely not." Hank drew a circle in the dirt at our feet with his finger—a simple-looking spell. The design was a circle with four symbols around it and a cross in the center like a compass.

Standing before the drawing, he placed the acorn between his palms and pressed them together. I stood back, holding my breath as he began whispering something in what sounded like a foreign language. The words were beautiful. They rang in the air like music, seeming to weave a harmony that turned slowly into the sound of bells. My skin prickled at the presence of magic. It always gave me that feeling.

The acorn began to glow between his hands, pulsing with a brilliant golden light that flashed in rhythm with his words. As he drew his hands apart, the acorn hovered in the air. It glowed like a small star. With the final word, it suddenly shot downward into the center of the circle Hank had drawn in the dirt. Nothing but a smoking hole was left behind.

"See? Pretty good messengers." Hank gave a small, sarcastic bow as he kicked dirt over the hole and messed up his spell circle with the toe of his shoe.

I wanted to learn that. No, I *needed* to learn it. "Who did you call?"

"Reinforcements," he answered cryptically. "I've still got a few friends in high places. Stay close to me."

I followed right beside him, deeper into the forest. The trees seemed to grow closer together, and the air grew so warm it was difficult to breathe. Hank panned the beam of his flashlight back and forth, following the tracks and looking for new evidence. I still hoped to see the children again. If we could find them we could get the heck out of here.

Then Hank stopped.

He snapped an arm out, blocking me from taking another step. I followed the beam of the flashlight upward as Hank shined it over the trunk of a *huge* tree—bigger than any I'd ever seen. The trunk was so thick you could have parked a car inside it. The massive branches spread out wide, stretching out above all the other trees.

Layers upon layers of intricate spells covered the whole trunk from top to bottom, even spiraling out toward its limbs. At first, it seemed beautiful, but the more I studied the marks, the more it almost seemed cruel to scar the tree like that. While I couldn't be sure without getting closer, it almost seemed like some of those spells were malicious. Like they were meant to be ...

"A trap," Hank snarled bitterly.

"What?"

He shook his head, as though he were too furious to answer. At the base of the tree, Hank's spotlight hesitated on a pair of objects propped up against the tree's giant base. They looked like baby dolls—but they weren't. They were a pair of lumpy, gnarled roots that almost looked like babies.

Both were swaddled in pieces of cloth, carefully placed side by side in a circle of spellwork etched into the dirt.

Something about this didn't seem right. It was as though someone had left them here specifically for us to find.

I took a step back, my heart stalling and starting. Where was Zeph? Why hadn't he and Eldrick come to find us yet?

Then I got my answer.

From far in the distance, something roared so loudly it shook the ground. It was a booming, monstrous noise. All the trees shuddered.

Hank suddenly shoved the flashlight into my hands. He grabbed my shoulders and gave me a violent push away from the tree. "Go back to the barn," he shouted. "Right now! Don't stop. The smell of the other humans inside might hide your aura!"

"B-but what about you? And Zeph! What if he needs me to—"

"I said *go*! I'll hold it off as long as I can!"

The booming roar shook the trees again. Whatever was making all that noise sounded really big and really upset. It even had Hank looking panicked. I didn't want to be anywhere nearby when that monster finally made its appearance.

My feet flew over the squishy soil. I tried shining the flashlight on the tracks, using them like breadcrumbs to lead me out of the forest again. However, the farther I ran, the more there seemed to be tracks everywhere. They led away in different directions, splitting and rejoining or doubling back. I was running in circles, and I was getting tired.

I stumbled to a halt in the middle of a big clearing. With no trees overhead to block it, the moon showered the ground in sterling light. There were tracks everywhere, making craters all around me, but leading nowhere.

My throat tightened so I could barely catch my breath. My legs went numb.

I turned, staggering in circles, looking all around for some sign of where to go. Nothing looked familiar. I couldn't even remember which way I'd come.

Oh god—I was lost.

"Zeph!" I screamed. "Eldrick! Hank!"

My voice echoed off all the trees. The roaring sound was gone. Even the sound of the chimes from the enthrallment spell had faded away.

Where were they? What if ... what if Zeph needed me? What if Fir Darrig had already found him and I was too late? He needed me. I had to find him.

I took a few shaky steps, trying to pick a direction to start running again.

Something *strong* grabbed my foot.

I screamed, dropping the flashlight. I hung upside down, staring right into the face of a huge monster I didn't have a name for.

A colossal, mashed-up mixture of rocks, roots, tree bark, and leaves held me up like a ragdoll by my leg. It stood upright, almost human in shape, with two big, gorilla-like arms and two stumpy hind legs. Its face was a featureless, eyeless mass with a big, gaping mouth that breathed blasts of hot, putrid, swampy breath over me.

I screamed again, kicking at the creature's hand that held my other foot.

"JOOOSIE," the monster boomed.

My name—it *knew* my name? How? Why?

"Zeph!" I kept kicking and fighting as the beast hefted me higher into the air, dangling me over its giant, gaping maw. I could see straight down into its nasty, moss-covered throat.

"Eldrick! Hank! Someone, please!"

Out of nowhere, the air seemed to explode into blue light. A blast of cold air sucked the wind right out of my lungs, and the monster dropped me. I fell, twisting and screaming. I glimpsed the ground as it rushed up to meet me—and then something snatched me right out of the air.

I was flying. There was an arm around my waist, and I could see the mossy creature wallowing around in the clearing below. Parts of it were covered in a thick layer of ice.

I looked up, trying to figure out who was carrying me. My head swam. All I caught was a glimpse of bright yellow eyes and glistening white wings.

We landed high on a thick branch of an oak tree at the edge of the clearing. My rescuer sat me down, and I straddled the tree branch and shut my eyes tightly. My body trembled as I dug my nails into the tree bark.

"Are you all right?" a merry, masculine voice asked.

I dared to crack one eye open and look up. He was squatting down so close to me that our noses were almost touching.

I screamed at him. I scrambled to get away, and almost fell off the tree branch.

"You can see me!" The stranger laughed. It was an infectious, rich sound. The sort of laugh that made you want to join in.

"W-who are you?" I whimpered as I slowly began inching toward the trunk of the tree. I felt safer when I could hold onto the trunk.

He cocked his head to the side like a confused animal. In fact, there was a lot about him that was animalistic. I mean, he was obviously a faerie. He had the face of a teenage boy with impish, mischievous features. He was tall and lean, with skin as pale as cream. His stark white hair was shaggy, and it fell sloppily over his long, pointed ears and golden eyes. A pair of black ram's horns peeked out of his hair and curled around his ears. On his back grew two big, beautiful wings with black and white feathers like a snowy owl.

He was wearing nothing but a pair of gray pants that were torn off at the knees because from his calves down, his legs didn't look like human legs. He had the big, feathery feet of an owl with huge black talons. Even his fingernails were long, black, and pointed like claws.

"Jack Frost," someone else answered my question.

The boy snickered and bobbed his head in agreement. He seemed pleased that someone recognized him, and fluttered away from me as another winged being landed between us.

Only, I knew this one.

"I owe you one," Zeph muttered like he wasn't thrilled about that.

"Someone sent me a message," Jack announced, springing nimbly from limb to limb around us. "It said there was a naughty Unseelie messing with my mother's handiwork here. Quite the understatement! Then I saw this one about to be gobbled up by a spriggan. Seemed a waste, since she's awfully cute." He winked one of his yellow eyes at me.

Zeph bristled. "Cool it, lover boy. You've got enough girlfriends, and this one's super high maintenance."

"Guys," I interrupted. Apparently, I was the only one still paying attention to what the monster was doing. "That thing is getting up again!"

Down below, the spriggan had managed to smash the ice off its arms. It was lumbering toward us with booming steps that shook the tree we were in. As it got closer, it let out a furious bellow that sent a blast of stinky swamp-breath straight at us.

Jack covered his nose. "A stubborn, smelly brute, isn't it?"

I gagged, too. Rotting sewage probably smelled better. "Where's Eldrick?"

"With Hank. The old geezer took a nasty crack to the head. I've about had it with this thing. We gotta find the centerstone." Zeph snarled as he bared his pointed teeth. He stood, his gleaming wings spreading wide as he flicked a wild-eyed glance in my direction. "Stay put."

I was still bear hugging the tree trunk for dear life, doing my best not to look down. "Do I look like a squirrel to you? We're twenty feet in the air—where exactly do you think I can go?"

He smirked. With his wings stretched out, Zeph dove from the tree and into battle. Jack Frost followed him, but not before conjuring up a fierce, bitter cold wind to go with him.

Zeph fought with brute strength, bellowing like a lion as he hurtled toward the monster. He landed on the spriggan's face and tried ripping it apart piece-by-piece. He must have been trying to conserve as much magic as he could.

Jack's approach was much more calculated. He zoomed through the creature's legs, building magical shackles of ice around its feet to keep it from advancing any closer.

"JOOOOSIE," the spriggan wailed. It snapped free of one of the ice chains and grabbed Zeph in a big, gnarled hand, plucking him off like an insect and throwing him to the ground.

I winced.

The spriggan raised its one free arm, taking aim with a huge fist. Zeph was still trying to stand, staggering with his wings drooping.

Power—he needed my power!

"Zeph!" I screamed, nearly losing my grip on the tree. My heart hit the back of my throat.

Everything went white as a burst of brilliant light exploded in the air. Cold wind squeezed at my lungs. The spriggan howled and stumbled backward, swinging wildly at Jack as he darted past.

I squinted through the spots in my vision, looking for Zeph. He wasn't anywhere on the ground. Had he escaped? Was he all right?

Jack's blast was already wearing off. The spriggan beat its fists on the ground like an angry gorilla. My tree shuddered with every impact.

"This isn't gonna work! Break the centerstone and it'll crumble!" Zeph's voice roared over the noise as he dove back at the spriggan's head again.

Alive—he was alive!

He beat his wings hard, hovering in one spot as he pressed his palms together. As he drew them apart, a complex circular design of pulsing violet light shimmered in the air between his hands.

Bells tolled in the air, hitting my body like waves of warm energy. My breath caught. My body shivered.

"Ready?" he shouted.

"On it!" Jack howled back as he swept in for another attack. His whole body began to gleam, radiating that wintry magic that turned the air ice-cold.

The giant earth-creature saw it coming. But rather than running, it ripped up trees and threw them. It hurled boulders and chunks of ice.

I shrieked as a huge rock went sailing past, missing me by only a few feet and smashing through the forest.

I should have stayed quiet.

The spriggan turned its giant head to look straight at me.

Oh god.

In the blink of an eye, the beast was hurtling toward me.

My body went numb. I couldn't move. I couldn't blink. I couldn't even scream.

"Josie! No!" Zeph was yelling.

The spriggan grabbed the trunk of my tree and plucked it out of the ground like a carrot. I hung on for dear life, my arms and legs wrapped around the trunk.

"TO THE MAAASTER!" The monster's thunderous voice left my ears ringing. It opened its big, smelly mouth again and prepared to eat me— tree and all.

Was this really it? Was I going to die like this?

Two strong hands closed around my wrists and yanked me away as the first half of the tree disappeared down the spriggan's throat. I yelped, clinging to the strong arms that reeled me in.

"Hang on to me," Zeph murmured as guided my arms around his neck. He soared higher, glassy wings beating hard as dove for the forest. His expression was fierce, his jaw tight, and teeth bared. But something wasn't right. His hair and face were dripping with sweat and his skin was flushed. The purplish runes on his skin were barely visible now. He was breathing fast, wincing with every wing beat as though he were in pain.

He was running out of energy. He couldn't last much longer like this.

Zeph stumbled into a rough landing in the woods just outside the clearing and put me down. His violet eyes stared at me for an instant, but he was breathing too hard get any words out. I didn't need to hear him speak to know what he wanted to tell me, though. I could see it on his face.

He wanted me to run.

"No!" I seized his arm. "Let me help you!"

Zeph frowned and started to pull away, opening his mouth like he was going to object.

Over the sounds of the spriggan bellowing in rage, I heard Jack Frost shouting at us. "Look out!"

I caught only a glimpse of what must have been the other half of my tree rocketing toward us through the air.

It was too late.

Zeph threw himself on top of me just as the forest around us seemed to explode. Branches cracked and popped all around us. The trunk smashed into the earth.

Then there was silence.

I opened my eyes, squinting into the moonlight. Alive—I was alive.

Lying on my back, the peaceful winter sky winked with a thousand stars above me. There was dust and twigs all over my face. I tried to cough, but I couldn't draw a breath because something heavy was on top of me.

It was Zeph.

He didn't move from where he lay, his arms hugged around me to shield my body under his. His wings were sprawled out, battered, and pinned by huge branches that had fallen when the tree smashed through the forest around us.

"Zeph?" I squirmed, trying to get him to wake up or move. I managed to get an arm free and pat the back of his head to let him know I was okay. I could feel all my fingers and toes. Nothing was broken or hurting.

I realized I couldn't feel him breathing.

As I tried shaking him, my hand bumped against something wooden. I couldn't see what it was because of how his heavy bodyweight was pinning me down, so my fingers traced it. I could feel what seemed to be a broken tree branch. As I followed the branch closer to Zeph's back, I realized it was wet with something—something warm and sticky. I felt around frantically, finding more and more branches that were wet, too.

My heart hit the back of my throat.

They were all sticking out of his back.

"Zeph?" I cried out again.

He didn't answer.

I yelled at the top of my lungs, pleading for someone to come help him. My eyes filled with tears. What if no one came? What if they came too late?

Suddenly, Eldrick's face appeared over us. I cried out for him to help, and he immediately pulled Zeph off me. My body felt hot and cold at the same time.

Zeph's eyes were open, but they looked glazed and distant. There was blood oozing from the corners of his mouth, staining his ashen cheeks.

My heartbeat thrummed in my ears, snuffing out every other sound. I couldn't breathe, I couldn't think. Pain ripped through me as a garbled scream tore past my lips.

I lunged for Zeph. I wanted to touch him, to see him wake up and give me that wonderful sarcastic smirk.

Hank grabbed me. "Stay back," he warned. He was staring past me down at Zeph, blood dripping from a deep cut on his forehead.

What? No! He needed me!

I tried to twist my arm free, but Hank held me back as Eldrick carefully laid Zeph's body facedown on the ground.

There were five, big, snapped-off branches sticking out of Zeph's body like jagged spikes. Eldrick stepped around him, testing the branches and giving some of them gentle tugs. Then he looked up at us, his gaze steely.

Hank nodded.

One at a time, Eldrick began pulling the branches out. It made a horrible, squishing, tearing sound.

It felt like someone was squeezing my lungs from the inside. My body went cold and my knees gave out. I crumpled to the ground. My stomach rolled. I wanted to vomit, but nothing came up.

Hank squatted down beside me. He put had a hand on the back of my neck, like he was trying to steady me. "It's all right," he muttered. "Breathe, girl. Just take some deep breaths."

All right? How the *hell* was this all right?

The gory ripping sounds stopped.

"Well?" Hank asked.

Eldrick was standing over Zeph, still examining the damage. When he met my gaze again, I saw his brows draw up and his mouth scrunch into an uncertain line. "It's bad."

My body shook with a sob. No—oh please, god no.

"He's not gone yet. But he doesn't have enough power left to regenerate from wounds this severe," Eldrick murmured. "We should let her try to revive him."

"If she does this, we won't be able to hide her anymore." Hank didn't sound hopeful at all. "There won't be anything we can do to stop Fir Darrig and the rest of the faerie world from finding her, even if it doesn't work."

Why were they talking about me like I wasn't even here? Shakily, I tried lifting my head. Zeph needed me to be stronger than this. But no matter how I tried, I couldn't steady myself. My chest burned and ached, as though someone were ripping my heart in half.

Eldrick stepped over Zeph's broken body. His silver eyes were focused upon the battle that still raged between Jack Frost and the spriggan. Magical explosions sizzled in the air, their chimes clanging and tolling, followed by the spriggan's thunderous roars. The earth shook and the trees groaned. Jack was holding his own, but it was obvious that all he could do by himself was keep the monster contained in one area.

Eldrick's expression sharpened. His hands curled slowly into fists and his head bowed slightly. The moonlight seemed to withdraw from him as though it were frightened. A whispering, sinister melody hummed in the air.

When he looked back down at me, our eyes met, and I saw something I wasn't expecting. There was wrath blazing in his eyes like silver fire.

"You have to do this, Josie," he said. "It's time."

Tears blurred my vision. I choked and fought for every breath. "B-but I've never tried to work a spell like this on my own! What if I mess it up? What if I do it wrong—what if I hurt him even worse?"

Eldrick bent down, grasping my chin and forcing me to meet his gaze.

"Either you do this or the man you love dies." His eyes narrowed. "Are you prepared to live with that?"

No—I couldn't let that happen.

I shook my head.

"Then you know what you have to do." Eldrick released my chin and stood, beginning to walk away, directly toward the rumble and roar of the battle. With every step, his tall frame flickered and dissolved, becoming something far more monstrous than a spriggan.

A colossal wolf with fur as black as a starless night sky took shape, standing almost as big as the moss-and-earth creature before him. His eyes and claws shimmered like platinum, catching in the moonlight with every stride. He stopped and threw his head back, unleashing a deafening howl. It filled the air with a piercing chime.

I covered my ears, clenching my teeth. The spellsong was so shrill, so intense. The vibrations made my skull ache and soul numb. I'd experienced Eldrick's power before, but never like this. He'd tormented me out of fear.

But I'd never felt him be ... angry.

The spriggan stopped, considering him with a tilt of its near-featureless face.

The ground flinched as Eldrick stamped his front paws. Magical energy snapped and popped off his fangs like an electrical current as his snout wrinkled in a snarl. The crown of long black elk-like horns on his head began to ignite with rings of intricate runes.

The spriggan lunged first, barreling wildly toward Eldrick with its giant mossy fists flailing. Eldrick surged forward, jaws open for the kill. Behind him, the white glimmer of Jack's angelic form made the air go cold again.

"We have to hurry," Hank yelled suddenly. "Are you sure you want to do this?"

My hands shook as I dug into my coat pocket and pulled out my Sharpie. I held it up where he could see, the chill of Jack's magic turning my tears to frost. "Yes."

Zeph's skin was cold to the touch.

Hank helped me roll him over, and I pulled Zeph's head into my lap. I took one of his hands in mine and squeezed it hard. I was hoping to feel him squeeze back, but he didn't respond. He wasn't breathing. His eyes were fixed. The purple runes on his skin had all gone dark.

Hank moved in closer, his expression was grim. Blood still dripped down the side of his face, staining the snow pink. "You know the spell?" he asked quietly. "I never did this one, I don't know the specifics. I can't help you."

I uncapped the Sharpie. "I don't need your help. I can do it myself."

I could. I believed that—I had to. Eldrick had taught me, I'd written this spell a dozen times. I'd even seen Zeph do it once before.

I could do this.

Behind us, the roar of the fight between Eldrick, Jack, and the spriggan raged on. Trees were snapped in half like twigs. Eldrick was slinging magic in a reckless fit of anger. He was big enough to take the spriggan on, and they rolled and brawled like two rabid dogs.

I struggled to push those sounds out of my mind. Whispers of doubt immediately took their place. What if I messed up? What if I killed us both? What if I couldn't save Zeph and was forced to face Fir Darrig without him at my side? Once I did this, they would come. Faeries and creatures far worse than spriggans would be drawn to me like moths to a flame, wanting to use my power or maybe even force me to do something terrible. I would see the darkest parts of the faerie realm.

But I was willing to face any measure of horror if it meant I could see Zeph smile again.

Putting the Sharpie between my teeth, I reached into the pocket of Zeph's pants to get his metal Zippo lighter. I took a piece of a broken branch and lit it on fire, letting in burn for a few seconds before I blew it out. Then I handed it to Hank and spat the marker back into my hand. "I need two spellsong circles—both for containment to keep the energy focused in this spot. You can manage that, can't you?"

He blinked in surprise. "Yes."

"Good."

While Hank used the ash from the burnt end of the stick to trace out the spell circles, I began drawing spellwork on Zeph's forehead. My thoughts raced and my body shivered with a cold sweat from adrenaline. My hands shook so badly I could barely grip the marker.

Peeling off my coat, I quickly rolled up the sleeves of my blouse and drew the runes onto the backs of my arms and hands. The sketches in my dad's journal had described how to do this in detail. I'd spent hours with Eldrick, reading every page and memorizing as many of those spells as I could. Why hadn't I brought the whole journal with me? What if this wasn't right? Was this even the correct spell? Was Zeph even still alive? What if I was too late?

I jerked back, uncertain, and accidentally dropped the stupid marker. I screamed a curse and dove after it.

Before I could reach it, Hank stepped in. He picked up the Sharpie and handed it back to me with a hard frown. "Breathe," he muttered. "You can do it. You're smarter than most people twice your age."

I flashed him a glare as I grabbed the marker. "I thought I was just a tourist."

"You were. But you pull this off, and I'll be forced to retract that." He nodded to the circular spells he'd drawn in the snow. "They're ready."

"Just a second." I unbuttoned the front of my blouse far enough to draw one last symbol ... right over my heart.

Hank shot me a startled look, his eyes wide.

It was excessive—I knew that. Not to mention it probably wasn't a good idea for me to start improvising on Dad's spell designs. But this would pour an immense amount of power into him at once. I had one shot. One chance.

If this didn't bring him back, nothing would.

Hank helped me position Zeph within one of the circles he'd drawn in the snow, and then he took a *big* step back.

My racing pulse made my chest ache as I knelt down on the other circle, so close to the edge I could reach Zeph's head. I put my hands on either side of his face and stared down into his lifeless violet eyes. I ran my thumbs over his cheeks. They were so cold. Tears blurred my vision. I gasped back another sob and bent down to press my lips against his—sealing the spell.

My heartbeat skipped and my fingers and toes began to tingle as though they were falling asleep. A numb, aching sensation swelled through my body, as though an icy riptide was dragging me under. It sucked all the air out of my lungs. Chimes clamored and thrashed in my ears, growing louder and louder. My body wanted to jerk away and break contact.

No—I'd come this far. His lips were still cold, I couldn't stop yet.

I gripped him harder, pouring every drop of magical power I could into his body.

A thundering crescendo of chimes boomed in the air. It sent spasms through every muscle in my body. My spine curled involuntarily as a wave of buzzing, tingling heat roared from my head all the way down to the ends of my toes.

My arms and legs ached, so numb I couldn't move them at all. My vision tunneled, going darker and darker. I couldn't hold on. I ... I wasn't strong enough. He was going to need more than that to regenerate from—

Zeph's lips moved against mine. Warm—they were growing warmer.

My eyes flew open in time to see the fires of life return to his. He took in a deep breath, and his hands shot up to grip my shoulders. His heartbeat pounded so loudly I could hear it like a crashing cymbal in my mind.

I gasped back, breaking the kiss as he groaned through clenched teeth.

His hold on me tightened and his whole body tensed and shuddered as the runes on his skin glowed to life. His wings lifted and grew as paw-shaped feet burst out of his shoes.

"Zeph," I rasped. Had I done it right? Was he going to be okay? If he got sick, I needed to be there. I had to take care of him.

"Josie—" his voice broke as his expression skewed. He sprang forward, arms closing around me with fierce urgency.

I buried myself against his chest.

"Are you all right?" he whispered against my ear. "Are you hurt?"

"Stop it. I'm fine." I hugged him tighter. "Don't ever leave me like that again."

I could hear the smile in his voice. "I'm sorry."

"No you're not."

A loud explosion from the clearing shattered over us.

I winced, looking up as the spriggan howled with fury. It had Eldrick's giant wolf-form in a headlock and was beating his head with repeated, crushing blows. Eldrick yelped every time, and yet continued to snarl and flail. Jack was still casting his frosty magic, trying to distract the monster long enough for Eldrick to get free.

How was this possible? I didn't know much about Jack, but Eldrick was faerie royalty. Was that mossy monster really stronger than him?

"Never seen a spriggan like this before," Hank murmured as he came to stand beside us.

"That's because Fir Darrig made it. He used a centerstone. It's an old sidhe trick. You can do whatever you want to the outside of it, but if you don't hit the centerstone, it doesn't matter," Zeph growled hoarsely. He tried to get up, but his knees threatened to buckle. "Eldrick can wail on it all day if he wants. It won't make any difference. I'll have to try—"

"No! You're not fighting that thing anymore. You can barely stand." I looped an arm under his shoulders to steady him.

"I'm fine," he muttered.

"Cut the crap," Hank barked. "She gave you enough juice to regenerate your wounds, but as long as the curse is sucking your life away, you can't hold enough power to fight a creature like that. You won't last two seconds."

Zeph shot him a glare. "Got a better idea, old man? I'm all ears."

I did. "So ... if we can destroy that stone, the magic holding it together will dissolve?"

"Basically." Zeph arched an eyebrow at me. "But the centerstone is hidden deep inside it. You'd need one hell of a blast to—"

I broke away from him, snatched up the burnt stick I'd used to draw my spellwork, and started running.

"Josie! No! Are you crazy?" Zeph shouted.

Yeah, maybe this time I was. But there wasn't time to think about it. I couldn't afford to second-guess myself now. I'd brought Zeph back from the brink of death. I could do this, too.

I could fight for the people I loved.

Okay, so this probably wasn't one of my better ideas. It was one thing to bring Zeph back using a spell I'd already seen in practice before. It was another to go charging headlong into a fight with a colossal earth monster that was slinging trees around like baseball bats.

A bad idea, really. Awful. Just terrible.

I sprinted headlong toward the clearing where Eldrick and Jack Frost were still fighting for their lives. The only weapon I had was the charred stick in my hand. That's probably why all my friends were staring at me like I was completely out of my mind.

Well—except for Zeph. He was trying to limp after me while Hank held him back, yelling curses at the top of his lungs.

But I had a plan.

Using my power to revive Zeph had made me an even bigger target, so as soon as I was out in the open, the spriggan whirled around and let out a bellowing cry. It tossed Eldrick aside before charging straight for me.

Eldrick was up again in an instant, shaking the snow off his back and taking up the chase. He wasn't going to make it. He was fast, but the spriggan had a head start.

I skidded to a halt, gaping up at the creature that was looming right in front of me, thundering closer and closer.

Oh god. I was … about to die.

I looked back at Zeph. His face had gone pale. He was flailing against Hank, shrieking my name.

A burst of blue light exploded in front of me, sending me sprawling backwards. I landed on my back in the snow, breathless. My head throbbed as I sat up, squinting at the figure hovering above me on gleaming white wings.

"You guys are fun." Jack laughed. He did an aerial front flip and started wheeling in circles around me. "We should hang out more often!"

Jack's blow had stunned the spriggan long enough for Eldrick to catch up to it. With his powerful jaws locked onto one of the creature's thick hind legs, Eldrick struggled to drag it backwards.

This was my chance.

"I need some clean snow!" I called after Jack. "I have to make a big spell circle!"

"Coming right up!" Jack grinned as he fluttered up, sweeping his hand toward the ground in front of me, conjuring up a fresh layer of untouched snow.

Perfect.

I used the charred end of the stick to draw a big circle in the untouched frost. That was the base of most spells, I'd learned. A framework to build from. This was one of the more complicated spells from Dad's journals— and also one of the most useful. It was the first one I'd even tried committing to memory. A failsafe, just in case.

Sweat made my hair stick to my face and neck as I scrambled, quickly adding symbols all around the outside of the circle. They had to line up perfectly outside the rim and there wasn't time to start over. I drew more circles within the first one like tree rings emanating from a central point. Some of them were a little crooked. It wasn't my best work—I mean, who can draw in snow very well?

It didn't have to be pretty. It just had to work.

A crash made the earth shake and I stumbled, nearly falling as Eldrick's massive wolf form hit the ground nearby. Blood dripped from his toothy jaws as he slicked his ears back, snarling at the spriggan as he stood again.

The spriggan was barreling straight for me again.

From the air, Jack called my name and dove toward me.

"No!" I yelled at both of them. "You have to run! Get out of the way! Now!"

Eldrick's silver eyes flashed to me, then to the design I'd drawn in the snow. His pupils went as small as pinpoints. Jack took one look at it, and his face went pale. Well, pale-*er*. He made an immediate turn, streaking toward Zeph and Hank to take cover with Eldrick galloping after him, tail tucked.

The spriggan was coming. The ground shook under its weight. It roared, reaching out for me. "JOOOOOSIE!"

I had five seconds—maybe six.

I stood in the center of all those circles, watching the spriggan get closer. Calmness washed over every part of me—a certainty I'd never experienced before—as I added the final symbol: an arrow pointing straight at the oncoming spriggan.

This was it; this was my chance to slap away the hands of fate that wanted to choke the life out of me.

Stretching my arms out wide, I took a deep breath. My gaze focused on the spriggan as every corner of my mind went quiet. No more doubts. No more insecurities.

No backing down now.

I stamped a foot on the star-shaped symbol in the center of all the circles. The rings lit up one-by-one, flashing to life. White light exploded into the air with a force that rocked me back onto my heels. There was a loud, concussive burst of sound like a cacophony of tolling bells. The spriggan's roars became broken and garbled as the force of my spell radiated outward, following the path of the arrow, and consumed the monster.

My vision spotted. The dull, tingling ache swelled through my body as more of that magical power was sucked out of me. My knees gave out as the ground shook. I fell forward, barely catching myself on my forearms. Everything was spinning and my stomach rolled dangerously as I wheezed for breath.

Had I ... used too much magic?

Everything was eerily quiet.

I raised my head, my vision still swimming.

There was a huge pile of rubble only a few yards away from where I lay. A mixture of crushed-up boulders, shredded roots, and bent trees was all that remained of the spriggan. At the very top of the heap was a single, smooth glittering stone the color of milky glass. It was about the size of a potato with something tied around it.

It was hair—a small lock of *red* hair. My hair.

How? How had Fir Darrig gotten his hands on ...

Lumi.

I clenched my teeth. When she'd tried to kidnap me from the fair, I'd heard a cutting sound. I'd almost forgotten about it. After all, almost suffocating to death had been a little more important.

She must have stolen it. It was such a small amount, I'd never even noticed.

"Josie!" A pair of arms lifted me up suddenly. The motion made my head spin again and I slumped against the familiar warmth of Zeph's chest. "What the heck were you thinking? Do you have any idea what would have happened if you had messed that spellwork up? How do you even know how to do that?"

I forced a drowsy smile. "You're not the only one with secrets."

He studied me with bloodshot eyes. "Shit. You *did* mess it up," he muttered through clenched teeth. "You have to put a cap on a spell like that! Otherwise it'll drain you completely and ..."

I couldn't hear the rest. My ears were ringing and my body shivered with a cold sweat.

Had I messed it up? I couldn't remember. Everything was getting hazy. My chest was heavy and everything was going numb. The harder I tried to focus, the more everything seemed to slip away into blurred shades of gray.

The next thing I knew, I was stretched out on my back staring up at the starry night sky. My back and legs were cold—cold and wet. From the snow? Yeah, that had to be it. I was lying on the ground like I'd just gotten finished making snow angels.

Something blocked my view. A face? Suddenly, a blast of warm air forced its way past my lips, directly into my lungs. My body jerked out of control. I pitched forward, sitting upright and sucking in a frantic breath of the frigid night air.

I coughed and wheezed, blinking away the blurriness in my eyes. "W-what happened?"

No one answered.

Zeph was kneeling in the snow next to me, his face blanched of all color and his eyes wide and haunted. His broad shoulders sagged and his head slowly dipped toward his chest. Behind him, Eldrick and Hank were gazing down at me with similarly tense expressions. Dried blood was smeared around Eldrick's frowning mouth as he stood with his arms crossed. Hank didn't look any happier as he combed his fingers through his goatee with one hand. In the other, he held the centerstone with the lock of my hair still tied around it.

"You almost died," Jack said quietly. He was crouched at my feet, his golden eyes glittering in the starlight. He offered me my coat with an uncertain smile. "Here, you must be freezing."

"Oh ..." I swallowed, reaching shakily for it. "T-thank you."

The silence was thick as I dared to look at Zeph again.

"Who taught you those spells?" he demanded in a low voice.

I stiffened.

Before I could say anything, Zeph was on his feet. He lunged for Eldrick, seizing him by the shirt collar. "*You!*"

The two men growled and bared their teeth like animals as Zeph slammed him up against the trunk of the nearest tree and pinned him there with a forearm under his throat.

"No!" I scrambled to my feet. "Stop! Leave him alone!"

"I told you *no* magic. *No* spellwork. None," Zeph roared. "You almost killed her, you son of a bitch. Now you basically have. They'll be coming for her."

Eldrick didn't fight back. "Don't be a fool. They were coming either way. Nothing about her situation has changed. The only difference is now she doesn't have to face that without you."

Zeph's face flushed and his mouth screwed up, brow twitching as he stared Eldrick down. At last, he took a step back, releasing his chokehold.

"Or maybe I should have told her there was nothing we could do to save you?" Eldrick snapped, his tone pure venom. "I am doing what you should have been every single day since her father's death—arming her for a battle that has always been an inevitability for her. You cannot change fate. You cannot change what you are. You can only change yourself and how well equipped you are to handle it. So far, you have failed miserably in that regard."

Zeph looked away, past everyone else, right at me. Our eyes met for an instant, and his expression skewed. His jaw went rigid and he squeezed his eyes shut. "I …"

"Don't speak. You've already made yourself look sufficiently idiotic for one evening." Eldrick straightened his shirt collar and walked away. He went straight up to Hank and held a hand out for the centerstone. "We must destroy it."

Hank didn't argue. He passed the hunk of crystal over, and Eldrick crushed it into dust with one squeeze of his hand.

I turned to look back at Zeph, who still hadn't moved. He stood alone in the snow, separated from the rest of us. His beautiful wings had melted away, leaving behind the tall, human-looking shape of the man I loved.

My footsteps crunched on the frozen earth, giving me away as I approached. "Zeph?"

He wouldn't look at me again. "He's ... right. I am an idiot. I just ..."

I took his hand and wove my fingers through his. "I know. You just wanted to protect me."

"I suck at it."

"Well, I guess I suck at spellwork." I gave his hand a little tug, coaxing him into looking back at me. "We'll both have to practice some more."

Zeph didn't smile.

His expression remained distant and bleak as he walked along with the rest of us out of the forest. My hold on his hand was all that kept him near me. I wondered if I let him go, if he would disappear altogether. That thought made my chest constrict, and I gripped his hand harder.

"You didn't tell me she was the vessel," Jack piped up as he fluttered by, spreading his lovely wings for a graceful landing on his birdlike feet. There was a mischievous twinkle in his eyes as he studied me. "I can sense you clearly now, though. You better be careful. Are you going to pick the next ruler this year? There's a Singing Moon soon, isn't there?"

My pulse stalled and started. That's right ... if everything Zeph and the others had told me about the vessel was true, then I was going to have to pick a new king or queen for the faerie court.

"I, um, I haven't decided." I stole a sideways glance at Zeph. His brow was furrowed and his jaw was clenched, like there was something he wanted to say.

Eldrick cleared his throat and changed the subject. "How is your lovely mother fairing, Jack? I haven't paid her a visit in quite some time."

Jack fluttered excitedly over to him, chatting with Eldrick like they were old acquaintances as we made our way back to the vineyard again. I spotted the ghostly outline of the barn and farmhouse through the trees.

Chills prickled over my skin as we got closer. The police cars were all gone. There was no sign of any of the guests, either. No lights. Nothing but the wind whistling through the bare limbs of the trees. The house itself bore no sign of life at all. Some of the windows were smashed out, and the doors had all been boarded shut. Even the barn looked like it was about to cave in from decay.

"It was all an illusion?" I stopped to stare at the abandoned house. My pulse was still racing as I tried to make sense of it. The wedding, the police cars, and the children—none of it was real.

"A trap is more like it," Hank answered gruffly. "And a damn good one. I didn't sense a thing."

"Ah, well, try not to take it personally," Zeph murmured. "You are getting pretty senile these days."

Hank scowled. "Yeah? Then what's your excuse?"

My head was throbbing as I climbed into the backseat of Hank's old Cadillac. I couldn't fathom it—how could *none* of that have been real? The policeman we'd spoken to had looked and sounded just like a normal person. I couldn't even comprehend the depth of the magical power Fir Darrig had used to create all that. And to fool Zeph, Eldrick, and Hank so easily? It made my insides tie up in knots.

Zeph got into the back with me, but neither of us said a word. He slipped his hand out of mine to light up one of his painkiller cigarettes, and I wondered if he was only doing that so he wouldn't have to touch me.

Outside, Hank was thanking Jack Frost for his help. The two shook hands, exchanging a few parting words. Jack leaned around to wink at me again before he took off into the sky.

My phone chirped inside my coat pocket. I took it out, and quickly checked the screen.

[CAMILLA]: Are you okay? Did something happen? We can sense you. Others are talking.

I tried to be discreet as I sent her a reply, turning so that Zeph couldn't see. I explained what had happened as briefly as I could, and assured her I was fine. I was about to put my phone away again when the screen flashed with another message.

[CAMILLA]: Be careful. Freddy says he has something for you. Let's meet soon.

Hank didn't like Eldrick driving his car. But with his head still bleeding from the scary-looking knot forming on his forehead, we all agreed he shouldn't be behind the wheel. Still, the tension in the air didn't let up for a second as we drove home in complete silence.

Eldrick parked on the curb outside our apartment building long enough for Zeph and I to get out. I didn't want to let it show, but I was still feeling numb and dizzy from the spells I'd used. No one had mentioned that there might be an issue with me using too much of my power at once. Now, I was feeling the full effect of it. My headache had gotten worse, like a pulsing pressure in my brain.

"I'll take him home and come straight back." Eldrick called after us.

I waved a hand to let him know that was okay.

Once we were back in my apartment, I shrugged out of my soggy winter coat. It was soaked through with melted snow and speckled with Zeph's blood. My head swam as I started for the kitchen. Aspirin—I just needed some aspirin and a glass of water. I'd be fine then ... right?

Zeph caught me as my legs gave out. "Easy, princess." His tone was softer, gentler, as he slipped his arms under my back and knees to carry me. "Let's get you to bed."

My head lolled against his shoulder. "You're angry at me, aren't you?"

"No."

"You are. I can tell."

He sighed deeply. "No, not at you. Let's talk about it later. You need to rest." He stopped at the edge of my bed and laid me down, carefully tucking me into the warm blankets.

"I thought you were the one who was supposed to get sick from using too much magic," I tried to tease him. "No puking this time?"

Zeph chuckled. "No. You gave me quite a jolt—enough to keep me sustained for a few hours unless I try any heavy spellwork. Last time I had to dump every drop you gave me into that boy. If I'm careful, I can make this last and taper it off gradually. No puking."

I reached up, brushing my fingers over his stubbly cheek. "I'm sorry. I would have fixed it before, if I'd known."

"Nah," he muttered and placed his hand over mine, holding it against the side of his face. "I deserved it that time."

No argument there. Maybe I deserved it this time, since I was the one sneaking around and learning spells behind his back. But if I hadn't ... he would have ...

"I thought I lost you there for a minute." My voice cracked. "Don't do that to me again, idiot."

Zeph didn't answer. His gaze met mine, riddled with intensity and emotion that never made it past his lips. Didn't he know I couldn't handle it? I couldn't lose another person I loved. I wondered if that was part of being the vessel; if there was some curse on me that said I was doomed to lose everyone I cared about because of it. Was it better just not to care at all?

Tears slid down the side of my face as I squeezed my eyes shut. A sob slipped past my lips.

"Hey, it's okay." The bed lurched as Zeph climbed in next to me. His body curled around mine, pulling me into that special place in the middle of his embrace. A place that was mine and mine alone. "I'm not going anywhere."

I hid my face against him, pulling my arms and legs in close to my body. "My dad did a lot of research about the vessels who came before me," I whispered. "His journals said they almost always had horrible, tragic deaths. It said that even after a vessel selected the new faerie leader, people and monsters continued to hunt them down because of their power. People tortured them, trying all kinds of horrible ways to steal all of their magic."

Until today I hadn't understood what that might feel like.

"I won't let anything like that happen to you."

"I'm scared, Zeph."

"I'm right here." His breath stirred in my hair. He kissed my forehead, my eyes, and the end of my nose. "Go to sleep."

"Stay here with me."

He ran a thumb over my lips. "There's nowhere else in the universe I'd rather be."

"We were severely outclassed," Eldrick muttered.

Around a small table at the back of the bistro near my school, I sat with Freddy, Camilla, and Eldrick. It was well past the bistro's usual closing hours, but a small bribe and a little eye batting from Camilla had bought us some extra time. We had to make this count, after all. Zeph had already gone to work at the bar, and as far as he knew, Eldrick and I were just out for dinner. Nothing suspicious about that, right?

"I find that hard to believe." Freddy's tone had an edge. "*You* were with her, weren't you? That's a lot of muscle for one spriggan."

Eldrick's eyes smoldered and he licked the front of his teeth.

I leaned in between them. "He's not lying." Now wasn't the time for them to have a pissing contest. "It was a trap from beginning to end, and none of us could see through it. Zeph was nearly killed. I was almost eaten. Twice, actually."

Camilla swirled her spoon in her coffee cup before looking up. "You said he used mandrake children?"

Eldrick seemed to relax. He nodded. "Two, to be precise. I speak not as an Unseelie, but as a fae, when I say that the amount of magic he had poured into that area was nothing short of grotesque. He disfigured an ancient tree. He turned the season on itself. It was abhorrent."

"A show of force?" Freddy looked surprised.

"If not a blatant challenge. Two weeks remain until the Singing Moon is upon us, and I have taught Josie everything I can." Eldrick gave a frustrated sigh. "I'm no scholar, and teaching spellwork is not my specialty. Whether out of stubbornness or pride—Zeph still refuses to be a part of her education."

"Both run rampant in his family, I'm afraid." Camilla smirked at her husband and gave his shoulder a nudge.

"We have been through her father's research from cover to cover. He believed the Fibbing Gate was our only chance to be rid of Fir Darrig, and I tend to agree with him," Eldrick continued as he fidgeted with his napkin. "The years have made Fir Darrig powerful, even beyond my own assumptions, and now he's recruiting others to his cause. Lumi has chosen to side with him. There are likely many others who would join with him if for no other reason than to avoid his wrath."

"You think he's planning a war?" Freddy looked pale. "Against the Seelie Court? Or humanity?"

"If he is able to take Josie, he could easily win both," Eldrick replied.

I held my breath, watching the light die out in Freddy's eyes. He bowed his head slightly. "That's … that's just madness."

"Is it? You know what he's like as well as I do." Camilla was swirling her coffee again. "Whatever happened all those years ago has changed him. He obviously has no regard for the old laws or the proper treatment of the earth now. Even the lowest of Unseelie rogues still have some respect for at least one of those."

Eldrick nodded. "He must be stopped—preferably before any of us perish because of him."

Wait, what? I stole a quick glance at Eldrick as he sat stiffly, scowling down into his own empty coffee cup. Was he worried about *Zeph*?

"I wonder if Aneira would join our cause, since it was her handiwork Fir Darrig defiled by having his summer overrun her winter," Freddy murmured as he rubbed his chin.

Camilla didn't look convinced. "She might, but if Jack already fought for her honor once, she might consider that more than enough. After all, she doesn't have much love for humanity."

I turned to Freddy and Camilla hopefully. "What about the Fibbing Gate? Have you learned anything else about it? Do you know where it is? Or how we can use it?"

They glanced at one another and then quickly looked away, shifting in their seats. Freddy cleared his throat. "Unfortunately, it seems to be a lot more complicated than I anticipated."

He glanced both ways before reaching under his seat to drag out the large duffel bag he'd brought along. As he unzipped it, Camilla began to explain, "Most faeries think it's nothing more than an old story. Those who do believe it also believe that it should never be spoken of. They fear the foul monsters that lurk beyond the gate, in our old world. They worry those horrors might follow us here."

"The skiia," I remembered aloud.

Beside me, Eldrick's hands curled into fists on the table.

"Only a very small portion of the faeries living in the world now actually remembers them from firsthand experience. As you know, there were only five pilgrims who made the journey," Camilla continued, her gaze softening upon Eldrick. "They did bring some of their family members and children along with them, but there were barely fifty in total. So for most of us, the skiia and the Fibbing Gate are little more than a scary bedtime story passed down from our elders."

The silverware rattled as Freddy dropped what looked like a big, rolled up tapestry on the table between us. "All record of the Fibbing Gate had been stricken from the whispering books. Heavy seals have been put in place so that those words could never be read again. But I did find this."

He unrolled the thick, musty smelling fabric onto the table.

The tapestry wasn't much bigger than a movie poster, and the colors of the threads and fabrics were faded and frayed at the seams. It depicted an arched doorway surrounded by a field of stars. A crescent moon hung over it, sending down streams of light that almost seemed to shimmer when the fabric moved.

The door itself was made of pieces of gray, cross-shaped fabric that had been carefully placed together like a patchwork quilt. Something about that shape was familiar. I took out one of my dad's journal and flipped through the pages, finally opening up to the one where he had sketched out a mineral called staurolite.

It had the same shape as the pieces on the tapestry.

"You called this a weeping stone before, didn't you?" I held the book up so Eldrick could see. Then I pointed to the tapestry. "It's the same shape."

Freddy and Camilla craned their necks to see, too.

"She's right," Camilla gasped.

Freddy frowned. "Weeping stones contain iron, which is completely resistant to all forms of faerie magic. That's a powerful deterrent for anyone who might want to open the gate again." He reached out, gesturing for me to pass him the journal so he could take a look. "It would almost ensure that neither side of the doorway could be breached by anyone."

"Unless they were human," I added as I handed it over. "If the gate is made of iron, then it's a safe bet faeries didn't make it by themselves, right? They had to have humans help them."

Freddy's eyes lit up suddenly. He dropped my dad's journal and dove back into his duffel bag and took out a large, yellowed piece of paper. One edge was tattered, as though it had been ripped out of a book.

He spread it out before me, tapping at a drawing in the center that was surrounded by faerie text—or at least, it must have been faerie text. Most of it had been scribbled out with red ink.

"D-did you tear that out of a whispering book?" Camilla sounded horrified.

Freddy shrugged. "Well, it's not like I could have carried the whole book out without someone noticing. It weighed nearly two hundred pounds."

I scooted in closer so I could see. "What's a whispering book?"

"One our ancient anthologies containing all of faerie history, even from our own world," Eldrick said.

"Think of it like a history book," Camilla added. "Only, it's been enchanted to continuously record major historical events even as the occur."

"So, couldn't we look there to find out what happened to make Fir Darrig do all of this? I mean, even if the parts about the Fibbing Gate have been stricken out, there must still be something about Fir Darrig's past in there, right?" Maybe if we could, I could find some way to reason with him.

Freddy shook his head. "I tried that. Seems I wasn't the only one who was willing to rip a few pages out. Someone had already removed everything about him from during that time."

I deflated, slumping back into my chair. So much for that.

My eyes wandered over the drawing, studying it. It depicted a very similar arched door to the one on the tapestry—a door made of little crosses, complete with a crescent moon at the top.

As my gaze traveled down the page, I noticed a normal, human-looking woman standing beside the door with flowing, curly hair. She was dressed in a billowing gown, wearing a heart-shaped necklace around her neck.

That wasn't the weirdest part, though.

She was holding hands with a strange creature—obviously some kind of faerie. It had a human upper body that looked like a young man, but its lower half was a lion—sort of like a centaur. He had two brightly colored bird wings, and a tall crown made of twigs and leaves on his head.

There were numerous paragraphs written beneath the drawing, but they had all been blotted out with that same red ink. I couldn't read any of it.

"Why are the words scratched out?" I asked.

"If you want to write something a faerie won't be able to read, you have to use old fountain ink. Old ink contains iron, which is why it appears red. It's simply rusted over time." Freddy explained. "They've covered the words so no faerie can read them. We call it sealing them, because it can't be reversed."

"These were undoubtedly sealed because someone didn't want the location of the gate compromised." Eldrick snorted. "Although it does seem to be made of weeping stones. That would make it impossible for any faerie to open it."

"Not without human help," Camilla guessed. "You would need both to open it again."

Freddy nodded in agreement. "A faerie to summon it, a human to open it."

"So how do we find it?" I glanced back down at the picture. "This guy, the one with the crown. He was the faerie king, right? If he's in the picture, he must know where to find it."

All eyes fell back to the page.

"It would seem so," Eldrick murmured quietly, his brow creasing. "But anyone versed in our history would know better. He has never actually worn the crown."

"Well, who is he? Is he still alive? Can't we ask him where the gate is?" I was already getting excited. This was a promising lead.

"That would be ill advised." Eldrick leaned back, his eyes never leaving the image.

They all looked reluctant, even scared. "Why?"

"Because that's Fir Darrig," a familiar voice growled from behind me.

My body instantly went stiff. I turned around slowly to meet a blazing violet glare.

Zeph shoved his hands into his coat pockets, his head turning slowly as he studied everyone sitting around the table one at a time. By the time he got back to me, I could barely breathe. My throat closed up, and I was gripping the edge of the table.

Then he gave one, small nod, and turned around like he was going to leave.

A wave of guilt come over me like an ocean tide.

Freddy raced out of his seat, stepping into the path of his much more dangerous-looking brother with a desperate expression. "Zeph, please listen to me. We only want to help. We—"

"I don't need your help," Zeph yelled.

"Don't be stubborn," Freddy snapped back. "Time is running out for all of us, not just you." He moved in closer, his hands curled into fists. "What will dying prove, hm?" He pointed back at me. "You'll be gone, and *she* will still be vulnerable. If Fir Darrig gets his hands on her, it'll be the end of us all. Don't think for a moment I'm not aware of that."

Zeph took an aggressive step toward his little brother. "What you do suggest? Maybe I should just stick a big apple in her mouth and serve her up on a silver platter just to save my own skin?"

"Why don't we take this outside, boys?" Camilla suggested as she stood and gathered her coat. "You're making a scene."

A few of the bistro workers were peeking out from the back kitchen to see what was going on.

They whispered and stared at us the entire time we were packing up and making our way out the door. I was so embarrassed I wanted to melt into the floor. We managed to get three steps from the restaurant before Freddy grabbed Zeph by the arm and shoved him up against the brick storefront.

"You act like this is your only option! We can beat this curse, Zephiel. We've overcome worse before! We can save you and destroy Fir Darrig," Freddy insisted.

Zeph gave a sarcastic chuckle. "Do you even hear yourself? Or does stupid come so naturally that you don't notice it anymore?"

"I hear plenty. Right now, all I'm hearing from you is angry noise." Freddy closed his eyes and rubbed his forehead before shifting the duffel bag of treasures tucked under his arm. "You're afraid. I know you are. Anyone would be. You've sacrificed everything and gotten nothing for it. You're about to die for the person you love, but you know it won't save her.

You don't think anyone can do anything to stop this. That's why you've … given up."

Zeph's expression faded from rage to anguish. His chin trembled as he looked down, stuffing his hands back into his coat pockets. I moved closer and looped my arm through his.

Freddy grasped his shoulder. "I can't undo what happened in the past, and I won't apologize for choosing my wife over you. Instead, I'd hope that now you'd understand that choice." He glanced at me. "But I'm here now. I want to help. Will you let me?"

Zeph slowly raised his gaze, his face expressionless as he stared at his brother. My stomach fluttered. He couldn't reject him—not now. Not like this. I'd always known Zeph to be stubborn, but he needed to let go of his pride just this once—for his own sake, not mine.

At last, he let out a noisy sigh, scratched at his forehead, and muttered a string of curses before giving a small nod. "Fine."

I sagged against him with relief, leaning my head against his arm.

"You're wrong about Fir Darrig, though," he mumbled. "He doesn't know where the Fibbing Gate is. No one does because it's not a physical place. It's a portal, like a spell circle. Only the crowned king or queen of the faeries can call it forth, and only human hands can open it."

"H-how do you know that?" Freddy sounded worried.

Zeph shrugged. "Because I was there when Josie's dad discovered it."

A hard knot formed in the pit of my stomach. I started to pull away. There was more to that story—something he wasn't going to talk about in front of them. I had a bad feeling I knew why he wouldn't, but I didn't want to talk about it in front everyone else, either.

Zeph flicked me a glance, his expression somber. "He'd gotten his hands on a wild tome. I tried to stop him, I swear. I told him it was dangerous— that we should just burn the thing. But he was … obsessed."

"What does that mean? What's a wild tome?" I looked around to all my friends for some kind of clue. Freddy and Camilla were staring down like they were avoiding my question completely.

Only Eldrick would meet my gaze. "Put simply, it's a book of unregulated spellwork." His mouth straightened and he cleared his throat. "Perhaps now isn't the time to go into that subject. I'm sure Zeph will be happy to explain more later when you two can discuss it at length."

I arched an eyebrow. Was he … actually showing Zeph a little respect? I couldn't think of any other reason he'd be giving us personal space like that. Usually he was happy to flex his superior knowledge of, well, everything.

Freddy shifted his weight, glancing up at Zeph again. "You'll help us, then?"

Zeph didn't answer right away. He moved away, letting my arm slide out of his, as he took a fresh cigarette out of his pocket and put it between his lips. "We're going to need four pieces of naturally occurring staurolite," he murmured at last. "They have to be perfectly shaped, like crosses, no cracks or faults."

It seemed ridiculously easy. Four crystals? That was all?

"Isn't there anything else?" Freddy asked.

Zeph shot him a scathing glare. "Of course. But that's not something we can get our hands on right this second."

"What do you mean?" Camilla frowned.

"Weren't any of you listening? Only a faerie ruler can summon the gate. As in, a king or queen." Zeph fidgeted with this Zippo lighter, snapping it open and closed. "Which we don't have because she can't pick one until the night of the Singing Moon."

"Genius," Eldrick murmured quietly. He sounded impressed. "That was why Fir Darrig designed your curse to coincide with the Singing Moon. He was confident you would surrender to his demands by bringing Josie to him on that night in order to save your own life. Without a king or queen, and no way to choose one until that night, no one would be able to call forth the only binding circle that might be able to contain him. It's quite brilliant."

Zeph snorted. "Not the word I would use to describe it, but yeah, basically. That's also why he'd love to get his hands on her before then.

Until recently, when little Miss Showoff decided to go nuclear on us with her spellwork, he didn't know exactly where she was."

I crossed my arms. "Well excuse me for not wanting to be the helpless victim anymore."

"So … this is why you think it's hopeless?" Freddy stood up straighter. "This is why you gave up? Because you didn't think we could find any way around it?"

Zeph narrowed his eyes. "I *know* you can't. What do you think I've spent all this time doing? There is no way around it. You can't summon the Fibbing Gate without a faerie king or queen. One can't exist until the Singing Moon rises and Josie picks one, which is a whole separate ritual unto itself."

I squeezed my arms around myself tighter. Maybe they'd just assume I was cold. Internally, my brain was in overdrive trying to remember everything from dad's research to come up with an idea of how to stop this. There had to be a loophole somewhere—some way we could get around Fir Darrig's carefully designed scheme. I needed more time. I needed to think.

"We should tread carefully," Eldrick suggested. "We will have to consider our next move with great caution. Until we can come up with a reasonable plan, we should turn our focus to acquiring the staurolite and keeping Josie out of Fir Darrig's hands."

"I think I can manage the staurolite," Camilla agreed. "Leave that part to us. You boys concentrate on keeping my goddaughter safe."

"Here, maybe there's more you can discern from these." Freddy handed the duffel bag to me with a thin smile that never reached his eyes. "We should get going. I have a meeting with Nagroot in an hour, and the last thing we want is for him to get suspicious. If the Seelie Court got wind that we were plotting against Fir Darrig … or even dreaming of summoning the Fibbing Gate …"

Camilla took her husband's arm and smiled at us warmly. "That won't happen. The secret stays between us."

I nodded and smiled back. "We'll be in touch. Take care of yourselves."

Standing between Zeph and Eldrick, I watched Freddy and Camilla walk away, hand-in-hand. So much about them was still a mystery to me. They were always kind, and they treated me like family. Even though they had shared a close relationship with my parents before, it was strange to be around them now. I still didn't remember them—but I found myself wishing that I did.

I watched them disappear down the street. The duffel bag in my arms felt even heavier once they were gone. I was nervous about what else I might find in those old documents, but more than that, I was afraid of how angry Zeph was that I had been having secret meetings with his relatives.

His silence was already making me a nervous wreck. Usually, when he was upset, he let the whole world know as loudly and with as much profanity as possible. But, he didn't say a word as we walked home. Even after he finished his cigarette, he didn't try to hold my hand or look my way. When we got to the front door of the apartment building, I hesitated to go in.

Eldrick turned back when he noticed I wasn't following them. "What is the matter?"

I couldn't look at him. "I just … need a moment by myself."

Zeph had stopped, too, but he didn't turn around.

"You shouldn't be alone out here," Eldrick said. "You know it's dangerous."

"Yes, but I'm okay. I won't be long. I'll be fine."

He didn't push it, although I caught a glimpse of a disapproving frown on his face as he followed Zeph into the building.

Standing alone on the curb, I looked up at the starry sky that peeked through the crowded buildings that towered over me. Jack had done a number on us tonight. Even under my layers of winter clothes and thick coat, I could still feel a tingling chill whenever the wind blew.

I turned around and sat on the front steps, dropping the duffel bag at my feet. It seemed like ages since the last time I sat here. Zeph had been angry with me then, too. A lot had changed in the past few months. My life had been turned upside down, shaken, and scrambled thoroughly. I had no regrets, and I cherished all of it. All the silly fights with Zeph, all the quiet coffee dates with Eldrick, all the stressful days of school watching Joe bask in the glow of everyone's adoration. Remembering it made me nostalgic.

"There's that weird smile again."

I winced as Zeph suddenly appeared. He sat down beside me, holding a fresh cigarette between his lips while he searched his pockets for his lighter. The pain was bad tonight.

"Zeph, I ..." I tried to speak, but the words got hung in my throat.

He arched an eyebrow at me curiously. "What?"

"Nothing," I sighed and leaned forward to rest my elbows on my knees. "I'm sorry about Freddy and Camilla. I shouldn't have gone behind your back like that."

"Relax, princess." He lit his cigarette. I watched as he puffed a few deep breaths and blew a perfect smoke ring into the air. "I'm not mad or anything. I get why you did it. I'd have probably done the same thing, in your shoes."

Somehow, that didn't make me feel any better. "I wish there was some way you could make up with them."

Zeph snorted. "I'm not mad at them, either."

"What?" I was stunned. "Then what was all that noise for? All the years of pushing them away?"

"Think about it this way," he interrupted. "If you had a sibling, a baby brother who was a mushy, emotional ball of insecurity who cried over everything and got pummeled on the playground all his life, what would you do? Would you drag him into a fight?"

"But Freddy thinks you're angry at him for not joining you when you first went to fight Fir Darrig," I told him. "He thinks you've blamed him all these years!"

"Freddy takes everything the wrong way." Zeph shrugged. "I never expected him to follow me. I'm not that stupid, despite what everyone says. And, I wasn't going to let him follow me into this mess after I went and screwed it all up." He took out his lighter and started playing with it again. "I wasn't about to ask my little brother to watch me die. I wasn't going to ask anyone to do that. But you meddling kids just wouldn't leave it alone."

"So … you've been trying to protect him?" I guessed.

"Trying being the key word there," he said. "Failing would be more accurate, I guess. Cause now you're all involved. Does it piss me off? Yeah, a little, but I'm not gonna fight you over it. Nobody wants to die alone. Hell, nobody wants to die at all."

I watched as Zeph dug his hand back into his coat pocket. He pulled out an old, battered envelope and handed it to me. On the outside, written in my dad's handwriting, was my name.

"He wanted me to give it to you when you were ready," Zeph explained. "Now seems as good a time as any."

My hands trembled as I opened the envelope. Inside, there were several sheets of paper covered in handwriting and a collection of old Polaroid photographs. I held the pictures up to the glow of the streetlights so I could see them more clearly.

The first two were of my parents. The sight of their smiling faces immediately made my eyes water. They were hugging each other, grinning happily.

Seeing her—my mom—made my heart hit the back of my throat. I'd almost forgotten how beautiful she was. Her hair was coppery red and she had lots of freckles, like me. She was wearing a red, heart-shaped pendant around her neck that caught the light. My dad had his hand on her round, pregnant belly, and a proud grin on his lips.

The next shot had my brother, William, in it as well. He looked like he was six or seven years old. His hair was dark brown and wavy, and freckles dusted his cheeks and nose. His eyes were a vivid shade of hazel, almost like green marble with streaks of amber. We didn't look much alike, except for the freckles. He favored Dad.

I flipped through the rest of the pictures. Most of them were family snapshots like that or silly pictures of my parents, but then I saw more familiar faces. There was one of mom and Camilla holding up little pink baby clothes. Another one showed Dad, Freddy, and Zeph wearing the most awful, ugly matching Christmas sweaters. They looked like they might be drunk.

I stopped at the last picture, stunned. It was the first one in the stack that I was in. I was a toddler, maybe three or four years old. But that wasn't why I stared at it for so long.

I stared because of who was holding me.

Zeph had me on his hip, grinning at the camera with that signature smirk of his. I had one of my chubby little arms wrapped around his neck, and my cheek pushed up against his. He appeared no older than twelve, lanky and cherub-faced in a way that reminded me of Jack somewhat. His hair and clothes were different, styled for another era, but I recognized those violet eyes right away. His smile was so bright, so full of life and joy.

My heart wrenched. Until that moment, staring at that faded memory, I'd never seen him smile like that before.

"I thought you were ancient? Why have you aged so much since this was taken?" I asked quietly. "Is it because of the curse?"

Zeph shrugged. "A face is just a face; I can change that easily enough. You always liked it better when I looked like a kid. And ... I would do anything if it made you happy."

My lips parted as I stared at him, wondering at all these memories that were somehow missing from my mind. Why? Why had I forgotten all of this? "Zeph, did something happen to me?"

"What do you mean?"

"I don't remember you, Freddy, or Camilla. I don't remember much of anything from before William died. It's fuzzy, and the further I try to think back ..."

He held out his hand for the photos and tapped a finger on the letter that had also been stuffed into the envelope. "Read first. Then we'll talk."

At least, I assumed it was a letter. The first two pages were, but the rest of the pagers were covered in faerie writing, diagrams, and descriptions. At first, I only glanced at them. I was more interested in my dad's letter. But as I read, I realized what was written on those additional pages, and in such extreme attention to detail.

Then, I understood.

Sweet Josie,

I'm giving this message to Zeph for safekeeping until you are old enough to understand what must be done. Perhaps I'll be lucky enough to give it to you myself, but if not, I wanted you to know how much your mother and I love you.

As I write this, you're still so young. I've done my best to protect you from the evil things in the world that will be looking for you soon. In some cases, that's forced me to make difficult decisions. Sometimes I worry that I'm not making the right choices, and I can only pray that your mother would agree with me when I do these things for your sake.

By now, I'm sure you know what you are. You also likely know how it is going to make your life complicated and dangerous. I've done everything I can to make sure you'll be safe if anything happens to me. Some of these things probably seem strange to you, but it's a strange world we live in, Josie. Strange, but beautiful.

Regardless of what he may tell you, I know Zeph is a good man. I know he cares for you. I know he would rather give his life than see you in danger, which is why I made him your legal guardian. I told him he could keep his anonymity, if he wished. I even suggested that it might be better if he did, because the more exposure you have to the faerie world, the more your power will begin to awaken. I gave him permission, if he believed it was best, to cloud your memories so that you wouldn't go looking for him or anyone else tied to his world until the time was right.

Eldrick is a good man, too. He just doesn't realize it, yet. I've seen him defy his heritage and choose to be honorable when he could have been as dark and treacherous as his bloodline would imply. That's why I have contracted him to remain by your side because there may come a day when you need his strength—not just for yourself, but for others, as well. He has much to learn about humanity. His past interactions with us have all but broken his ability to trust any human. But I know you can change that. Until then, try to be patient with him and remember that it is often the hearts that lash out with rage and bitterness that have suffered the most. Anger isn't just an emotion; it's a reaction. It's most often the voice of pain.

What I have to tell you now is difficult. As I write this, Fir Darrig is relentlessly hunting what remains of our family. I admit I'm not as brave as your mother was. She smiled until the very end. She had faith that I would be able to protect our family. But, when Fir Darrig took your brother's life, I lost myself in grief. I poured every ounce of my energy into the pursuit of a way to destroy him so that you, my sweet girl, could be safe.

You are the vessel. It's not something you or anyone else chose. You were born with this gift, and you can never be rid of it. It's true that in the past, most vessels have suffered tragic lives only to die miserably at the hands of some slave master. I believe this cycle will end with you—not because of anything I do, but because you have your mother's fighting spirit. I pray you never lose that fire.

By now, I'm sure you know it's very hard to kill a faerie. It's almost impossible to destroy one as old and powerful as Fir Darrig. Many have tried and failed. They all insist it's as though he's found some way to make himself immortal. If that is the case, he cannot be killed.

Banishing him, however, is much more easily done. The Fibbing Gate may be our only chance to accomplish that. I've risked quite a lot to learn about it, how to summon it, and how it can be opened and closed again. Enclosed in this letter are all the instructions you'll need. Read them carefully. Memorize them. After that, you must destroy them because such knowledge is too dangerous to endure.

You must choose the next faerie ruler, regardless of what else happens. Understand that this choice will change the course of history, not just for faeries, but for mankind as well. You'll be ending a dispute that has existed for thousands of years. Will it end the fighting? No, absolutely not, but your power extends beyond simply being a source of energy for faeries. Vessels have *always been a symbol of unity, which is a far greater thing than any magic circle or spell. You can become the beacon that will call together both humans and faeries in resistance to Fir Darrig, even if the Fibbing Gate fails. So take care when you choose the next king or queen. It should be someone capable of making tough decisions for the sake of the greater good, but with enough conviction of conscience to show mercy. I know you'll choose well.*

Sweet Josie, I love you more than anything. Sometimes I worry I don't tell you that often enough. You are my greatest treasure, and not a moment goes by when I don't feel proud of you. Stay strong. Remember, it's okay to follow your heart, as long as you don't leave your head behind.

Your loving father,
Marcus Barton

I carefully folded the letter back up with the rest of the papers and tucked them into the envelope. For a moment, we just sat in silence. I didn't know what to say, and my mind was struggling to absorb and process everything. I'd known I would have to choose a new faerie ruler for a while, but I hadn't had time to give it any actual thought.

It was a terribly big choice to make on a whim.

"Zeph, can I ask you something?" I glanced sideways at him.

He was staring down at that old Polaroid picture of us. There was a soft, nostalgic look of sadness on his features as he nodded. "Sure."

"Did you cloud my memories so that I wouldn't remember you and the others?"

Zeph gave a heavy sigh. He brushed a thumb over that picture and then placed it back on top of the stack. "Yes."

My heart ached and my stomach twisted. I almost didn't want to know. "Will I ... ever get those memories back?"

"I gave them back a long time ago," he answered quietly.

"What?"

"The feather. The one you've kept on the windowsill." He looked away.

"You didn't think it was strange it never dissolved away?"

I frowned, trying to understand. "My memories are inside that feather?"

"Burn it. Or wait until after the Singing Moon. It'll dissolve on its own then, and you'll get your memories back."

"You mean after you die?" I grabbed his arm, forcing him to look back at me. "You really have given up, haven't you? You don't believe we can win against Fir Darrig."

The depth of the sorrow in his eyes made my throat close up and my confidence crumble. "Josie, he's taken people I've loved from me before. He took my dignity. And now I only have this one chance to keep him from taking the one person in the world who means the most to me."

People he loved? Was he talking about someone else or ...

"What was it that killed my dad? What started the fire?" I asked shakily. "Was it Fir Darrig?"

Once again, he wouldn't meet my gaze. "To be honest, I'm not sure. Magic can have strange effects on human minds. It can be as addictive as any drug. I think your dad was beginning to reach that point. He was consumed with saving you and stopping Fir Darrig. Once he got his feet wet in the world of spellwork, he couldn't get enough. He got his hands on a wild tome somehow. Those books are like hazardous waste."

"What are they?"

"Basically what Eldrick said before—unregulated scripts with original spellwork in them. Sort of like diaries that fae have kept over the years, writing down their own personal spells and charms or things that have been passed down. Because no scholar has ever checked them over to validate if the spells would even work, it's dangerous to use anything you find in a book like that. In most cases, you don't know who wrote it or what their intentions were. It can just as easily kill you as help you." He handed the stack of pictures to me. "He never would tell me who gave it to him. I had my suspicions it was connected to Fir Darrig, and I made the mistake of leaving him alone with it. I didn't have a choice, really. You came home from school early that day. Your dad and I had agreed that you shouldn't see me or any other faerie again until you were ready. We didn't want to provoke any more of your power to surface. When I came back later that night, the whole damn place was up in flames."

Zeph's strong shoulders tensed up. His lips were pressed together like he was trying to keep his emotions from reaching the surface. He shut his eyes tightly and bowed his head before he continued. "I couldn't save him. I was too late. I found you passed out in the hall. You had breathed in too much smoke. I carried you out so the firefighters would find you on the lawn, and I sat beside you until they arrived. Then I had to disappear."

"It wasn't your fault." I put a hand on his back. "You did everything you could, right? But Dad wouldn't listen? I don't know who told you that you had to be everyone's personal bodyguard, but that's not true at all."

He put his head on my shoulder and wrapped one of his arms around my waist. "How can you be so nice to me? I messed everything up. I ruined your whole damn life."

I kissed his forehead. "Don't be such a drama queen. It wasn't your fault that I was born the vessel. My life would have been messed up regardless. Even if you'd never provoked him, Fir Darrig would have come for me anyway, right?"

He didn't answer.

I jostled his shoulder a little, trying to get a response. "Right? Isn't that why you confronted him in the first place?"

"Fine," he grumbled. "Yes, you're right."

Leaning over, I rested my head on top of his. "Besides, the best parts of my messed-up life are the ones with you in it. I want those memories back. So as soon as this is over, that feather is toast."

Zeph cleared his throat. "I should probably forewarn you about the makeup incident, then."

"Makeup incident?"

"Uh, let's just say you wanted to play princesses and William didn't. You did the damn lip trembling thing so … I let you put makeup on me. Tiaras might have also been involved."

I smiled. "Okay, I definitely want *that* memory back."

He groaned. "Figures. Well, as long as there's no repeat performances."

I laughed, but heavy questions hung in my mind like boat anchors, keeping me tethered so that I couldn't feel hopeful. Could we even hope to beat Fir Darrig? Just thinking about the consequences of our failure made my lungs constrict with panic. Zeph's life hung in the balance. If he didn't take me to Fir Darrig on the night of the Singing Moon, then he would die from his curse. That couldn't happen. I could *not* lose this man.

That's when I had an idea.

A bad, terrible, reckless, super dangerous idea.

"Sloppy." Zeph leaned over me. "Start over."

I seriously wanted to ram my pen into his forehead—especially since I knew it wouldn't kill him. Instead, I crumpled up the piece of paper I was practicing my spell circles on and threw it at him.

"Yeah. That's really mature." He scoffed and turned around to drink milk straight out of the gallon.

"You've been at this for six hours. Perhaps she has earned a break?" Eldrick was peacefully sipping his seventh cup of coffee, flicking through the TV channels until he found a medical drama I was beginning to suspect he liked.

"No breaks." I took out another piece of paper to start over yet again. "I can get this."

Eldrick frowned over the rim of his mug. "That's an extremely ancient and complex spell. It's useless to keep trying if you're already exhausted. You won't make any progress that way."

I slammed my hands down on the table. "No! We don't have much time left. I have to memorize this perfectly! I can't screw it up like I did with the focused blast!"

Zeph and Eldrick glanced at one another wordlessly. Abandoning his half empty gallon of milk, Zeph came over to sit down across from me. He put a hand on my arm. "You're not gonna screw it up."

"Yeah? And what if I do?" In the back of my mind, I knew Eldrick was right. If anything, I was getting worse. Fear jumbled all my thoughts. I couldn't concentrate for more than a minute or two without starting to imagine all the things that would happen if I messed this spellwork up.

I stared down at my ink-speckled hands and the mountain of balled up papers spilling out of the garbage can next to me. Everyone was counting on me, and for our plan to work, I had to be able to do this on my own. And right now, my brain probably resembled an old raisin, all shriveled up from stress and worry.

"As you were, then." Eldrick's eyes never left the TV screen, but I could tell from his tone that he was up to something. "Say, wasn't that school dance tonight?"

I flinched.

Zeph perked up. "What dance?"

No—*no*!

"Oh, what do they call it … these human words escape me," Eldrick stalled.

I squeezed my pen so hard I thought it might crack in half.

Zeph hadn't gone to school as Joe in a while, so he had no idea it was prom week. Of course, I'd still been going the extra mile to make sure he wouldn't find out. Eldrick was *supposed* to keep it a secret—that jerk. He was selling me out!

"Prom?" Zeph guessed.

Eldrick smirked, his silver eyes twinkling with mischief. "Ah, yes. I believe that was it. I heard someone mention it just the other day when I walked her home from school."

I could feel the heat of Zeph's glare without looking up to see it. "Prom is tonight? And you didn't say anything?"

I tried to sound blasé. "Must've slipped my mind. Too late now, though. I didn't buy tickets."

I could hear the wicked smirk in Eldrick's voice without having to see it curl up his lips. "No, you didn't. So I took the liberty."

I ground my teeth, frantically trying to devise any excuse to get out of this. There was a faint, magical chime of bells before the pen in my hand morphed into a long, green snake. I screamed and threw it on the floor. "Ew! I hate snakes!"

"You," he said, pointing at me. "Go get ready. Now." He pointed at Eldrick and then held out his hand. "You, tickets. Now."

Eldrick was still smirking as he took out his wallet and passed them over.

I glared at him. "We don't have time for this. This is the last night before the Singing Moon and we can't afford to waste one of our last nights—"

"Going on a date together?" Zeph finished for me.

My heart wrenched and I snapped my mouth shut. Of course I wanted to go out with him again. It didn't even have to be to prom. But I was barely keeping it together as it was. Time was running out. I needed to practice—I had to get a grip on this.

"I don't have anything to wear to a dance like that," I muttered as I started digging through my backpack for another pen.

He stepped in and snatched my backpack away. "That's too bad. Shoulda thought of that before you decided to get all sneaky on me. Now go, or I'll turn your hair into snakes, too."

"B-but seriously, Zeph, I don't have any dresses like that. Please, let's just forget about it," I begged. "It's not a big deal to me, I promise."

He didn't budge. In fact, he didn't speak at all. He just pointed over my head, toward my bedroom, and scowled harder.

I wasn't going to win this fight. I could tell by the furrow of his brow that Zeph already had his heels dug in. One way or another, I was going to the prom tonight.

"Fine." I grumbled.

"Good. Meet me downstairs in two hours."

"Two hours?" I gaped in horror. "That's absurd!"

He arched an eyebrow, apparently unconvinced. "Two hours."

I didn't say anything else as I watched him leave for his own apartment. It wasn't that I didn't want to—there was plenty I wanted to yell at his back as he swaggered out my front door. But it wasn't going to change anything.

People spent months getting ready for prom. I had two measly hours. I didn't have a dress, my hair was a wreck, and my hands were splotched with blue ink from my pen. I was so tired I couldn't think straight.

Basically, I was a hot mess, and it would take more than two hours to fix it.

I trudged back to my bedroom and began digging through my closet. I'd never had much reason to keep a lot of fancy, dressy clothes around. I never went on dates before Zeph came along. No boys my age ever gave me a second look thanks to my reputation as the schoolhouse nutcase. I didn't know how to do super fancy things with my hair or makeup because my mother had never been around to teach me. I didn't even own a pair of heels.

Pulling a plain, khaki, pencil skirt and one of my nicest sweaters from my closet, I laid them out on the bed, and went to take a bath. I couldn't get all the ink off my hands no matter how I scrubbed. When I glimpsed my reflection in the foggy bathroom mirror, I shuddered at my own haunted appearance. There were dark circles under my eyes from not getting enough sleep.

My face burned with humiliation as I came back into the kitchen, dressed like I was going to visit a relative in the nursing home instead of my senior prom. I couldn't even bring myself to look at the mirror hanging in the living room. I didn't want to see what I looked like again if I could help it.

Eldrick was leaning in the kitchen doorway, holding a coffee mug as his silver eyes glanced me up and down. His dark, handsomely defined eyebrows knitted together like he didn't approve.

"I hardly think that is appropriate evening attire," he observed between sips of coffee.

"It's all I have." I was trying to keep up a cool front, but simply admitting that out loud made my throat feel tight and uncomfortable. I swallowed back the emotion and blinked the tears out of my eyes.

"Hmm." Eldrick set his mug on the counter and walked over to stand right behind me. "I can't reasonably allow any ward of mine to go to a ball looking like this."

"You were the one who threw me under the bus, remember?" My chin trembled. "And it's not a ball. It's just a stupid dance."

"I'm told there's little difference between the two."

Suddenly, Eldrick put his hands over my eyes. Everything went dark, and I could feel his presence standing very close behind me. His scent was complex, like a mixture of old books, rich coffee, and crisp eucalyptus.

"W-what are you doing?"

"Hush," he scolded.

Chimes of magic whispered in the air, humming over my skin. It made my pulse race as I took in a shuddering breath.

Slowly, Eldrick took his hands away from my eyes.

My breath hitched. A beautiful silk gown the color of platinum hugged my body in all the right ways. It flared at the knees, and fit like a glove everywhere else. The bodice was encrusted with little sparkling bits that looked suspiciously like diamonds. There were black satin gloves on my arms, and a big, black diamond pendant hanging against my chest.

When I went to look in the living room mirror, I realized even my hair had been twisted into a fancy half-updo. There were matching black diamond studs in my ears. My makeup was perfect and my lips were an alluring shade of ruby red.

Eldrick's reflection appeared in the mirror, standing behind me with his head tilted to the side. "This will do, I suppose."

"This ... this is ..." I couldn't get the words out. Tears welled in my eyes, threatening to smear all that beautiful makeup.

"It isn't free, I can assure you. I'm not some godmother sweeping in to grant all your desires without any expectation of payment." He grasped one of my hands and turned me around to face him. "I'm not that generous."

I smiled. "Figures there'd be a catch. What do you want?"

He drew me in closer and put his other hand on my waist. I stiffened. My heart raced and my face started to feel hot.

"I will settle for a dance. The first dance, mind you. Be sure you make that imbecile downstairs aware of that fact."

I smiled wider, and nodded.

As we danced in the living room, swaying slightly to a nonexistent melody, I laid my head against his shoulder. For someone who emanated an aura of darkness and cold bitterness, he was incredibly warm to the touch. To call him mysterious would have been the understatement of the century.

I didn't know how to tell him how much he meant to me. I didn't know if he cared about that, or if he even wanted to know. He had become family. I loved him. It wasn't the same love I had for Zeph, but it was every bit as strong. Eldrick was the brother I'd never truly known, and the father who'd been taken from me too soon. He was my teacher, my protector, and my friend.

"Thank you," I whispered as our dance slowly came to an end. I stood up on the toes of my black glass slippers and kissed his cheek.

Eldrick grasped my chin with his hand. Before I could pull away I felt the touch of his warm, firm lips as he kissed my forehead gently. "Enjoy yourself tonight." His silver eyes lingered on mine as he slowly, reluctantly let me go.

"I'll try." With my hand on the doorknob, I paused and looked back. "Does this spell end at midnight, too?"

Eldrick stood with his hands deep in the pockets of his dress slacks. He was still staring at me, and there was something strangely sad in his expression. I didn't quite understand it. "Of course not."

"I'll be back soon," I promised.

He turned away, almost as though he didn't want me to see his face. "I'll be waiting."

I stopped in the doorway of the apartment building, looking around for Joe. After all, I assumed that was the disguise Zeph would be sporting for the evening.

Only, it wasn't.

Zeph stood on the curb, smoking a cigarette in a black tie tuxedo like a young James Bond. His hair was styled back, and he'd even shaved the stubble off his chin. This must have qualified as a super-special occasion if he'd bothered to shave for it. Anyway, it made him look younger, sharper, and so handsome that it caught me off guard.

He looked like himself—not Joe.

My heart pounded and my stomach fluttered as I lingered there to watch him for a moment. He was pacing back and forth and chain smoking like a freight train. He had a tense expression, like he was concentrating.

"This is a pleasant surprise," I said to get his attention as I stepped outside. My bare shoulders were hit with a blast of cold night air and I immediately regretted not grabbing my coat on my way out. "I was expecting Joe."

Zeph stopped pacing and turned to face me. He flicked his cigarette away, and our eyes met. Suddenly, his anxious frown vanished. His cheeks turned more and more red as he studied me.

"That's … uh." He cleared his throat. "That's a nice … I mean, you look … really good."

I laughed as I wobbled toward him on my high heels. "Thanks. You don't look half bad, yourself."

"Sorry, that was lame. I don't speak fashion." He fidgeted with his bowtie nervously. It was totally adorable. "This is probably even lamer, though. I … I got you something."

I narrowed my eyes. "Got me something? What for?"

He shrugged as he reached into jacket pocket and took out a clear plastic box. Inside was a corsage—a beautiful purple globe amaranth with a sprig of baby's breath.

I knew what this meant to him. The language of the flowers was important to faeries. Each blossom had a meaning as unique as the bloom itself.

Globe amaranths meant undying love.

"This is what humans do, right?" he asked as he slipped the corsage onto my wrist.

"It's not lame," I whispered.

When I looked up at him again, guilt made my throat tighten and my lungs constrict. Maybe this hadn't been important to me, but it was obviously important to him. I was being selfish. I had been so caught up in trying to save him I'd forgotten to cherish these moments. "I'm sorry I didn't tell you prom was tonight."

Zeph gave me that candid, roguish grin of his. "You're sly, I'll give you that, but you'll have to get up pretty damn early in the morning to get one past me."

"That wouldn't be very hard. You sleep late every day." I looped my arm through his, warming my body against his side.

"Hey, wait a minute." He pulled away and took off his tuxedo jacket. He draped it over my shoulders, helping me into the sleeves. Suddenly, I was surrounded by his familiar warmth and smell.

"All right, let's go." Zeph took my arm again and walked me to the school.

I'd never been more thankful he had picked an apartment so close to Saint Augustine's. The tall, black glass heels Eldrick had put on me were hard to walk in on the icy sidewalks. Zeph had to hold me up more than once to keep me from falling, but I didn't mind the walk. It was nice to be the one being stared at when we passed other couples on the street. Zeph was right beside me, holding my hand and smiling while he cracked jokes about being the only old guy at the prom. It felt perfect. It felt right. And in that moment, my heart was full.

To be honest, I hadn't even thought about how he was going to be the only 20-something-year-old man at a high school prom. That was bound to get some interesting looks from my classmates, who were all expecting me to arrive with Joe. But Zeph was just a few days away from the Singing Moon now. He barely had any magic at all at his disposal, so he couldn't maintain the ruse of being Joe for long. I knew it must have been hard enough for him to keep up his usual "human" disguise instead of slipping into his natural form.

"I'm glad it's you tonight instead of Joe." I squeezed his hand tightly as we walked up the steps to the school. "I mean, I'm glad you look like you."

He arched a brow. "That so? You don't like being with the popular jock type?"

"No. I like being with you."

Zeph didn't have a sarcastic retort for that. His haughty expression faded into boyish, embarrassed surprise again as he held the door open for me. Loud music thumped through the gloom of the dark school halls, and there was a big purple banner hanging over the doors that led into the gymnasium. I'd forgotten that the theme was a masquerade until some of the kids from the theatre department greeted us at the door with boxes full of hand-painted masks. They must have been working on them for weeks.

Zeph was already getting a few stares as he tied a black and silver mask over his eyes. He was right; he was bound to be the oldest person here— well, except for the teachers. I was going to have to come up with one spectacular story to explain all this, but at that moment, I didn't care. I was starting to have fun.

"Hey, stop squirming around," Zeph scolded me as he tied a purple and black mask over my eyes.

I was nervous as we entered the gym together. Everyone was dressed up in beautiful gowns or flashy suits and wearing their painted masks. The whole room was decorated with streamers and balloons. Couples were dancing under the flashing lights that came from the DJ booth. Even more kids were hanging out in the doorways chatting, or sitting at some of the dining tables munching on snacks and drinking punch. A few bored-looking teachers serving as chaperones stood against the far wall. I was relieved to see Ms. Grear wasn't one of them.

"What's with that face?" Zeph had to shout over the music so I could hear him. "You look petrified."

I leaned closer to him, holding onto his arm. A few of the popular girls gawked at us, whispering. They were eyeing Zeph and probably wondering why I had come with someone else—not to mention a grown man.

"I've never been to a dance before," I admitted, although it was only half-true.

I was way more worried about getting attacked again. I hadn't gone anywhere except school by myself since the night Fir Darrig's spriggan nearly crushed us all. Even then, Eldrick had gone back to his old ritual of camping out in the coffee shop across the street in case anything went wrong.

I scanned the faces of my peers for anyone who didn't look like they belonged here—well, besides my date, that is. What if this was all just an illusion, too? What if Fir Darrig was here, somewhere, waiting to kidnap me. Or maybe he'd send one of his minions like Lumi …

Zeph was right; I was a nervous wreck.

Zeph put an arm around my waist and smiled. "Relax. It's supposed to be fun."

"Explain to me again why you think this isn't corny?" I curled up closer against his side.

He was grinning like a kid in a candy store. "I dunno. Maybe it's that primal faerie urge to cause mischief."

"Just don't burn anything down, please."

After visiting the banquet tables stacked high with delicious food, Zeph and I sat down to eat. He had practically taken all of the spinach-stuffed croissants. He'd also snatched up three pieces of cake, and then helped himself to the chocolate fountain. I was afraid he might go back and try to stick his whole head under it. Apparently, chocolate was his second favorite thing next to honey.

A few other kids from my class joined us. They were friendly, which I knew was only because they were eager to find out why I had come with a much older man instead of Joe. The pretty and extremely nosy girl, Anna, from our calculus class plopped down in the seat next to mine and flashed a spiteful glance in my direction. I could recognize her easily by that look, even if she was wearing a mask.

"Nice dress." She was obviously forcing herself to be at least slightly nice.

I pretended not to notice. "Thank you. Yours is pretty, too."

"So, who is this? I thought you were coming with Joe. Did you guys break up?" She cut straight to the chase. I had to give her some credit; she didn't mince words.

"You talkin' about my kid brother?" Zeph's eyes sparkled with mischief. I guess he thought this was his golden opportunity to indulge some of those primal faerie urges he had mentioned before.

Anna blinked in surprise. "Oh. You're Joe's brother?"

Zeph's smirk was as cocky as ever. "Yep. He won't be coming tonight, though. In fact, you'll probably never see him again."

I had to turn my face away so no one noticed my panicked expression. All the kids sitting around us leaned in closer, eager to hear Zeph's story.

This wasn't good.

"What?" Anna looked genuinely upset. "Why not?"

"Well, it's sort of a private family matter. But hey, you're his friends, so I'll let you in on it." Zeph sat back in his chair and adjusted his cufflinks proudly. I could tell by his tone that he was just getting tuned up. "My mother left the family business to him when she passed away. I guess he

289

just couldn't take the pressure. He ran away, leaving behind a note that said he was never coming back and that I should take over the company instead. At first, I didn't want anything to do with it. I'm not exactly the business type. I've never liked living my life with that kind of responsibility hanging over my head." He put a hand on my shoulder with an exaggerated sigh. "But then I got one look at the beautiful girlfriend he'd just abandoned … and I just knew I had to step up. She needed someone she could count on."

I blushed and looked down—not because I was flattered, but rather because he was telling even crazier lies than ever before. I was so mortified I wanted to dive under the table and hide. The worst part was everyone believed it! They were buying everything he was selling, and all the girls sitting around him swooned when he stroked my arm affectionately and described how he'd fallen in love with me right away and had been counseling me through a broken heart after his "little brother" ditched me. It was ridiculous.

"That is *so* romantic," one of the girls said with a dreamy sigh. "It's like a movie or something."

Zeph brushed a lock of hair behind my ear with a feigned wistful smile. "Maybe she'll never love me the same way she did him, but I just can't give up on her. I'll do whatever it takes to make her fall in love with me."

Under the table, I kicked the side of his leg as hard as I could. He squirmed and shot me a glare.

"He's just going to have to convince me that he's not just some womanizing cradle-robber who only tells people what they want to hear," I said calmly.

Anna nodded in agreement. "He's a little old for you."

She had *no* idea.

"Age is just a number, sweetie." Zeph winked at her. Now he definitely sounded like a dirty, old creep, but his good looks got him another round of dreamy sighs from his captive audience.

He went on and on with this story, basking in the attention as usual. Even a teacher came over to see what all the fuss was about—or maybe she got concerned with why there was a grown man sitting with a bunch of high school girls. She got caught up listening to him, too. I didn't hear any chimes, but his stories seemed to work like magic on these people. They believed anything he said, and he obviously loved every second of it.

Watching him be a showboat was annoying, at first. I'll admit it made me jealous seeing all those other girls, and now an adult teacher, fawning all over him. At the same time, watching him pander to a bunch of hopeless romantics was kind of funny. He never failed to drag me into the story, professing his undying adoration for me over and over. Even if it was mostly just an act, it made me blush.

It was so subtle; I barely noticed it at first. Before I knew what was happening, I was sitting with a bunch of other kids from my school, smiling and laughing. We were talking like nothing had ever gone wrong, like I'd never been crazy. The other girls complimented my dress and hairstyle. They all wanted to know if my jewelry was real. Of course, I told them it wasn't. People usually didn't go to prom dripping with black diamonds—but then again, most people didn't have faeries for roommates, either.

We talked about normal things—about good restaurants, movies, and final exams. It was wonderful. Anna even invited me over to her house for a group study session. I couldn't remember smiling that much since before my dad had passed away.

I was comfortable. I was being myself. I couldn't remember the last time I'd been able to feel that way at school, even with Zeph or Eldrick there.

I was so busy making new friends, I didn't notice Zeph stand up until he put a hand on my shoulder again. "I'm gonna step outside for a minute. To grab a smoke and take a breather," he whispered in my ear.

"Are you okay?" I was worried something might be wrong. Was he in pain? Was he running out of magic? "Do you want me to come with you?"

He smiled and shook his head. "Nah. Have fun, princess. I'll be back in a few."

I watched him duck out one of the side doors of the gym, a cigarette already between his lips. That's when I realized … this was all part of his master plan. I'd been suckered into it from the beginning right along with everyone else.

All this time, I'd assumed that Zeph pretending to be Joe Noble was just a way for him to get attention and feed that desire to cause mischief. But his antics in my so-called romantic life had caused such a stir that everyone had long forgotten about my crazy outbursts. I wasn't a pariah anymore. I had a fresh start and a chance at a normal social life again, all thanks to him.

There was a smile on my lips I couldn't have hidden even if I wanted to. I went back to talking, confident Zeph would come back once a few of Hank's special cigarettes had taken the edge off. I was exchanging phone numbers with a few girls from my history class when I felt someone tap on my shoulder.

I assumed it was Zeph.

I turned around with a big grin still plastered on my face. "That was fast. Too cold out there for—"

I stopped short, staring directly into the bright, brilliant green eyes of a boy I didn't recognize. It was hard to tell much about him because of the mask that covered his face around his eyes and nose. His wavy blonde hair fell over his forehead in a beautifully casual way. "Would you like to dance?"

I blinked. Was he talking to me? I glanced around for a girl or anyone else standing nearby he might be talking to. Nope. It was definitely me.

"Um …" I glanced back at the other girls sitting at the table. They were all staring at me with wide, mystified eyes. Anna shrugged her shoulders slightly, indicating she didn't know who this guy was, either.

"I-I'm not sure," I stammered, still glancing around for some clue as to who this guy was. Maybe he was dating someone from our class? If so, she might not be too thrilled about seeing us together like that. "Won't your date be upset if you dance with someone else?"

He smiled and adjusted the red silk tie of his tuxedo. "No, I'm sure it's fine. What about you? Where's your date?"

My date would *definitely* mind if I danced with someone else, but I didn't want to be rude. It was just one dance, right? One dance didn't mean anything. Besides, Zeph might not be back for another half hour if he decided to have a second cigarette … or a third.

One dance wouldn't hurt.

"Okay then," I agreed. He offered his hand, and I took it.

I watched the door as the boy led me out onto the dance floor, half hoping Zeph might suddenly appear and intervene, but he didn't come.

A slow, soft song was playing as the boy placed one hand on my waist. He looked straight into my eyes as we swayed together. I couldn't help looking him over. It wasn't hard to imagine he'd be good looking under that mask. His teeth were perfect and his hair was a beautiful shade of wheat gold. He was only a little taller than I was, which made him pretty short for a guy. He was lean and his hands were soft, so he probably didn't play sports at all.

I wasn't used to boys approaching me even for casual things, so my stomach was spinning. Something nagged at the back of my mind—an anxiety I didn't quite understand. There was something about him that seemed almost … *too* perfect.

"You don't talk much. Am I making you nervous?" He chuckled.

"N-no! I'm sorry. I was just trying to remember if I had seen you at school before."

"Oh," he said. "No, I doubt it. You're Josie Barton, right?"

"Yes." It was a little creepy that he already knew my name. I was starting to worry my reputation as the city's teenage nutcase had spread to other schools. "How do you know that?"

He shrugged lightly and sent me another smile that made his light green eyes sparkle behind his black mask. They were so beautiful it was almost enchanting. "I've heard a lot about you. I thought we should meet."

Something about him made me relax. Maybe it was his casual, soft smile, or the gentleness of his voice. He had such a meek, comfortable demeanor, and it made me feel calmer—as though I'd known him all my life.

"My name is Raleigh," he continued. "Although I do have a lot of other names."

Other names? Like nicknames?

I studied him more closely, watching the way his gaze wandered away. His smile faded as he began observing the other couples dancing around us. There was a glint of something in his eyes—something quietly angry. It was subtle, just a fleeting spark, but I could see it.

My hands started to get clammy and there was a dull ache in the pit of my stomach. Something wasn't right about this. Why had he asked me to dance in the first place? And why had he waited to do it after Zeph had walked away? How had he heard about me if no one else at the school knew him?

"What other names?" When I asked that question, his sparkling peridot-colored eyes focused directly on me again.

"Fir Darrig," he replied evenly. "Not that I've ever been fond of that name in particular."

No ... *no*!

I couldn't move. My heart felt like it had stopped beating.

He didn't force me to keep dancing. In fact, he seemed perfectly content to let me stand there, gaping at him with my mouth open. His expression never changed as he studied me, the other couples still swaying and twirling around us.

"Were you expecting a bent old man?" He tilted his head to the side slightly. "Or perhaps a monster?"

I swallowed. In my mind, I was screaming for Zeph to come back. I was also mentally kicking myself for even being in this position. How could I have been so stupid? This was the second time I had fallen for one of Fir Darrig's traps.

"I didn't come here to kidnap you, if that's what you're worried about," he announced. His ancient eyes narrowed a bit through the holes in his mask, and his beautiful lips curled into a smirk. "I simply wanted to ask you something and introduce myself formally before we … inevitably find our paths intertwined again."

I gathered my courage and took a deep breath. "So ask, then."

"You don't have to act brave. I can feel you shaking." His smirk widened, and he pulled me closer until our noses were nearly touching. "You aren't the first vessel I have met. Did you know vessels can only come from royal bloodlines?"

I could feel his breath on my face and his body heat burning against me. I squirmed to try to get away from him, but he was much stronger than he looked.

"That's what you went to all this trouble to ask me?" I snapped in defiance.

"No." He shook his head, making his golden bangs swish over his brow. His expression sharpened, becoming serious. "I came to ask who you are going to choose to rule the faerie court. Have you made your selection?"

I hesitated. What? He had me in his grasp and *that* was what he wanted to ask?

As I stared into his eyes, I realized I didn't see any of the evil I'd expected to find in his visage. I could feel the power wafting off him like rays of warm sunlight, sending chills over my body like crashing waves. But there was an unmistakable essence of gentleness ebbing off him, too. It was hard to keep in mind that he was a monster—the one who was killing the man I loved.

"I-I …" I stammered. "I don't know."

"This is a very important decision, Josie," he spoke calmly. Little by little, he began coaxing me back into a gentle swaying dance. I saw his dazzling gaze flicker to my lips for an instant. "Are you sure you don't have anyone in mind? You only know a few faeries well enough to call them candidates. So wouldn't you give it to the one you love?"

"You mean Zeph?"

He resumed a calm, knowing smile. "You are in love with him, aren't you?"

"Yes. But that doesn't mean I'll choose him."

That shrewd smile vanished in an instant. Now it was his turn to stop, freezing in place as he stared down at me. "If you love him, why wouldn't you choose him?"

"Because one thing has absolutely nothing to do with the other. A ruler should be someone who is fair in all things, and who can make critical decisions under pressure without letting their personal feelings or vendettas get in the way. They have to be gentle and kind, merciful and understanding, but firm and unyielding to pressure when it comes to upholding laws." I squared my shoulders and looked up at him with confidence. "Zeph is stubborn. He has a bad temper. He has horrible people skills when it comes to resolving conflict, and he likes to pick fights just for the entertainment. He can be selfish and rude, and he has basically no self-control at all. Maybe it sounds strange, but I love those things about him. They are precious to me because they're a part of who he is—but they're the same things that would make him a terrible king."

My answer obviously wasn't the response he had anticipated.

Fir Darrig didn't speak for several long, awkward moments. I wondered if there was any possible way he could understand that. Could he be reasoned with? Could I change his mind somehow?

"Have you thought about how that is going to impact him? That maybe he's expecting you to choose him?" he asked quietly.

Of course I hadn't. Those words struck me. I knew my surprise was bound to be obvious as I stared up at him. Never once had it even crossed my mind that Zeph might actually *want* to be the faerie king.

"Is that what happened to you?" I countered.

He cut me a dangerous glare, and that sense of gentleness in his aura vanished.

"No one knows your story. Or if they do, they aren't talking. All I've been able to learn is that something happened with a princess. She did something to hurt you. Was that what happened? You said vessels only come from royal bloodlines. So that princess, was she a vessel, too? Did you get angry because she didn't choose you to be the faerie king?"

His pale green eyes narrowed dangerously. He stood straight, and took a step away from me as though I'd threatened him. "That was how it began," he replied stiffly. "I believed as strongly—as I'm sure Zeph does—that our love was unshakeable. That she could be trusted with all the intimate secrets of our world. But human beings are all the same. You are consumed by greed. You see nothing. You feel nothing. My people are fools to continue to trust you."

I'd obviously struck a chord, and I could tell by the look on his face that he wasn't eager to go into any further detail. His voice was shaking, and his words became sharp and furious.

Before he could move farther away, I grabbed his hand to stop him. "You know that isn't true. We're not all like that! I know it must seem that way. Even Eldrick thought so, once. I know she must have done something truly horrible to make you feel like this. But it's not true—I would never do anything to hurt Zeph."

"And what about me?" he snapped. "You want to kill me, don't you?"

I frowned. "That's not fair. You started this. You've preyed upon my entire family and now you're killing the man I love. And I'll do whatever it takes to stop you."

He smirked, and for the first time, I saw malice in his eyes. I saw centuries of hatred, anger, and grief all boiling together with a thirst for revenge. He had been hurt; so he was going to make everyone else suffer with him.

"You're a brave girl," he purred as he stroked my hand. "Brave, but foolish to challenge me. The life of one changeling means nothing to me. On the night of the Singing Moon, you will be mine, and only then will you choose a new King of the Faeries. You are going to choose me, or I will crush all that remains of your meaningless, brief human life. I will destroy everyone you love, starting with the one you hold most dear."

Narrowing my eyes back at him, I squeezed his hand back as hard as I could. I was hoping it might hurt him, even if just a little. I wanted him to know I wasn't scared of him anymore.

"Maybe you've met other vessels before, but I guarantee you've never met one like me. If you want my power, then you better bring more than a moldy old spriggan to do your fighting for you."

"Is that so?"

I smirked. "Absolutely. And I'm going to enjoy kicking your ass."

We glared at one another long after the song ended and the dancing had stopped. Was I scared? Of course. But I wasn't about to let him know that. I couldn't back down now. I refused to show any weakness as he leered at me like he was waiting for me to flinch.

If he'd come here to size me up, I wasn't going to let him see any of the kinks in my armor.

"Josie!" Someone called my name over the noise of the party.

A cold pang of fear shot through my body, piercing me to the core. I looked back to see Zeph coming toward me, weaving through the other couples and kids who were bouncing around on the dance floor to an upbeat song.

When he saw my dancing partner, Zeph stopped halfway across the gymnasium. All the color drained from his face. His lips parted and his eyes went round.

"He really is a fool, isn't he? His power is all but gone. He can't even sense my presence anymore, and yet here he comes to save his damsel in distress," Fir Darrig hissed with a wicked grin on his lips. He leaned down to put his mouth close to my ear. "But then, so are you. Do you, a pitiful human whelp, honestly think you can stand against me?"

Chimes of magic began whispering in the air. Every hair on my body stood on end. They hummed louder and louder, and the kids around us suddenly all stood still—as though they had been frozen in time.

As Fir Darrig backed away, he pulled the mask away from his face and tossed it aside. I sucked in a breath, bracing myself. His true form began to unfold before me like the rising of the sun. Golden light filled the air with such intensity that I had to cover my eyes.

He was a majestic creature, half an angelically handsome man and half a golden lion, with glorious wings with feathers in every color of the rainbow. His golden hair was long and braided into long dreadlocks, interwoven with clay beads, twigs, and leaves.

I stumbled back and almost tripped over my dress and high heels. The kids around me were staggering like zombies straight for me. Girls in prom dresses, boys in tuxedoes, and even teachers were all lumbering toward me with glazed eyes and drooling mouths.

It was an enthrallment spell!

The zombie crowd grabbed at me, rushing me from every side. They ripped off my jewelry and tore my dress while dragging me closer to Fir Darrig. I tried to push them away, but more of them came as fast as I could pry others off me. I screamed. I kicked and punched, holding nothing back.

From somewhere nearby, I could hear Zeph shouting. Through the crowd, I caught a glimpse of his horrified face as he reached for me. I kicked harder and bit down hard on someone who tried putting a hand over my mouth. Zeph was so close. I stretched my arm out, desperate to reach him.

The crowd converged, swallowing me and tearing him out of my reach. I was shoved, mauled, wrenched, and flung down to the gymnasium floor at Fir Darrig's feet. Battered and bruised, I looked up into his sneering face.

"Foolish little princess." He narrowed his wild green eyes and brandished a tall staff made from three branches woven together. "You have barely sampled the true power of magic. You know nothing of my world. What's to stop me from taking you now? Your hero can't even save himself."

I took off one of my black glass shoes and hurled it at him. He grunted when the heel caught him right over the nose.

Fir Darrig roared, raising his staff toward me threateningly. The jagged tip warped and twisted, extending into a long spear.

"You will choose me as the faerie king, or you will die!" Fir Darrig bellowed, thrusting the point of his staff straight at my heart.

I tensed, preparing for the worst, but I didn't look away. I wouldn't give him the satisfaction of cowering before him. I waited for it to end—to feel the pain.

Purple light bloomed in the dark gymnasium. My vision spotted, and my brain ached at the sound of bells chiming out of tune. Zeph appeared right in front of me, holding the end of Fir Darrig's spear at bay with his bare hands. His human disguise was gone. His wings sagged lifelessly to the floor, feathers falling and turning to smoke before they ever touched the ground. His whole body shook and he cried out, his feet sliding over the floor as Fir Darrig leaned in harder against his staff.

It was futile. Zeph couldn't last like this. He'd been no match for Fir Darrig even without the curse. And now ...

I clenched my teeth and reached into his pocket for the lighter he always carried. I tore off a piece of my dress and set it on fire, blowing it out as soon as there was enough to use for ash.

"How long do you dream you can hold me back?" Fir Darrig chuckled. "I will have her. There is nothing you can do to stop it. And when I am finished with her, I'll carve my name upon her heart. Then no one else will ever be able to touch her. She will know no other love but mine."

Zeph yelled, his shoulders flexing and his wings lifting to spread wide. He gave a violent shove, sending Fir Darrig rocking back in surprise.

This was my chance.

I used the ash to draw a quick circle and series of symbols on the floor.

I snatched off my mask and put it in the center, drawing out a few specific symbols around it, and then a few more on my hands.

"Please work," I muttered as I pressed my hands into the circle, pouring my energy into it. The runes began to glow red, spiraling inward until the mask was engulfed in an eerie red light. It twisted and spun, before rising up into the air and sprouting fiery wings.

The mask soared straight for Fir Darrig. All around the gym, the other masks began to glow bright red, too. One by one, they jumped from people's faces, sprouted glowing wings, and flew straight for the enemy. They jumped off tables, and out of boxes and trashcans, buzzing through the air to attack Fir Darrig like a flock of angry birds.

Fir Darrig roared, jerking his staff out of Zeph's grasp. He swung at the masks and pried them off as they stuck to his body wherever they landed. Not bad for my first attempt in battling an ancient faerie lord. I kicked off my other shoe and grabbed Zeph's arm. Together we sprinted for the exit.

I couldn't run very fast in my fancy dress and by the time we got to the door, Zeph was fighting for every breath. His pace had slowed to a stagger and his wings had all but dissolved till only a few clusters of feathers remained. This wasn't going to work. We needed a different escape plan—*now.*

I hit the exit door first, flinging it open and looking for the first running vehicle nearby. Car, truck, limousine—it didn't matter which.

A giant, mossy hand grabbed me by the legs and snatched me off the ground. Fingers like thick tree branches squeezed around my knees until I screamed. The ground fell away, and the stench of rotting wood and sulfur blasted me right in the face.

Another spriggan.

Zeph yelled my name, diving forward to catch my hand before I was pulled out of reach. My fingers brushed his. And then he was gone—left somewhere far below as the spriggan held me up by the legs like a mouse by the tail.

I struggled and clawed at its big, gnarled fingers as the creature lumbered away. Oh god, where was this thing taking me? I screamed until I couldn't breathe. Zeph—where was Zeph? We were leaving him behind. He barely had any magic left at all. He probably couldn't even fly. He wouldn't be able to help me now.

Then I remembered—I still had his lighter in my hand.

As hard as it is to work a Zippo lighter upside down, I managed to get the flame going and lit the spriggan's hand on fire. It took a few seconds for the monster to realize it. The flames spread quickly over the moss, leaves, and sticks that made up the creature's body.

It let out a booming yelp of pain and dropped me, crashing around in a frantic circle, waving its arm around to try to put out the fire. From twenty-feet up, I plummeted toward the ground, smacking into tree limbs all the way down.

Right before I hit the earth, something soft cushioned my fall. It let out a loud "Oof!" as we landed right in the middle of a patch of prickly, holly bushes in the city park.

Beneath me, Zeph was lying on his back with his arms, legs, and flimsy wings spread wide. "Have I ever mentioned ... I really hate spriggans," he groaned.

"Nice catch," I gasped as I crawled off him and stumbled out of the bushes. My heart pounded and my body shook from all the adrenaline surging through my veins. "Hurry up! We have to call Eld—"

I stopped short because there was already a car pulling up the street, screeching toward us at an alarming speed. It flashed its bright lights and honked repeatedly to get my attention. When it got closer, I got a better look. A black Cadillac.

"Hank!" I cried in relief as I ran for the car, holding up the tattered ends of my dress.

As the Caddy pulled up to the curb, the rear door opened and Eldrick stepped out. My legs almost buckled with relief. He had a no-nonsense frown on his face as he caught me in his arms and practically tossed me into the back seat. He waited for Zeph to climb in behind me before he ducked into the passenger's seat. Talk about perfect timing. He patted the back of Hank's headrest, and the car zoomed away from the curb.

Behind us, the spriggan ran in circles, almost totally engulfed in flame as it knocked over trees and crashed through power lines. It shrank into the distance as Hank sped down streets toward his bar, taking turns I thought might sling the hubcaps off. I didn't have to ask why we were going there. He'd already told me once that it was the most magically shielded place in the city. It was our only safe place now. Fir Darrig was getting bolder. Time was running out.

"H-how did you know?" I managed to ask as I turned back around and slumped into the seat.

"A giant burning spriggan was a pretty good beacon to follow." Hank chuckled. "That's usually how I find Zeph anyway. Just look for something burning and people screaming."

Zeph grumbled a few curses as he picked holly leaves out of his hair. "Very funny. Laugh it up."

"Before that we were just cruising the area, just in case. Kinda figured Fir Darrig might try something nasty. He's in a time crunch," Hank explained.

"And so are we," Eldrick agreed. "I took the liberty of packing a bag for you, Josie. I also contacted Freddy to let him know we are changing locations in light of the danger. He informed me that he and Camilla want to join us as soon as they can slip away."

My whole body was shaking as the adrenaline left me cold, and I noticed my shoulder hurt. There was a deep cut right across my shoulder, probably from a tree branch. It was bleeding down my chest. I put a hand over it, trying to stop the bleeding.

"Here, hold still," Zeph spoke quietly as he scooted closer to me. He took a handkerchief out of his pocket and pressed it over the cut. I winced, and when he put pressure on it to stop the bleeding, a whimper made it past my clenched teeth.

"I'm sorry I couldn't stop him." I could sense the weight of guilt in his voice. Zeph wouldn't even meet my eyes. When we got to the bar, he came around the car and insisted on carrying me inside. I was glad about that since I wasn't wearing any shoes. As we ducked into the bar, Eldrick retrieved our bags from the trunk, and Hank got busy sealing magical wards on the doors as soon as everyone was inside.

Hank's bar was dark and empty. Nothing had changed since the last time Zeph had brought me here, but it still made me nervous. Before, this place had intimidated me a little because it was a bar—a place for adults. Now, it felt like a foxhole in a war zone. I just hoped the magical wards would hold.

Zeph carried me behind the bar, through the kitchen and into a back room that was set up like a tiny, one-room apartment. There was an old, single bed and a few shelves stocked with clear glass jars filled with all kinds of bizarre things—things I assumed were for working spells. There were herbs, dried flowers, bones, and even animal teeth.

Eldrick came in only long enough to drop off the duffel bag he'd packed for me. He flicked me a tense frown, but didn't stick around to chat. He was pacing like a caged animal, and it didn't take him long to decide he'd rather be up front in the bar area. Not that I blamed him, really. This room was cramped, windowless, and felt more like a prison cell. Even the tiny attached bathroom barely had enough space for a shower, sink, and toilet.

Zeph placed me carefully on the bed, handling me as though I were made of glass. The old iron frame creaked under my weight and somehow it made the silence between us seem even more awkward. He didn't say a word as he went to shut and lock the door. We were alone in that tiny room, but he still wouldn't look at me.

I watched him bite down hard, a vein standing out against his neck as he pulled himself back into his human form. It seemed to take an eternity, and his expression skewed like each second was agony. Eventually, his horns and wings melted away. Then Zeph sagged against the door, struggling for breath.

We were both a wreck. His tuxedo jacket was gone, and the white shirt underneath was tattered and stained with my blood. My dress was in shreds and I was smeared with ash.

But we were alive.

Once he caught his breath, Zeph went to the bathroom, opened the medicine cabinet behind the mirror, and took out a small first aid kit. He rinsed off a washcloth and came back to sit on the bed beside me. It creaked loudly again.

"Is this where Hank lives?" I tried desperately to break the silence.

Zeph focused on wiping the blood away from my shoulder. Every time he touched the cut or bumped my arm, it made me take a sharp breath.

"No," he answered at last. "This is a safe house for emergencies only."

"Oh, right. He told me something like that before," I remembered aloud.

Heavy silence settled over us again. It made my throat feel thick and my body tremble no matter how hard I tried to hold still. I watched as he cleaned my wound, disinfected it with antibacterial cream, and applied a thick layer of bandages. He was touching me, being so gentle and careful, but I could feel him withdrawing. That expression of cold thought was pulled over his features like a mask. It didn't fool me anymore. He didn't want me to worry. He didn't want me to see his weakness or pain. Tonight, I'd seen both.

As he tried to get up, I put my hands on the sides of his face and forced him to look at me. "Zeph, please don't do this," I pleaded. "Don't shut me out. I can't take it. If this is our last night together …"

His strange violet eyes stared directly at me. Couldn't he tell I was struggling, too? I'd spent so much time reading, studying, and memorizing spellwork so I would be prepared. And in the end, I'd been duped like a rookie. I was out of my league when it came to Fir Darrig. Sure, I'd managed a diversion long enough to save us tonight. But what about next time? And the time after that?

Doubt swallowed all of my faith, all the confidence that the Fibbing Gate would work, and all the hope that I could even save him at all. He was precious to me. The thought of losing him because I might fumble a spell or do something stupid like I had tonight—letting my guard down and getting tricked so easily—was unbearable. If I kept making mistakes like that, it wouldn't matter what tools I had packed with me. Now, to top it all off, Zeph was closing up on me again. He was scared. I could see it all over his face. But he wouldn't even talk to me. It felt like he was slipping through my fingers already.

Tears filled my eyes until I couldn't see him anymore. A sob escaped me, and then suddenly, his arms were around me. Zeph pulled me against his chest and began running his fingers through my hair. I clung to him, my face against his neck while I squeezed him as hard as I could.

"Hey, calm down," he whispered against my ear. "I'm sorry, okay? You're right. I'm just being an ass, as usual. I just get mad at myself when I can't protect you like I'm supposed to."

"I know. But it wasn't your fault." I pulled away sniffling and trying to compose myself again. I tried to wipe the mascara out of my eyes, but it was too late. All that fancy makeup Eldrick had put on me was running all over the place. It was embarrassing. "I guess I should change and clean myself up."

Zeph gave me that wonderful half-cocked smirk of his. "Nah, I kinda like this look. It's like you're going to a grunge metal concert. Or a Halloween party," he said as he tousled my already ruined hair.

"So not funny."

"Don't be like that. You know I think you're beautiful, right?"

I glared at him. "Sure. Maybe when I'm all dressed up."

"No. I mean, I do like it when you're all dolled up, but not because it makes you any prettier than you already are," he murmured as he brushed his hand down the side of my neck. "I like it because when you wear something you think makes you look good, regardless of what it is, it puts a spark in your eyes. You're more confident. You hold your head up and prance around like you own the place. It's the sexiest thing I've ever seen— and it has nothing to do with whatever you've got on."

My mouth opened, but I couldn't come up with a snappy reply to that.

I gulped, my face getting hotter by the second. I waited for him to laugh, or to turn it into some kind of joke ... but he didn't.

"I don't prance," I muttered.

"Okay, fine. Maybe it's more of a strut."

I grinned and leaned forward to let my forehead rest against his. "Well, I'm still taking a bath. So you'll just have to admire my strut with my hair in a towel."

"I can do that." He had that mischievous glint in his eyes again.

Standing up, I went to the bag Eldrick had packed for me. I took out a change of clothes and a baggie with all my toiletries arranged inside in an obsessively neat order. I tried not to think about Eldrick going through my underwear drawer to pick out clean panties and bras. At least I could be fairly sure he hadn't enjoyed it. I seriously doubted Eldrick saw me as anything but a bothersome human girl he had to look after like a nanny.

I started for the bathroom with my stuff. Maybe once I'd calmed down, I could practice the Fibbing Gate spell again. I wanted to study some more, and make sure everything was still going as planned.

But there was a Zeph-shaped object in my way, blocking the bathroom door.

"Come on, what're you doing?" He took the fresh clothes out of my hands and tossed them aside. He did the same thing with my toiletries. "I feel gross. Seriously, there's makeup running all over my face and I just want to—"

He silenced me with a finger over my lips. He was holding up his cell phone, staring intently at the screen.

I waited. One minute ticked by. Then another. I tapped my foot.

Then Zeph turned his phone around so I could see. It was midnight. "Happy birthday."

I blinked. "I-I—"

He tossed his phone into my bag and shrugged. "This wasn't exactly what I'd hoped we would be doing for it. I know I agreed to throw a party and lavish you with gifts, you know, as payback for past sins. Sorry about that."

I smiled. "I'll let it slide. Just this once."

He moved in closer, his gazed fixed upon me. "Going easy on me because I might die tomorrow?"

"No, of course not." I laughed. "I'm just too tired to put up with—"

He kissed me.

I thought he was just teasing me again, so I bit at his bottom lip and tried to pull away.

His kiss deepened, becoming hungrier. He'd only kissed me like this once before, and the ringing of a cell phone had ended it much too soon.

Nerves made my body feel tangled and awkward. I stumbled as he pulled me closer, almost tripping over my own feet. His rough hands touched my waist, and his fingertips grazed my back as he pulled at the zipper on the back of my dress.

I gasped against his mouth and tried to pull away again. "Wait."

"I thought you wanted this," he murmured with his lips still against my neck.

"I do …"

His teeth grazed a sensitive place right under my ear, making my stomach flip and my body shudder with delight. "Since you came back into my life, I've thought every single day about what it would be like to finally join your spirit with mine. Now you're gonna make me wait even longer?"

My insecurities roared through my mind. What if I couldn't live up to that expectation? What if he was disappointed?

"B-but I look horrible. I need to take a bath first."

His mouth moved over my skin to kiss my uninjured shoulder. The sensation made my fingers clench at the fabric of his dress shirt and my skin prickle with wild excitement.

"Okay, then," he conceded, and stepped away.

Whew. At least now I could prepare for this. Then I caught the tail end of a mischievous smirk.

Nope. He was up to something.

Zeph picked up my toiletries and went into the tiny bathroom. He turned on the shower, and began loosening his tie. I gawked shamelessly as he unbuttoned the front of his dress shirt, giving me a generous view of his muscular body. It had been a while since I got a view of those sculpted, tattooed arms. The rest of him was no less perfect ... or utterly intimidating.

He flicked a devious grin in my direction as he curled a finger, beckoning me to come closer. My heart was beating so fast I was afraid it might launch right out of my chest.

Did I want to go? Absolutely.

Was I nervous? Definitely.

I wobbled into the bathroom. Inside that tiny space, we had to stand so close that our noses were almost touching ... even after he shut the door. Steam from the shower made the air hot and thick, but my teeth wouldn't stop chattering.

He leaned in close, his mouth almost touching my ear. "Turn around."

Before I could respond, Zeph grasped my hips and spun me so that my back was against his bare chest. I focused on the feel of his warm hands on my skin as he slowly slid the zipper down on the back of my dress. Every inch and the dress slid a little lower, until it fell around my feet. My pulse boomed in my ears. I knew what was coming—where this would end—and I wanted it so badly I could hardly stand it.

The touch of his lips against my shoulder made me gasp, and I went stiff in surprise. That feeling, his mouth investigating me like he intended to taste every part, made my insides flutter. My skin was sticky from the hot steam that filled the room, and yet I shivered as he combed his fingers lightly down my spine.

"It's okay. Try to relax," he whispered as he brushed my hair away from the back of my neck. His short stubble prickled and scratched my skin as he kissed me there, gently at first. Then his mouth opened and I could feel the light scrape of his teeth as he reached around to press his fingertips against me—right between my thighs.

Tingling heat bloomed through my body. A loud, elated breath escaped me.

"Want me to stop?" Zeph chuckled darkly. He slid his fingers under the hook of my strapless bra.

"No," I whispered. "Don't you dare stop."

My bra hit the floor. I heard him unfastening his belt. Then Zeph turned me slowly back around to face him, wrapping his thick arms around me and pulling me in. The feel of his body against mine, bare and slick with the moisture from the steam, sent waves of tingling heat through me.

"Look at me, Josie."

Slowly, I raised my gaze.

Zeph's expression was difficult to read. The hand still touching my chin shook.

"I'm serious. If you don't want this, you can tell me," he said. "I'm not trying to force you into something you're not ready for."

Words failed me. I took another deep breath. Then I closed my arms around his neck and planted a slow kiss against his lips in answer.

He made a deep, satisfied, growling noise as he snatched me off my feet and carried me into the shower. The glass door closed behind us, sealing us within our own world.

Horrible things like spriggans, Fir Darrig, and life-ending curses didn't exist. There was only the euphoria of my skin sliding against his while the stream of hot water from the showerhead poured over us. The only sounds were our deep, ragged breaths. There was urgency in the way his strong hands gripped me and earnest excitement in the way his brawny, solid body explored mine.

It was like we were alone in the universe.

And for a few precious, fleeting moments I was able to taste perfect bliss.

"Zeph?"

"Mmm?"

"Can I ask you something?" Lying on my side in the small creaky bed, I listened to the sound of his panting breaths. He was stretched out with his arms wrapped around my waist like a kid hugging a teddy bear. There was barely enough room for both of us, and he was essentially draped around me so we could both fit—not that I minded. It meant his warm, bare body was still touching mine all over.

"Sure," he murmured as he started planting soft, slow kisses against the back of my shoulder again.

I took a steadying breath. "When I was little, and you said I made you promise to make me happy ..."

He paused. "Yeah? And?"

"Did you hear a heart-chord between us?"

The bed groaned as he sat up on an elbow, staring down at me. "Who told you about that?"

"Oh, um, no one. I just read about it in one of Dad's—"

"It was Camilla, wasn't it?"

My cheeks flushed as I turned on to my back so I could gaze up at him. "Sort of. She said it might have been the reason you felt so attached to me. I was just wondering ... Did you really hear one?"

"Would it make any difference if I didn't?"

"No. I guess not." I loved him, either way. "I just wanted to know. I want to hear it, too."

Zeph swept his fingers over my forehead, pushing some of my damp hair away from my face. His expression softened and his eyes grew distant as he traced a thumb along my bottom lip. "It's not something humans can usually hear, even if they are the vessel. Statistically, you're more likely to get struck by a meteor than find someone you share a true heart-chord with."

"That's not an answer." I grasped his hand, holding it against my face. "Did you hear one between us or not?"

His brow creased a little. Fear flickered through his violet eyes as they searched me. "Yes," he answered quietly.

"Why can't I hear it, too?"

Zeph's jaw set. "Because I'm nearly dead. My aura is almost gone. I can't even hear it myself, anymore. And until tonight, when I couldn't sense that Fir Darrig was at that dance waiting to ambush us, I didn't realize ... I can't sense anyone else's now, either."

My stomach cramped and soured. I gulped against the pain in my throat. Doubt like a cold shiver ran through my body. What if we failed tomorrow night? What if I never got to hear that sweet sound, or lie with him again like this?

"Hey, don't make that face." He leaned down and kissed my lips, some of his wet hair tickling my cheek. "You need to rest."

How was I supposed to rest? Every time I closed my eyes, all I could see was Fir Darrig's sneer. His voice was etched into my memory. I squeezed myself closer to Zeph, hiding my face against the side of his neck.

"All right, we'll do this the hard way, then." He closed his arms around me and held me close. "I was saving this back for an emergency when I needed to cheer you up."

I fought back a smile. Tears flooded my eyes. It didn't matter what he said, as long as I could listen to his voice.

"This is the story of how I saved your dad from getting beaten up by an elf at the mall on Christmas Eve ..."

I still couldn't sleep.

Even with Zeph holding me close and the slow, peaceful rhythm of his breathing in my ear, my brain wouldn't shut off. My thoughts raced, blurring between my encounter with Fir Darrig and all the spellwork I needed to remember.

Finally, I couldn't take it anymore.

I slipped quietly out of Zeph's arms. He didn't even stir. He had to be exhausted after what had happened at prom. I'd seen him struggle before—but never like that. He couldn't protect me anymore, not in this state.

Pulling on a sweatshirt and jeans, I wound my damp hair into a braid over my shoulder to hide the fresh hickeys on that side of my neck. I tiptoed out through the kitchen and into the bar area where the lights from the streetlamps outside cast eerie shadows across the tables and chairs.

Hank sat by the door, leaning up against the wall, sound asleep. I looked around for Eldrick, and finally spotted his tall silhouette sitting in one of the booths against the front window. His elbows rested on the table, and his silver eyes stared out into the night with a sharp, serious frown.

When I sat down across from him, he looked at me through his long black bangs. His strange eyes reflected the light like a cat's, and his frown deepened as he pinned me with a punishing glare.

"Keeping watch?"

He nodded slightly. "Why aren't you sleeping?"

"I can't," I said with a shrug. "I really messed up today."

He arched an eyebrow. "How so?"

"I used one of the spells I was saving for Fir Darrig," I confessed. "Now he'll be expecting it. He'll be prepared. And I don't have time to come up with something new."

Eldrick didn't answer, and I was too humiliated to meet his gaze again.

"This is impossible, isn't it? To think that we can beat Fir Darrig?" I asked. I knew he would tell me the truth about what he thought. Eldrick wasn't cruel, but he was brutally honest.

He let out a slow, deep sigh and turned his face back toward the window. "That depends on what your true intentions are. If you intend merely to save Zeph's life, then that is easily done by keeping to your original plan. Whether or not we will be able to summon the Fibbing Gate and force Fir

Darrig through it ... has been questionable from the beginning."

That certainly didn't make me feel any better.

I sank back in my seat, thinking about my brief interaction with Fir Darrig again. He hadn't been quite what I was expecting. He had been so disarming at first. Now all he wanted from me was my power and to be named king of all the faeries. I didn't want to give him either of those things, but if my plan failed, I might not have a choice. There wouldn't be anything my companions could do to help me. Fir Darrig was ancient and powerful, and I was just a puny human girl. What chance did I stand?

"Stop that," Eldrick growled suddenly.

I looked up, surprised to find him glowering at me again.

"Now is not the time to be doubting yourself. I can see it in your eyes. We have come this far because we all believe as you do. It is true, no one has ever successfully stood against Fir Darrig." He glanced away, back out the window. "But then again, we don't know that a human has ever tried. Let alone a human vessel."

"What can a human do that a faerie can't?"

One corner of his mouth lifted. "Apparently, *some* of you are far better at denying your base instincts than I originally suspected."

I smiled. "Oh? Is that your way of saying you might be wrong about all humans being so terrible?"

"Let's not get carried away." He flashed me a look. "There is another instinctual trait that all faeries share besides our desire to be close to mankind. Tomorrow night, we will exploit this trait as his greatest weakness."

I shifted uncomfortably in my seat. "And what is that?"

Eldrick smirked and sat up a bit straighter. "Pride."

His words gave me something to consider as I sat in the booth with him. Together, we watched the sun rise over the city while I went over my plan again and again, wondering if it would work. Eldrick was right—I couldn't let myself crumble under all my doubts. I'd come this far, learning so much in such a short amount of time.

This had to work—it *would* work.

Freddy and Camilla arrived just a few hours after daylight. Hank broke down the protective wards long enough to let them both inside.

Zeph staggered bleary-eyed out of the back room. He was dressed, at least, wearing jeans and an undershirt. He looked at me curiously with a groggy frown, like he was wondering why I hadn't been in bed with him. It wasn't that I didn't want to be close—I did. That's the whole reason I was still awake. I wanted to make sure we stayed close. Just the thought of it made my heart skip a beat and my face feel warm.

Freddy came into the bar armed with several bags of supplies ... including a few from a local bakery that smelled divine. As soon as he sat everything down on the bar top, Zeph made a beeline straight for the food. He snatched up a box filled with fresh pastries and started inhaling them.

I was hungry, too, but I couldn't think about food just yet. Still sitting at the booth with Eldrick, I had all my papers spread out before me. He'd been keen enough to pack those, as well, so I could continue to practice up until the very last moment. I kept my eyes fixed on my work, perfecting my spell designs. I didn't stop practicing until Camilla strolled over and draped an arm over my shoulder. She hugged me tightly and planted a motherly kiss on my temple.

"How is it going?" she asked as she peered down at my papers.

"I wish we could do a trial run, but I know there isn't time for that." I sighed and slumped against the table, resting all my weight on my elbows.

"Here, these might help." Camilla smiled wistfully and sat a small, black velvet purse in front of me.

I opened the soft fabric and poured the contents into my hand. Four pieces of black staurolite landed in my palm. Each one was about the size of a silver dollar and shaped like a perfectly formed cross. I handled the crystals carefully, lining them up on the table side-by-side. These were the last missing pieces to my spellwork to summon the Fibbing Gate. I needed them—all four of them—for it to work.

"We can't wait to hear the details of your plan," Camilla added as she picked up a few pieces of paper where I had been practicing the spell circles.

She began looking them over like she was critiquing them. "My, you do have a knack for this!"

"Of course she does," Freddy said. He came over with a big, friendly grin on his face. "Both her parents did. It's only natural that she be a talented spellworker, too."

Camilla shot him a punishing look. "Calling Marissa Barton merely a spellworker hardly does her justice."

Freddy got pink around the ears like a child who'd been scolded. "I suppose you're right. She was a force to be reckoned with by humans and faeries alike. And, it seems her young daughter is already following in her footsteps."

"I-I don't remember anything about my mom," I reminded them. "She died when I was a baby. My dad never liked to talk about it. I think it was too painful for him."

Camilla grasped my shoulders, radiating an enchanting smile. "Your mother and I were the very best of friends. She rescued me, and I will be eternally grateful for her compassion. She was the bravest human I've ever known, and lovely as a star."

In every picture I had ever seen of my mom, she had looked elegant, beautiful, but fragile. Her porcelain skin seemed to shine in every photograph and her long red hair looked like mine. She had been petite, like me, and willowy. However, I didn't know much about her personal life—where she'd come from or who her friends had been.

"Am I really like her?" I heard myself ask quietly.

"In more ways than you realize," Camilla spoke quietly. "Your mother always expressed a great conviction that justice be upheld in the faerie world— justice in situations that have always been carefully overlooked by both Seelie and Unseelie." She moved to the bag of supplies Freddy had brought in. "Her passion for protecting the people she loved and learning about our culture was a breath of fresh air. It's not often humans take so much interest in our world anymore. Your mother acted as sort of a liaison, and sometimes ... even a vigilante. She was a truly unique and wonderful person."

Everyone gathered in closer to listen. Even Zeph was no longer stuffing his face with pastries. He stood behind me, taking up a position like a bodyguard with his arms crossed.

"I'm sure you've heard plenty of faerie tales. Most humans have. Those stories have been made into myths and legends. They tell of magic, curses, kings, and princesses. They happen in beautiful kingdoms and faraway places." Camilla's voice was hushed as she opened her bag, taking out two large bundles of dark red velvet cloth. She sat them on the table, and gestured for me to open them. "But every story, even faerie tales, have a bit of truth to them. Your mother understood that better than most."

I swallowed. I wasn't sure I wanted to see what was in those bundles, but something struck my memory—something Fir Darrig had said to me the night before.

"Vessels always come from royal bloodlines," I remembered aloud. Realization hit me like a punch to the gut. Turning slowly, I looked back up at Zeph.

The corner of his mouth quirked up. "That's right, princess."

My jaw went slack. He … had called me that from the first time we'd met. I'd just assumed it was a silly nickname.

Camilla was smiling, too. "Such knowledge is usually kept secret to protect the families who might bring forth the next vessel in later generations. As the world moved into the modern age, many countries have turned their back on the monarchies of old. Kings and queens have been forgotten, or reduced to nothing but mere celebrity figureheads."

"Or high school students with fluffy red hair." Zeph chuckled.

I elbowed him in the ribs.

"Princesses and princes have been lost to the pages of history, no longer needed in a human world where magic has no place. However, some royal families still remember the precious gift that might come from their bloodlines," Camilla continued. "Your mother's family remembered, and she had been prepared to stand against the dangers and the rampant injustice that now casts a dark shadow over the faerie world. She was fearless and bold, but honest and gentle; a true princess. She entrusted me with these things with the promise that I would pass them on to you."

I unwrapped the first bundle and drew out a slender dagger about eight inches long. The long blade was made of a dark, heavy metal while the hilt shimmered like gold. The sheath for the dagger was wrapped separately and much lighter compared to the blade itself. Its golden surface was engraved with the image of a medieval lion and numerous swirling rings of spellwork. Some of the characters had almost been completely rubbed away, but I could still make out the design of a containing enchantment.

"Your mother used it to protect herself. Perhaps you can, too," Camilla suggested. "The sheath is spelled so that faeries can't sense the presence of the iron blade. A secret weapon, if you will."

Putting the dagger aside, I took the second, much smaller bundle from her. As I pulled back the velvet, I caught another glimmer of gold. It was a beautiful little jewelry box covered in intricate engravings of archaic designs, swirls, and a heart with a crown over it. Just the sight of it took my breath away.

My heart raced as I opened it. My chest tingled and my breath caught at the sight of a large, heart-shaped ruby resting on a green velvet cushion. I brushed my fingertips over the pendant, noticing the strange coloration in the center of it. It looked almost like a white star.

The instant I saw it, I got a wave of déjà vu. I *knew* I had seen this necklace before.

"Your mother told me this is the last of her family's jewels. She wanted me to give it to you when you ..." Camilla's voice trailed away as she watched me digging through my papers. I guess she realized I wasn't listening anymore.

I had seen that necklace before, and now I remembered where. Pulling out the book page with the drawing of the Fibbing Gate and Fir Darrig on it, I spread it out next to the necklace. The woman in the picture who was holding Fir Darrig's hand was wearing a necklace—and it looked like the exact same one.

I pointed to the picture. "Who is this woman? Why is she in this picture?"

Everyone leaned in closer to get a better look.

"This was drawn many centuries ago, Josie," Eldrick growled in reminder. "Her name has been stricken out, sealed along with the rest of the text. It can't be read. You know that."

"But if I were gonna guess," Zeph interrupted as he leaned over me to see the picture. "I'd say it is the princess who caused Fir Darrig to turn against everyone."

My palms started sweating. This couldn't just be a coincidence. "Look at her necklace. It's the same, isn't it? Is it ... is it possible that the princess is a distant relative of mine?"

"It would have to be very distant. Your mother never mentioned anything like that, but perhaps she didn't know. It might just be a coincidence." Camilla picked up the necklace carefully and ran her fingers over the intricate design. "There is something odd about it, isn't there? Almost as though it has an aura all its own. It must have had great significance to your family to have survived this long."

"Not to mention it being depicted in a drawing this old," Freddy agreed.

The mystery of this princess, and what had happened between her and Fir Darrig was growing more and more bizarre. I'd already figured out that she had been a vessel, too. And I'd also learned that the spark that had ignited all of Fir Darrig's wrath had been the moment when she didn't choose him to be the faerie king.

Now to think that same princess was somehow related to my family only made it even more troubling, but it also sparked a curious suspicion in my already frazzled brain: there might be another chink in Fir Darrig's armor.

Camilla passed the necklace to me, and I cradled it gently in my hands. It was a rich-looking piece that sparkled beautifully in the light, and the color of the red stone was as deep and vibrant as blood. When I turned it over, I realized there were dozens of teeny little spell circles and symbols engraved onto the back of the stone. They were so small you'd need a magnifying glass just to see them. I'd have to look into it later, but for now … this was the first real piece of my mom's belongings I'd ever had. Somehow, it made me feel closer to her. No one said a word as I put it around my neck, letting the heavy pendant fall against my chest.

"It suits you." Eldrick was looking at me strangely.

I tried to smile, but I couldn't.

"Wait—wait a second!" Zeph interrupted the moment, pushing past everyone and disappearing into the back of the bar at a jog.

When he came back, he was holding the old envelope that contained my dad's letter and all the old photographs. He flipped through the pictures, finally holding out the one of my parents when my mom was pregnant with me.

Suddenly, I saw it, too. My mom was wearing the necklace in the picture—the exact same one I was wearing now.

I closed my hand around the pendant. It was like touching her, somehow holding her hand across all the time and space that separated us. Camilla was right, there was something odd about it, though. Just having it against my chest, touching my bare skin, made my skin prickle. It was as though some invisible presence were there with me—something I couldn't see, touch, or even explain.

"Time to get down to business?" Freddy suggested, jarring my thoughts. He was looking at the stacks of papers on the table where I had been practicing my spells over and over.

We'd been keeping things very brief in our text messages and phone calls. None of us were willing to take the chance that Fir Darrig might overhear our plans. So now, in the safety of Hank's bar, we all settled around the table to talk things through.

First, I had something to own up to. "Last night Fir Darrig approached me at the prom. He said he just wanted to ask me a question."

Zeph sat right next to me with one of his arms draped along the back of the seat. He sat up straighter, scowling when he realized I had been holding out on him. "What question?"

I told them about my dance with him, about how he'd come introduce himself, and to ask me about whom I was going to choose to be the faerie king. I couldn't meet Zeph's glare as I repeated the conversation—even the parts where I insisted I wasn't going to pick him to be the king. My stomach did nervous backflips, wondering if he would respond with the same rage Fir Darrig had when he wasn't picked.

"Shit." Zeph let out a huge sigh and slumped back in the seat some. "Thank the stars for that. I was hoping you wouldn't do that to me."

I blinked in surprise. "You're not upset?"

Zeph smirked. "Do you honestly think I'd *want* to be in charge of anything like that? Hell no. Pick someone else."

All the worry about that potentially catastrophic argument drained out of my body immediately. It left me even more tired than before, and I leaned against him while I let it sink in.

I went on to tell them about what I suspected when it came to Fir Darrig and the princess. All the time, the necklace felt somehow heavier around my neck—like a ball and chain, connecting me to whatever tragedy had come between them.

"The point is I ruined a key element to my plan," I admitted. "The only way to break Zeph's curse is for him to take me to Fir Darrig, as the curse demands. After he hands me over, and the curse is broken, I need a distraction. I need some way to get away from Fir Darrig so he can't use me as a hostage or keep me from opening the Fibbing Gate. I was going to use the same spell I did on the masks, but now he'll be expecting that."

"Only the king or queen of the faeries can even summon the gate," Zeph interjected. "So she'll have to make that choice before it can even be opened."

All eyes were on me, and though no one said it out loud … I knew they were all wondering the same thing: who was I going to pick? Most of the faeries I knew were already sitting in the room with me.

I stared at my mom's dagger sitting on the table. I was determined not to reveal my choice until I was absolutely sure. "There's something else, though," I said in hopes of changing the subject. "Fir Darrig obviously has more than one spriggan at his disposal. He probably won't come alone once we arrange the rendezvous. We might be outnumbered."

"I believe we can count on it," Eldrick sounded certain. "Making spriggans isn't a difficult task for a sidhe of his caliber. Not to mention he has been actively recruiting from within the Unseelie community."

I sank lower in my seat. One spriggan was almost more than we could handle. How on earth were we going to take on more than that?

"Quit looking so depressed. It's bumming me out. I'll be back in the ring for real, this time." Zeph puffed out his chest proudly as he reached over and messed up my hair. "I've got a few tricks up my sleeve that not even Fir Darrig knows about."

"A lot of good that did you last time," Hank muttered.

Zeph deflated. You could practically hear it, like someone letting the air out of a party balloon.

"Hey! I was emotionally distraught which, by the way, was *her* fault." Zeph jabbed an accusing finger in my direction.

"Ah yes, bewitched by a three-year-old. You poor creature." Camilla giggled. Beside her, Freddy had a hand over his mouth to hide his own smirk. Too bad it did nothing to hide how red his face was.

"I suppose I can send another message to Jack. That kid always likes an excuse to sling some ice around and we're gonna need some backup." Hank combed fingers through his long white beard, then flicked a meaningful glance at Eldrick. "What about you, pretty boy? Your daddy still sitting on his royal fanny on the throne of nightmares? We could use some of his strength."

Eldrick rolled his sterling eyes. "My father resents my existence and quite frankly, I'm not all that enamored with his, either. We don't speak. I assure you, he would not agree to see me, even if I went to the trouble of seeking him out," he snapped bitterly. "Besides, I have no intention of debasing myself to groveling before him like some sniveling child."

"Right. Cause nothing you do is childish or pathetic." Zeph had that devilish, taunting grin on his face.

"I might be able to call in a few favors." Camilla tapped her lips thoughtfully. "After all, we only need to stall him long enough to open the Fibbing Gate."

Looking around at all my friends, I found myself hopeful again. Everyone was working so hard.

Well, almost everyone.

My eyes fell to Eldrick, who was still sulking his seat with his arms folded. He and Zeph were spitting insults at each other from across the table, which wasn't anything new, but hearing Eldrick refuse to aid in our cause by asking his dad for a little help made my skin feel flushed and my teeth clench. How could he refuse? Didn't he care if Fir Darrig captured me and took the faerie throne? Didn't he care about any of us? We could all die in this fight!

As I went back to explaining the rest of my plan, I found it hard to make eye contact with him or even look his way. He was acting like a pompous jerk. How could he go from being encouraging and supportive one moment to being so cold and stubborn the next? Were his issues with his dad *that* bad?

The only thing that distracted me for even a fleeting second was when a crumpled piece of paper fell out of the book Freddy was frantically flipping through. The yellowed, faded page fluttered through the air, landing right in front of me. Before he could snatch it back, I caught a glimpse of what was written on it. It was a diagram—a design for what looked like a fancy revolver.

I flicked him a curious glance.

Freddy colored and winced, like I wasn't supposed to see that. "I-it's just a basic design," he stammered. "Something your mother and I were working on a long time ago."

"My mother wanted a gun?"

"Not just any gun!" Freddy's eyes sparkled with excitement. "A magical revolver. A Claidheamh Soluis."

My brow scrunched at the sound of the strange word. "A what?"

"It means 'Sword of Light,'" he replied and wafted a hand in the air dismissively. He picked up the page and stuffed it back into his book. "A story for another time, maybe. Besides, it's not like I actually got to make it. It was just an idea. I didn't even finish the prototype."

"Probably for the best." Eldrick snorted. "Handing a human a magical weapon like that would likely be catastrophic."

I cut him a glare, biting my tongue. Angry words lodged in my throat, and I could practically taste fire in my throat.

Zeph must have noticed my change in mood because after our makeshift war meeting was over, he followed me back to the tiny room in the back of the bar. Everyone else had dispersed to send messages, call in favors, or—in Eldrick's case—do nothing. I didn't trust myself to be in the same room with him. I knew I would say something or my temper would get out of control.

I waited until Zeph had closed the door behind us in the privacy of that small back room to let out a deep sigh of surrender. I knew what I was in for even before I turned to face Zeph. He was standing right behind me with that persistent slant to his frown.

"You gonna tell me? Or are we doing this the hard way?" He widened his stance like he was preparing to tackle me.

Stepping toward him, I hugged my arms around his waist and laid my head against chest.

"No fair," he grumbled as he put his arms around me.

"Eldrick is only fighting with us because of the contract, isn't he? If he wasn't spelled to stay with me, he'd be long gone by now."

Zeph put a hand on top of my head. "Why the hell are you worrying about that idiot at a time like this? Who cares why he's fighting with us? If he has his butt out there doing something useful, what does it matter?"

"Because I thought he was my friend." I'd been carried away, thinking the contract wouldn't matter to Eldrick. I'd fooled myself into believing he wanted to be around me. The coffee dates, the prom dress, the help studying—he hadn't wanted to do any of it. He was just following orders because of his contract with my father.

"Don't let it get to you." Zeph combed his fingers through my hair. "Eldrick's always had his own agenda. He's got a shitload of baggage. Major daddy issues. Probably some mommy issues, too. Trust me; the last thing you want is for him to dump it all in your lap. Quit worrying about him."

"Right. Cause my lap is already full of all your baggage."

"Exactly." He obviously hadn't caught the sarcasm in my voice. "And hey, if his motives mean that much to you, then ask him straight out. Or better yet, give him a test. Let him out of the contract. If he sticks around to fight with us, then you'll know he really is a friend. Otherwise, good riddance."

I leaned back so I could stare up at him. I had to be sure he wasn't bleeding from the ears or suffering from a psychotic break. Didn't he realize how badly outmatched we were? Hadn't he been listening at all? We'd need all the help we could get in order to stand a chance against Fir Darrig. "But we need him, don't we?"

"I dunno about you, but I'd rather die in the midst of my friends than live surrounded by people who don't care about me. Otherwise, what's the point, right?" Zeph gave me that crooked smile and kissed my lips firmly. "But it's your call, princess. You do what you think is right."

I had been expecting the day of the Singing Moon to seem different, but when the sun rose on that frigid spring morning, it felt like the start of a normal day. The air was bitter cold. There was a fresh dusting of snow on the ground. People in business clothes were walking to work, yammering into cell phones, and carrying trays of paper coffee cups.

As we loaded our bags of gear into the trunk of Hank's car, I was a nervous wreck. I sat in the back seat next to Zeph while Eldrick and Hank sat up front. Behind us, Camilla and Freddy followed in their sporty, white sedan. We left the downtown area, driving past the suburban neighborhoods out into the countryside.

We passed houses where I vaguely recalled my childhood friends had lived. Horse pastures and large barns dotted the landscape, all blanketed in frost and snow. The wind carried the musk of livestock and the faint hint of smoke from chimneys. I'd lived in the city so long it felt like I didn't belong here anymore. Or maybe that was just because my memories of it were so blurred.

We drove for another half hour, far away from any other sign of civilization, before Hank turned down a long driveway. It twisted and snaked through a line of hardwood trees, over a small bridge, and emerged in a large, open field surrounded by forest on all sides. When the house appeared through the naked tree limbs, a torrent of confused emotions swelled in my body; I hadn't seen my family home in so long.

The beautiful old farmhouse looked like a cracked memory, standing at the crest of a hill overlooking a sweeping pasture. Parts of the roof had caved in from the fire. The whitewashed porch was charred, and the windows had been broken out.

Of course, it was abandoned now. My father had left it to me in his will, but I had never come back after his funeral. The fact that it was so far out on the outskirts of town, hidden away from the public eye, was probably the only thing that had saved it from being demolished. Seeing it made my head hurt—as though someone were driving a spike right between my eyes. I whimpered and sat back, rubbing at my forehead. When I squeezed my eyes shut, memories flickered to life from some dark, forgotten corner of my brain. Playing hide and seek in the trees with William, drawing on the front steps with sidewalk chalk, and blazing down the twisty driveway on my bicycle with pink tassels on the handlebars.

"What is it?" Zeph put a hand on my arm.

"I-I … remembered something. Something from when I was a little." I squinted up at him, my head still pounding. "I thought the memories wouldn't come back until the feather was destroyed?"

His mouth was set in a hard line. That's when I realized—his hand on my arm felt colder than normal. "My time's almost up," he muttered. "In a few hours …"

"In a few hours it won't matter," Hank interrupted. "The curse will be broken, you'll be fine, and then our only problem will be shoving Fir Darrig's big ass through that gateway as soon as possible."

I took a steadying breath. Hank was right—now was not the time to lose my focus. Too much was riding on this. I had to be clear. I had to stay calm. Lying back in my seat, I kept rubbing my forehead until the throbbing pain gradually faded.

We stopped at the front of the house, and I peered past my reflection on the car's window at the place that had been my childhood home until a few years ago. My stomach twisted into knots and no matter how hard I clenched them, my hands wouldn't stop shaking.

My legs tingled as I climbed out of the car. I helped take the bags of supplies out of the trunk and spread them out on the driveway. Hank stalked off a few yards and began sending out his acorn messages—one to Jack and one to Fir Darrig on Zeph's behalf. When he was finished, he came back to join me in emptying the trunk. He pulled out a familiar large duffel bag packed full of supplies and an even longer gun case.

Camilla and Freddy set off to walk the perimeter of the property to put up alarm wards so we would know when we had company. Eldrick and Zeph started going over battle plans. There was a lot to do, and plenty I needed to prepare, but my mind still raced. My palms were sweaty and I couldn't concentrate. I crouched before one of the open bags, arming myself for battle with the spellwork materials. I packed my coat pockets with a Sharpie, Zeph's lighter, and a few twigs that I had already charred on the ends so I could use them to draw spellwork in the snow. Two little bags of salt, the staurolite stones, and a travel size can of hairspray completed my collection.

I tucked my mom's iron dagger into the side of my boot where it wouldn't be so obvious. Having it made me feel strangely confident, like I could stand a bit taller. But I couldn't help but think about that drawing of the magical revolver I'd seen in Freddy's book. What would it be like to fight with a weapon like that? Better question—what was it going to take to get Freddy to actually make it for me?

"There's that prance." Zeph smirked as he walked past.

"Strut," I corrected.

"Tomayto, tomahto."

Regardless of how I walked, I wasn't a helpless waif anymore. I could pack my own punch.

Now that I was outfitted, all I had to do now was wait. Everyone else was still busy preparing. Eldrick and Zeph were staring down at a crudely drawn map of the property, arguing about where to make our final stand if things went bad. Hank was checking his shotgun and packing his pockets full of shells. Freddy and Camilla hadn't come back from putting up wards yet.

My gaze wandered away, pulled as if by gravity to a place at the far edge of the property. With everyone concentrating on other things, it wasn't hard to slip away unnoticed. I walked through the snow, past the house, to a small grove of poplar and evergreen trees on the far corner of the clearing.

There, sheltered by the arms of the trees, were three gravestones.

I stared at the names engraved on each one: Marcus, Marissa, and William Barton.

This was all that was left of my family—three cold stones almost buried by the snow. My mother's ancestors had owned this property, almost a thousand acres, for a long time. As far as I knew, most of it was just untamed forest with a few lots sold here and there. I'd never suspected it had anything to do with being some kind of royal descendant—and maybe it didn't—but it was sort of a family tradition to have a home burial here on the family land.

Beside William's grave there was an empty spot, a place meant for me. My stomach fluttered at the sight of it.

I pulled out my mother's necklace from under my shirt, slipping it over my head to run my fingers over the beautiful blood-red stone. The tiny spells etched onto the back made me wonder what they were for. It couldn't just be coincidence that Fir Darrig's princess had been wearing this, too. It had to mean something.

And that strange presence about it, as though it had an aura all its own, still pricked at the back of my mind …

"Been a while since you came back here, huh?" Zeph's voice came from right behind me. I jumped in surprise.

"I just couldn't bear to see this. The house, the property, these …" My voice faded in my throat. It hurt to look at them. I put the big heart-shaped ruby back around my neck.

"Perhaps it is good to remember now," Eldrick spoke up suddenly. I was stunned to find him standing behind me, too. "Remembering what Fir Darrig has done to your family may give you courage."

My heart skipped a beat, but not because of anything Eldrick had said. His presence reminded me that there was something else I had to do—something I'd been psyching myself up for all day. Today was going to change my life forever, for better or worse. I didn't want to go into this battle with any lingering doubts about who I could trust.

"You're right," I said as I turned to face them. "My family deserves vengeance, Zeph deserves saving, and I have to stand up for myself. This is *my* fight."

My eyes met Zeph's for a moment. He knew what I was about to do. I could see it in his expression, but instead of giving me any reassurance or confirmation that this was the right thing to do, he just looked down. He couldn't make this choice for me.

"Which is why I'm letting you go, Eldrick," I added.

He frowned. His silver eyes narrowed, and his head tilted to the side, as though he suspected he was misunderstanding.

"Your contract has been fulfilled. You've been a good friend to me and ... and there will never be any way I can repay you for everything you've done. I'm so grateful for every moment." I forced a smile as I extended a hand toward him. "Well, except for the ones where you tortured me and trapped me in the closet."

His frown hardened and his glare became as sharp as steel. "Why?"

"You're risking your life by getting involved in this. And I don't want you to do that because you have to, or because my father's contract demands it. If you fight with us, I want it to be by your own choice. So, you are hereby released from your contract. Eldrick, you are free."

Eldrick didn't move. His eyes went wide. He gaped at me for a few seconds, and then his gaze moved down to my hand. Slowly, he reached out to take it.

The instant our palms touched, I felt the prickle of magic on my skin. Whispering bells echoed in the air, and Eldrick shuddered hard. His hand gripped mine harder, strong fingers squeezing tightly. Then he sucked in a sharp breath and abruptly snatched his hand away.

His silver eyes flashed wildly as he glanced between Zeph and me. He looked confused, like he wasn't sure what to do. His chest heaved and his nostrils flared as he sucked in deep breaths.

I took a small step back. I wondered if he might attack me again. The feral expression on his face certainly made that seem like a possibility. Before I could say another word, a column of swirling black shadows rose around him. The darkness engulfed his tall form, and in an instant … Eldrick was gone.

I had my answer.

"I'm sorry, princess." Zeph put a comforting hand on my shoulder. "Loyalty isn't something his bloodline is known for."

My throat constricted. I set my jaw and I shook my head. "It's okay. I wouldn't have asked if I wasn't prepared for either answer. At least now I know where he stands."

Only, it wasn't okay. He'd been like family to me. And now I didn't know what to think. Had it all just been an act? Was our entire friendship a farce?

I was still biting back tears when we rejoined Hank and the others, they gathered around with curious expressions. I guess they could tell something was up.

"Eldrick won't be fighting with us," I announced.

Camilla's expression paled. "Why not?"

I hung my head. I felt like such a coward, I couldn't even find the words to explain to them what had happened.

Zeph squeezed my shoulder and stepped in to rescue me. "It doesn't matter. He made his choice. But we don't need him anyway."

I wanted to agree with him; it shouldn't have mattered that Eldrick abandoned us, but it did. Mentally, I was scrambling. My plan was falling apart already.

Preparations continued and I tried to swallow my sorrow and concentrate. The wrenching feeling of betrayal made my stomach turn sour. I wanted to be angry, but I was angrier with myself than I was at Eldrick. I felt stupid for believing he liked me or wanted to help us. I had been so blind.

At dusk, everyone began to take their places. It was almost time. Freddy, Camilla, and Hank stood inside shielding circles that were spelled to make them invisible, both to humans and to fae. They would be undetectable until they stepped outside those circles. It would be a surprise ambush—we hoped.

In the middle of the pasture behind my family's house, I stood with my hand in Zeph's. Together we watched the horizon turn gold and red as the sun set behind the forest. My hands were sweating and trembling like crazy. I tried to at least look composed and confident, but I couldn't stand still. It felt like my chest might explode as my pulse hammered and skipped.

"Hey." Zeph tugged on my hand. "You know I love you, right?"

I exhaled shakily as I squeezed his palm harder. "Yeah. I know."

"Good. We've gotta make this convincing. So just … you know, play along." He sucked in an anxious breath. "Damn, I hope you're a good actress."

I managed a quick, teasing grin. "Oh sure. I got you to think that I liked those tattoos, didn't I?"

"Easy, tiger. Just remember to keep your head on straight. Don't let fear get the best of you. Stick to the plan. After I hand you over, wait for the curse to break. Then give 'em hell."

I nodded. I wanted to be confident so badly. My friends needed me, but all I could think about was the fact that Eldrick had left us. Did we even stand a chance now? I wanted to believe Zeph was right; that we didn't need his help. We could handle this on our own.

I needed to believe that.

Minutes passed as the last few rays of the sun melted out of the sky. As night drew in, the stars began to wink through the twilight. The cold air made the sky seem crystal clear, like I could have dipped my hands into the heavens.

"W-what if he doesn't come?" I wasn't sure if it was the cold or my nerves that made my teeth start chattering. "What if he knows it's a trick? What if he refuses your invitation?" I'd never been a very good liar and now my life and the lives of all my companions depended on it. The irony was cruel.

Zeph was sporting a fearsome scowl. "He'll come." His brilliant violet eyes narrowed on the tree line ahead of us, as though he were waiting for any sign of movement. "His pride won't allow him to refuse. He'd never pass up the opportunity to see someone groveling at his feet."

Something moved in the forest.

My heartbeat stammered and stalled. I could hear twigs snapping. Between the trunks of the trees, delicate little lights were floating toward us like fireflies. My common sense told me that wasn't possible—it was far too cold for fireflies. But what else could they be?

Out of the corner of my eye, I saw Zeph bristle like a guard dog ready to attack. He moved, but it wasn't against whatever creature was coming our way. He lunged at me suddenly, snatching my arms behind my back and forcing me to my knees. I cried out in genuine surprise at how rough he was as he held me, twisting my arms painfully every time I tried to struggle.

"Louder," he murmured so quietly even I barely heard him. "This is an Oscar-winning performance, not an audition."

I let out the loudest scream I could. I cursed at him, demanding that he let me go. I was afraid it sounded fake, but I didn't have to play pretend for very long.

Those floating lights weren't fireflies—they were eyes. Monsters emerged from the forest like phantoms. Their eyes glowed like golden embers, and they all stared straight at me. They looked like wolves, or at least that's what I thought they were. They were about the same size as a wolf—or a giant dog—but as they got closer, I saw that they weren't animals at all.

They were made of plants, roots, rocks, and gnarled branches all twisted together, just like the spriggans.

A dozen of them prowled toward us, snapping their jagged, stone teeth and twitching with eager ferocity. It was as though they had been designed only to fight, hurt, and kill. I had a feeling they were going to be a lot harder to kill.

"Moorhounds," Zeph scoffed loudly. "Seriously? It's not like you to be so cautious."

A deep, musical laugh echoed through the trees. It made my whole being shudder. Tears filled my eyes, and I let out another scream. I struggled, but Zeph just squeezed me harder.

"I had to be sure you were being honest, boy. One can't be too careful," Fir Darrig's voice chimed. It seemed to come from everywhere at once. "You understand my skepticism, don't you? How can I be sure this is even the right girl? Perhaps you're simply trying to use a bit of that changeling magic to save your own neck."

Zeph grabbed a fistful of my hair suddenly and jerked my face upward, forcing me to look toward the dark forest.

"That enough proof for you?" Zeph snarled angrily.

There was no reply.

Instead, the forest seemed to shudder. The trees groaned as though they were in pain. Their trunks began bending and twisting, parting like a living curtain. Fir Darrig stepped into view wearing his natural form—that strange combination of lion, man, and bird. He carried his staff and wore a shining golden breastplate. His vivid eyes fixed on me, scalding me under a vengeful glare.

It was bad enough to see him again, but he hadn't come alone. The forest rumbled again, and out stepped four huge spriggans. They were even bigger than the ones we had battled before, flanking Fir Darrig like colossal, moss-covered mountains. Their gaping maws steamed in the cold air, and they beat the ground with their boulder-sized fists.

I didn't have to pretend to be scared anymore. I was terrified. I screamed and struggled. My curses turned into sobs, and I began pleading with Zeph to let me go. I begged him to reconsider, to remember his love for me, but his gaze was so icy and detached it made me wonder if he was acting or not.

He wasn't … going to let Fir Darrig take me, was he?

"Tick tock, old man," Zeph snarled. "The moon'll be up any second. I've upheld my end of the curse. Give me back my power."

Fir Darrig sneered. "Do I look like a fool to you? Hand her over first."

Zeph spat at the ground. He murmured a few profane things, obviously not happy about being bossed around. Then he forced me to walk. When we were only a few yards away from Fir Darrig and all his horrible monster-minions, Zeph gave me a violent shove. I stumbled, tripped, and fell face-first into the snow at Fir Darrig's feet.

"Good luck with that whiny little bitch." Zeph snorted and crossed his arms. He gave me a disgusted look. "She wouldn't make me the faerie king, either. I don't see why you think you'll have any more luck with her."

I had barely staggered back to my feet when I felt the humid breaths of the moorhounds staring me down. They snapped at my legs and forced me to cross the rest of the distance to Fir Darrig. He waited for me with a smug grin on his lips, holding out a hand as though he were inviting me to dance again. "Of course she will."

Oh yeah, I thought as I took his hand. *Let's dance, you bastard.*

I glared at him with every ounce of courage I had left. He smiled back cruelly, as though it amused him. With a violent jerk, he yanked me closer and snagged an arm around my waist. He sniffed me like an animal, puffing his filthy breath all over my face and neck.

It was all I could do to keep from coming unglued.

Then I saw it—a glimmer of silver light through the trees.

In the distance, a radiant full moon was rising. It was shaking free of the horizon, filling the sky with rich, sterling light, and making every snowdrift and icicle shine like platinum. The air resonated with energy so strong it made my body shiver as it sizzled over my skin. A faint sound like glassy music echoed through the air, carried on the crisp wind.

It was the Singing Moon.

My trance of breathless awe was broken when I heard Zeph cry out. He roared in panic and agony, hunching over suddenly as though he'd been shot. I almost broke my act. My heart twisted painfully as I watched. All he managed to get out were desperate, agonized sounds. I couldn't watch. I bowed my head, clenched my teeth, and shut my eyes tightly.

"Don't be a coward." Fir Darrig grabbed my chin suddenly. He forced me to look.

Zeph had crumpled to his knees. Even from a distance, I could see something wasn't right. His whole body shook erratically. He crawled across the snow as though he were trying to get away from something, but with every move he made, his body—clothing and all—was slowly turning a strange shade of gray. First were his feet, then his legs and waist. Soon he couldn't move the lower half of his body at all.

He yelled out, his eyes crazed with terror as he tried to retreat.

"What's happening to him?" I tried to sound calm and complacent. My heart was pounding so loudly in my ears it almost drowned out Zeph's tortured cries.

"When we are completely drained of magic, fae cannot live. We turn to stone." Fir Darrig laughed with pleasure like he was enjoying this. "Does it pain you to watch him suffer?"

On the inside, I was screaming. I was falling apart, but I couldn't let that show—not now. This was it. This was the moment of truth. One slip up might blow our entire plan.

I stared back at Fir Darrig. "He betrayed me," I answered coldly. "He's nothing to me."

It was probably only a few seconds, but we stared at one another for what felt like hours. With every passing moment, I grew braver and more frantic all at the same time. Zeph's life was slipping away. He couldn't move his arms now, but I couldn't show any emotion—at least, none other than hatred and anger. Fortunately, I had enough of both for Fir Darrig, so it wasn't hard to look at him like I wanted to rip his pointed ears right off his head.

"Young hearts are such fickle, useless things. They are turned so easily, it's delightfully revolting," Fir Darrig mused. He chuckled darkly and raised a hand toward Zeph. "But how you feel is irrelevant, I suppose. A deal's a deal. You belong to me now; the curse is appeased."

The snap of his fingers cracked like lightning. It made a shockwave ripple through the air, spreading out and striking Zeph's nearly lifeless body with great force.

He collapsed into the snow and didn't move.

I couldn't breathe. I stared at him, waiting for something—anything—to happen.

Nothing. He was completely still. I couldn't even see him breathing.

It was as though someone were tearing my soul in half. I couldn't stop the tears.

And then, there was light—bright violet light that blinded me. A swell of tolling chimes filled the air, growing louder and louder until I was forced to cover my ears. I shrank back, unintentionally pressing myself against Fir Darrig in the process. Before I could react, he snatched me up and carried me off into the forest.

"See that he doesn't follow us," Fir Darrig commanded his army of monsters.

The spriggans and moorhounds bellowed in reply.

My vision was still spotty as the dark forest engulfed us. I twisted in Fir Darrig's grasp, trying to look behind us to see anything—any sign that Zeph was still alive. All I could see were the shapes of Fir Darrig's monsters as they began to converge upon that vibrant point of light. A glimmer of white fur caught my eye, and I stiffened in terror as a familiar white wolf galloped past. It was Lumi.

"I've a nice spot picked out for my crowning," Fir Darrig laughed with wicked delight. "We won't be disturbed there. Come, little vessel. It's time we put the faerie crown where it is most richly deserved."

I pretended to struggle again. In the process, I twisted my body slightly, bringing my knees up until I could reach my foot. I slipped my fingers into the side of my boot and closed a fist around the hilt of my mom's dagger. It wasn't a fancy spell or an intricate enchantment, but hopefully it would work ...

I ripped the dagger out of my boot and stabbed Fir Darrig in the side with all my strength. The iron blade sank deep into his flesh—all the way up to the hilt. Immediately the air filled with a putrid burning smell.

Fir Darrig threw me away like a bad apple.

I skidded over the snow, slamming into the trunk of a tree. The impact cracked my head so hard that everything spun. He roared in pain, throwing away his staff and clutching at his side where the dagger had left an awful black wound. So much of his blood poured out onto the snow that I could practically taste it in the air.

When I got up, I was still seeing bright specks, but I never let go of the dagger. If he came at me again, I was prepared to stab him as many times as it took.

"You want to get me back, you bastard? You'll have to catch me first!" I spun and ran full speed back toward the clearing. Thankfully, we hadn't made it very far, and there were plenty of radiant bursts of light to guide me in the right direction.

I broke the tree line and emerged onto a battlefield. Freddy and Camilla were running around, trying to cast spells while dodging the swinging arms of spriggans. Hank had taken a wide stance, firing round after round from his shotgun. The percussion of each blast cracked like thunder in the air and was usually followed by the agonized wail of a moorhound. Most of the moorhounds seemed more focused on Zeph, however, who stood in their midst like a gleaming, violet angel.

Only, I'd never seen him shine like that before.

With his power fully restored, his true form bloomed in the night with more beautiful strangeness than ever before. His horns were longer, his wings were larger, and the once sparse runes on his skin now covered him like stripes on a tiger. He bared his fangs, prowling on hind legs like a lion's. He even had a long lion's tail. He fought the moorhounds like a wild animal, ripping them apart one by one as they swarmed around him.

"Head's up!" someone shouted suddenly.

Another moorhound sprang toward me, ready to tear me to shreds. I raised my dagger again, but the instant it leaped, ice climbed the monster's body and froze it in midair.

"Jack!" I cheered as he swooped low on his wintry white wings to give me a playful wink.

"Don't get too comfy," he warned with a merry chuckle. "The spell will wear off quickly! Fir Darrig was ready for me this time. He warded them all against my frost."

I ran straight for an open patch of snow. The curse was broken, Zeph was free, so now it was time for phase two of my plan.

I had a new royal to crown and a gate to open.

With Jack flying defense to keep the moorhounds at bay, prepping the crowning spell was easy. It was just a simple circle spell with a few symbols around it and a mark in the center that looked sort of like a crown. I drew them out quickly and perfectly with one of my charred twigs. Then, I scribbled more spellwork on my arms with the Sharpie. I was working fast, but I didn't mess up. My mind was a steel trap, remembering every symbol in perfect detail.

A familiar enemy came striding toward me right before I finished the last symbol. Lumi stood only a few yards away, her white fur bristling and her pale blue eyes shining like stars. Her snout wrinkled, lips drawing back into a snarl as she flattened her ears. I looked around for Jack—but he was already preoccupied with two moorhounds.

This was up to me.

I scowled, sticking the Sharpie between my teeth before I took out Zeph's lighter and the little can of hairspray from my pocket.

Lumi sent a blast of cold air at me when she snapped her jaws, her legs coiled for the attack.

Wait for it—wait for it.

The white she-wolf sprang, surging toward me with fangs flashing in the moonlight. I tensed, holding firm until she was only a couple of feet away. Then I sprayed a burst of hairspray through the open flame of Zeph's lighter.

Fire belched out into the night and blasted Lumi right in the face. Her fur caught fire immediately. She yowled and scrambled to get away, pawing at her face.

So I advanced. This was personal; I wanted some payback. She'd only just managed to douse her face in the snow when I hit her again, blasting another wave of fire over her body.

Lumi yelped and shrieked. I threw down the lighter and hairspray and drew my dagger again. Seizing her charred snout with one hand, I held the iron point right between her eyes. "Move and I'll ram this right through your brain."

Lumi froze, her pale eyes wide as they stared back at me.

"If you *ever* come near me or any of my friends again, I swear I will kill you. Got me?" I pressed the point harder against her hide. "This is your only chance—leave now and never come back."

As soon as I let her go, the white wolf stumbled back with her tail between her legs. I kept the blade of my dagger poised, ready to strike if she decided to test me. Lumi snarled one last time, her eyes blazing with anger, and disappeared into a whirlwind of snow and white mist.

I smirked, slipping the dagger back into my boot before I went back to my spellwork. No time for a victory dance now. I still had to pick someone to be the new faerie ruler ... someone new. My mind raced as I finished drawing the symbols on my arms and hands. Who should I pick? Freddy? Camilla? Jack? Those were my only choices except for Zeph. I didn't know any other faeries to choose from.

Suddenly, I couldn't breathe.

Something hit me so hard it sent me flying like I'd been struck by a car. I sailed through the air, flipping helplessly over the ground. Something snapped. I felt my leg hit awkwardly, knocking my dagger free of its hiding place. It was lost somewhere in the snow—my only effective weapon against these monsters.

I landed facedown on the frozen earth. My whole body ached. Every time I tried to take a breath, sharp pain pierced my chest like I was being stabbed.

I stared up through my delirium to see what had hit me. As my eyes focused through the haze, I saw a pair of wrathful, green eyes glaring down at me with utter hatred.

Fir Darrig wrapped a powerful hand around my neck. He plucked me out of the snow like a naughty puppy. I gasped for air, clawing at his arm. My chest was already hurting so badly that I knew I must have broken something, and now Fir Darrig was crushing my windpipe so I couldn't even speak.

"You wretched little shrew," Fir Darrig rasped. He was still bleeding from that wound in his side where I'd stabbed him. The flesh around it was turning black and rotting away faster than should have been possible.

"You *will* name me as faerie king and *maybe* then I won't crush the life out of you." He squeezed my neck even harder. I thought it might snap at any second.

It took every ounce of my strength to suck in a tiny breath. It was just enough for me to wheeze, "Go to hell."

Fir Darrig bellowed in frustration, squeezing my throat harder. I flailed in his grasp. The world began to go dark. I couldn't breathe. I couldn't see. He was … going to kill me.

Something slammed into us.

The impact jarred Fir Darrig enough that he let me go. I landed in a nearly unconscious heap in the snow at Fir Darrig's feet, choking and wheezing. My neck ached and my throat spasmed with every rasping, desperate breath I took. With vision still blurred, I glanced up to try and figure out what had happened—and if I had time to get away.

A huge, furious black wolf had his jaws locked around Fir Darrig's arm and was shaking. My jaw dropped. Tears welled in my eyes.

"Eldrick!" I screamed.

A flick of Fir Darrig's free hand summoned his staff again. He smacked Eldrick over the snout with it. It didn't work—Eldrick didn't let go. Instead, he pitched violently, shaking his head with his teeth still digging into Fir Darrig's arm. Blood spattered the snow, and Fir Darrig raised his staff again, his face twisted with rage.

The crack of his staff over Eldrick's head sent a burst of chimes roaring through my eardrums. I stumbled back, clamping my hands over my ears as a flash of blinding green light lit up the night.

Eldrick hit the ground running. He shifted forms mid-stride as he sprinted over the ground straight toward me, plucking me out of the snow just as a blast of magic roared past us. The heat of the spell sizzled against my face and singed some of my hair.

Fir Darrig lost it. He started casting wildly, sending bursts of raw magic in our direction like tongues of green lightning. Each one left a patch of scorched, naked earth behind.

I gripped Eldrick with all my might as he ran. He ducked and dodged, moving as quick as a shadow over the frozen ground. When we reached spell circle I had been working on for the crowning, he skidded to a halt and whirled around.

"I can draw him off." Eldrick panted as he set me down inside the circle. "Who is it that you've chosen? Give me the name and I will try to clear the way for them."

Eldrick started to pull away. His wild eyes flashed around the battlefield as he waited for my word before he sprang into action. I grabbed the front of his sweater to keep him from charging back into battle.

"Why?" So many emotions swirled through my head. Most of them could wait, but this I needed to know right now. "Why did you come back?"

He stared down at me as though I had completely lost my mind. "I didn't leave," he corrected me sharply. "I simply had to run an errand."

An errand? Seriously? What could he possibly have to do that couldn't wait until—

Horns blared in the distance. If not for Eldrick's smug, almost evil grin, I might have thought I was hallucinating.

On the horizon, a churning black cloud rose up like a dark tidal wave. It blotted out the sterling light of the moon and swallowed the stars, generating a thrumming energy that sent cold pangs of fear through my body. At the crest of the wave, in a chariot drawn by two ghostly black horses, rode an older man wearing a sweeping black cape and a crown made of black glass. There was a cruel smirk on his lips as he drove his horses on, snapping a whip that cracked like thunder.

Fir Darrig stopped. Even the spriggans seemed curious and confused at first, but that was before the charioteer descended into the clearing, steering straight for one of the colossal monsters with a sword drawn. Behind him, the toiling black cloud split into a hundred smaller, ghostly fragments. Some looked like horses, others like panthers, wolves, or skeletal soldiers with bat-wings. Their ghoulish forms flickered like black shadows, but their claws, fangs, and swords were very real.

"Your dad?" I guessed.

Eldrick sighed and put his hands over mine so I would let go of his sweater. "We weren't going to survive this without sizeable reinforcements."

"But you said you would never ask him—"

"That was before you set me free. After that I was ... forced to acknowledge something I had taken for granted," he cut me off quickly and touched one of his warm hands to my cheek. "You are precious to me. I am indeed your friend. I will not forsake you now. Your battles are mine, as well."

That was all I needed to hear. I'd made this decision days ago, and now

I knew it was the right one after all. "I have made my choice."

The moment those words left my lips, the spell circle beneath our feet ignited. Fir Darrig shrieked, hurling another bolt of green lightning in our direction. Before it could hit, Jack Frost and Zeph swept in, melding their powers to create a protective shield around us.

The crowning symbols lit up one by one beneath my feet, burning as brightly and softly as candles in the darkness of the night. The marks on my skin did the same, gleaming to life until I could feel the swell of magic surging through my body.

"I didn't understand it before. I thought Dad contracting you to me was a mistake, or some kind of cruel joke. But … I get it now. I believe he wanted me to see you for who you truly are, and for you to learn that not all humans are stupid, selfish, and cruel. This is why he brought us together—because I needed you as much as you needed me."

Eldrick seemed mute with shock as I stood on my toes, taking his face into my hands. His eyes were wide and his cheeks flushed as I kissed his forehead. Ignoring the battle that raged on around us, Fir Darrig's magical blasts sizzling against the barrier, I whispered the final bit of the spell. "From now until the eve of the next Singing Moon, you alone shall bear this responsibility and sacred blessing. I crown you, Eldrick Dorchaidhe, to rule as King of the Faeries."

A string of glowing golden runes ignited across his forehead, forming a band that blazed like fire. They faded quickly, melting as though they were being absorbed into his body. Eldrick's eyes rolled back and he took in a deep breath. He shivered, his body tensing, broad shoulders flexing, and hands slowly curling into fists.

When he opened his eyes again, they weren't silver anymore—they shone like molten pools of gold.

"*No!*" Fir Darrig thundered. He lunged, his expression twisted with a look of insane fury, and swung the staff again. The spear-like tip glowed and sizzled with raw magical energy, sending out a wave of power aimed directly at us.

I cringed against Eldrick as the blow rocketed over the snow like a blazing comet. There was no outrunning it. We couldn't dodge this one.

Eldrick straightened and stretched out a hand. He caught the blast as though it were nothing, his expression never changing from perfect calm. As he snapped his hand closed, the sphere snuffed out with a puff of smoke.

Fir Darrig froze in place, his mouth falling open. His eyes went round and his face blanched. Gradually, his whole expression began to twitch and his grip on his staff tightened.

He swallowed hard and took a wobbly, limping step backward.

Eldrick's mouth curled into a smirk. "I will keep him occupied," he repeated, although this time his voice carried a sense of pride and authority that made me blush. It suited him. "Prepare the spellwork to summon the gate. I will return shortly."

I grinned. It probably looked goofy considering our circumstances. "Right away, Your Majesty!"

Eldrick's father stormed the battlefield in his chariot, snapping his whip around the arms and legs of the massive earth monsters. The whole time he laughed like a complete maniac. He seemed to be the only one enjoying himself.

As much as I wanted to help them fight, I had my hands full. All my studying and practice boiled down to this one moment. I couldn't mess this up. My forehead was sticky with sweat and my chest ached and throbbed as I began drawing the complex series of spell circles. The fight raged on around me, threatening to distract me or break my focus. I had shut everything else out.

Suddenly, a pair of strong hands grabbed my shoulders.

I screamed, rearing back for a punch since I'd already lost all my battle hardware.

Zeph didn't wait for me to recover. He went through my pockets until he found another charred twig. "I'll start over there," he growled. "Hurry up. We're not doing so hot."

What? But we had Eldrick and Erebos fighting with us now, didn't we?

Shouldn't that have least evened the odds?

I glanced around through the bursts of magical spells that bloomed in the night and the twisting, earthy bodies of Fir Darrig's monsters. As quickly as my friends were cutting them apart, spriggans and moorhounds were reassembling and diving right back into the fray. Hank fired shot after shot, sending wood splinters and shards of rock in every direction. Each time, a moorhound dropped ... but didn't stay that way. The creature writhed and hissed, its body rapidly regenerating until it could stand and charge again.

Freddy was squaring off against another spriggan. It swung at him, its giant fists slamming down hard enough to make the ground rumble and my teeth rattle. He dodged and jumped at the last second, narrowly escaping. He was soaked with sweat, barely able to stay on his feet.

Then he tripped. The spriggan drew back for a killing blow.

I screamed.

Out of nowhere, Camilla landed on the spriggan's fist. Her whole body shimmered like it was covered in blue and white diamonds. She dug her fingers into the spriggan's hand and immediately it started to melt, turning to sludge and watery mud.

The spriggan was still studying the stump where its hand had been as Camilla darted down to drag her husband away. Her expression was skewed and desperate, her eyes darting toward me.

They were tiring. They wouldn't last much longer.

Zeph's wings brushed against me as he stepped over and began hurriedly writing the proper runes around the other side of the circle. "Come on, slacker. Less watching, more working!"

I tried to focus again. But another quick glance at the battle made me hesitate. There was *another* Zeph still locked in combat with a group of moorhounds. No—more than one. I saw three Zephs scattered across the field, ripping Fir Darrig's monsters apart as fast as the gnarled beasts could reassemble themselves.

"Told you've I've got a few tricks. The illusion will stick as long as they believe it's real," he said with a quick smirk. "Good thing spriggans are dumb as hell, right?"

We finished the markings together in half the time it would have taken me alone, even with my injury was slowing me down. I winced, unable to suppress a whimper of pain as I bent over to press the staurolite stones into the earth at the proper places in the innermost part of the central circle. Then I stood back to double-check my work. It was perfect—it had to be. There wasn't time to do it over.

"All right, princess. Now we just need the king," Zeph spread his wings, glassy violet feathers catching in the moonlight. "Eldrick, right?"

"H-how did you know?"

He tapped his temple. "Got my senses back. A Faerie King puts off a powerful aura. He's stronger than Fir Darrig now."

Good to know, but I didn't see Eldrick or Fir Darrig anywhere.

A sudden chorus of snarls made me turn—right into the oncoming teeth of a lunging moorhound. I screamed and threw my arms up to shield my face. My feet tangled as I pitched backwards.

In one fluid motion, Zeph yanked me out of the moorhound's path and rammed his arm into its open jaws. His eyes blazed with wrath as the creature gnawed on his forearm, still trying to get to me. Two more of the monsters were closing in, ready to join the fight.

"Stay behind me," he ordered.

No argument there. I scrambled out of the way as Zeph flared his wings and grabbed the moorhound dangling from his arm by the scruff. A chilling toll of bells rippled through the air as the vibrant runes that striped Zeph's whole body flashed brighter. The moorhound in his hand stiffened and yelped as though it had been electrocuted. It kicked and flailed, trying to get away from him—but Zeph didn't let go.

Not until he'd taken aim, that is.

He hurled the moorhound through the air, using it like a bowling ball to knock over the other two. The crashed end over end, the first one exploding like a grenade of purple magic that sent the other two flying.

Four more moorhounds were already charging in to pick up the fight, though. Zeph dropped to his hands and feet in a crouch, wings spread wide and pointed canines bared. His lion tail lashed and the stripes on his body strobed and pulsed.

The advancing pack skidded to a halt, their wicked eyes flickering as they stared past Zeph at me. One of them took a daring step closer.

Zeph's body rippled, his runes gleaming brighter as he let out a thundering roar. All the moorhounds flinched back. They made yipping sounds as they cowered, finally turning to run with their tails firmly tucked.

"W-we don't have much time …" I wheezed as Zeph stood and faced me again. The pain in my chest was getting worse and making me feel strange. My fingers tingled. Everything was spinning.

Zeph caught me as I started to fall. One of his hands touched my chest, right at my ribs. I whimpered and clenched my teeth.

"What's wrong?" His expression was riddled with concern. "Are you hurt?"

I had to use his arm to steady myself. "Don't worry about it. I'll be fine. Where is Eldrick?"

Zeph nodded and pointed into the distance, his expression somber.

Eldrick had slipped back into his beastly, wolfish form. He and Fir Darrig clashed in the moonlight, the bursts from their magical attacks lighting up the dark like fireworks. They brawled, two giant faerie gods— Fir Darrig wielding his staff to send bolts of power that Eldrick snagged in his teeth or let bounce off his shaggy black hide. Each hit made him falter, but only for a moment. He struck back, seizing Fir Darrig's staff in his jaws and trying to wrench it out of his hands.

My stomach twisted. Eldrick was king now, wasn't he? Couldn't he crush Fir Darrig—or at least hit him hard enough to buy us enough time to open the gate? Why was he holding back?

"That idiot," Zeph growled under his breath. "He picked a fine time to get heroic. He must be worried about us getting caught in the crossfire. He's not using even half of his power."

"What can we do?"

He frowned, his eyes going steely. "*You* aren't moving from this spot. I'm gonna mix up a distraction so he can get back over here. It won't hold him for long, though, so you better be fast."

My skin prickled at the presence of Zeph's magic as he sprang into the sky, wings catching a frosty gust of wind. Jack swooped in to fly beside him and then the two broke away as though they were coordinating some kind of attack.

Zeph lined up, pumping his wings hard as he hovered in place. Jack circled wide, streaking through the sky and summoning up a concentrated blast of his icy power. It made the air around me crackle with energy and the rising swell of chimes.

Drawing his hands apart, Zeph made a glowing purple spell circle that hung in the air—hovering right above his hands. It grew and expanded until it shone like a glittering bullseye in the sky ... right above Fir Darrig.

Jack Frost hurled his own spell straight through the center. The instant his ice magic met Zeph's illusionary power, the spell imploded with concussive force. It sent snow and wind howling through the air like a blizzard. I had to cover my eyes from the stinging, blinding wind.

When the whiteout dissipated, Fir Darrig had a new opponent—a giant replica of himself made of solid ice. The frosty giant lumbered forward, catching Fir Darrig off guard with a swing of its staff. It sent the faerie lord staggering, barely able to raise his own staff in time to block another swing. Overhead, Zeph and Jack were already lining up to do the same spellwork combination again.

Eldrick caught on right away. He backed up two steps, turned, and galloped back to the spell circle, still in his giant wolf form. He lowered his head to me, then put one of his massive paws into the circle and howled so loud I had to cover my ears.

The ground shook. I stumbled onto my rear end as the runes in the Fibbing Gate circle slowly came to life with soft, gentle, white light. The more marks that glowed, the more they seemed to emanate a fine, shining white mist. The shimmering vapor gathered in the center of the circles, swirling like a million pin-prick sized stars.

Slowly, it drew together into the vague shape of a ghostly white door that hovered in the middle of the circle. It looked just like the door in the picture Freddy had stolen out of the old whispering tome.

The time had come. I had to open the gate, and somehow, we had to get Fir Darrig through it.

My whole body shook as I got to my feet and took timid steps toward the door. It towered over me, seeming to glisten somewhere between reality and a floating, misty dream. I shivered, reaching for the giant handle—a snarling metal gargoyle with a ring through its teeth.

The moment my fingers touched the translucent ring, it solidified. A ripple went out from the handle, drawing the whole door into this dimension. The four staurolite stones began to rattle and shake as though they were shivering in place.

The earth rumbled again. I cringed back as more of those cross-shaped gemstones burst out of the earth and shot toward the gateway, stacking themselves rapidly. Several hundred cross-shaped gems all formed together, interlocking like a giant jigsaw puzzle in the shape of the door itself.

"Open it!" Eldrick shouted. "Do it now!"

I clenched my teeth, grasped the handle with both hands, and pulled.

The giant door didn't move. I couldn't budge it at all. Then the wooden edges began to creak and groan. I pulled harder. My feet slipped on the icy ground and my chest hurt so badly I could barely stand it, but I'd come too far to give up now.

Slowly, I dragged the heavy gateway open.

I expected to see light from within, like a gateway to heaven or something. Instead, bitter cold wafted through the opening like a gust from a deep freezer. The darkness beyond the doorway churned and moved as though it were alive. It emanated the worst sort of feeling I'd ever experienced. It was a harrowing mixture of terror, sorrow, and complete hopelessness.

My heart pounded—or at least, I thought it was my heart. Something was tugging at my neck. I looked down to see that there was a strange lump under my clothes. My mother's necklace slipped free of my shirt collar, levitating and pulling straight toward the open doorway as if it were being drawn in by a magnet.

I closed my hand around it, bringing the heart-shaped ruby close enough that I could see the tiny engraved runes on it. They were radiating a pulsing red light in rhythm ... like a heartbeat.

That eerie feeling tingled through me again—the sense that someone's aura was here with me, so close and strangely comforting. Why? What was it about this pendant that made it feel so *alive*?

The words burst from the depths of my memory, making every joint in my body lock up.

Fir Darrig found some way to make himself immortal.

Oh god ... could that really be it?

Slowly, I turned around. Through all the chaos and magical explosions, I saw Fir Darrig. He was still wrestling with the fire-breathing dragon version of Zeph. Our eyes met briefly.

Then he noticed what I was holding.

All the color drained from his face. His eyes went wide in horror.

The pendant's pulse had begun racing faster, as though with fear—the same fear I could see on his face that very moment. He hadn't made himself immortal. At least, I suspected that hadn't been his original intention. Somehow, he'd bound his life, his very heart and soul, to this little trinket. Then he'd given it to that princess.

He had literally given her the most precious part of himself—but that hadn't swayed her opinion at all when it came to crowning the new faerie ruler.

And now I knew. This little heart-shaped necklace was why no one could defeat him. This was why everyone thought he was immortal. His life was magically tied to it. His body would regenerate over and over, no matter what you did to him, just like his earthen monsters, so long as this necklace was still intact. Even the wound I'd cut into his side had already begun to heal now. That shouldn't have been possible. Iron was supposed to hurt faeries beyond the ability of their magic to repair it.

Fir Darrig let out a panicked scream as he bashed past the ice giant. He hurled his spear through the air, ramming it straight through Zeph's chest. It made a horrible, gory sound as Zeph crashed back to earth, the spear pinning him to the ground.

"Zeph!" I screamed, pitching forward and almost losing my focus.

He was still snarling and cursing, yelling my name and trying to reach for me while pinned under the staff. Jack landed and began trying to pull it out to set him free.

Fir Darrig sprinted for me at blitzing speed, his wings spread wide and his teeth bared.

There was nowhere to run. I was going to die. Unless …

I stumbled back and caught myself against the gate.

I held the necklace out toward the open doorway again. The big heart-shaped ruby floated in the air as it was pulled in toward the darkness beyond the Fibbing Gate. I could still sense it pulsing. It was such an innocent, delicate feeling.

But there was nothing innocent about the person it belonged to.

"*No!*" Fir Darrig boomed desperately.

I met his gaze. "Enjoy hell, you monster."

Then I closed my eyes tightly … and let it go. The necklace shot out of my hand and was sucked through the gateway. The darkness swallowed it whole.

Once it disappeared, the whole door began to shudder. The staurolite stones rattled, and the hinges groaned. Darkness licked out from beyond it, boiling over like black smoke from a cauldron. A wisp of it slipped past me, zipping out and dissolving into the night. Weird …

The ground tremored as the eyes of the gargoyle handle began to glow bright red. The door was closing. I backed away, staring up as the Fibbing Gate began to deconstruct. The runes melted away like liquid starlight. The staurolite stones crumbled and turned into dirt. The door closed with a deep, resounding *boom*.

And then Fir Darrig hit me.

Just like before, I went flying several yards before landing in the snow. I sat up in a daze. Eldrick clamped his jaws around one of his hind legs, trying to hold Fir Darrig back.

The crack of a whip snapped in the cold air. Eldrick's father drew his chariot close enough to snag the business end of his whip around Fir Darrig's arm. He yelled at his ghostly horses, and together they kept him at bay while I got to my feet.

As I stood, my fingers brushed against something solid. It was the same object I'd hit my head on when I landed. Buried in the snow, I closed my fist around the hilt of my mother's iron dagger.

Feeling that cold metal in my hand made courage surge through my body. I turned toward Fir Darrig and ran—well, it was more like fast limping. I couldn't stand up straight anymore without the pain in my ribs bringing me to my knees.

"Josie!" Zeph's voice called out to me an instant before I felt his arms close around me from behind. "Are you suicidal? The Fibbing Gate didn't work! They can't hold him forever—we have to get out of here now!"

"No!" I screamed as I struggled to fight him off. "I can do this! Let me go!"

Zeph squeezed me harder and growled in my ear. "Stop it. I won't let you kill yourself."

"I'm not," I growled back, twisting so I could look him in the eye. "Didn't you see? He's mortal now!"

He obviously hadn't seen because Zeph just gawked at me in bewilderment.

His hesitation gave me a chance to wriggle free of his arms. I ran for Fir Darrig, blade in hand.

Fir Darrig shouted furiously, and reared on his hind legs. When he stamped his front paws down again, it sent out a concussive shockwave of magical energy that threw Eldrick and his father off at once.

Then he turned on me. Murder blazed in his eyes. He leapt through the air with his wings spread wide and his claws outstretched.

I braced for impact and squeezed the dagger in my hand. Behind me, Zeph was yelling.

It was too late.

He couldn't save me now.

Fur and feathers smothered me. Something sharp—claws or fangs—dug into my shoulder. I clenched my teeth, squeezing the dagger's hilt and ramming it upwards with all my might. The musky, coppery smell of blood flooded my nose. I couldn't tell whose it was—mine, Fir Darrig's, or both.

Then an unbelievable weight crushed my body into the ground.

White hot agony shot through me. I pushed and shoved, anything to get that weight off my ribs. It didn't work. I couldn't breathe or scream. Something hot and wet, most likely blood, started soaking my clothes.

I was running out of air. No—this wasn't how it was supposed to end. I'd come so far. I couldn't die like this—suffocating under Fir Darrig's giant carcass where I couldn't even call for help.

All of a sudden, Fir Darrig's giant body rolled off me. Cool air rushed in, and I sucked in a frantic, deep breath.

Zeph, Eldrick, and Jack stared down at me, their human faces all showing a similar look of horror.

I slumped back onto the cool ground. I managed a hoarse laugh.

"You really are crazy," Zeph's voice cracked as he pulled me up to my feet. His brow quavered as he looked me over like he was trying to decide if he was going to shake me or kiss me.

"I-I'm okay," I rasped.

He yanked me in and hugged me tight against his chest. "You are … the most … I can't even …"

"I know," I whispered as I draped my arms around his waist. "Sorry about that."

"Never again." He was trembling as he buried his face in my hair.

I petted the back of his head. "I promise."

For a moment, everything was quiet. And that's when I felt it— something like a stirring deep inside. It started out small, like a quiet whispering melody in my mind. But as he held me close, it grew stronger. It was a simple coupling of chimes, and yet much more. Their perfect harmony hummed through my chest, deep in my bones, seeping into my soul. My eyes welled up. It felt like my soul had touched his somehow. They were entwined—woven together and never to be separated.

Our heart-chord.

"Zeph, I …" My voice caught as tears ran down my face. "I can hear it."

He pulled back slightly, his eyes searching me. Then he drew me in again, his lips meeting mine with triumphant excitement.

Someone cleared their throat behind us.

Pulling apart, we both turned to look. I hadn't noticed that everyone was gathered around us.

Freddy and Camilla looked like they were about to drop with exhaustion. Hank was picking twigs out of his hair. Jack was wiping soot off his feathery white wings. Despite that, most of them were giving me these weird little grins. Even Eldrick's father had an odd, approving smirk on his lips.

"I guess I've been out of casting for too long," Freddy panted.

Camilla gave him a sympathetic pat on the arm. "It seems both of us have, sweetie. We're a tad out of shape."

"That's what you get for choosing the scholar's path." Jack grinned at them impishly.

The conversation died as we stared across the quiet battlefield. All over the snowy hills around my family home were piles of dirt, rocks, and roots. Without Fir Darrig, the spells that had fused them together had fallen apart. Spriggans and moorhounds were reduced to nothing but heaps of earth. That's all that was left of his army now.

Well, except for Lumi … but she was nowhere to be seen.

Before us, Fir Darrig lay motionless on the snow. My mother's dagger was sticking out of his chest, right over his heart. I barely remembered stabbing him as he'd fallen on me, but there was no denying the evidence.

Seeing him that way was a relief. It was over. He was gone. He couldn't hurt anyone else I loved. And yet … I wondered how something so innocent, a beautiful gesture of love, could have gone so terribly wrong. My eyes wandered to Zeph, who was still gripping my hand as though he were afraid I might try something else reckless.

What was going to happen to us? Could a faerie and a human really be together and everything work out?

Little by little, Fir Darrig's body turned gray like stone. It reminded me of the way Zeph's body had changed when the curse was draining his life away. As soon as all of Fir Darrig had turned that color, his body crumbled into a sparkling chalky dust.

In the end, all that was left of him was a little powdery, silver ash and my mother's dagger.

I reached down to pick it up and carefully dusted it off.

"I don't understand," Eldrick muttered quietly. He was the only one who wasn't smiling. "You stabbed him once before and it only slowed him down slightly."

"It was the necklace," I said as I looked at Camilla.

She tilted her head to the side in confusion. Everyone else looked puzzled, too. I tried to explain. The more I did, the more the mood seemed to shift. Everyone was staring down at the pile of silver dust left where Fir Darrig had been.

"As long as the necklace endured, he couldn't be destroyed." Eldrick's eyes were a piercing shade of gold now when they gazed at me. It gave me chills. "What a clever girl you've turned out to be."

I blushed. "I wasn't even sure I was right. I just hoped I was."

Camilla gave a shaky sigh and leaned against her husband. "It's a good thing I remembered to give you those things. Imagine if I'd forgotten!"

Freddy stroked her hair. "Now that's what I call good luck."

She smiled and leaned her head on his shoulder. "Or a small touch of destiny."

"This is never going to work. No one is going to believe that you're *my* Ben." I was halfway hoping a car would hit me or maybe I'd get kidnapped. Anything, really, as long as it kept me from having to go to school today. I knew there was humiliation in store for me unlike anything I'd ever faced before. We were just walking down the sidewalk and people were already giving us funny looks.

"Relax." Zeph was as blasé as ever as he walked hand-in-hand with me toward the school. I was the only one who knew it was him, though. He'd whipped up another disguise to explain why my legal guardian had been so absent … and also why I'd been missing so much school lately. He seemed confident that this would work, but I wasn't convinced anyone was going to buy that my legal guardian was a famous movie star. This was ridiculous, even by his standards.

I guess I had forgotten how good Zeph was at being ridiculous. He sold some wild story to the principal and Ms. Grear about how he couldn't be available because he was filming a new movie. Then he told them I had fallen down the stairs at my apartment and broken some of my ribs, so he had insisted I come stay with him in L.A. until I had recovered. Of course, they bought it. They ate it up like a fattening dessert. It shouldn't have surprised me, but I still couldn't believe it.

The principal was apologetic and eager to make accommodations for me to make up all the work I had missed so I could still graduate on time. Ms. Grear looked like she might be sick. I guess she didn't like having to face the reality that Ben did exist.

Zeph worked his magic on them like a pied piper. Meanwhile, I sat in mortified silence while the entire faculty took turns finding excuses to peek into the meeting room where we were talking. They were obviously starstruck and looking for a chance to get a glimpse of the famous actor. It was absurd, so of course Zeph loved every second of it.

As we left the school, I gave him a good punch in the arm. My ribs were still sore though, so it probably hurt me more than it did him. Camilla had shown me a healing spell to help speed things along with my recovery, but it didn't do much for the pain. "First Joe Noble, and now this? Are you trying to make sure I'm treated like some kind of freak show attraction?"

He laughed and ruffled my hair. "Just go ahead and thank me. It's like ripping off a Band-Aid. It'll only hurt for a second."

I tried to scowl at him, but I just couldn't. I loved that wry, smug grin on his lips. I loved the way he walked with his arm draped over my shoulders so that my side was pressed gently against his. He handled me more carefully now, and I loved the way he leaned down to plant a firm, scratchy, stubbly kiss on my cheek.

I only had a few weeks left until high school graduation. After that came Eldrick's formal coronation and the official dissolving of the two faerie courts. Things were going back to the way they had been before— the way they were supposed to be. A king I had chosen because I knew he could be strict, stern, fair, just, but compassionate and loyal would now rule a *united* faerie court. Eldrick really was the best candidate, and so far, he seemed to be flourishing in his new role.

Eldrick had extended a personal invitation to Zeph, Freddy, Camilla, and me to attend his coronation ceremony that would reveal him as king to the rest of the faerie community. He'd invited Hank, too, but the old shaman insisted he'd had enough faeries to last him a while. He was taking a vacation, or so he claimed. Honestly, I think he just didn't want to wear a suit and tie.

Weeks passed like a blur. The day of my high school graduation seemed to come a lot sooner than I expected. Fortunately, I managed to catch up on all my schoolwork before then. Not having to worry so much about being kidnapped by an ancient, evil faerie opened up a lot of free time for me. Being the one who killed Fir Darrig gave me quite a reputation. I wasn't to be trifled with, so for now, they left me alone. Not that I believed for a second it would stay that way for long. I was the vessel, after all. My life would always be complicated and dangerous.

On the day of the ceremony, I walked across the stage and accepted my diploma with my head held high. I wasn't crazy Josie anymore. I was a lot of weird, bizarre things—a popular boy's girlfriend, the kid of a famous actor, a faerie's princess, and an aspiring sorceress—but I wasn't crazy.

That was enough for me.

Zeph sat in the audience along with the rest of my mismatched, would-be family. Freddy had on an expensive suit and tie and Camilla was wearing a dainty cocktail dress, pumps, and lace gloves. They looked like a rich couple on their way to the horse races. Hank had come, too, but he still dressed like a scary biker Santa Claus. Some of the other parents sitting near him in the bleachers stared, obviously a little concerned. It didn't help that he sat right beside a boy who looked like he was about my age— an abnormally beautiful, cherub-faced boy with shaggy platinum hair and eerie yellow eyes. They made an odd looking pair. Still, I was glad to see Jack again.

I looked for Eldrick sitting with the rest to them ... but he wasn't there. I was determined not to let it get to me. I hadn't expected he would come, after all. He had a lot of responsibilities now. His people were looking to him for answers and guidance. There were things he had to deal with that were a lot more important than a high school graduation.

I was a little nervous as I made my way outside the school gym to meet up with everyone. Zeph had mentioned that we were all going to lunch afterward to celebrate. All the families and graduates began flocking to the gym exits. I was getting pushed around by all the people trying to funnel through the doors when I felt a hand on my elbow. I looked up just in time to see Zeph looking down at me with a weird, proud smile on his lips.

"Like a little lost lamb," he chuckled as he pulled me close and guided me outside. "Nice hat."

I blushed and pulled off my graduation cap. "Where is everyone?"

"I told them to go ahead and leave. They'll be meeting us for lunch," he answered quickly—too quickly. He was hiding something. "We're gonna stop by the apartment first. I gotta grab some stuff."

"Where are we going? I'm starving."

He wouldn't look me in the eye. "It's kinda far. Hank's gonna drive us, though."

My stomach was doing anxious somersaults as we walked home together. I couldn't figure out what he was up to, and it was actually starting to make me worried. He sure was going to a lot of trouble, and now it seemed like everyone else was in on it, too.

When we got to our apartment building, Zeph went up the stairs ahead of me. He walked straight to his own front door and gestured for me to stay put. "I'll just be a sec, so hang tight."

I did, for a few seconds. Then I decided I wanted to take off my graduation gown before I went anywhere. I took out my own keys and ducked into my apartment. I got about two feet inside before I noticed …

My apartment was completely empty.

There was not a stick of furniture anywhere. My couch, my TV, my kitchen table, everything was gone. The pictures were gone off the walls. The rugs on the floor were missing. Even the cabinets were empty.

My first thought was that I'd been robbed. Robbed in the most extreme sense of the word. They'd taken everything that wasn't nailed down.

"Zeph!" I screamed as I ran back out into the hall. I threw open Zeph's front door in a panic. "My stuff is gone! Someone broke into—"

His apartment was empty, too.

I froze, staring around the room at all the spots where furniture used to be. His place was just as bare as mine.

"What're you yelping about?" Zeph was standing there with a box under his arm.

"What happened to our stuff?"

He shrugged and herded me back out the door. "I moved it. Here, gimme your keys. We've got to turn them back in to the landlord."

My mind swirled with confusion as I shakily took my door and mailbox keys out of my pocket and handed them over. "Moved it where? What's going on?"

Zeph just grinned. "Chill out, will you? Just trust me."

I didn't know what else to say, and I didn't have much of a choice. All my stuff had gone somewhere and he was the only one who knew where. I followed him as he walked back downstairs. We stopped off at our landlord's room. Zeph thanked Mr. Bregger for everything, and gave him a thick envelope and all our keys. They shook hands, and that was it. I didn't even have to say a word.

We left the building just as Hank's Caddy pulled up to the curb. Zeph loaded his box in the passenger's seat and climbed in next to me in the back. As we pulled away, I knew better than to ask where we were going. I was twirling my graduation tassel around my finger anxiously as our apartment building disappear behind us.

"I almost forgot." Zeph pulled a bandana out of his pocket and started tying it over my eyes. "No peeking. I'm serious."

It seemed like we drove for a long time. Even though I couldn't see, I kept fidgeting with the tassel on my graduation cap until I felt Zeph's big, rough hand close around mine. As nervous as I was, I had almost forgotten this was supposed to be a good surprise.

My stomach did a backflip when I felt the car stop at last. My palms got sweaty, and I squeezed Zeph's hand as hard as I could. Leaving all my graduation stuff in the backseat, I wobbled forward blindly and tried to feel my way out of the car. Immediately my senses ran wild. I couldn't see, but I could smell the fresh, crisp spring air. I could smell the trees, the grass, and something like lumber and fresh paint. I could hear the wind rustling in the leaves, and the sound of our footsteps.

Zeph led me a few feet away from the car, and then he stood behind me with his hands on my shoulders. "All right." He sounded nervous.

I pulled the bandana off my eyes and squinted into the evening sun.

At first, I didn't recognize where I was. Everything looked so new and clean. The winter snows had finally melted away, and everything had fresh green buds on it. Then it hit me.

I knew this place.

My family home stood proudly at the crest of the hill. There was no evidence of fire damage, no smashed-out windows, and no holes in the roof. Everything had been fixed, and the house looked brand new. Brand new—but just how I remembered. There were rocking chairs and a swing on the broad front porch. Big pots filled with fresh flowers sat on the front steps.

My knees were shaking as I walked toward it. I barely touched the railing of the front steps and big tears welled up in my eyes. When I got to the front door, I stopped and stared. It was painted a deep, rich red. Through the windows, I could see lights on, but I couldn't bring myself to go inside.

My chin trembled. I'd walked into my apartment hundreds of times over the past few years. But going through that door had never been like this, even after Zeph and Eldrick came into my life.

It had never felt like coming home.

"What's wrong?" Zeph asked as though he were afraid I might be upset. "Don't you want to see it?"

I couldn't speak. I opened my mouth, but no sound would come out. I looked up at him with tears running down my cheeks, and tried to at least smile. Of course, I wanted to see it.

Zeph frowned uneasily. "I, uh, I guess I should have asked you first."

I grabbed his arm. "N-no. It's perfect. It's wonderful. You … you really did all this for me?"

I felt his body relax, and he dragged me into a hug and put a hand on the back of my head. "I can't take all the credit. I mean, it was *my* idea, but I did have some help. Come on. The inside's the best part."

As I pulled away, he held something up in front of my face—a single purple feather that twinkled in the light. "But we might want to deal with this, first."

I swallowed hard. That feather contained a spell, one that he'd used to suppress all my childhood memories. It had made me forget him, Freddy, and Camilla completely. Zeph had asked me not to destroy it after our battle with Fir Darrig. He'd said he wanted me to wait, that there was something else he needed to do first.

"Ready?" He smiled.

"O-okay." I took a deep breath. "Is it going to hurt?"

He held the feather up, using a touch of power to make it float above his palm. "Not a bit, princess."

With a quick, shrill chime the feather burst into flame. It burned with tongues of bright green fire and was gone in an instant.

At first, I didn't feel any different. There was no headache or pain this time. I blinked at him, confused.

Then I *remembered*.

I couldn't stop the swell of childhood memories from carrying me away to games of tag in the front yard, evenings spent building forts out of sticks and branches, and mornings when Zeph would make stacks of blob-shaped pancakes he insisted were supposed to look like animals.

I walked slowly beside him as he opened the door and led us into the house. I was greeted by the scents of fresh paint and wood, and food. There were furniture pieces from both of our apartments scattered about, paired in a stylish but traditional way with new things. It was simple, but cozy.

And it was teeming with more memories.

I remembered sitting in front of the fireplace in the living room, curled up with Dad while he read stories to me. I remembered doing homework at the kitchen counter and running down the stairs from my bedroom when I was late for the bus. So much of my life was connected to this house, and I thought it had all been lost in the fire, but Zeph had brought it back. It was new, and a little different, but it was still perfectly the same.

When we peeked into the dining room, a loud cheer almost gave me a heart attack. Everyone sat around a long table decorated with lots of flowers and streamers and plenty of food to share. Everyone—even Hank—was wearing a party hat. His was the only one shaped like a giant foam strawberry.

Camilla hugged me tightly. "We are so proud of you! Do you like the house? I picked out all the new décor!"

"Yes, it's incredible," I cried as I hugged her back.

"Just wait till you see upstairs," she whispered as she pulled away. I wasn't sure how to take that, but the mischievous grin on her lips made me wonder what she was up to.

Everything seemed so surreal as I sat at the head of the table, surrounded by my friends. We talked, laughed, and ate together like nothing at all was strange about this—about me eating with faeries and a shaman. I looked around at everyone, watching how they smiled as they told stories and teased one another. I wondered how I'd gotten here and how things had changed so dramatically. Just a few months ago, I had been completely alone in that apartment. My life had been caving in all around me. I'd been afraid and full of despair, ready to give up on any semblance of happiness. Now my heart was filled with love for these people.

One in particular.

Zeph was sitting right beside me, joking with his brother. He was the one who had changed everything. He'd taken my world, shaken it up, and turned it upside down.

Under the table, I felt the familiar touch of his fingers lacing through mine. I couldn't imagine where I would have ended up without him. And I couldn't imagine ever loving anyone more than I loved him. He turned those bizarre violet eyes in my direction and gave me that perfect, roguish, lopsided grin.

"You should show her the upstairs," Camilla suggested. "You haven't yet, have you?" Her tone was totally suspicious. So was the way she was glancing coyly over the rim of her wine glass.

Zeph cleared his throat and nodded. "Well, she was crying so—"

"So show her now!" Jack chimed in. He had a big smear of icing on his cheek. "Come on, that was the hardest part, wasn't it? You should be proud!"

After an uneasy glance around the table, Zeph stood up. He turned to me without a word and offered his hand again. "Shall we?"

There were four big bedrooms, but the one at the end of the hall was the largest. It had been my dad's before, but Zeph explained that now it was mine. It certainly looked more luxurious than what I'd had before.

A huge four poster bed stood against one wall with beautiful blankets and plush pillows arranged on a deep blue comforter. On the opposite wall, a pair of wingback chairs faced a fireplace and a big sheepskin rug stretched across the floor. It was like something from a magazine.

"It's beautiful. So where will you be sleeping? On the floor? Or maybe the couch downstairs?" I teased.

"Oh, I'll be in there with you," Zeph didn't miss a beat. "But I doubt there'll be much sleeping."

My cheeks burned. He laughed and kissed my cheek before continuing his tour.

The other bedrooms had normal sized beds and modest decorations. I even recognized some more of the stuff from my apartment.

The last room wasn't a bedroom at all. There was no bed. Instead, a big wooden desk sat under the long bay window. Against the back wall, a series of tall bookshelves were packed with all kinds of old books, scrolls, and artifacts. There was a familiar series of pictures framed on the wall next to the desk. The first few were the Polaroid pictures my dad had put in his letter. But the last three … those were the ones I'd taken with my phone. One was of Eldrick wearing my pink apron, another was of Zeph in that ridiculous strawberry hat, and the last was of the pair of them sitting at the kitchen table.

I ran my fingers over the glass of the frame, smiling at those memories.

Apart from those personal touches, it looked like any normal study. The only thing that seemed out of place was the closet door. The knob looked like it was made of solid gold and it was covered in beautiful swirling spellwork. All around the frame of the door, more symbols were engraved into the wood.

Zeph nudged me toward the door. "Go on."

As soon as I touched the warm gold, the soft sound of chimes whispered through the air. The more I turned it, the more it made all the tiny hairs on my body prickle. The last time I had opened a magical door, things hadn't exactly gone as planned.

This time was different.

A radiant green light came from inside—a garden like something straight out of one of my romance movies. Beautiful hedges blossomed all around, trimmed to perfection. The warm wind flowed over a manicured field of grass that was spotted with colorful flowers. Fruit trees dropped soft pink and white petals into pools of crystal clear water. In the distance, a stunning castle rose up out of the garden. It didn't seem real. Castles like that didn't exist, right? I mean, maybe they did in some places, but not anywhere near here. It looked like it had been cut straight from a storybook about princesses and knights. Banners of gold, purple, and red fluttered from all the towers, rippling against a perfect sapphire sky.

There was something off about this place, though. I felt it right away. Everything was a little *too* perfect. There were no clouds in the sky. No birds in the trees. When I began looking around, there was radiant warm light pouring down from overhead … but I couldn't see the sun anywhere.

"What is this place?" I whispered. I didn't realize Zeph had stopped just inside the door and left me to wander on alone.

"Nowhere," a deep voice answered.

I spun around and gasped sharply.

Eldrick was standing right behind me. He looked different, although still as elegant as ever. His black hair was a bit longer, so it blew around his face and eyes as he gazed down at me with warm, golden eyes. He wore a tailored black suit with a golden and red sash across the breast. There were golden aiguillettes on one of his broad shoulders, and the high collar of his jacket was set with a golden pin in the shape of a coat of arms.

"I would like to apologize for missing your ceremony," Eldrick said quietly.

For some reason, seeing him like this made me proud. It was weird, but it was almost a motherly feeling. "It's okay. You look great. And this place … I didn't realize you'd have a real castle."

He gave me a faint, bemused smile. "Calling it real is a bit of a stretch. It is an illusion. It was made from spellwork, and can only exist here, outside the realm of the normal world. It is a place without a destination—a dream made solid."

I was struggling to wrap my mind around that. "Are you alone here?" Looking around, I didn't see anyone else here.

"Hardly. Though I'd much prefer it that way sometimes." He offered his arm, like he always did, and began walking with me through the gardens. "I have a staff of servants to look after me and delegates of the courts are always coming and going. My father is by far the worst. He's keeping himself thoroughly entertained by exploiting every last drop of my patience and visiting on the weekends."

"Did you make this place? It's unbelievable. I've never seen such beautiful flowers." Just when I thought we had reached the edge of the gardens, more paths, hedges, and blossoms popped up to greet us. It was as though this sanctuary was enchanted to be endless. It would last as long as we cared to walk.

Eldrick snorted. "Although I do wish I could claim authorship, there is only one faerie alive capable of illusionary spellwork of this caliber."

He tipped his head toward Zeph, who was following us from a distance. I could see him watching us with a strange, uncomfortable frown on his lips. He almost looked a little jealous.

"Why is there a door to it in my house?" I dared to ask.

Eldrick flicked a quick glance down at me again. He stopped walking, and I could tell he was having a hard time deciding how to answer. "I wish my motives were entirely pure. But apart from simply enjoying your company, and offering you an invitation to come here whenever you like, I need to ask something of you."

"Of course. Anything."

He gave an uncomfortable sigh, and then began to explain, "There is a lot of unrest between the Seelie and Unseelie. Years and generations of quarrelling have built up many grudges. Even worse, there are some Unseelie fae who have begun unsavory but highly lucrative practices forbidden by our laws that are trying to go underground to hide from me. These fellows don't want to answer to anyone, not even their king. Finding them is a challenge, and things are already in chaos as we try to unite as many powerful fae to our cause as possible. My father has agreed to rejoin the court, and many are following his lead. But many more are still doing heinous things with magic that, as king, I cannot allow."

I tensed. He hadn't said it yet, but I had a feeling I knew where he was going with this.

"I'd like to ask for your help, yours and Zeph's, in bringing some of these fae to justice. You have experience now, and you are a talented spellworker. It will be dangerous, especially when your position as vessel is taken into consideration. However, I wouldn't ask this of you if I wasn't sure you could handle it," he finished.

I wasn't sure I understood completely what he was asking me to do, but it sounded like he wanted me to become a faerie-hunting secret agent for him. As cool as that sounded, I knew it wasn't a small favor. I'd glimpsed some of the horrors of the Unseelie world, and I could imagine there might be far worse things out there.

"What did Zeph say about it?" I asked as I stole a glance at my changeling. No wonder he looked so sulky.

"He said it would be your choice. Naturally, I'm sure he doesn't approve of the danger, but being what you are puts you in a degree of danger already. This would almost certainly exacerbate things." Eldrick hesitated, and then put a hand on my shoulder. "I wish I didn't have to ask this of you. After what you've lived through, you deserve peace. However, I can't imagine a better candidate for this task. I need someone who knows our laws, respects them, but isn't bound by them. I also need someone I can trust."

I took a deep breath. "Yes. I'll do it."

Eldrick looked relieved. "I'll compensate you for your time, of course. You will be outfitted for each case with the best resources we can assemble. I've appointed Freddy into his former position as master engineer. He'll be developing specialized weaponry for you."

Visions of that magical revolver danced in my mind. Was I actually going to get to use something like that?

Stepping in close enough to put my arms around his middle, I gave him a big hug. "I'm not worried. I know you'll take good care of us. I have faith in you, Eldrick. You're a good man."

He hugged me back and brushed an affectionate hand over my cheek, which was sort of awkward to do in front of Zeph. I didn't care, though. I'd missed him so much. Not having my friend around the apartment to brew coffee and complain about my romance movies while Zeph was working made things especially lonely.

He let me go quickly and straightened his collar. "Very well. I'll see you both at the dinner tonight, then?"

I laughed. "Sure. My house or yours?"

Eldrick gave a little smile. "I would prefer your cooking, if it's not too much trouble."

"All right, then. I'll make sure the coffee's on," I said as I began strolling away back to where Zeph was waiting. He took my hand and together, we walked back through the gardens. At first, I wasn't sure how we would find our way back to the closet door, but as soon as we started looking for it, it seemed to appear around the next corner.

"Looks like he survived his first months of Faerie King training," Zeph murmured.

"Yeah …" I looked back to catch a glimpse of the tall, dark, and handsome King of the Faeries one more time. I'd picked him because I knew he would take this job seriously. I knew he'd do the best he could. But leaving him there all alone … it made me a little sad. It made me wonder if he would be happy with this life or not.

The look in his eyes as his gaze caught mine made my heart ache; it almost seemed like he was missing me, too.

"Why did you put Eldrick in my closet?" I asked, glancing back to Zeph.

He flicked me a wry grin. "Seemed appropriate, since that's where he used to stick you."

"I didn't think of that." I giggled and gave his hand a squeeze. "So what now?"

Zeph suddenly stepped in front of me. I yelped in surprise as he swept me up into his arms. He carried me like a new bride toward the closet door.

Resting my head against his shoulder, I draped my arms around his neck and combed my fingers through his hair. It made him growl with satisfaction whenever I did that, like a lion who liked being scratched behind his ears.

"What happens next?" I asked quietly. "I mean, do you think everything will be okay now? Will we be safe?"

Zeph only stopped long enough to open the door. "We may never be safe, princess. Especially if Eldrick wants to use us as glorified bounty hunters," he reminded me. "But as long as I'm alive, I'll do whatever it takes to keep you safe. You're mine now. And I'm never letting you go."

"Because you got trapped in a love contract by a toddler?" I teased.

"No," he said as he carried me through the door and back into our house. "Because that's how our story is supposed to end—with you and me together forever. Happily ever after'n all that crap."

I couldn't hold back my smile. "Sounds like a faerie tale ending to me. Some people might think that's a little cheesy, you know."

Zeph waggled his brows mischievously. He planted a firm kiss against my lips as the door slowly swung closed behind us. "What can I say? I'm a faerie. It's the only kind of ending I know how to do."

The First Floor

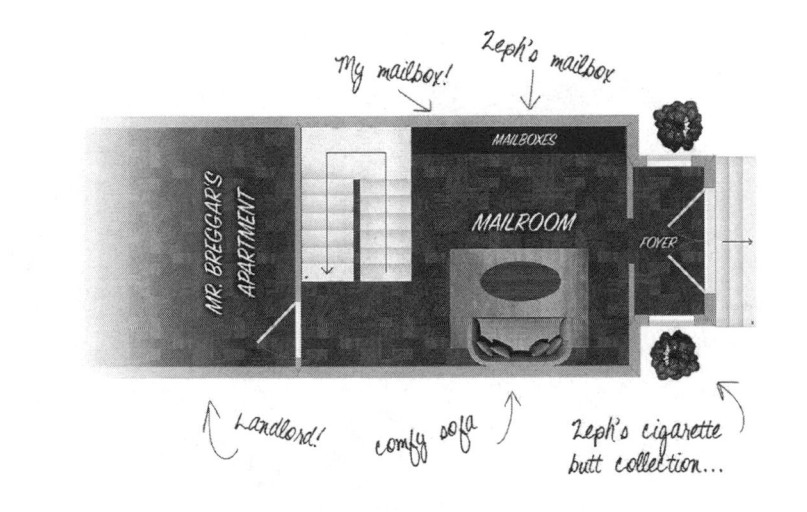

My mailbox!

Zeph's mailbox

MAILBOXES

MR. BREGGAR'S APARTMENT

MAILROOM

FOYER

← Landlord!

comfy sofa

Zeph's cigarette butt collection...

Josie's Apartment   ## Zeph's Apartment

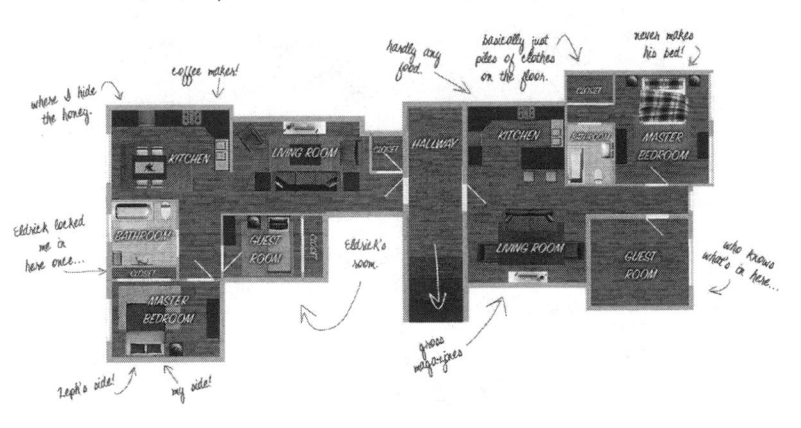

where I hide the honey.

coffee maker!

hardly any food.

basically just piles of clothes on the floor.

never makes his bed!

KITCHEN

LIVING ROOM

CLOSET

HALLWAY

KITCHEN

BEDROOM

CLOSET

MASTER BEDROOM

Eldrich locked me in here once...

BATHROOM

GUEST ROOM

CLOSET

Eldrich's room

LIVING ROOM

GUEST ROOM

who knows what's in here...

CLOSET

MASTER BEDROOM

Zeph's side!

my side!

gross magazines

Claidheamh
Solus

Otherwise known as the "Sword of Light"

This is a highly flexible weapon usable by humans and faeries alike. All casting spellwork on the artifact is internal, so that it cannot be tampered with. Rounds can altered for specific results, but all require a magical source to fire and activate the internal spellwork.

The Five Pilgrims

While only five known faeries survived the journey to our world, this chart depicts only a fraction of their offspring—particularly those who are openly acknowledged or were sired during a legitimate faerie marriage. There are countless others scattered and hidden throughout the world, and while they come in a wide variety of shapes, sizes, and with varying magical abilities, all can trace their lineage back to one of these common ancestors.

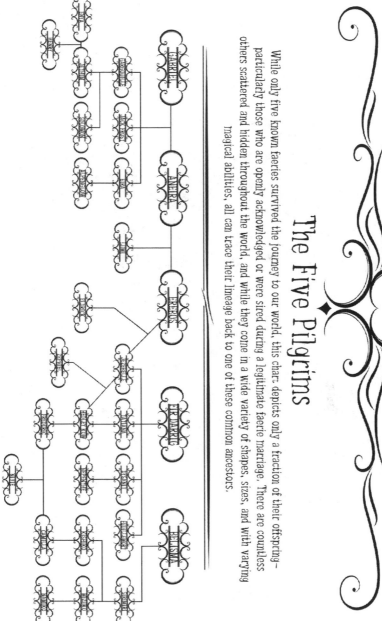

ACKNOWLEDGEMENTS

Special thanks to my rock star beta readers:
Heather, Jennifer, Jaime, and Pam. Thank you so much for keeping me
on track!

***

To my agent, Fran, I want to say thank you for keeping me grounded,
calm, and always being there to lend an ear when I need to talk
something out.

***

To Aileen, for helping me through the brainstorm process. You've always
been amazing about humoring all my crazy ideas. Miss you lots!

***

Thank you to my husband, for all your love and support. You'll always be
my faerie prince charming!

***

To the editing staff, and designers, I can't thank you enough for all the
hours you put into this project. Your dedication to making sure this book
was the best it could be is truly humbling. I'm so blessed to be working
with you!

OTHER MONTH9BOOKS TITLES YOU MIGHT LIKE

FLEDGLING
AVIAN
TRAITOR
IMMORTAL
SAVAGE

Find more books like this at http://www.Month9Books.com

Connect with Month9Books online:
Facebook: www.Facebook.com/Month9Books
Twitter: https://twitter.com/Month9Books
You Tube: www.youtube.com/user/Month9Books
Blog: www.month9booksblog.com

DRAGONRIDER CHRONICLES 1

Fledgling

NICOLE CONWAY

DRAGONRIDER CHRONICLES 2

Avian

NICOLE CONWAY

DRAGONRIDER CHRONICLES 3

Traitor

NICOLE CONWAY

DRAGONRIDER CHRONICLES 4

Immortal

NICOLE CONWAY

DRAGONRIDER LEGACY I
SAVAGE
BESTSELLING AUTHOR OF THE DRAGONRIDER CHRONICLES
NICOLE CONWAY